VARYING *Paramour*

A. L. Rose

Order this book online at www.trafford.com
or email orders@trafford.com

Most Trafford titles are also available at major online book retailers.

Printed in the United States of America.

ISBN: 978-1-4669-9611-3 (sc)
ISBN: 978-1-4669-9612-0 (e)

Trafford rev. 05/29/2013

www.trafford.com

North America & international
toll-free: 1 888 232 4444 (USA & Canada)
phone: 250 383 6864 ♦ fax: 812 355 4082

For Michael,
Who has made Christmas,
Christmas again.
I love you

&

For Naomi,
Who wouldn't quit begging me
to finish this book.

Chapter 1

David Smith awoke to the sound of his alarm. He slowly rolled over to look at the soft blue numbers on its face. It read seven thirty and he yawned.

"Wow, that sucks." David said aloud as he reached for his package of cigarettes. He popped it open in a wrist flicking action he had learned from his father. He took one light brown filter into his teeth and pulled the package away. He let his hand fall back on to the table and let the package flip out of his hand. He looked at the clock again. 7:31 the numbers read. "God, one more year" He said as he grabbed his lighter and rolled over on to his back. He yawned again then lit the smoke. He took a long pull off of it and blew out the blue toxin in a giant heave. He stared at the ceiling and listened to his mother turn on the shower. He took another puff of his cigarette and closed his eyes.

Another year at that school with those insufferable idiots. How can I be expected to survive? David thought to himself and smiled. *God, please give me a new history teacher. I promise to pay close attention if they don't suck this year.* David mock prayed. He took another drag from his cigarette. He remembered the idiot that called himself a history teacher from last year. He seemed to have had it out for David right from day one. He had to admit that he certainly didn't help matters much, but, never the less, a more learned professor was definitely in order. *God, make it a young, female professor straight out of collage that has a soft spot for young, hopeless, good looking students.* David added to his prayer and smiled again. He squinted his eyes open and looked at his cigarette. The blue smoke danced around the end of it and then disappeared into the sun struck space in his room. He took another puff and slid himself up to lean against the head board of his large twin bed. He tapped the ashes of his cigarette off into the ashtray then leaned his head back against the cool wood of the head board. He stared at the desk in the corner of the room. On it was the new journal he had purchased for the year. In front of the desk was the folding chair he stole from the kitchen. On its seat was the backpack he had picked out when he and his mother went shopping for endless school supplies. Hanging on the back was his favorite leather jacket. It had been a gift from his father. Just before he died, he gave it to David and told him that it had been worn by some of the greatest guitar players of their generation. It hadn't meant that much to David until 3 months after, when his father's life ended suddenly with a bathroom, pill assisted suicide. Then all of a sudden, that stupid leather jacket became his most prized possession. That and the journals he had started keeping 2 years prior. His father had told him that keeping a record of life events can sometimes change the course of one's existence. *Fuck, whatever dad.* David thought and put his cigarette out. He stood up and stretched. He walked over to the closet and found a clean white tee-shirt and a pair of blue jeans. He walked over to the small dresser next to the desk and dug out a pair of black socks and a new pair of boxers. He opened his bedroom door and listened down the hallway.

"Bathroom free mom?!" He called in the direction of the bathroom.

"Go ahead dear, good morning" His mother called back from behind him in her room. He smiled and headed to the bathroom. He closed the door behind him and stood in front of the toilet. He closed his eyes and tilted his head back as he emptied his bladder.

Dear God, give me the strength to last the day. It would make mom happy. He prayed. He finished and let his boxers hit the tile floor. He turned the water on to his favorite temperature and stepped into the shower. The warm water felt good against his chest and face. He stood there for a while thinking about the wish he had made for a new history teacher. He snickered at the thought of co-ed shower rooms and young, history professors. He washed his hair, and then his body. He stepped out of the shower and dried off. He looked at himself in the full length mirror on the door. His almost shoulder length hair sent tiny drips of water down his chest and stomach. He looked at the goose bumps forming on his arms and legs. The muscles in his abdomen flexed as he shivered slightly.

"Damn, your good lookin'" David said to his reflection. He reached down for the towel he had dropped and dried his hair. He watched the muscles flex in his arms as he dried his hair and drops it had left in his chest and shoulders. He quickly dressed, added deodorant and cologne, and then headed back to his room. He stood in front of the mirror that rested on his desk. He combed his hair, straight back like always. He grabbed the leather jacket off the back of the folding chair and slid it on. He then grabbed his backpack and slung it over one arm. He took one last look at himself in the mirror, grabbed the pack of cigarettes off the night stand, and headed out of him room.

His mother had a cup of coffee on the table for him. He sat down at the table and set his bag on the floor next to him. He lit a cigarette and took a sip of his coffee. His mother came into the room then. She was dressed in her nurse's uniform. Her hair was tied back in a tight pony tail and she had a light covering of makeup.

"Good morning Dave, ready for your first day back to school?" She asked as she refilled her coffee cup and joined him at the table. She sat at the opposite side of the table from him, closer to the coffee pot than him.

"Oh, you bet, mom. Practically jumped out of bed." David said sarcastically. His mother smiled and shook her head.

"Oh, it's not that bad dear. Two more years and you're done . . . unless collage . . ."

"Not this morning mom. Bug me about collage next year, kay?" David said. He took a sip of his coffee and a drag off his smoke. "Besides, who would remind you of the time if I ran away to some collage?" David added gesturing his eyebrows to the clock above the stove. It read 7:45.

"Oh shit," She breathed and hurried with her coffee cup to the sink. "Don't be late for school dear and don't wait up. I am going out with girls tonight." She said. She kissed his forehead and hurried to the door.

"Wouldn't dream of it mom, have a good day" David answered then took another sip of his coffee.

"Bye dear!" His mother's voice called as she slammed the door behind her. He smiled and shook his head.

My mother, the wing nut. He thought to himself. Just then the phone rang. David leaned back in his chair and grabbed the phone off the wall.

"Yellow" He answered.

"*Good morning gorgeous*" The voice on the other end said. David smiled and shook his head.

"Good morning, Amanda." He answered. Amanda was David's dearest friend. She lived 2 doors down from him and they had known each other since they were very young. They had experienced all of life's little journeys together. They even had each other's virginities. She had been there for him through his dads drinking and then through his death. She was very dear to him.

"*Ready for another riveting year at North Hill High?*" She asked.

"Oh, you bet. Can't hardly contain myself"

"*You're such a bull-shitter David.*"

"Isn't that why you stick around?" David asked smiling and downing the last of his coffee.

"*Nope, I plan on being in the will when your rich and famous and need someone to leave all your money to.*" Amanda said playfully.

"Classy. Walking with me this morning?" David asked getting up from the table and taking his cup to the coffee pot.

"*I was planning on it, I called to make sure you were up.*" Amanda teased.

"Nice of you to think of me."

"*I'll head right over than. Got coffee on?*"

"Breakfast is served my dear" He could hear Amanda giggle.

"*Kay, I'll be right over. Bye*"

"Chow" David said and hung up the phone. He grabbed a cup out of the cupboard for his friend and poured them both a cup. He added the appropriate measurements of cream and sugar and headed back to the table. He set Amanda's cup where his mother had sat and returned to his place at the table. He lit another cigarette and waited for Amanda to arrive. It wasn't long before he heard the door open.

"Are you decent?" Amanda called from the door. David smiled and shook his head.

"Nope, Monday is naked coffee day. Didn't you know?" He called back. He could hear her giggle as she walked into the room. She was wearing an unbuttoned jean jacket over a black tee-shirt and blue jeans. Her hair was pulled back in a ponytail but she wore no makeup. She wasn't the makeup type. David liked that about her. He hated the girls at school that layered it on like hookers.

"Well, you look normal" She said as she sat down at her coffee cup. David smiled and looked down at his cloths.

"And here I thought I dressed up."

"Me too. First day back and all that." She said smiling back at him. David shook his head and took a drag off his cigarette. Amanda sipped her coffee and winced at the heat. "Who are you hoping to get this year?" She asked sipping at the hot coffee again. David sighed.

"Don't care as long as Felch the history prick is gone." He answered sipping at his coffee too.

"Well I hear he was replaced." Amanda answered. David raised his eyebrows.

"Really?" He asked in a bad English accent.

"Yea, some young guy from the city or something."

No hot and bothered female professor in your future David. He thought to himself. Of course the selfish praying of a dead rocker's son would only be half answered.

"Crap, I was hoping for someone worth staring at for 80 minutes at a time." David sighed out and Amanda laughed.

"I suppose some young, French, just out of school sex kitten huh?"

"ooooo, never added the French part in the equation. What would I do without you Amanda?" David joked. They added more and more tantalizing features to David's dream teacher as they drank their morning coffee. Amanda's imagination, being much more interesting than David's, soon changed the teacher into a sex goddess David hid in the basement. Used only for his sexual pleasure.

"Well, that's a lot more fun than a teacher anyway" Amanda said finishing her coffee and grabbing both cups. David was often finished his coffee before Amanda.

"No shit. Never a dry spell with something like that in your possession." David said smiling and getting up from the table. He glanced at the clock and read 8:20. "Better go" He added handing Amanda her backpack and throwing his over his shoulder again. They left the house together and headed toward the high school. It was nice outside and everything was still as green as summer.

"Why can't school wait for crappy weather?" Amanda asked taking a deep breath through her nose.

"Maybe we should start a petition?" David kidded.

"I'll get started on it right away." Amanda kidded back. They turned on to 7th ave where they could see the school at the end of the block. Busses lined the front and students laughed and talked as they went inside. David and Amanda stepped through the doors side by side. They could see where the home room lists where posted. They scrolled for their names.

"Room 9, Mrs. Coldiron." David read aloud.

"Hey me too! Things are looking up." Amanda said. They walked together to room 9 and sat at desks that where beside each other. The bell rang and the room filled with the rest of their home room class. Mrs.Coldiron handed out the first semester class lists to every one while taking attendance. David read over his carefully.

Period 1, Math with Mr. Jackson in room 10, 40 minutes. Period 2, Science with Miss Walker in room 1, 40 minutes. Periods 3 and 4, Phys-ed with Mr.Ernswild, 80 minutes.(fuck, woo hoo) Lunch. 11:30 to 12:30, (I'll be looking forward to that) Period 5 and 6 History with Mr. Black in room 19, 80 minutes. (Black, how original) Period 7, English with Mrs. Coldiron in room 9, 40 minutes. Period 8 SPARE (Fuck, I love this school! Always a short day!)

"Hey, check this out! A spare for last period!" David said pointing it out to Amanda.

"Lucky duck! My spare is after lunch." Amanda said pouting.

"No 80 minutes of hell in history? Gimme that." David said switching schedules with Amanda.

Period 1 and 2, History with Mr. Black in room 19, 80 minutes.

"Oh that sucks! First thing in the morning." David teased switching schedules back. Amanda wrinkled up her nose.

"No classes together this whole semester." She said.

"Hey, we'll always have home room." David teased again. Amanda giggled. Just then the bell rang and the class set out for their first morning back.

To David's enjoyment, the morning went by quickly and before he knew it he was at his assigned locker, which was right next to Amanda's, getting his books away and getting ready for lunch.

"How was your morning?" Amanda asked doing the same with her books at her locker.

"Fast Thankfully. How was yours?" David asked closing his locker and locking it up. Amanda did the same and then answered,

"Well, for what it's worth, History class is a lot better for the girls." She said smiling. David rolled his eyes as they made their way to the side doors of the school.

"How wonderful for you. Is he interesting?" David ventured conversation. Amanda smiled and sat down at the picnic table designated for the smokers.

"Don't know. Too busy looking." Amanda giggled at her own answer.

"Oh, shit Amanda. I'll have to tutor you history so you pass. How wonderful." David smiled at his smitten friend.

"Oh please. Just wait till you see him. He's so pretty." Amanda said giggling again. David lifted one eyebrow.

"I doubt I'll see what you see Mandy."

"Oh come on, remember when we used to pick out the best looking actors in movies? It's the same as that."

"If you say so." David answered. They spent the rest of the lunch break discussing Mr. Black and how lucky Amanda was for having something to look forward to. They slowly walked towards the doors when the bell rang.

"Just keep an open mind David, tell me what you think after school. I'll come by your place after and you can tell me all about the great taste I have." Amanda planned as they headed to their lockers. David finally agreed after great begging and pleading on Amanda's part. He collected the appropriate books and headed to room 19. Mr. Blacks name was on the door. David rolled his eyes and stepped in. He chose a desk at the front of the room.

Man this sucks, first thing I gotta do is get glasses so I don't gotta sit up at the front any more. I mean come on, I gotta be the only dude that actually picks a spot at the front of the . . . . David's thought was cut short. Mr. Black walked through the door and set a stack of paper on his desk. He turned and wrote his name on the board then faced David. David's eyes grew wide and his breath caught in his throat. Mr. Black smiled and began to speak.

"Hello, I'm Mr. Black. I'll be your history teacher. And you are?" His voice cut right into David's soul.

What the fuck is going on with you David? Wake up! Don't just sit here! SAY SOMETHING!!!!!

"UH, David, David Smith." He answered clearing his throat between David and David Smith.

"Well, Nice to meet you David." Mr. Black said offering his hand to the young man. David looked at his hand and then up at his face.

David!!! Shake the man's hand for fuck sake!! David reached up and shook Mr. Black's hand.

"It's a pleasure David." Mr. Black said smiling then went up to the papers at his desk. The bell had rung and class had started. David listened as Mr. Black started the lesson. He wanted to start the year off with a little show and tell so to speak. He asked everyone to stand, introduce themselves and say a little bit about themselves. David hardly listened to the other students and their ridiculous 'look at me' speeches. He watched Mr. Black as HE listened to the stories and smiled at what must have been humorous anecdotes.

What the hell is with this guy? How am I supposed to get through a year sitting up at the front of the class where I can practically smell this guy's cologne? Wait. Why am I smelling his cologne? And why do I even care how close I am to him? Why am I even thinking about this? It's irrational and weird. What's with the hard on? FUCK!!! I have a hard on??!! Oh God! Great. He's a dude! Nice timing. Just frigging perfect. How much time is left?

David looked up at the clock. There was still 35 minutes left of class.

Oh God!! 35 minutes! What the fuck is going on? How can this be happening? I'm not gay. Oh god . . . . Gay? Why? Wait wait wait. I can't be . . . . It would have turned up before this. Yea, just a weird day. Just a weird guy. Maybe I can switch classes. That's what I will do.

David soothed himself with thoughts of a new class schedule. He had even found himself listening to the other students talking about their summers and their plans for the future. He made a constant effort not to look at Mr. Black. Derik Hanson was next. He talked about football and camp. David listened to his exceedingly poor grammar boring story. He realized the erection he had been sporting for the last 30 minutes had finally subsided. He sighed a breath of relief and continued listening to each student's story. He chanced a glance to the clock. 5 minutes left.

Thank Christ!

Mr. Black got up from his desk and stood at the front of the class again. David watched him move. His broad shoulders heaved with a yawn. He thanked the last speaker and looked at the clock. David stared into his eyes careful not to look anywhere else.

"Well class, good first day. I will be looking forward to hearing the other half of your stories tomorrow. I would like everyone to keep in mind that this *is* history class and it won't always be so fun." He smiled at his own dry humor. David still stared hardly blinking. Mr. Black made eye contact with him finally just as the bell rang. David didn't move,

Get up you jack ass! The bell rang!

"Everything ok, David?" Mr. Black asked as the room emptied. David took a deep breath and stood up grabbing his books all in one movement.

"Uh, yea. My leg was asleep." David lied. He flashed a quick smile at Mr. Black and headed for the door.

"I hope my class is more interesting for you tomorrow. Wouldn't want anything else falling asleep on you would we?" Mr. Black said to the back of David's head. David stopped walking. He raised an eyebrow and turned to face his teacher. He was still standing in the same spot.

"Sorry, I didn't mean you. I get bored easy" David answered holding Mr. Blacks gaze.

"Well, I have an interesting semester in store for you, don't you worry about that." He said and winked.

Oh fuck!! Don't wink at me you weirdo!

"Great, can't wait." David said then left. He made his way to room 9 for English class. He stared at the floor thinking about what just happened. He sat down in the same desk he had sat in when he and Amanda had started this strange day.

Oh shit, Amanda! She's gonna know what I think of Him.

David thought as Mrs.Coldiron got right down to business and handed out novels to read. It was some world war two story. She directed the class to start by reading the first 2 chapters. David opened to the first page but didn't read.

What do I think of Him anyway? What do I say? She's gonna know something's up as soon as I see her. Its Amanda though, David thought, *She'll have an explanation for this. She always knows what to say in a weird situation. I'll have to say something to her. But what? God, dad, if you could only see me now.*

David's father was the kind of man that would rather beat a gay man to death than look at him. He had told David from a young age that being gay was genetic. That it came from retarded cells. Of course David knew that wasn't true but he wondered,

How could I get turned on like that by some dude when a man like MY father had anything to do with my upbringing? God, he would disown me. He would beat me half to death and THEN disown me, just so I could live with it.

David shook his head and tried to concentrate on the book in front of him. It started out in a small village outside of Berlin. A family had been running from the Nazi's for months but they knew that this General Balkoneve was gaining on them. They had to protect themselves but mostly their eldest son Hans, who was different than the other boys his age. He was intelligent and had angelic like beauty. (*oh please. That's one chapter done at least).* They had taken refuge in a Jewish farmer's barn. The Jews that lived there had helped some Nazi soldiers a while back so they were exempt from any capture for the time being. During the night, Hans left the barn to go urinate on a nearby tree. He was not alone. One of the Jewish farmer's sons, Anthony, snuck up behind him and startled him. They got into a childish wrestling match that ended up with a roll down a hill and Anthony lading on top of Hans. Hans's lip was bleeding from the tumble and Anthony leaned down and kissed him. (*OF COURSE HE DID!!)* Hans pushed Anthony away and got up off the ground. (*Good Boy!)* Anthony slowly rose off the ground and they got into a real fight this time.(*Kick his ass Hans!)* Anthony quickly got the upper hand and was on top of Hans again. They stared at each other. They were now both bleeding from the lip. They breathed heavy into each other's faces, tired from their battle. Anthony held Hans down by the wrists. Hans tried to move but he was no match for the farmer's son. Soon he quit struggling and lay still under Anthony's body. Anthony loosened his grip but did not let go. They stared at each other for quite some time. Then Hans tilted his head forward and kissed Anthony deeply. *(Great)* Anthony released Hans's wrists and ran his fingers through his hair. They kissed until the sun touched the horizon. Then they made their way back up the hill to the farm yard and snuck back into their beds. (*Really? This is what is going to follow history class EVERYDAY?)*

David closed the book and raised his hand. Mrs. Coldiron came to his desk with a question sheet for chapter one and two. She walked back to the front of the class.

"Please finish these pages at home. We will be discussing chapters one and two tomorrow." David looked at the clock to see that the bell was about to ring. He packed up his things and got ready to leave. The bell rang and he hurried to his locker. As he loaded his back pack, he caught something in the corner of his eye. It was Mr. Black. David watched him walk closer to him. David closed his eyes and tucked his chin into his chest.

Please don't be coming to me.

"David, I'm glad I caught you." Mr. Black's mystical voice said. David sighed and looked at Mr. Black. A loose strand of hair had fallen into his eyes. In his hand he held David's leather jacket. His heart jumped. He looked back and forth between the jacket and Mr. Black's gorgeous face. "You left this hanging on the back of your chair after class today." He said handing the jacket to David.

A guy that gives me a . . . Some dude that I . . . HE touched my coat. Dads coat.

"Uh, thanks." David said slowly taking the jacket from Mr. Black.

"Looks expensive, better keep a closer eye on it hey?" Mr. Black said winking again. David sighed.

"Yea, uh, thanks." David said quietly.

"You don't really say much do you?"

"Not really." David said sliding the jacket on over his shoulders. He could smell Mr. Black all over it and gritted his teeth.

"I suppose the talking in front of the class thing won't be easy for you?" Mr. Black asked putting a hand against the lockers. David could see the muscles on his chest ripple through his tight tee-shirt. He cleared his throat.

"Yea, uh, I'm really no public speaker." David answered looking around for the closest exit.

"Well, you don't have to say much. Just let us know you exist okay." He answered smiling. He moved his hand off the lockers and put his hand out for David again. David shook it this time without hesitating. "Guess we'll see you tomorrow then."

"Yup, tomorrow." David answered and headed toward the door.

Don't look back, just walk.

But he looked back anyway. There was Mr. Black talking to another student. He looked up from their conversation and looked at David. David nodded and tugged the lapel of his beloved jacket. Mr. Black smiled and did a half salute then looked back at the student he was speaking with. David turned and went through the doors. He lit a cigarette and quickly walked home staring at the ground the whole way.

Ok. One day down. But It ISN'T! I gotta talk to Amanda still!

"Shit," David said out loud as he turned the corner for home. He could smell Mr. Black's cologne again.

Fuck, he does smell good, I'll give him that.

David shook off the thought and walked up to the door of his house. He unlocked it and walked in. He headed right up the stairs and into his room. He through his bag onto the folding chair and fell back onto his bed. Mr. Blacks scent shrouded him like a silk sheet of sex. He closed his eyes and clenched his teeth.

What the fuck is wrong with me? It's a dude's cologne. Come on David, Snap out of it!

David got up off the bed and took the jacket off. He through it onto the chair and stared at it. He stood there for quite some time.

Amanda, Think about Amanda. You fucked her twice. That's gotta count for something! Just remember what that was like. Think of her hard little nipples and her shaky breathing. Come on David. Remember her voice moaning your name.

David smiled and looked down at the growing bulge in his jeans.

"There! That's when you do it!" David scolded his penis and walked downstairs to the kitchen. He got a pop out of the fridge and stood at the window, staring out side.

Ok, now that we have YOU trained, gotta start on my brain. Wonder what Amanda is gonna want to know. Is he attractive? Yea, for a dude, of course. Does is voice sound sexy? Well, yes. EVERYTHING about him is sexy Amanda!!!

"Fuck, I'm doomed." David said aloud opening his pop. He took a big sip and walked over to the kitchen table. He opened his bag and dug out the question pages for English class.

Number one, Why would the runaway family feel their oldest son, Hans, would need more protection than the others?

(Are you kidding woman?)

David worked quietly at his homework answering the questions the best he could. He used as many politically correct words as he could muster without sounding smarter than the teacher. He read over his answers a few times before loading his bag back up. He tossed the bag close to the door so it would be ready for the next day. Then he went up to the bathroom to pee. He stared at himself in the mirror as he washed his hands. He shook his head and turned the water off.

"You need to get laid David . . . . By a chick." He said to himself then walked out the door. He went back down to the kitchen to find Amanda sitting there with a pop of her own.

Bingo! There's one now.

"Hi." David said sitting down at the table.

"Well, how was history class?" She asked staring right into his eyes. David swallowed hard and laughed.

"No hi or anything first?"

"Yes yes, hi. Now, Mr. Black. Hot or Not?" She asked sipping her soda but never breaking eye contact. David leaned back in his chair and sighed.

"Well, he's . . . . Interesting"

"INTERESTING? Are you kidding? He's gorgeous!"

"If you say so Mandy" David said looking down at his pop can. Amanda gasped. David's eyes shot up to meet hers.

"I know that look . . . . Where is your mind at David?" He sighed and looked down.

Fuck, she knows.

"What do you mean?" David tried.

"You get that look for only two reasons, hot car or hot chick. What's going on?" She leaned closer to try to look at him. He sighed and looked back up at her. He couldn't fight the tears that filled his eyes and he looked back down. "David, why . . . what's wrong?" She asked and moved to the chair next to him. She put her hand on his leg and stared at his face.

"Bad day" He answered and lit a cigarette.

"And here I am going on about some guy. God David, Talk to me." Amanda said moving the hair out of his eyes. "Did something happen with a girl or something today?"

David frowned at her and took a drag off of his cigarette.

"When have you known me to tear up over a girl in one day?"

"Well, what is it then?" Amanda asked again. She sat quietly as David gathered his thoughts. He looked at her and searched his mind for an answer. Then it came to him.

"I lost dads coat today." He said. It wasn't entirely a lie.

"Oh my god David. Why didn't you say something? We can go to the school and look for it if you want." Amanda offered. David shook his head,

"No no, I got it back."

"Than what's the matter?"

"It just freaked me out a little that's all." He answered knocking the ashes from his cigarette. Amanda leaned back in her chair and frowned.

"What do you mean, *got it back?* Did someone steel it?"

"No, I left in in history class and someone brought it to me." David answered suddenly aware how close he treaded to the Mr. Black subject again.

"Well, that was nice." She said reaching for her pop. David felt relieved when she sipped at her pop and didn't seem to have any more questions about it until, "That's a nice coat for someone to just, return it, like that. Who was it?"

Damn it Amanda!

"Mr. Black" David choked not looking up at her. Amanda sat quietly for a minute and then started to laugh. David looked up at her puzzled. "What? What's so funny?" Amanda laughed harder and held her ribs. "What?"

"You like him don't you?" She asked trying to keep a straight face. David gasped and stumbled over his thoughts.

"Well, sure, he's more interesting than that other jack off history teacher from last year." David said calmly. Amanda squinted at him.

"That's NOT what I mean David." They sat silently for a long time. Neither one of them looking away from their gaze. David could feel a bead of sweat trickle down from his brow but he held his gaze. It was Amanda who spoke first, "Are you gay, David?" David's body shot arrow straight and he started breathing rapidly. Amanda's eyes grew wide and she sank down in her chair. He looked at her and shook his head slowly. He bit his bottom lip and ran his sweaty hand through his hair. It pulled and it hurt.

"Ouch! Fuck!" David cursed and through his pop across the kitchen into the sink. Brown foam splashed the window. Amanda jumped in her chair but didn't get up. She looked over at her friend. He held his cigarette in one hand and rested his head in the other. She quietly cleared her throat and inched closer to him. She gently touched his shoulder. David's body tensed and he spun his head to face her. She gasped but never moved away. He stared at her for a while before he grabbed her by the back of the head and pulled her in and their lips met. He hungrily kissed her, pushing his tongue farther into her mouth deepening their kiss. She moaned and moved onto his lap. She straddled him and kissed just as deeply as he was. They lightly tugged at each other's hair as they kissed. Amanda could feel David hardening underneath of her. She moaned and pushed against him. David moaned with her and grabbed her hips. He moved her with his powerful hands to counter the grinding movements of his hips. She moaned and through her head back. She raked her long nails down his arm. He countered by lightly biting her hard right nipple through her shirt. She squealed and pulled his hair till his head snapped back. She met him with another powerful kiss. He pushed his swollen penis hard against her.

"God David, we cant." Amanda said putting her hands on his chest.

"Why not?" David asked looking into her very sexually frustrated eyes.

"My period. I'm sorry. I should go." She said now looking a little embarrassed.

"Hey wait. You don't have to go. So you got your period, so what?" David asked trying to kiss her again. Amanda sat herself up and moved off of David's lap and more than ready erection.

"I can't David, I'm sorry." She said and moved toward the door. David looked up at the ceiling,

What? Really?

"Wait Amanda don't go." He said and caught her at the door. She spun around in the door way. Her face was fire engine red and she wouldn't look him in the eye. David tilted her head up with a finger under her chin. He leaned down and kissed her cheek. She smiled and looked away. He tilted his head and smiled at her embarrassment. She finally looked at him and sighed. He had his arms reached out for a hug. She answered with one and he pulled her close to him. She could feel his still, very hard penis push against her. He smelled her hair and whispered in her ear. "At least you know what's waiting for you when you CAN." His voice was like satin to her. She shivered and hugged tighter.

"Thank you for understanding David." She whispered back. He smiled and kissed her hair.

"I have a question." David said still whispering.

"What?" She asked with her eyes closed leaning her ear into his lips.

"How many gay guys do that for you?" He asked thrusting himself against her. She moaned and kissed him sweetly on the lips. She pulled her head away and looked into his eyes. She thought for a minute than hugged him.

"Well, you're the first." She said and cringed but didn't let go. David sighed and rubbed her back. He was quiet. "Sorry, that was rude." She said pulling away to stand in front of him. He looked into her eyes and seen her apology was sincere. He sighed again and shook his head.

"Let's not be calling me gay just yet beautiful. You still get me up in a big hurry." He said smiling. Amanda blushed and smiled back.

"bi then?" She ventured. David stuck his hands in his pockets.

"Look, I don't know what it is okay? I just got a lot to think about. Let's call it, left horny for too long for now okay?" David said smiling at her. Amanda giggled and nodded.

"Okay, Horny for too long it is. Am I picking you up tomorrow?" She asked in her sweet 'never been kissed' type voice.

"How would I get there without you?" David asked shrugging.

"Great, 7:45 then, see ya." She said and half skipped away. David shook his head. To think just minutes ago she was straddling him and shoving her tongue down his throat and now she's skipping away like a 7 year old who has no idea what a kiss like that even feels like. He walked back into the house and shut the door. He leaned his back against the door and looked down.

"Well, you're having fun today aren't you?" He said to the bulge in his jeans. He shook his head and headed up to his room. He shut the door and got undressed. He sat down at his desk and lit a smoke. He opened up his journal and stared at the blank page. "Well, Mr. Black. Welcome to my journal." David said and he began to write.

Sept. 5 Monday,

Well, skip the boring shit shall we? Mr. Black. History teacher/ sexiest creature on earth. I can't believe I think this way about this guy. Amanda thinks I'm bi. We have decided what I have is to be called 'Horny for way to long' Witch, let's face it, Amanda was the last time and that was over two years ago. What kind of guy am I? I am 17 years old and I've had sex twice . . . with the same girl. GOD I'm a loser. I bet Mr. Black fucks all the time. I bet he's got a woman in his bed right now. But then again . . . What if he is gay? What if I picked up on it and that's why I feel this way? Anyway, either way, he certainly gets more tail than I do I bet. Could have done it tonight but Amanda is a girl. What I mean is, girls come with periods and this one happens to have hers. I told her it didn't matter, it wouldn't be the first time she bled on me. She was so embarrassed that time. That's probably why the brakes were on tonight. Well, she knows where I am if she changes her mind I guess.

Anyway, This Mr. Black had me hard during class today. Wonder how come feelings like this never surfaced before? Was it because of dad and how he felt about it? Then again, it could be nothing. Guess we'll see how it turns out tomorrow.

Thanks for listening.

Chapter 2

David was awake the next morning before the alarm. He sighed as he could feel the very familiar tight tug of a morning erection. He looked down at his very swollen penis and shook his head.

"Nope, not gonna happen this morning. You want satisfaction, you can wait for Amanda." He scolded.

That's all I need to start doing. Jacking off about HIM.

"Nope, no way will that ever happen." David said and looked over at the clock. 7:15. He grabbed his smokes and had his ritualistic morning cigarette and stared at his erection. He lay there and flexed it a few times. "God, this sucks." He said and sat up. He ran his free hand through his hair while the other one tapped the ash into the ash tray. He stared at the floor thinking about the day before.

Its only Tuesday. After yesterday, you would think it could be a weekend or something? 4 more days of this.

"God this sucks." He said again and stood up. He stretched and realized he was still hard. "Why are you such a morning person, huh?"

He asked his dick and shook his head. He opened the bedroom door. "Bathroom free mom?" He called.

"In a minute, dear." He heard his mother's voice say from the bathroom. He went back into his room and picked out his clothes. An Iron Maiden tee-shirt today and a pair of black jeans. He grabbed some under wear and socks and sat on the bed. He took the last couple puffs off of his cigarette and crushed it out in the ash tray. There was a quick knock at the door,

"Bathroom is free dear. Good morning." His mother said from the other side of the door.

"Thanks mom." He said and got up. He looked down at his relentless erection. He shook his head and decided to give his mother a few seconds to get out of the hallway and down the stairs. He cracked open the door and looked both ways. She was gone so he hurried to the bathroom. He closed the door behind him and looked down again. "I'm gonna have to pee sooner or later you know. Before or after the shower?" He shook his head and took his boxers off. He started the water and stood in front of the toilet. He waited for a few minutes. Standing there waiting for the need to pee to be stronger than his erection. Finally after a while, standing in the cold bathroom, he was limp enough to urinate. When he was finished he jumped into the shower and quickly cleaned his body. When he shut the water off, he could hear the music from his alarm clock. He wrapped the towel around himself and grabbed his clothes. He walked down to his room and through the cloths on the bed. He shut the alarm off and sat down on the side of the large double bed. He yawned and looked at the time. 7:40. "Holy shit! I must be gay! I take as long in the bathroom as a woman." David jumped up and dropped the towel. He quickly got his clothes on and grabbed his jacket. He slid it over his shoulders and got a strong whiff of Mr. Black. "Oh yea. HE is on you isn't HE?"

He asked his prized possession. "Well, we can fix that." He said and went out of his room and back to the bathroom. He sprayed his own cologne on his jacket and then chased it with deodorant. "That's better." he said and turned to see his mother standing in the door way. She smiled at her grown son.

"You look just like your father when you wear that jacket." She said and approached him to fix the collar.

"Nah, I look better." David teased and hugged his mom. She was dressed for work the same as always. She smelled like some kind of flowers, like always.

"Well, I guess you do. Certainly younger." She teased back and stepped out of the room. David followed. "I gotta run. Have a good day." She said as she walked down the stairs.

"No coffee this morning mom?" David asked as they reached the bottom of the stairs.

"Your coffee companion this morning is a little younger and less related than I am today." She answered grabbing her coat from the stair rail and headed for the door. She winked at him and opened the door. "Have fun." She said and did a funny little finger wave at him.

"Bye mom." David said rolling his eyes. He walked into the kitchen and saw Amanda at the table. She had a coffee in front of her and one at his seat at the table. He sat down and looked at her. She was wearing a low cut tank top and low rider jeans.

"Good morning." She said in her signature 7 year old voice. David raised his eyebrow and sipped his coffee.

"I thought we agreed I was already horny enough?" David said lighting a cigarette. Amanda's face spread with sarcastic shock.

"Whatever do you mean?" She asked sticking out her chest, "This old thing? Hardly." She said and giggled.

"Yea, yea. Always the innocent one, aren't you?" He asked smiling at his friend.

"Of course. Anyway, now that all that stuff is out of the way. Let's talk."

"About what?" David asked taking a sip of coffee.

"You and Mr. Black's lusty romance." David choked on his coffee and Amanda laughed.

"Our what?" David coughed. Amanda laughed and repeated herself.

"Your lusty romance. Don't you wanna talk about it?"

"Not really." David said taking another drag off his cigarette.

"Why not? You must have come up with something to say since I was here yesterday." She prodded and David smirked.

"Sure, thanks for the huge hard on that seemed to last all night."

"Oh come on, David," Amanda laughed, "You have hands." She teased and raised her eyebrows.

"Yea well, that's not gonna happen for a while." David said sipping his coffee again and swallowing it before she could open her mouth again.

"Why? Isn't that like a guy's favorite pass time?" David laughed at her question.

"It used to be." He said tapping his ash into the tray.

"Ok, that's ominous. What did you do? Miss a stroke and hurt yourself so now you're scared to do it?"

"NO!" David laughed.

"Then why not?" Amanda asked frowning. David sighed and looked at his cigarette.

"You wouldn't understand Mandy." He said quietly.

"Try me." She said and leaned forward in her chair. David smiled and shook his head. "OH come on. I'm your bestest friend." She said sticking out her bottom lip and batting her eye lashes. David leaned back in his chair and looked into her sad pathetic face. She continued looking at him like that until he broke.

"Uh, fine." He sighed.

"Yes!" She breathed and fixed her face. She sat practically at the edge of her seat and waited for him to speak. David shook his head and had another sip of his coffee. He stared at the swirling black liquid. Amanda sat quietly waiting to hear him speak. He looked up into her eyes and was instantly nervous.

What am I doing? I can't explain this to her. What will she think of me? Am I crazy or something? This is all happening so fast. But what is even happening? One weird day and I'm ready to think I've got a mad crush on some guy? And this guy is my teacher. I have half a school year with him. She wants to know why I refused to jack off last night. How can I answer that? Scared to cum to the thought of Mr. Black? Afraid of what she'll think of me? Afraid of what I'll think of myself? How can I word this so I don't sound crazy? David held his gaze on Amanda's eyes as he thought. She shifted slightly in her chair as he stared at her. She could tell that whatever it was that was keeping David from satisfying himself must be important. She suddenly felt terrible for pressing the issue.

"It's hard to explain." he began saying but she stopped him.

"Then don't David. I don't need to know. Give yourself some time to figure this Mr. Black thing out."

"Okay, that's weird. It was so funny to you yesterday." David said gulping the last of the coffee out of his cup. Amanda sighed and drank hers too.

"It was a surprise. And it was still a little funny this morning to me too till you got that look on your face. I can tell you don't want to talk about it."

"Well, you're right. I don't." David said and took his cup to the sink. Amanda came up behind him and slowly wrapped her arms around his waist. David closed his eyes and smiled.

"And . . . I'm sorry about yesterday." She said and kissed his right shoulder blade. He turned around and looked into her eyes. She stared up at him like she did the last time they made love. He sighed and looked up at the clock. 8:25.

"I hate time." He whispered and looked back down at her. She rested her head on his chest.

"Why?" She whispered her question smelling his intoxicating cologne.

"Time for school."

"Oh, I hate time too then." She said and leaned up to kiss him. He met her kiss and gently caressed her tongue with his. He ended the kiss with a few little pecks and smiled.

"We better go." He whispered but didn't move. Amanda opened her eyes and stepped away from the tall, dark, gorgeous man she had just kissed. He touched her cheek then held her hand and led her to the front door. They walked in silence to the school. Clouds covered the morning sky. A light fall breeze blew and Amanda shivered.

"I guess some one read our petition." She joked. David smiled and stared at the doors of the school.

"Crappy weather just as you ordered Mandy."

"Are we going in, or are we just gonna stand here staring at the doors?" Amanda asked nudging her friend. David looked at her and then back at the doors.

That was a fast walk. We're here already.

"I guess we are going in. We'll freeze if we don't." They walked through the doors and collected the appropriate books from their lockers. They headed to homeroom and waited for Mrs. Coldiron to do attendance.

"Maybe it's nothing? Maybe it was just a weird day?" Amanda whispered across the aisle to David. He looked at her lovely face and smile.

"Yea, maybe." David whispered back. The bell to head to first class rang. Again the morning flew bye as if it was only minutes. David felt sick as he got ready for lunch break. Amanda met him at the lockers. She bit her bottom lip and stared at him before opening her locker. "What?" David asked looking at her almost guilty expression.

"Come on, we gotta talk." She said, dumping her books into her locker quickly and grabbing his hand. They walked swiftly to the smoking table and she waited as David lit his lunch.

"Ok, what?" He said taking a long drag off his cigarette and sitting down at the table. She smiled at him and then looked down at the ground. She picked at the peeling paint on the seat between her legs. "Fuck Amanda, what's going on man?" He asked with a giggle in his voice. She looked up into his dark blue eyes.

"You're frigging doomed, dude." She said holding her gaze. David raised one eyebrow and spit on the ground.

"That's cryptic."

"Oh God, David! I want to warn you but I'm not sure how." Amanda said with pleading in her voice.

"Warn me about what?" David asked more interested now in Amanda's strange behavior.

"It was terrible, man." Amanda said taking in a deep breath and looking back down at the chipped paint. David slid closer to her and put his hand on her leg. She looked up at him and pursed her lips. He half smirked and raised both eye brows in a questioning gesture.

"David, history class is gonna suck. That's all I can say." She answered his questioning eyes and patted his hand.

"And why is that, Amanda?"

"Look, whatever you thought was sexy about him yesterday has just been trumped."

"Tsk, Amanda." David frowned and got up from his seat. He paced in front of her and then stopped to face her. "I thought we weren't going to talk about it?" She could tell he was angry or nervous or something.

"I'm sorry David, but he's like . . . ." David was pacing again and lifted his hand in front of her.

"Amanda, I don't wanna hear what he's like! I just wanna get through the day with my mind in one peace and my cock limp, ok?" David said in an angry voice.

"Don't yell at me David. I'm trying to help. I'm trying to be your friend."

"You wanna be my friend, Amanda? Don't talk about HIM any more okay?" He said and stopped pacing to stand in front of her again. She looked down at her feet.

"You know, we used to talk about everything. Now all of a sudden, you don't wanna talk? This is a big 'must have friend to talk to' event. Why are you being like this?"

"Amanda, I don't even know what there is to talk about. It's the second day and your acting like I got this guy's name written all over my binder."

"David, I knew your dad okay. I just feel like your beating yourself up and I want to help. Why is that such a crime?"

"Haven't even thought about it." David lied.

"Come on David." Amanda said standing up in front of him. "I know you too. Sometimes I think I know you better than you know yourself. You've probably done nothing BUT think about it."

"Fuck, Amanda. It's not what you think. If my mind was on HIM, why did what happen yesterday after school happen then?" Amanda shook her head and looked away.

"So for 5 minutes out of your life you had me on your mind." She said and sat down at the other side of the picnic table with her back towards David. He squinted his eyes and pursed his lips.

"What is that supposed to mean? We spend like every day together." He said to the back of her head. Amanda sighed and wiped a tear from her cheek. David's shoulders fell and he walked over to sit beside his best friend. She turned so not to look at him. "Are you crying, Amanda?"

"No." Amanda sniffled through her lie. David put his hand in the low of her back and kissed her hair.

"Don't cry Mandy. I'm just not sure that there is anything to talk about right now." David said now calmed by the sadness in his friend.

"God, David!" Amanda scolded and turned to face him. "Who cares WHAT you are? I feel like you don't even notice me unless your cock is hard! Ever since the first time."

"Amanda! What are you talking about? We've been together like that twice! And what do you mean by WHAT I am?" Amanda looked deep into his eyes and shook her head.

"David, I'm talking about yesterday."

"What about it?" David asked confused with Amanda's argument.

"You were ready to fuck me right there at the table. And as far as WHAT you may or may not be, I would still have done what I did yesterday with you." David had a confused look on his face.

"What do you mean, 'what I may or may not be?"

"Ask me that after History class today, David." David sighed and stood up.

"I'm sure you're not referring to my sexuality, Amanda." She looked at him and shook her head.

"David, if it were up to me, YOU wouldn't be questioning it." David stared at her and shook his head again.

"Well then, Amanda. Where are you with that period thing?" David asked with an answer or die look in his eyes. Amanda hated it when he looked at her like that so she thought it better not to keep quiet.

"It should be gone by the weekend. Why?" She shot a look of answer or else of her own. David half smirked and leaned in close to her ear and whispered,

"Then I guess this Saturday would be a good time to defend my sexuality then wouldn't it?" He stood up slowly and watched her face turn three shades of red. He smiled and walked back to the doors of the school. She waited until he was inside before she got up and went into the school herself.

David found his desk in room 19 and sat down. He quickly wrote a note to Mr. Black pleading his case about public speaking. He got up and quickly took it up to the desk.

"Note from mom?" Mr. Black's voice hit David's back like a knife. He wheeled around and looked at the man in the door way.

Oh my God!

Mr. Black was dressed in a tight white tee-shirt he tucked into a pair of incredible looking blue jeans. His hair was parted in the middle and a strand of it hung down in his eyes. The front of his jeans all of a sudden caught David's attention. Just below the button on his fly, his jeans bulged from the package they held. David swallowed and cleared his throat. He met Mr. Black's eyes again but stayed silent.

"A fake maybe?" Mr. Black smiled as he walked toward David and the large oak desk. David could feel sweat beading on his forehead as the man approached. His walk was more of a sexy strut. David's stomach was in a knot and he felt sick. Mr. Black stopped next to David and reached for the paper on his desk. David could smell his cologne and it hit him like an aphrodisiac. He stepped slowly to the side and watched Mr. Black as he read. The sweat that had beaded on his brow now slowly trickled down the side of his face. He swallowed again and took a small step back. Mr. Black looked up from the page. "I see." He said and put the note back on the desk. David shifted where he stood concentrating on not becoming erect. "You know, everybody has to do it David. I need a pretty good reason to exempt you." Mr. Black explained. He crossed his arms across his muscular chest and leaned back against the desk. David looked into his light green eyes.

Come on David. What's a good reason? How can I get out of this? Come on think! David begged his mind for a reason to tell Mr. Black. His mind raced and tripped over its self. *Because YOU will be listening and staring at me while I talk. Because the very thought of YOUR eyes on me makes me hard as a rock and I can't live with that.* David quickly spun around and sat at his desk. Sitting seemed like a good idea if he was going to be thinking like that.

"Well, David? What you got for me?" Mr. Black asked still leaned against the desk.

A cock so hard it would KILL YOU! David thought. Then suddenly his dad popped into his head.

"Well," David said. "Everybody in this school already knows me pretty much."

"And?" Mr. Black said not convinced this was a good exemption reason.

"And," David continued, "The only thing they wanna know is what happened to my dad." David said looking down at his desk. Mr. Black knelt in front of David's desk. David looked up at him and his closeness was like staring death in the face. He looked back down at the lid of his desk.

"Is your dad gone David?" He asked in a half whisper. It almost sounded like the kind of voice used for pillow talk. David nodded but never looked up. "Good reason." Mr. Black said and patted David's back. He started the class then and when it was David's turn to talk, Mr. Black sent him on an errand to the office that would keep up the rest of class. When the bell rang he headed back to room 19 to collect his books and jacket. He walked into the room to find it empty. He walked over to his desk and collected his things. He took his jacket off the back of his chair and folded piece of paper fell to the floor. He put the jacket on and grabbed the sheet of paper. The second bell rang that notified students that they had better be to their next class. He slipped the paper into his pocket and headed to room 9.

"Alright class. There were questions that went with chapters one and two from yesterday. Can we take those and our books out please." Mrs. Coldiron said as David sat down at his desk. He did as the teacher instructed. "Ok, so class. With a book like this, the answers are subjective. You see, there are two reasons why Hans needs more protection. One is obvious. His choice of sexuality. But there is another, what could it be?" David listened to the other students try out several different, some fairly farfetched answers until she called on him. "David, dare to venture a guess?" David sighed and thought for a second.

"I think he's the only blonde in the family." David said shifting in his chair.

"Why do you say that?" Mrs. Coldiron asked leaning against her desk the same way Mr. Black had in his earlier class.

"Well, his description was angelic. I'm guessing that means blonde hair and blue eyes." David answered.

"Very good David." She said and continued with the class. The other answers were a lot like the first one. But at least she picked on the other students for them. When the bell rang, David wasted little time collecting his things and heading out doors. Instead of heading home, he went the other way toward the town library he endearingly called 'the big library' as it held a lot more books than the schools. He walked through the doors and went directly to the mid-evil section. He scrolled through until he found one he hadn't seen there before.

"Turn of the century torture methods hey? Cool." He said to himself and went up to the counter. He checked out his book and headed for the door. Patty Wells was standing there.

"You know, David, those methods aren't practiced anymore." She sneered. David rolled his eyes and walked by.

Duh you idiot. He thought as he walked out the door. David and Patty had been enemies since second grade. She always had some kind of stupid, rude, or idiotic thing to say to David whenever he was around. He walked home in the frigid cold breeze carrying his new heavy book. Mrs. Coldiron had asked the class to read chapters 3 and 4 of their novels but he was hoping to get that done quickly and get to his new book.

He walked through the door of his house and into the kitchen. He tossed his bag next to the table and headed to the fridge for a pop. There was a note:

> David, I have a date tonight so I will be late getting home. Dinners in the fridge. Mom.

"Dating now hey mom?" He asked the note and opened the fridge. He grabbed a pop and the dinner and headed back to the table. He sat down and sighed.

I guess a couple years is as long as you wait now a days after your mate dies. David thought and dug into his book bag for his novel. He turned it open to chapter three and began to read again. He picked at his dinner as he read. The Jewish farmer had given Hans's father a job on the farm so they would be allowed to stay as long as there was work. Hans and Anthony became closer and closer as the weeks went on. They often went swimming together in the creak that passed through the farm yard but at night, they always found themselves together in each other's arms. Their nights together became more and more passionate. (*Dear god)* They touched each other in new and more exciting ways every time they were together. The young men were falling in love. Even their afternoon swims in the creak became more of a lustful adventure than a leisurely splash in its cool water. (*Of course it did)* One night, when the young men were together, Anthony's father was awakened by the quiet giggles and moans of the two young lovers. He stormed from the house with a large gun. He followed the sounds he heard. What he saw dropped him to his knees. The two boys were lying on the ground on their sides with Hans in front of Anthony. Anthony slowly trusted his hips as he made love to Hans. (*Oh GOD)* Hans's moans filled the night air and soon Anthony's own cries of pleasure joined him. Anthony stopped moving then and the two boys lay on the ground panting. Anthony's father was out raged. He flew down the hill with gun in hand and tears flowing from his eyes as he cursed at Hans. The boys jumped up from the ground and grabbed their clothes. They ran to the creak and swam across. They reached the other side and found refuge in a large thicket where they quickly got dressed. They could hear the angry cries from Anthony's father across the creak. They decided it was too dangerous for them to remain near the farm so they headed off north.

David finished the forth chapter and threw the book into his bag.

"Thanks for the riveting novel Mrs. Coldiron." David said and lit a cigarette. He flipped open his new book of torture and settled down for a better read. Just as he started to read about the Iron Maiden, his favorite, the phone rang.

"Hello" David said

"*Hi.*" a familiar voice answered.

"Hi, Amanda." David said and sighed.

"*I'm really sorry about earlier today. I wish I could just keep my mouth shut sometimes.*" She said quietly. It sounded like she was very upset. David rolled his eyes.

"Amanda, its ok."

"*No its not, David. None of this is any of my business. I don't want to fight with you.*" Amanda said in a pleading kind of voice. David smiled. Amanda was so passive aggressive.

"I'm not willing to fight with you either Amanda. And besides, I was thinking. Your right."

"*About what?*" Now she was puzzled but at least sounded happier.

"This is a 'need friend to talk to' thing I think." David said flicking the long ash of his cigarette into the ash tray on the table.

"*And, about this Saturday?*" Amanda sounded afraid to ask.

"You know me better than I know myself remember? If you aren't interested in having a night with me, I won't make you."

"*What? I thought you had a sexuality to defend?*" Amanda mused. David smiled at his friends unwavering ability to start arguments over nothing.

"Fine, have it your way. And by the way, I like it when you shave." David teased.

"*You are a pig, David.*"

"I know. I'll talk to you tomorrow morning." David said trying to cut the conversation short.

"*Ok, see you.*" Amanda said and hung up on her end. David smiled and shook his head. He put out his cigarette and grabbed his things from the kitchen table. He slowly walked up the stairs to his room. He thought about how easy it had been to proposition Amanda. He set his bag on the folding chair in his room and hung his jacket on the back. He walked over to the bed with his torture book and slumped down on to his side. He flipped open to the page he had been reading and studied the mechanical wonder of the Iron Maiden. As he read how the machine worked, something caught his eye. A folded piece of paper peeked out from his jacket pocket.

"Oh yea." David said and got up to get the note. He pushed his bag on to the floor and set the still folded piece of paper on the desk. He sat down on the folding chair and stared at the paper for a second.

Open it David. It's not from him. And even if it were, what would it say? How he wants you? How he wishes to run his long fingers through your dark hair? How he wants to feel your naked body against his? He wouldn't say those things. He's a teacher. He would lose his job and any way of ever teaching again. You're letting your mind play tricks on you. Just open it. It probably isn't from him anyway.

David opened the note and read,

David,

I let you out of class today because I understand where you are coming from. I know that losing a parent can be *difficult and you wouldn't want to share those feelings with a bunch of people who call themselves your peers. I am a very understanding man, David and I will listen if you need to talk. Hope tomorrow will be a better day.*

Alan Black.

David read the name several times before sitting back in his desk chair and lighting a cigarette.

"Alan Black." David said out loud. The name slid off his tongue like satin. It felt like saying something in a long forgotten language. He set his smoke in the ash tray and grabbed his journal.

Sept 6, Tuesday

His name is Alan Black. He is the most incredible thing I have ever seen. These things I can't say out loud. I need to do something about these feelings before it kills me. I am having an evening with Amanda on Saturday. I plan to fuck her. God I hope she wants to. My body is fighting me and I can't let it win. I can't be gay. No matter what happens or how he looks or even what it feels like to be around him. I WILL NOT BE GAY! My dad would kill me if he were here. Speaking of dad, mom has apparently moved on. Or is trying to. She is on a date with some guy tonight. I hope for his sake it goes well. My mom is still damaged goods. I'll kill him if he hurts her. Anyway,

This weekend with Amanda will be good for me. I look forward to letting her work her magic on me. Thanks for listening.

Chapter 3

"God, not again." David said to the feel of a morning erection. He rolled over on to his back and stared at the ceiling. He could hear the shower turn off in the bathroom. He looked over at the clock. 7:29. "One minute till the alarm hey?" David said yawning. He flicked the off switch and lit a cigarette. He sat up on his elbows and looked over to his desk. The note hand written by Alan Black sat there staring back at him. He sat up never taking his eyes off of it. He slouched in his sitting position and could feel his penis dig into his gut. He looked down. "This is bad." He said and stood up. He could hear the bathroom door open and his mother walk past his room. He walked over to the desk and grabbed the note. He scrolled down to the name. "Alan Black" He read aloud. He took another drag off his cigarette and stared at the name on the page. "What's the deal with you, huh?" He asked the name on the paper. He shook his head and dropped the page back down on the desk. He went to the closet and picked out his clothes for the day. His socks and underwear were next. He put the cigarette out in the ash tray next to his bed and headed down the hall to the bathroom. He turned the water on and looked at himself in the full length mirror. "What is up with YOU?" He asked his reflection. "Besides that thing?" He said looking down at the reflection of his dick. He shook his head and jumped into the shower. He washed his hair and his body. He stepped out and dried himself in front of the toilet. He dropped the towel and stood there looking down. "So I can pee now? How nice of you." He said and emptied his bladder. He sprayed on his cologne and put on his deodorant. Then he got dressed and headed back for his room. He grabbed his school bag but left the torture book behind. He threw on his jacket, grabbed his cigarettes and headed down to the kitchen. His mother was standing at the counter talking on the phone.

"I will see what I can do." His mother said as she listened to the voice on the other end. David sat down at the table and sipped at the coffee his mother had prepared for him. "Yes, I'm sure he would have but I don't think now is the time." She said to the phone. There was another long pause and she sighed. "Well, he won't but I'll talk to him ok?" She said and looked at David with apologetic eyes. David mouthed 'what?' but his mother shook her head and lifted one finger up. "Ok, yes and you to. Ok bye now." She said and hung up the phone.

"What was that about?" David asked as his mother sat down at her side of the table.

"Well, it was your uncle." She said.

"And?"

"And he thinks you should have some man to man time." She said taking a sip of her coffee.

"Man to man time? What is this? An after school special?" David joked and lit a cigarette. His mother smiled and shook her head.

"I thought you might feel that way about it." She said.

"I might feel differently if he were around more. The last time we saw him was when dad died." David said taking a drag off his smoke and realizing how upset that actually made him.

"I know dear. I said I would ask. What would you rather do?"

"Why? When is he coming?" David asked sitting back in his chair.

"This weekend." She answered quietly. David leaned forward in his chair.

"What!? Are you kidding? I have plans. Tell him that! Tell him he should give more notice than 48 hours!" David yelled.

"Calm down, son. I'll tell him. What's got you all fired up today?" She asked glancing at the clock then taking her cup to the sink. David shook his head and took another drag from his cigarette.

"Ah nothing mom. Sorry I yelled. Just been some weird days, that's all."

"Wanna talk about it? I have some time if you make it short." She said leaning on the counter.

"NO! Ah, no, that's ok mom. I'll figure it out." David said taking a big sip of coffee.

"Okay." His mother giggled. "Maybe tonight then?" She said as she walked passed him and tossed his hair lightly.

"Uh, no mom. Not this time. It's a personal thing." David said slicking his hair back with one hand and leaning over his chair to see her at the door.

"This wouldn't have anything to do with Amanda, would it?"

"HA! You know my trouble with Amanda mom. She's a girl." David said smiling. His mom smiled and put her jacket on before opening the door.

"Well, David. That GIRL is growing up to be a nice looking woman. You have your hands full I'm sure." She said and blew him a kiss. David smiled and waved.

"Bye mom." He called as she walked through the door. He could hear her call 'bye' as she closed the door. "Amanda. Huh. If she was my problem I could jack off when I wanted to." David said and leaned back in his chair. He glanced at the clock. 7:45. He took another big gulp of coffee and took his cup back up to the pot. He got down a cup for Amanda and fixed them both a cup. She walked in as he set the cups down.

"So I was thinking." She said as she sat down. David smiled and sat down at his seat. "About this Saturday."

"Uh, huh." David said sipping his hot coffee. Amanda shifted in her chair and cleared her throat.

"Defending your sexuality means having sex right?" Amanda asked and David giggled.

"Yes." He answered. Her face blushed a bit but she went on.

"And this is something you really, really, wanna do?" She asked sipping her coffee gingerly. Her face was still a little red.

"Yes." David answered in a sexy bedroom voice. She sighed and shifted in her chair. David could tell she was uncomfortable but he thought better of asking what the 20 questions were about.

"How badly?" She asked sipping again and turning an even deeper red. David half smirked and sucked his front teeth.

"Pretty bad." He said in his bedroom voice again and bit his bottom lip. She sighed a shaky breath but continued.

"Then will you do something for me first?" She asked looking down at her jacket buttons. David tilted his head wondering what on earth she would have him do. Deciding she would not be cruel, he answered.

"Ok, what do you want?" David asked. Amanda took yet another nervous sip from her cup then looked at him in the eyes.

"I want you to tell me everything."

"About what?"

"Everything about Mr. Black." She said and waited as David's eyes grew wide and he seemed to search for the English language. He sighed and looked down at his coffee cup.

What is there to say? I can't even figure out what is REALY going on. Is she really going to use sex as a tool to get me to talk? He glanced up at the clock. 8:00. *GOD! I can't even use time as an excuse to get out of this. I could always say no. What's sex anyway? A quick fix? If I say no, am I admitting I'm gay? If I say anything I sound gay. GOD! What do I do?*

"Why don't you start with what you feel like around him?" Amanda ventured.

"You're assuming I wanna talk about it, Amanda." David said and lit another cigarette. Amanda slumped back in her chair.

"I just need to know what's going on with you."

"Nothing, really." David said staring at his cigarette. Amanda leaned forward in her chair and sighed.

"David, I know you. I know something is up. You want me to LET you defend your sexuality, or whatever. Then I need to know what you're defending it against." She made a valid point, David thought. He leaned back in his chair and took another long drag off the smoke in his hand.

"Fine!" He said. Sounding a lot angrier than he meant but he didn't apologize for it. "If you need to know, I find him very . . . ." David thought about the answer before he spoke. Amanda looked into his eyes. There was no use sugar coating it. She would see right through it. He shook his head and sighed.

"Very what, David?" She said not moving in her chair. David could feel a lump growing in his throat.

Why is this so hard? It's nothing right? Just tell her what you think. David took another puff of his cigarette and looked back at Amanda.

"Very, attractive." David whispered and looked back down at his coffee cup. The black liquid sat unmoving in its little white vessel. Amanda sat back in her chair and shook her head. "WHAT! What Amanda? What do you want me to say, huh?" David barked at his friend.

"You're really going to expect me to accept ATTRACTIVE?" She asked.

"Why not? That's what I think, okay?"

"David, You think Brad Pitt is Attractive in Interview With a Vampire. Attractive isn't good enough." Amanda said staring at David. David sighed and shook his head.

"Okay . . . . Better than attractive then." David answered and took a sip of his coffee. He looked up at the clock again. 8:09. *Come on clock!*

"Ha! Like sexy? Hot maybe?" Amanda said noticing his constant eye on the clock. David looked at his friend. She was obviously upset at his last outburst but she wasn't giving up. He said nothing. "Look, you said this was a 'need a friend to talk to' thing. Why won't you talk about it?" She asked softening the look on her face.

"I don't know what to say Amanda." David said looking back down into the black abyss of cooling coffee in front of him.

"I have never known you to not be able to talk about something." She said sitting back in her chair again and drinking her coffee. David shrugged his shoulders.

"This is a weird thing. It's hard to talk about it."

"Even to me?" She asked.

"Especially to you." David answered and butt out his cigarette. He gulped the cold coffee out of the cup and got up from his chair.

"Why?" Amanda asked following his lead and going up to the sink with her cup.

"Because, aside from being my best friend, your also the only woman I ever . . . you know?" David said and sat his cup in the sink. Amanda raised her eye brows.

"REALLY? Wow, I didn't know that." She said and walked over to pick up her bag. "How is that a reason for not talking to me about this?" She added as she watched David gather his things as well. David shook his head and opened the front door.

"Well, Because." David answered and let her walk out first.

"*Because?*" Amanda said sarcastically. "Because why?" She added. David locked the door and walked with his friend down to the sidewalk. They slowly made their way down the street to the 7th ave. corner. "Because why, David?" Amanda asked and stopped walking. David stopped in front of her and turned to face her. She shivered in the fall breeze. David sighed.

"Because, it's kinda the same as you." David said.

"What does that mean?"

"He is the same as you." David said and grabbed her hand to get her to walk forward. She followed with a puzzled look on her face.

"What am I then?" She asked looking at the ground as they walked.

"You?" David asked and smiled. "You are the kind of thing that keeps a guy awake at night. You have a killer body, which makes me a little *uncomfortable* at times." David said smiling and Amanda giggled.

"Anything else?" She asked remembering that she was being described side by side with Mr. Black. David sighed and stopped at the doors of the school.

"Very, very sexy." He said and winked. Amanda giggled again and went in before David. She stood in front of her locker without opening it. David looked at her and was puzzled. "What?" He asked as she stared at her locker. She looked at him and smiled.

"So . . . this is what you think of him?" She asked quietly for only them to hear. David raised his eyebrows and finished in his locker. He waited for her to finish collecting her things then said,

"Those are the things that are the same as you." Amanda's jaw dropped open as he walked away to home room. She hurried to catch up to him. She quickly sat down at her seat and leaned across the aisle.

"There are *other* things?" She asked in a loud whisper. David giggled and leaned over to her.

"How bad do you wanna know?" He asked and winked. Her face went red and could already see were this was going.

"Really bad." She whispered giggling. David smiled.

"You'll have to do something for me first." David said

"Okay, what?" She asked as the bell rang. David got up from his desk and winked at her again. "What, David? What do I have to do?" Amanda called after him as he walked the other way down the hall than she had to go.

"I'll tell you at lunch time." He called back and disappeared into his math class.

The lunch bell rang and David made his way to his locker where he saw Amanda waiting for him. He shook his head and smiled as he unloaded his books into his locker. Amanda said nothing as he slowly put his jacket on and walked with her to the doors. They sat down side by side at the table. David lit a smoke and sat silently. Amanda waited for a while before finally saying.

"Okay, David. You promised lunch time." David looked at her and squinted his eyes. She squinted back and they both laughed.

"Are you above hooking yourself out for information?" David asked and laughed. Amanda smiled and answered

"That depends how good the info is my dear." David raised his eyebrows and took another drag from his cigarette.

"Oh, it's pretty good." He answered and laughed again. Amanda laughed now too but said nothing. They sat in silence for a few minutes before David added, "It's so good, you'll never hear anything like it again in your life."

"I doubt that. But I'll play along." Amanda said looking at her friend.

"Hey. You're the one who wants to know so bad." David said lifting himself up to sit on the table and put his feet down on the seat. Amanda did the same and sighed.

"Yea I do." She said and looked at him again. David took another drag from his cigarette and looked down at his feet. "I'll tell you what, David." Amanda said. "You tell me the other stuff, and I'll tell you if it's worth hooking me out for." David laughed and looked back at his friend.

"Ok, let's see." David said and looked out on to the school yard. "He has this smell." David began.

"A smell?" Amanda asked. She looked like a young child settling down for a bed time story.

"Yea, a smell."

"What about it?" She asked trying to be gentle although she knew if she pried he would stop talking.

"Well, it's kind of powerful."

"How do you mean?"

"It's like . . ." David thought about it for a second. He wasn't even quite sure want it was like, but he went on. "I don't know. But he smells *really* good."

"Okay, so he smells good. What else?" Amanda asked getting closer to her friend.

"Well, his voice is what gets me I think. That smell and his voice."

"Can you explain it?" David still looked out into the school yard as if the answers were out on the football field somewhere.

"Not really Mandy. It's like a spell or voodoo or something." He said taking the last puff of his cigarette and tossing it away.

"Voodoo?" Amanda asked trying to keep him focused. David sighed and got off the table. He paced back and forth for a while still thinking. Amanda watched him careful not to push any more than needed.

"It's like my body can't help but react to him, Amanda." David said still pacing in front of Amanda and the picnic table.

"What do you mean, react?" Amanda asked. David stopped walking and looked at her.

"What do you think I mean Amanda?" He asked. She sat there for a moment and her eyes grew wide with realization.

"OH! You mean you get . . . *hard?"* She asked. Shock struck her face when he nodded. "Wow, that's . . . weird." She said and David laughed.

"I told you it was worth hearing."

"It certainly was. But there is something I still don't get. How come never before?"

"That's the weird thing Amanda." David answered. "This is the only time anything like this has ever happened." Amanda thought about it for a while.

"Maybe it's always been there but it just took the right guy?" She asked. David sat back down on the table.

"I don't know." He said and leaned back on his hands and closed his eyes.

"So now what?" She asked and moved a loose hair off his face. David sighed and rested his elbows on his lap.

"I don't know that either." He answered.

"How much thought *have* you given this thing David?"

"Like I said before, Amanda, not a lot." David answered. Other than the fact that Mr. Black turned him on for some reason; he really hadn't thought about what happens next.

"Here's what we do David." Amanda said and patted his leg. "Come to my house Saturday and we decide what you do next. But you have to really think about this thing."

"*We* decide what I do next?" David asked half-jokingly.

"You know what I mean David. We'll discuss it and see what we come up with for things for you to do or not do about this little *uprising.*"

"Cute, Amanda." David said and playfully nudged her with his shoulder. The bell rang and they walked in together. They decided on pizza to eat when he went over on Saturday and Amanda said she would call tonight to see how the rest of his day went. They went their separate ways to their class rooms. David stopped in front of room 19.

He'll be in there. You can't stand out here all afternoon. Just walk in and go right to your desk. David thought and took a deep breath. He walked into the room and went right to his desk. He sat down and then looked up at Mr. Black's desk. There he sat reading a pamphlet of some kind. He looked up and met David's gaze.

"Good afternoon David." He said and smiled.

GOD! You're gorgeous. David thought then answered.

"Hi."

"Ready to learn something today?" Mr. Black asked.

"You bet." David answered and put his forehead down on his arms. He could hear Mr. Black put the pamphlet down and get up from his desk. He wrote something on the board and clapped the chalk off his hands.

"Does anyone know what October 31st is?" He asked the class. David kept his head down and listened. A couple students said Halloween.

Fucking rocket scientists. David thought but waited for Mr. Black to continue.

"Yes, but it is also the 25th annual Mid-Evil fair." David shot his head up and read the chalk-board.

Mid-Evil War Tools

David read the board and raised his eyebrows. Mr. Black smirked at him and continued speaking.

"This year they have invited our school to make the War Tools demonstration. I have been asked to put a group of students together to work on this project with me. Now before everybody signs up, you should know. This will not be done during class time. This is an after school and maybe some weekends kind of thing. It *is* however worth extra credit." He said and picked up a piece of paper from his desk. "This is the sign-up sheet. I will be collecting this after school." He said and pinned it to the board. A student in the back lifted his hand. "Yes Derik?" Mr. Black said allowing the student to speak.

"How many people are you trying to get for this thing?"

"Excellent question. I need a group of 6 students that I can split into groups of two. So if you all put your names down, you won't all be chosen. But, I am always prepared for these kinds of things so . . . ." He said and grabbed a text book from his desk. It read *The tools of War.* "We will be doing a short unit on Mid-Evil war tools and torture and the like so . . . . The students with the best marks at the end of next week will be selected." He said and handed the text book out to the students. David stared at the cover as if it were the first copy of the Bible. He watched Mr. Blacks strut as he walked back up to the front of the room. He looked at David and smiled then started the class.

They started at the beginning with the invention of the chain and how it could be used as a weapon. When class was over, many students wrote their names on the signup sheet. Mr. Black thanked them and watched them leave. David had remained at his seat still reading the literature on chain maces and armor.

"Don't you have an English class to attend?" Mr. Black said smiling at the young man engrossed in his book. David looked up at him and rolled his eyes. He packed up his things and stood up. He walked over to the door but was stopped by Mr. Black's sexy rock star voice. "Did you get my note yesterday, David?" He asked. David sighed and turned around.

"Uh, yea I did." David answered and pulled at the strap of his book bag.

"I would have just told you I was here to talk to but you seem to prefer your conversations on paper." He said and smiled.

"Yea, kind of." David answered. He could feel the palm of his hands starting to sweat. Mr. Black tapped the sign-up sheet.

"Not interested in joining?"

"I'm sure you'll find 6 students that will do just fine." David answered.

I have to endure you at school. That's quite enough for me. He thought.

"We'll see." Mr. Black said and sat down at his desk going over the list. David shook his head and stepped out of the room. He went to

English class and plopped himself down at his desk. Again he rested his head on his arms.

GOD! What am I gonna do? Amanda said give it some thought. Ok, brain, think. What are we gonna do. Live with an itch I can't scratch for the rest of my life is certainly an option. What about cutting out my eyes and blowing up my ear drums so I can't see him or hear him? It's doable.

Fuck! He is so hot! Why is he, huh? What does he have no other guy ever did? What makes him so sexy? The smell? I wear cologne and I don't turn myself on. That voice? Other guys probably sound like that. What is it David? What is it about HIM? Why is he such a big deal? Why does he turn me on so much? Fuck, I'm doomed.

Mrs. Coldiron had started the class and was asking questions about chapters 3 and 4 of the ridiculous history class chasing novel. Many students were upset over the reaction of Anthony's father. The obvious out bursts of 'He should accept him no matter what' comments were popping out all over the room. The class soon turned into a debate of sexuality differences during WW2. Not a lot had been accomplished but the teacher was happy with the class's determination to rewrite history. At the end of class she sent chapters 5 and 6 for home work. David got up and went to his locker. He quickly got what he needed for the night and headed out the doors.

When he arrived home he could see his mother's car in the drive way. He walked in.

"Hi mom!" He called.

"Hi dear. I'm in here." She called from the living room. He stepped in and seen his Uncle Carl sitting on the couch next to her. He looked at the young carbon copy of his deceased brother.

"Hi sport. How have you been?" He asked and smiled his crooked smile. David rolled his eyes and looked at his mother. She had a pleading look on her face so he decided to play nice and sat down in his dads reclining chair.

"I thought you weren't coming till the weekend?" David asked and lit a cigarette.

"I thought I would surprise you and your mom." He said and patted David's mothers leg. David could feel the hair on the back of his neck stand on end.

"Your Uncle Carl might be moving to the area dear." David's mother said and shifted in her seat.

"Is that right?" David asked in the nicest voice he could muster through clenched teeth. His mother smiled and pleaded with her eyes again. David bit his lip and looked down at the arm of his father's favorite chair.

"I thought since you guys had such an empty house and no body taking care of things around here, I would stay here and whip this place back into shape." Carl said and placed his hand back on Nancy's leg. David's blood boiled but he waited for his mom to speak.

"Really, Carl, we haven't got the room. And David does a good job keeping up with the things that need to be done." Carl squeezed Nancy's leg and smiled. David could feel every muscle in his body screaming to rip this guy's head off.

"Don't be silly Nancy. You have plenty of room. We could chuck out all that old band equipment from the room down stairs and . . . ." David jumped off the chair.

"LIKE FUCK you will!" David yelled and Carl got up from where he was sitting.

"David, stop." Nancy said and got up as well.

"What did you say to me, boy?" Carl sneered at David. David shook his head and looked at his mother. There was fear in her eyes but she seemed to beg him to deal with this pig who had been touching her leg since David walked in the room.

"I said . . . Like FUCK YOU WILL!" David spat into Carl's face. Carl pushed David back by the shoulders.

"Carl! Stop!" Nancy cried and grabbed his arm. He looked back at Nancy and then turned his head to look at David. He was met by a powerful right hook. He fell back onto the couch and started to laugh.

"Great work, BOY! Just what I needed to get you out of here!" Carl said and hurried to the door. David stared at him with death in his eyes.

"Carl, what are you talking about?" Nancy asked following him to the door. Carl looked back at David and then said.

"Mike stole you from me and nothing, not even that LITTLE FAGGOT of your's is gonna stop me from getting you back!" David practically jumped on him and pushed him out the door. Carl fell off the step and drug David down with him. He jumped on top of David and whispered in his ear. "You gonna let your sweet mother stay lonely just because YOU can't get over your drunk father?" David fought underneath of him and Carl laughed. "You think you're so tough don't you? I'm gonna make you a promise you little puke." David lay there and listened as tears filled his eyes. "I'm gonna get you hauled out of here for that little stunt you just pulled. Then I'm gonna come back here and . . . console your poor sweet mother. All . . . Night . . . Long." He said and spit in David's face as he got up. David kicked him in the back of the leg and Carl fell.

"David! Don't!" Nancy yelled and ran over to him. She grabbed his arm and held it tight. Carl got back up from the ground and smiled.

"Your mine, you little fuck!" He said and got into the car on the other side of the street. David watched him drive away and shook his head.

"What the FUCK was that, mom?" David yelled and turned to walk into the house. She caught up with him and stood in front of the door.

"How was I supposed to know he would do that?" She asked and started to cry. David shook his head again and went for the door handle. Nancy stepped out of the way and let him go in. She followed him into the kitchen and sat down at the table.

"Okay, The truth mom. WHAT was he doing here?" David asked and sat down at the table. He was vibrating from anger. Nancy shifted in her seat and cleared her throat.

"David," she said and paused, "It would be nice to have some help around here." She said quietly. David shook his head and grinned a very pissed off grin.

"Nice, mom. What do you need help with huh? Your lonely nights?" David barked and slammed his cigarettes down onto the table.

"David! Don't speak to me like that." Nancy said and wiped a tear from her face.

"Then what? Mom."

"Things aren't as easy as just getting up for school in the real world you know." She said and lit a cigarette. David rolled his eyes and stood up.

"Mom, don't patronize me. Dad left money." He said and walked over to the sink.

"Yes he did but it's almost gone. I can't afford this place on my wages." She said and tapped the ash from her cigarette into the ash tray.

"So I'll get a job or something. Don't you DARE let that fat FUCK into dad's house again!" David yelled pointing his finger at his mother.

"Who do you think you are, David? You can't talk to me like that! I raised you better than that I hope!" She yelled back at him from the table.

"MOM! The guy just wants to fuck you and take over dad's life! GOD only knows what else!"

"David! How dare you? He is your father's brother. He is only trying to look out for his family." Nancy began to cry. David came back to the table and sat down.

"Mom, listen to me." David said and grabbed her hand. She wiped the tears from her face again and looked at him. "We don't need him. You don't need him. He's just looking for a free ride. Don't do this." David pleaded. Nancy looked down at her son's trembling hand. She knew he was angry enough to kill someone.

"Oh, David. What am I supposed to do? I miss having a man around. I need a companion. I can't be alone anymore." She whispered through her tears. David sighed and squeezed her hand.

"What about that guy from last night or whatever?" He asked hating the thought of his mother with anyone but Mike Smith.

"Oh, that's not going to go anywhere dear." She said and pulled her hand away. She wiped her face with both hands and sighed. David leaned back in his chair and closed his eyes. He had no idea what to say to his mother. "There's this fellow Roger who wants to take me to dinner but he's a business suit kind of guy. I feel like he's way out of my league." She said. David kept his eyes closed and sighed.

"Why? You're a high class lady stuck in a lower class life mom. You should go." He said.

"Oh, David. The things you say." She said and laughed. He opened his eyes and smiled.

"Go mom. Go on ten thousand dates with ten thousand guys; just don't let him back in this house. Okay?" David said smiling at his mother's tired looking face. She sighed and shook her head. "Got Rogers number?" David asked handing her the cordless phone. Nancy stared at the phone for a moment and then sighed.

"Go get my purse." She said. David did as he was told and fetched the black purse from the stair rail. He brought it to her and set it on the table in front of her.

"Good luck." He said and grabbed his bag and headed up stairs.

"What should I say?" She called at him from the kitchen. David peaked his head around the corner to look at his mom and said,

"How about hello? And then yes to dinner." Nancy smiled and waved him away as she dialed the phone. He stood on the stairs until he heard,

"Um, hello, Roger? Its Nancy, Nancy Smith from the Hospital." He shook his head and headed to his room. He could hear her laughing as he shut the door. He tossed his bag on the floor next to the desk and sat down on the bed.

Fucking Carl. What a shit head. He thought and snuck down the stair to the fridge. He stood hiding behind the fridge door and listened to his mother talk.

"Yes, I have a son. He's almost grown . . . . No, he is in school. Grade 11 actually . . . . No, he's the only one. And he's nosy." She kidded. David looked over the door and smiled. He grabbed some leftover meatloaf and headed up the stairs again. He sat down at his desk and opened his journal.

Sept 7, Wednesday

What a day. Carl was here and I had to throw him out. Fucking jerk was feeling up my mom and thinking he was all that. GOD! I should have kicked his fat ass. I seemed to have talked mom into a date with some dude named Roger. Sorry dad. I guess she NEEDS to move on more than she's ready to. History class has taken an interesting turn. Mid-Evil stuff, as if being sexy wasn't enough to keep my attention. He's putting together some extra credit thing for the fair. I thought living through 80 minutes a day with him was lots long enough for me to be around him. I didn't sign up. I did how ever tell Amanda pretty much everything there is to know about how I feel about him. I never mentioned the note, I need to keep something secret. The note thing is going to turn into a regular thing I think. He seems to really want to talk to me about dad or something. Anyway, the new plan is to meet up at Amanda's and discuss what to do next. Still hoping to get laid, but we'll see.

Thanks for listening.

Chapter 4

Amanda was there bright and early as always. She was laughing and talking with David's mom as he came into the room. David smiled at them and sat down at the table. He yawned and lit a cigarette.

"So, how did it go last night mom?" He asked eyeing up Amanda's very revealing shirt. Nancy giggled and sipped her coffee.

"Well, we are going out on Friday." She said and smiled. David sighed,

"That's good mom. I'm glad." He said and sipped his coffee too. Amanda giggled and sipped her coffee.

"I hear you had an interesting night of your own." Amanda said looking at her friend across the table. David looked at her and smiled.

"What? Carl? Whatever. No biggy." He said and tapped the ash from his cigarette.

"You're so modest David." Nancy said and smiled. David shook his head and drank his coffee.

"God, everybody's late this morning huh?" he asked as he looked at the clock. 8:15. Nancy looked at it too and sighed. She got up from the table to get ready to leave. David walked her to the door.

"Thank you for talking me into calling Roger last night." Nancy whispered as she put her coat on.

"Whatever mom. Just have a good time. Okay?" David said and opened the door for her.

"I hear you have a date of your own on Saturday?' She mused and stepped out the door. David rolled his eyes and smiled.

"Something like that mom." He answered. They said their good byes and David shut the door. He turned to see Amanda standing behind him.

"I was wondering" She said as he walked by her and collected his things for school.

"What's that?" He asked and handed Amanda her bag. She threw it over her shoulder and walked over to the door.

"What do you think of the novel in English class considering all that is going on?"

"OH SHIT!" David said, "I forgot to read the next two chapters." He said and went to the door. Amanda giggled and followed him out.

"5 and 6?" She asked as they walked. David nodded.

"Nothing exciting. They ran, and ran, and ran some more." She said. David shook his head and kept walking. "What do you think of it?" She asked again.

"It sucks is what I think." David answered and smiled. Amanda shook her head.

"Come on David, full disclosure."

"It's true. It sucks to have to read that shit right after History class." David answered as they turned the corner.

"I see. It's not so helpful huh?"

"Not really." David answered and sighed. "The school is against me Amanda. I'm telling you. It's a conspiracy." David joked as they approached the school. Amanda giggled then said,

"Yep! I'm in on it too." David looked at her with a puzzled gaze.

"Oh, really?" He asked and opened the door for her.

"Uh huh." She said in her little voice and walked in. David shook his head smiling and followed her to their lockers. They made their way to home room class and sat down. Mrs. Coldiron sent them away after attendance and they went on with their morning. It went by slowly. David felt as though he would fall asleep in period 4 but he was saved by the bell. He met Amanda at her locker and they headed outside.

"So, in on the conspiracy huh?" David said lighting a cigarette and sitting down at the table. Amanda sat down beside him and smiled.

"Kind of." She said.

"Ok, What's 'kind of'?"

"I'll tell you on Saturday." She mused. David rolled his eyes.

"What ever happened to full disclosure?" David asked lifting one eyebrow. Amanda giggled and answered,

"Are you above hooking yourself out for information?"

"That depends on the info." David said laughing. Amanda laughed and looked into her friends eyes.

"This is so good. You'll never hear anything like it again in your life." She laughed again and twisted her hair in her fingers. David shook his head and shoved her playfully with his shoulder. Deciding she was kidding about the info., David spent the rest of lunch break discussing his mother's date with Roger. When the bell rang they headed in to their lockers.

"Will I see you after school?" David asked as he shut the door to his locker.

“Mmmmm, Babysitting detail. My parents have some ‘grownups only’ diner thing to go to. I’ll call you though.” She said and turned to head to class. David did the same but heard her call from behind him, “Have a good time in History class today! You should find it extra spicy!” She laughed. David smiled and flipped her the finger. He walked to his class but didn’t hesitate at the door today. He went straight to his desk and sat down. Then he looked up at Alan Black. He was wearing a tight red shirt that left very little to the imagination. He wore tight blue jeans that looked like they would burst at the seams around the fly.

Oh dear GOD!

David thought and put his head back down on his arms like he did the day before. He could hear Mr. Black walk over to his desk. He felt him lightly tap him on the shoulder. David looked up into his eyes.

“Are you tired or not feeling well?” Mr. Black’s voice was like sex by itself never mind the tight cloths and incredible looks. David sighed and leaned back in his chair.

“A little of both.” David answered and looked to the front of the room.

“Anything I can do?” Mr. Black asked as he walked to the front of the room. David was quiet but his mind thundered in his skull.

Take off that shirt!

“No, I’ll be fine.” David answered and opened his books. Mr. Black handed out work sheets on the chain stuff they had read about the day before. David didn’t look up as Mr. Black set his on his desk. He got right to work on it. The questions seemed far too easy for grade 11 History. He filled the questions in anyway. It took him almost the whole class. When he finished, he took the pages up to Mr. Black’s desk.

Thank god for baggy jeans. David thought as he could feel the erection forming beneath his pants. Mr. Black looked up at him as he set the pages down.

"Done already? I was hoping to send it for homework." David shrugged.

"They were pretty easy Mr. Black." David said and turned to head back to his desk. Mr. Black smiled and went over the questions. David watched him as he bit his bottom lip slightly as he read. David ran his hand through his hair then put his head back down on his arms.

Holy fuck! I'm gonna die! You'd think I was old enough to fight a fucking chubby! GO AWAY!

"David, come up here please." Mr. Black said. David froze for a minute and looked up. Mr. Black looked at him and waved him forward. David closed his eyes for a second.

Please go away! He pleaded in his mind and stood up. He quickly glanced down to see that his erection was not noticeable. He sighed a breath of relief and walked forward to Mr. Black's desk. He patted the seat beside him. David felt sick but he sat down.

"These answers are perfect David." He whispered. "This took you no time at all. You really know your Mid-Evil war fair." David could feel every muscle in his body begging him to run. Or at least get a little farther from this man. But he held his ground and just shrugged. Mr. Black continued whispering, "Join the group David, put your name on the sheet. I can see from this bit of work that you would be an asset." David could smell Mr. Black's cologne and he felt dizzy. The powerful throb in his jeans was almost impossible to ignore. It was almost painful. Mr. Black waited silently for David to answer.

"My mom needs help with the bills. I gotta get a job. I won't have the time." David answered and took a deep breath. His lungs filled with the smell of Mr. Black. He fought back the whimper that hung in his throat. Mr. Black sat back in his chair.

"That's really too bad. Your knowledge on the subject sure would have been helpful." Mr. Black sighed and placed David's work on a pile of other papers that needed to be graded. Then he turned back to face David. David studied his features like an artist studied his art. His light green eyes were like shiny emeralds artfully placed into his perfectly chiseled face. His jaw line was strong and cut arrow straight. His blonde hair was almost shoulder length and had a slight wave in it. He leaned on his desk and spoke. "Is there something I can do to help you and your mom?" His voice was quiet and sincere. David shook his head and answered,

"Thanks but no. I can deal with this."

"Bills and mortgages and groceries aren't a child's responsibility, David." Mr. Black whispered as not to alert the class of their discussion.

"I agree. Good thing I'm not a child." David whispered back. Mr. Black smiled and leaned back in his chair.

"No, I suppose you aren't David. But still. These things shouldn't be held on your shoulders alone." Just as Mr. Black finished his sentence, the bell rang. David stood up and headed for his desk. He gathered his things and headed for the door. He let the other students go first then he turned and faced Mr. Black.

"I'm not alone. I have my mom." He said and turned back toward the door. Mr. Black smiled and let him go. David made his way to English class still very aware of the excitement Allan Black had caused in his body. He thought about the way Mr. Blacks eyes seemed to cut into him like sand in a desert storm. His body knew what it wanted and only his mind fought it.

God! What am I gonna do? David thought as he sat down at his desk in English class and got ready for the lesson. *Why can't I just have a normal day where no man gives me a hard on and makes me sweat like a 10 year old looking at his first set of tits?*

"Ok class. Chapters 5 and 6 where a little slow, granted, But I would like to discuss the authors reasoning for describing the distance they traveled." As the class offered their reasons for the two apparently boring chapters, David's mind was elsewhere.

If only I could get him out of my head for 10 minutes. Ok, Think about Amanda and her hot little shirt this morning. Think about how her mouth and tongue feel when I kiss her. Remember her hands on my body, pulling my hair. Imagine what it would be like if Allan Black did it. SHIT! Really David!

He decided it was better to pay attention to the class discussion.

"I think what they are doing is romantic. it's a love story really." One of the girls at the back said.

"*I* think they should go back." Another student said. Mrs. Coldiron looked at David.

"What do you think David?" She asked. The room was quiet. David cleared his throat and then answered,

"Well, I think the author has a demon or two in his closet." The students giggled at his answer but Mrs. Coldiron seemed interested in what David had to say.

"Why do you come to that conclusion after only six chapters, David?" David shifted in his chair then answered,

"Actually, I thought of that after only four chapters. It seems to me that the author felt a need to add even more heart ache than already existed during the holocaust."

"Why would he do that?" A student asked from the back. David looked at Mrs. Coldiron to see if he should go on. She raised her eyebrows as if to ask the same question.

"The holocaust has been over written. This guy wanted to write something that wasn't all Hitler and A-Bombs. Something that was real. That's just what I think anyway." The class exploded with their own interpretations of the authors reasoning for writing about two gay boys instead of concentration camps and Hitler. The whole period went on like that until the bell rang. David collected his things and went to the door. Mrs. Coldiron stopped him at the door.

"David, it's nice to see you participating in class. You are very bright."

"It's only the beginning of the year Mrs. Coldiron. I hope to disappoint you yet." David said and walked toward the door.

"Bright and funny huh? There isn't a class clown in there somewhere is there?" David stepped through the door and smiled.

"I promise no class clown." He said and walked to his locker. When he opened the door, a folded piece of paper fell to the floor. He picked it up and shoved it into his jacket pocket. He quickly gathered the rest of his things and hurried home. He busted through the door and went straight up to his room. He dropped the book bag on the floor and pulled the note out of his pocket. He sat down at his desk and slowly opened it.

David,

I hope I didn't offend you today. I understand that you wouldn't want to talk about these kinds of things with your teacher. I just hope you're not in over your head with whatever problems you and your mom are having at home. And I also hope you reconsider your decision not to join the Mid-Evil group. Anyway, please reconsider.

Alan Black

David leaned back in his chair and sighed. He stared at the note on his desk.

Another note. Why does he care I wonder. It's his job to care I guess. If only he knew my biggest problem was HIM. What words of wisdom would he have for that I wonder?

"Whatever it is, it would sound awesome I bet." David said aloud and stood up. He walked down the stairs and to the fridge. He grabbed a pop and sat down at the table. He lit a cigarette and stared out the window.

What am I supposed to do with all this? I was practically in pain today. What the heck is going on with me? Am I gay or what? I wish I wasn't but what else could it be? I've never been this turned on by anybody. Not even Amanda.

"Why can't I figure this out?" David said aloud. He stared out the window for the better part of an hour before the phone rang. "Hello." David said.

"*Hi honey*" It was David's mother.

"Hi mom."

"*How was your day dear?*"

"Long. How was yours? Aren't you on your way home about now?" David asked looking at the clock. It read 3:45.

"*Oh, I have to work a second shift today. I won't be home until early morning.*"

"You HAVE to or you ASKED to?"

"*I have to dear, Lisa called in sick and there is no one else to work for her. Besides, we COULD use the extra money.*" Nancy said.

"Ok, mom. Just don't work yourself to death. I said I would get a job if you needed help."

"*Oh David, that won't be necessary. You have school. I won't let you ruin your education because we are a little tight.*"

"A job won't ruin my education mom. A couple hour a week after school won't kill me." David said.

"*Let's talk about it tomorrow sometime ok son?*"

"Ok, mom. Need anything done tonight?" David asked.

"*Well, you'll have to feed yourself. I don't think there is any left over's in the fridge. Could you do some laundry maybe?*"

"Sure mom. No problem." David said and got up off his chair.

"*Thanks Dear. Listen. If I'm not too busy later I'll call ok.*"

"Ok, mom. Don't work too hard."

"*Oh I'll try not to. Bye dear.*" Nancy said.

"Bye mom." David said and hung up the phone. He went down the stairs and stepped into the laundry room. His mother had clothes in the wash already so he moved them to the drier and threw a new load in the wash. He started the machine and went upstairs to the kitchen. He dug through the cupboards and found some Kraft dinner. He started a pot of water on the stove and walked back over to the table where his pop sat. He lit a cigarette and waited for his pot of water to boil. When it started he cooked his dinner and took it upstairs with him. He went into his room and sat down at the desk. He stared at the name at the bottom of the note while he ate.

I bet Amanda is wondering if I'm thinking about you. What should I tell her if she asks when she calls? I wish I was sure about how I felt. I wish there was a way to turn back time and take my wish back. I would almost give anything to get Mr. Felch back. I hated that guy.

David finished his meal and set his bowl aside. He lit a cigarette and cleaned his teeth with his finger. He sat still staring at the note on his desk when the phone rang. David got up and went downstairs and grabbed the cordless phone off the hook.

"Hello" He said.

"*Hi David.*" Amanda said.

"How's babysitting?"

"*Fine. Just finished super.*"

"Me too." David said and took the phone out into the living room and laid down on the couch. He took a long drag off his cigarette and tapped the ash off into the tray.

"*How was your afternoon?*"

"Uh, interesting."

"*Do tell.*" Amanda coaxed.

"Well, your spicy comment was right on. The red shirt right?" David asked. He could hear Amanda giggle on the other end.

"*Yea, I thought if fit him nicely.*"

"It sure did." David said thinking about the rippled frame of his History teacher.

"*Any . . . physical reactions?*" Amanda asked with a slight giggle in her voice.

"Of course." David answered and shut his eyes.

"*Wanna talk about it?*"

"I thought we were?" David asked and puffed on his cigarette again.

"*I mean . . . Do you want to talk about your . . . reaction?*" Amanda stumbled over her question.

"What's there to say? For the last three days it's been the same thing every History class. I get hard and stay hard till I leave." David answered his friend. She was quiet for a few seconds and then answered,

"*Remember when you said you wouldn't be jacking off for a while?*"

"Yea, I remember." David said tapping the ash off his cigarette.

"*Why won't you?*" Amanda asked.

"It's hard to explain Amanda."

"*Can you try?*" She asked. It sounded as though she had also lain down on the couch. David sighed. He took another long drag from his cigarette and put it out in the ash tray.

"Well," David said putting his arm behind his head and closed his eyes. "I'm not sure I want to do it."

"*Why though?*"

"I feel like it's a big step in this whole thing."

"*What do you mean?*" Amanda asked. Her voice sounded kind of sensual on the phone. David smiled and sighed.

"I don't want to jack off thinking about HIM." David said quietly.

"*Oh.*" Amanda said, "*But isn't that the beauty of masturbation David? No one knows what you're thinking about.*"

"I would know." David answered. He opened his eyes and stared at the ceiling.

"*You have to live with the hard on he gives you, why not do something about it?*" She asked. It sounded like she took a sip of something.

"It's hard to explain why I don't. I feel like I would be allowing myself to give into being gay or something." David tried to explain.

"*David, only you can turn jacking off into something complicated.*"

"It's an art." David said and laughed. Amanda laughed with him and then sighed.

"*I think you should just do it and get it over with.*"

"Witch is why you do not control my hands." David joked. Amanda giggled.

"*Still, I think you should. It might help.*"

"How can cumming over a guy I wish I didn't feel like this about going to help?"

"*It would relieve some tension or something. It might help you come to grips with all this.*" Amanda said. David thought about that for a second.

"What if I like it too much?"

"*Then . . . you've got your answer. And what do you mean like it too much? It's YOUR hand David.*" Amanda said. David rolled his eyes.

"Ever came harder thinking about one person than another?"

"*I guess.*"

"Well, what if I cum really hard?" David asked.

"*David. I was your last right?*"

"Yea."

"*That was like over two years ago.*" Amanda said.

"Yea, so?" David asked.

"*After that long of going without, don't you think you would cum really hard no matter who you thought about?*"

"Probably. Why risk it though, huh?" David asked closing his eyes again.

"*New plan David.*"

"What's that?"

"*Saturday is now gonna be a sex date.*" Amanda said.

"What?" David asked with a slight laugh in his voice. "Why?"

"*Well, for one thing, I would like to.*"

"Okay." David said.

"*And you need to.*"

"That's very true." David said smiling.

"*Well. You could jack off after something like a sex date and know whether or not its cause you really like it or because it's been too long. We take the 'been to long' out of the equation and it's like regular masturbation.*"

"Well. Taking the 'been to long' out of the equation is a good idea. I'm game for that."

"*You're such a pig David.*" Amanda said giggling. There was the sound of crying on her end of the phone. "*Uh, the baby is awake. I gotta go. I'll see you in the morning ok?*"

"Sounds good. I'll see you." David said.

"*Kay, bye.*"

"Bye." David answered and hung up the phone. He shook his head and took the phone back to the charger. He did up his few dishes and went downstairs to change over the laundry. He set the dry clothes in the basket and put the wet clothes from the washer into the dryer. He stretched and yawned. "What a day." He said out loud. He folded the laundry and took the basket to the top floor of the house. He set his mother's cloths on her bed and took his into his room. He hung his two pairs of jeans in his closet along with the few shirts that were washed. Then he sat down at his desk. He looked at the note again and shook his head. He took both notes from Mr. Black and put them in the drawer at the front of his desk. Then he opened his journal and wrote,

Sept, 8 Thursday.

Sex on Saturday seems to be a go. I think it's funny that Amanda and I plan these kinds of things. It's always been that way with us though. At least that little part of my life is easy. Today Mr. Allan Black had me so hard I thought I would puke! I might if this keeps up. I refuse to jack off about the guy but Amanda thinks I should. I think she is crazy. Oh well, I got another note from him. He seems to care about me and mom's home life I guess. He's paid to care. But I have to say, I like his writing. And I think its sexy that he signs his notes Allan Black. I don't know why that's sexy, but it is.

Anyway, thanks for listening.

David closed the journal and sighed. He was tired from these past few days. Since his mother was working through the night, he thought it would be best to shower now so he didn't wake her up in the morning. He quickly showered and came back into his room. He read chapters 5 and 6 of the WW2 novel. Amanda had been right. It was run, run, run some more. He put the book away in his bag and lay down in bed. His last thought was of Mr. Allan Black.

Fuck, you're gorgeous. I wish I could just kiss you to see what it felt like.

Chapter 5

Friday morning was quiet in the Smith house. Since David had showered the night before, the only thing for him to do was get dressed and do his hair. He snuck to the bath room and quickly wet his hair down. He slicked it back like he did every morning. He sprayed on his cologne and applied his deodorant. He quietly walked back into his room and put on his jacket. He grabbed his book bag and cigarettes and headed downstairs. It was 7:40 and David knew Amanda would be there soon. He made half a pot of coffee and sat down at the table waiting for it to brew. He lit a cigarette and watched the fall rain run down the window. He grabbed a piece of paper out of his binder and took a pen out of the cup in the center of the table.

Mr. Black

Please don't worry about me and my mom. We will be fine. I am going to start looking for an after school job *next week. I'm sorry I won't be able to join your group. Maybe next time, if I have time.*

David.

He stared at his note and decided it would have to do. Mr. Black would have to accept this. David wasn't lying about looking for a job. He knew his mother needed help of the monetary type. Plus, he was really sure that any more time with Mr. Black would be unbearable. This was the best thing. He folded the paper and stuck it in his pocket. He could hear the coffee brewer spitting out the last bit of coffee into the pot. He set his cigarette into the ash tray and walked over to the pot. He took down two cups and poured the black liquid into each one. He put cream and sugar into each and took the cups to the table. He could see Amanda come by the window with her jacket held over her head. He shook his head and went to the door.

"Come in here before you melt." David said pulling Amanda in the door.

"Uh, I hate rain." Amanda said as she hung her jacket on the rail. They walked into the kitchen together and sat at the same chairs they had all week for their morning coffee.

"How was babysitting?" David asked taking the last puff from his cigarette and putting it out in the tray.

"Uh, the baby stayed awake until after 12 midnight. Mom and Dad got home by then and took over."

"That's sucky."

"Oh well. How was your night? And where's your mom?"

"She had to work a double shift. I heard her come in at around 4 or something this morning. She's sleeping."

"Oh, did you give any thought to our talk last night?" Amanda asked warming her hands on her coffee cup. David took a sip of his and rolled his eyes.

"I thought the beauty of masturbation was that no one knew about it?"

"So . . . you did it then?"

"No." David said and took another sip from his cup.

"Oh." Amanda said sipping at hers. David looked at his friend. She was wearing a heavy sweater and blue jeans. She wore her hair down today and it hung straight down her back and over her shoulders. David thought she was very attractive. She was the only girl he was interested in. There were pretty girls at school but they seemed so superficial. Amanda had real looks that makeup would ruin. When she was young, she would wear her hair in pig tails that bounced around when she ran. She used to have a lot of freckles but they seemed to fade as she got older.

"Are we still on for tomorrow?" David asked taking the last sip from his cup.

"Well, you can come over and we'll see what happens when you get there."

"Oh, Amanda." David said with a smirk. They put their cups in the sink and headed to the door with their book bags. They stepped outside into the rain and hurried toward the school. They laughed as they splashed each other with the water in the puddles they passed. They hurried into the school. They were still laughing when David ran right into Mr. Black. He stopped and stared at the man in front of him.

"Well, where's the fire David?" Mr. Black asked and handed Amanda back the book bag she had dropped during the collision.

"Oh thank you." She said and took the bag from him.

"Sorry, Mr. Black." David said and smiled at Amanda. She blushed and turned to head toward her locker.

"It's fine, David. Just slow down next time, hey?" Mr. Black said and patted his shoulder. David stood still as Mr. Black walked away. He felt a tap on his shoulder. It was Amanda.

"Are you going to just stand here like an idiot or are we going to home room?" She asked smiling.

"Yea, right." David said and hurried to his locker. He hung his jacket inside to dry and gathered his books. They rushed to home room and sat through attendance. Math class for David was a test that apparently was going to happen every Friday. He found it fairly easy. It was straight forward algebra. Science class was more notes and looking at slides of the inside of frogs. The girls were grossed out but David found it very interesting. The rugby game for gym class was called on a count of rain. They played their own version of ultimate dodge-ball instead. When the bell rang, David met up with Amanda at their lockers. They looked out the window to see that the rain had slowed to a sprinkle so they stepped outside. David had his hands in his pockets. He could feel the note addressed to Mr. Black. His stomach flipped and he pulled his hands out. They stood next to the smokers table. They had both decided it was too wet to sit on today.

"So, are you signing up for that extra credit History thing?" Amanda asked as David lit his lunch time smoke.

"Nope. Plan on getting an after school job instead." David said making smoke circles. Amanda poked her finger through one.

"But you love this Mid-Evil shit. AND, it would be more time with Mr. Black."

"That's exactly why I'm getting a job instead." David said rolling his eyes.

"Wouldn't it be nice to see him outside of school?"

"Not really. I have a *hard* enough time with the 80 minutes of History class as it is. Why add to it?"

"Well, you could see what makes him tick. He seems to really be into this stuff. Just like you." Amanda teased winking at her friend. David rolled his eyes again.

"Oooo, something in common."

"See, and it's at the big library . . . At night." She added.

"Where did you here that?"

"I heard him talking to Mr. Relling from the library this morning. Sounds like he has the group picked out already too." Amanda said.

"Well then it's too late to join, isn't it?" David smiled and flicked the ash off his cigarette on to the ground. Amanda sighed,

"I bet he would add you if you wanted. No one knows more about this stuff than you do."

"Well, if it's at the library, they will know everything I do. I got it from the books in that place."

"It's not the same as hearing it from you. You get so into it." David smiled at his friend. Amanda was never into the Mid-Evil war fair or torture things that he was into. When they were young, she used to say it was yucky and gave her night mares.

"I'm sure they'll do fine without me, Mandy." He said and turned to look at the school. He stared at the big doors and wondered,

Do you know how hot you are? I mean, do you look at yourself in the mirror in the morning and admire the incredible looks you have? I bet you do. I bet you have a full length mirror over your bed so you can look at the marvel that is your naked body. Why can't you just gain 100 pounds and get a scruffy looking beard? Maybe wear clothes that are too small for your fat gut so it hangs out the bottom. That wouldn't be so nice to look at. But no, you have to be so fucking sexy, don't you?

"What are you thinking about?" Amanda asked noticing that David's mind had drifted off.

"Fat guys." David answered not looking away from the doors. Amanda laughed,

"I thought you were into muscular, History teachers." She teased. David looked back at her laughed.

"Yea, that's why I'm thinking about gross fat guys."

"That makes no sense David."

"Sure it does. Think about what you don't like to keep your mind off what you do like." David said and smiled. Amanda raised her eyebrows.

"So . . . You're admitting to your crush? That's the first step to healing you know?"

"Nice Amanda." David said.

"What? It's true. That's what the T.V. says about drug attics and alcoholics." Amanda teased.

"I know what it says. And I never *denied* my crush or whatever you wanna call it."

"Well, you never said it out loud either."

"No, I guess I haven't. Telling you he gives me a hard on doesn't count?" David asked putting his hands in his pockets.

"Well, it sort of does I guess." She answered. They could see people starting to go back into the school. They looked at each other and both sighed.

"Any post History class warnings for today?" He asked as they went through the big glass doors of the school.

"Well, it should be . . . Interesting." She said and smiled. David shook his head and dug his books from his locker. He pulled the note out of his jacket pocket and tucked it into his Tools of War text book. He hung up his jacket and locked his locker. The second bell rang as he stepped into room 19. Mr. Black was standing at the chalk board writing notes. David went to his desk and sat down. He opened his binder to the History section and began writing. Mr. Black spoke as he wrote.

"There will be an exam on this stuff next Friday so please get it all down. The questions will come right from these notes." He said. David watched the muscles in his shoulder flex as he wrote. His hair was longer than David had first thought. He noticed that Mr. Black combed it straight back a lot like he did. It was a light brown with blonde highlights. It went really well with the light tan he had. His shoulders were very defined and David surmised that he must work out or something. He continued with his notes on the first beheading. David giggled to himself when he heard some of the girls say 'ewe' when the part came up about how sometimes the eyes of the victim's stay open afterwards. The notes Mr. Black wrote took up about two and a half pages by the time he was finished. It was stuff David already knew so it was really just a waste of paper.

"How are we supposed to remember all this?" A voice from the back of the class asked. Mr. Black raised his eyebrows and smiled,

"Did you sign up for the after school group Mr. Peters?" He asked.

"Uh, no. I have football sir." Stan Peters answered.

"Well, that's good." Mr. Black said and chuckled. There were a few giggles from the rest of the class. "You study it Stan, that's how you remember all this stuff." He added and sat down at his desk. "Any questions on these notes?" There were a few hands that went up. Mr. Black answered the questions and wrote the really interesting ones on the board. When the bell rang, David collected his books and waited for the class to clear out a little. He got up and walked up to Mr. Black's big oak desk. He had the note in his hand. He set it in the center of Mr. Black's desk and headed out the door.

"Another note?" Mr. Black asked. David turned to see him looking at the paper on his desk. He turned to face David.

"Yea, well. I like notes better than conversation remember?" David answered and turned to leave.

"Have you reconsidered the Mid-Evil project?"

"It's in the note." David said and walked away. He slowly made his way to room 9 for English class. He walked into the room and went to his desk. Mrs. Coldiron was handing out the latest question sheets she had prepared for chapters 7 and 8.

"Ok, we are reading today class. I am very impressed with your debates these last couple of days, but the show must go on. I would like you to read chapters 7 and 8 and start on the questions I've given you. If you don't get them done, they will need to be completed for Monday." Mrs. Coldiron said and went to sit behind her funny shaped pine desk. David hadn't noticed the differences between the teacher's desks before today. Mr. Black's seemed like a historic oak relic from the 19th century or something. Mrs. Coldiron's desk, on the other hand, seemed like it had just been purchased from Ikea or something like that. He shook his head,

Seems fitting. Fantastic looking piece of colonial furniture for Allan Black, and a through away at the end of the year looking piece of crap for Mrs. Coldiron.

David smiled at the thought and opened his book to chapter 7. After weeks of running from Anthony's father and random Nazi soldiers alike, Hans and Anthony found themselves lost in some forest 120 miles from Berlin. They built a make shift lodge from old branches they had collected around the spot they had chosen to build the thing. It had taken them days to build. They covered the roof with large pieces of bark and long dead grass. They had fashioned a small broom out of a short stick and some of the dead grass they had collected. Hans swept out the inside of the little house when they were finished building it. Anthony made a bed from moss and soft ferns. The boys fished with a long piece of string from Anthony's overalls and a pin from Hans's shirt his mother had given him to patch a small hole. They managed to catch fish for days to feed themselves. Soon the fear of the Nazi's and Anthony's father were fading. Anthony playfully teased Hans at night hoping to make love to him again. Hans was still afraid at night and would often scold Anthony for even thinking of such things. One night, soon after the young men fell asleep. Two Nazi soldiers found themselves stumbling upon the strange camp sight. They quietly snuck around the camp. They looked into the small window in the lodge and snickered at what they saw. The two young men lay half naked in each other's arms. One Nazi went for his gun but the other stopped him. They devised a plan to rape the boys before they killed them. The soldiers crept into the little house and put their sweaty hands over the boys' mouths. Hans tried to scream but it was no use. Anthony fought with the Nazi that held him. He bit the soldiers hand and the soldier hit him. He fell to the ground at Hans's feet. Hans cried still being held by his large captor. Anthony's Nazi pulled off the young boy's underwear. Anthony kicked at him and cursed Hitler. The soldier slapped Anthony's mouth and swore at him. He undid the front of his pants and released his frightening penis. Hans screamed and fought the large Nazi that held him. Anthony tried to crawl away but the soldier grabbed him. He laid himself on top of Anthony's squirming body. Anthony screamed when the man pushed himself inside. Hans cried as he watched. Anthony's screams were terrifying to him. The Nazi that held him laughed and cheered on his friend. Soon, the man was finished with Anthony and rose up. Anthony curled himself into the fetal position and lay there shaking. Hans's Nazi did the same to him but made little Hans bleed. The Nazi's laid the boys naked on the ground beside each other. They pointed their large riffles at the faces of each boy. Suddenly, a loud holler could be heard from the tree line. The solders looked behind them to see Anthony's father come from the trees holding a rather large gun of his own. The Nazi's engaged the farmer in an epic battle the boys knew he would lose. They grabbed what clothes they could and ran into the trees. They ran all night until exhaustion beat them and they could not make another step. They found a small thicket of bush to hide in. It was daybreak. They held each other and cried until they both fell asleep.

David raised his eyebrows and closed the book at the end of chapter 8. He looked at the question sheet and then at the time. It was almost time for class to end so he put the question sheet into his binder and waited for the bell. When it rang, Mrs. Coldiron reminded the class that the sheets were due for Monday and reading chapters 9 and 10 would also probably be a good idea. David went to his locker and gathered the rest of his things. He headed out the doors of the school. It had stopped raining but the sun was hidden behind a thick cover of clouds. He shivered and lit a cigarette. He slowly walked home. He was in no hurry because he knew when he got there, he would have to listen to his mother going on about her date tonight with Roger. He was happy she was going but still felt like it was too early since his father's passing for her to be seeing other men. He hated to think of someone trying to take his father's place in their lives.

"Anything is better than Carl." David said to himself as he made his way up the side walk to his front door. He opened it and called out,

"Hi mom. I'm home!"

"I'm in the kitchen Dave." Nancy answered. He hated being called Dave by anyone but his mom. He preferred David because it sounded tougher. Dave was a sissy sounding nick name. Amanda used to call him Wizard, but like her freckles, that to faded with age.

"Did you get any sleep?" David asked as he stepped into the kitchen and tossed his bag on the floor next to the table.

"Oh, a little. I must admit, I'm a little nervous about tonight."

Here we go.

"Why?" David asked as he got himself a pop and sat down at the table with his mom.

"I made coffee, if you like dear." Nancy said gesturing with her cup.

"And ruin my routine? Never." David said as he cracked open the can. "So, why are you nervous about this date? He a weirdo or something?"

"Oh, no, no, nothing like that. I just can't help but feel like he's just too good for me."

"HA! He should be worrying about that mom, not you."

"You know something? I don't think men get nervous about dates." Nancy said sipping her coffee. David smiled and shook his head.

"Sure we do mom. We don't wanna look like idiots or something."

"Really? Do you get nervous before a date?"

"Well, no. But I'm gorgeous and never date girls smarter than me. No risk of looking stupid." David joked and lit a cigarette. Nancy giggled at her sons comment. She knew that David didn't date much if at all.

"Well, it's different when your older. I don't think I remember how to date, to tell you the truth."

"What about that guy who wasn't gonna work out?" David asked remembering the note from earlier in the week.

"Well, he was a colleague from work. And I knew it wasn't gonna be more than a first date. I just went so he would quit asking." Nancy said and blushed. David laughed,

"Wow, that's classy mom. So what's so different about Roger then?"

"He's a really nice looking man. And what if I would like a second date? What if I like him? What if he tries to kiss me? What if I want him to?" Nancy babbled.

"Well, go on a second date then. But I don't wanna hear about it if he kisses you. I've been in enough fights over your virtue this week." David said referring back to his toss with Carl. Nancy smiled but said nothing. They sat in silence for a while until David spoke.

"When's he coming?"

"Actually, we have agreed to meet at the restaurant at 5:30."

"He's not picking you up? That's weird." David said looking out the window. It was 3:00 now and he was hoping Amanda would stop by after school.

"I thought better of it, after what happened with Carl." Nancy said and got up to refill her cup. "Want one now?" She asked David holding a clean coffee cup in his direction.

"Sure mom." David said and thought about her last statement. He wondered if he had really scared her that much. "I'm not *gonna* beat up *every* guy that comes around, mom. Just the ass licking fuck heads." He said and smiled as she handed him his coffee. Nancy shook her head and sat down.

"You know, your dad would have been proud of you." She said and carefully sipped her hot coffee. David sighed.

"Let's not talk about dad hours before you go on a date, kay mom?"

"David, you need to move on. He's gone." She said in a sweet, maternal voice. David looked at her and struggled for something to say.

"No I don't." He said and looked back out the window.

"Ok. You can miss him, David. But you have to accept the fact that he won't be coming home or something."

"I know that mom, I'm not stupid. I have a pretty clear understanding of death." David said hoping she would change the subject. Unlucky for him, she did.

"Like any of your teachers this year? You despised the teachers last year." David sighed and thought of Mr. Black.

"Uh, well. The gym teacher is the same jack off from last year." David complained. Nancy choked on her coffee,

"DAVID! Must you be so . . . . *fowl?"* David laughed and sipped his coffee.

"Sorry." He giggled.

"Any *new* teachers then? I heard Mr. Felch retired."

"Yea, he did." David answered. That was the killer thing about a high school in a small town. The teachers shared the work load by teaching their subject to every grade.

"So, is the new teacher any good? I know how much you *loved* Felch." Nancy joked. David sighed. How was it that every woman in his life wanted to know what he thought of Mr. Black.

"Oh, he's alright I guess." David said, trying to remain brief.

"Well, I seem to remember you saying something about a horses ass or something the first day with Felch, so 'alright' is quite the improvement."

"Actually I said, cock sucker with a taste for horse meat."

"DAVID!" Nancy choked. David laughed and noticed Amanda Coming up the walk. He smiled as he felt the sweet relief of a subject change coming on. Amanda walked in as she always did.

"Hi mom!" She called from the door way.

"Hello dear." Nancy said as she stepped into the kitchen. "Can I get you a coffee?"

"No, I'll get it. Hey David." Amanda said as she dug through the cupboard for just the right cup.

"Hey." David answered and lit a cigarette.

"We were just discussing the teachers for this semester." Nancy said as Amanda sat down at the table with her cup. David rolled his eyes.

What ever happened to subject change? He thought as Amanda answered

"Oh, really?"

"Yes, any favorites this year?" Nancy asked. Amanda smiled and shot a look at David. David glared at her as if to say, '*mention him and die!!'* Amanda was never good with telekinesis and said to Nancy,

"Well, I would have to say Mr. Black." David felt his stomach flip and thought he would be sick.

"Oh, I haven't heard of him. Is he new?" Nancy asked. She seemed so interested that David felt like he would sink into a black hole that formed under his chair and die.

"Oh, yea. He's the new History teacher." Amanda said sipping her coffee and smiling at David. She did love her petty torments.

"I see. Well he must be good because David hasn't thought of any distasteful things to say about him yet." Nancy said giggling. David's legs went numb. He glared at Amanda. She giggled and shook her head just enough for him to see.

"Well, he is a lot smarter than Mr. Felch and a lot nicer to look at." Amanda said and winced.

"Is that right?"

"You know girls mom, ga ga over the latest thing." David said taking a long drag from his cigarette and blowing the smoke at Amanda's face. She swished it away with her hand and frowned.

"Well, you haven't said anything mean or gross about the fellow yet. That must stand for something?" Nancy said defending girls. David lifted his right eyebrow and sucked his cheeks in. Amanda giggled and waited to see what her friend would say.

"Well, mom. He's a great . . . big . . . hard-on" Amanda spit her coffee across the table and Nancy laughed. David held his gaze on his friend. She apologized for the mess and jumped off the chair to get a cloth.

"DAVID! I will hear no more of that talk. You can be so disgusting." Nancy said with a smile under her scolding. David smiled and got up to help Amanda clean up her mess.

"Nice, David." She whispered and smiled at him. He smiled back and tossed the coffee soaked rag over to the top of the stairs to be taken down with the rest of the laundry. The three of them chatted about the rest of the teachers and left the Mr. Black subject alone. At 5:00, Nancy thought it would be best to leave so she wouldn't be late for her date with Roger. David and Amanda had gotten out of her that he was a Lawyer from the big Jackson & Roth firm in the city. She had met him at the hospital where she worked when he went in there to see a client that had allegedly cut himself going through a window of a house he was robbing. Now he was suing the home owner for pain and anguish. Never the less, they got a good laugh out of it. After Nancy left, David and Amanda went up to his room,

"You know, David, for a guy, you have a really clean room." Amanda said as she sat down on the bed. David shook his head and sat his book bag next to his desk. He hung his jacket on the folding chair and came to join her. He lay back against the head board and she did the same. They both stared up at the ceiling. "Have you ever considered hanging posters above your bed?" She asked as David puffed quietly on a cigarette.

"Why?" He asked looking over at his friend.

"It would give you something to look at. I have posters on my ceiling." She said. David looked back up at the roof above them. It was yellowed from smoke.

"It's an idea." He said. "Of what though?"

"How about war lords or something?" David laughed,

"Why war lords?" He asked

"Well, I read in Teen Magazine, that if you are going to hang posters on your ceiling, they should be of things you like."

"I see. Aren't your posters all of that singer dude Steve Tyler?"

"Like I said. Stuff you like." She said smiling. David remembered the posters from the last night they had together. He could remember thinking how weird it was having sex and staring at sweaty pictures of some guy. "Besides, it's supposed to help you think or something." She added.

"Well, I think just fine. I like my bare ceiling. It's like a blank canvass."

"Sure, if you're going to paint it." Amanda joked and nudged David with her arm. David smiled and put out his cigarette before rolling over to face her.

"Why did you mention Mr. Black to my mom?" He asked. She rolled over to face him.

"She asked about the teachers." Amanda answered and picked at David's quilt.

"I know she did. But why did you say he was nice to look at?"

"Because he is."

"Were you trying to irritate me?" David asked smiling. He liked having Amanda in his bed. Amanda giggled.

"No, I didn't think it would work so easily actually."

"Me neither. I had to say something. Sorry I made you spit out your coffee everywhere."

"Yea, that would have been pretty embarrassing if it were a public place or something." Amanda said still picking at the quilt. She seemed nervous.

"Are you okay?" David asked putting his hand on the hand Amanda picked at his blanket with. She smiled and looked at him,

"Yea, I'm ok." She lied and looked back down at their hands. David let go and rolled back over onto his back.

"I scare you don't I?" He asked as he stared at the ceiling. Amanda cleared her throat and went back to picking the blanket.

"Why would you say that?" She asked.

"We used to lay in here like this all the time. Do you think I'll try something or something?"

"I don't know. It's been a long time David. We were kids then. We're grown up now and from what I felt the other day, you're *a lot* bigger." Amanda said quietly. David looked over at her. Her face had gone red with embarrassment. That was one thing about Amanda that David found amazing. No matter how embarrassing a statement or a question was, she would always force herself to say it. He looked back up at the ceiling and sighed.

"Oh, I see." He said. He wasn't quite sure what to say to something like that. He thought size didn't matter or something like that. Apparently it did, just not how he thought. "So, are you scared I'll hurt you or something?" He asked.

"Well, yea." Amanda said. David didn't look back over. He knew what he would see. An embarrassed little red face that used to be brave, beautiful Amanda.

"Well, I wouldn't." David whispered. This time he rolled back over to face her again. She looked at him and smiled.

"I know you wouldn't mean to David, But have you been paying attention in the gym class shower room? Your sort of a cut above the rest." David giggled at Amanda's words. He hadn't paid that close attention at all. He knew she was with a couple guys since him so she would know.

"No, I haven't been looking." David said smiling.

"Well, maybe you should. Don't you guys compare them or something?"

"Sure, when we were like 10. Not anymore. Fear of being upstaged or something." David said and moved a piece of stray hair from her face. She smiled at him and sighed.

"You should have no fear of that." She said and rolled over to face the ceiling again. David watched her chest move as she breathed. Then it suddenly dawned on him,

"Did you really have your period? Or did you lie because you were scared?"

"No, I really had my period, David. It was a good save then, but I don't know how I'll get my way out of tomorrow." She said. Her face reddened again. David smiled.

"You could try saying no." He said.

"Would that work?" She asked closing her eyes.

"Of course it would work, Amanda. What's gotten into you?" David asked and propped himself up on his elbow. He saw a tear come from her eye. "Amanda, it would work. I won't even touch you if you don't want me to." He said suddenly concerned for his oldest, dearest friend.

"Oh, its not you David. It's just that, not all guys take no for an answer." David's heart sank and he could feel an anger come on like the one he felt when he watched his Uncle Carl feel up his mom.

"What happened Amanda? Did someone hurt you?" He asked trying to sound sympathetic but his anger shone through. Amanda's eyes popped open and she looked at him.

"No, David, not really." She said putting her hand out for him to hold. He put his hand in hers.

"What's 'not really'?" He asked hiding his anger much better this time. She looked at their interlocked hands and smiled.

"It was when I went to go see my Gram. There is this boy there that I used to hang out with when I would go to see her in the summer." Amanda said and squeezed David's hand.

"What happened?" He asked holding her hand tightly.

"We went to this party that his friends were having, for summer holidays?" David nodded, "anyway, we were drinking and I started to not feel so good. I didn't drink a lot but it had been super-hot that day and I really didn't eat anything." She explained still staring at their hands.

"Okay, so what happened next?" David asked.

"Well, I told him I wanted to leave. He was kind of a jerk about it but he decided to take me home. But we didn't go home."

"Where did you go?" David could feel his blood getting warmer as she spoke.

"He parked his car at some farmer's gate. We started making out and stuff. It was kind of nice actually." She said remembering the boys kiss. "Then, he started touching me. I asked him not to but he wouldn't stop. He just kissed me harder and kept fighting with my pants." She said. Tears filled her eyes again and David had her in his arms faster than she could blink. He held her and listened to her light sobs. He rubbed her back. He wanted to be consoling but he needed to hear the rest.

"What happened next?" He asked in a whisper. She sniffled and wiped her tears on his shirt but she didn't pull away.

"Well, when I knew that yelling wasn't gonna help, I punched him in the crotch and jumped out of the car. I ran all the way back to Grams. I told her about it and she called the police."

"What did they do?" David asked still rubbing Amanda's back.

"Nothing, they said he had a different story so it was my word against his, and unless I had some kind of evidence like cum or spit or something. They couldn't do anything else."

"That figures." David said holding his friend. They lay quietly like that for a while. David thought about what kind of guy you would have to be to do that kind of thing. Amanda stirred after about 30 minutes. David instantly let go.

"Thanks David." She said. "No one else knew besides Gram."

"Why didn't you ever tell me this?" David asked getting a tissue for her from his side table. She blew her nose and tossed it into the trash can.

"It just happened, David. I still haven't really gotten over it yet."

"It happened this summer?" David asked shocked.

"Well, yea. If it happened a year ago don't you think you would know by now?" She asked sitting up to sit cross legged on the bed. David sat up too and ran his hand through his hair.

"Wow. That's really heavy Amanda." David said lighting a cigarette. Amanda sighed and nodded. "Look, we don't gotta do nothing tomorrow, Amanda." David said looking into his friends tear reddened eyes.

"I know. I know you wouldn't expect it David." She said.

"It's a nice thought though." He said smiling. Amanda threw an invisible object at him and giggled.

"You're such a pig David." She said smiling. He dodged the make believe projectile and laughed.

"I know." He said. Amanda looked over at the clock,

"Crap, its 6:30. I had better go." She pouted.

"Ok." David said and got up. He pulled Amanda up to her feet a little harder than she expected and she landed right in front of him. Almost nose to nose. David smiled at her. Her face went red again she giggled. "Under different circumstances, that would have been a good time for a kiss." He whispered and backed away from her. Amanda giggled and walked to the door.

"It's too bad you never capitalize on these little moments David." Amanda teased and stepped out of the room. David smiled and followed her out. He walked her to the door and went out on to the step with her.

"Still wanna hang out tomorrow?" He asked looking at the still cloud covered sky.

"Yea, you still need to hear my involvement in this conspiracy." Amanda joked as she walked down the side walk.

"Oh, Yea! Can't wait!" David called to her. She waved at him and continued walking. He turned and went back inside.

Poor Amanda. What a dick. He thought as he went into the kitchen and made himself a sandwich. He went into the living room and turned on the T.V. A gangster movie was on so he watched that. It ended at 9:30. There was nothing else on so he decided to go up to his room. He sat down at his desk and opened his journal,

Sept. 9 Friday,

Amanda was apparently attacked by some idiot this summer. She wasn't raped, thank god, but it was close enough. This has apparently made her afraid of guys. Me even. She says my cock is too big for her or some shit. Who knows? I think I would feel good but it looks like it might take a little while for her to get over fuck face so, no sex this weekend.

Allan Black was sexy today of course. I noticed the differences in desks today. It's kind of funny how his is so cool and the other teacher's desks look like crap. Amanda had mentioned that I should hang posters on my ceiling to stare at. Guess what I thought of? Anyway,

Mom is out on her date with Roger. I hope she has a good time. I wish I could be happier for her but I hate thinking about her with someone else. Guess I'll have to deal.

Thanks for listening.

Chapter 6

David loved Saturdays. He had such a knack for sleep that he could seldom exorcize having to get up for school and things. When he had finally awoke, it was 10:37. He yawned and rolled over on to his back with cigarette in hand. His morning erection however, never took a day off. He lay there staring at the ceiling picturing the life sized, naked poster of Mr. Black he didn't have when he heard his mother laughing downstairs. He got out of bed and went to the door. He cracked it open and he could hear the faint voice of a man talking in the kitchen.

HE STAYED THE NIGHT?? David thought. He shut the door and leaned against it for a second. He quickly rushed over to the night stand and put his cigarette in the ash tray. He threw on the clothes he was wearing the day before and grabbed the smoke from the tray. He pulled off the last couple puffs and put it out. He took a deep breath and slowly opened his door. He could hear his mother laugh again. He creped down half the stair case when he heard familiar voice say,

"Please, call me Allan." David could feel the blood run from his face. His heart jumped in his chest as though he had just been caught stealing.

HE is at my house? David thought. Panic struck him and he sat down on the stair.

"Well, Allan. I hope David isn't giving you a hard time in class." He could hear his mother say.

"No, actually the opposite. He is very bright and I would say the best in the class." Mr. Black's voice was like an unforgivable punch in the gut.

"Oh, well that makes me very happy to hear that." Nancy said. It sounded like she put two coffee cups down.

He's staying for coffee? David could feel sweat forming on his brow.

"Thank you, Mrs. Smith." Mr. Black said.

"Please, Nancy." She corrected.

"I am here, Nancy, because I have started an after school project for the renaissance fair and David has been reluctant to join." David held his breath.

"That's odd. He loves that kind of stuff." Nancy said.

"And it shows in his work. I have asked him to reconsider, but he says he wants to get a job instead." Allan Black said as he sipped his coffee. David waited to hear what his mother had to say about that. He knew it would not be in his favor. And he was right.

"Well that is ridiculous. Is this group for extra marks or anything?" She asked.

"Well, not marks, but it's worth three extra credits."

"My goodness that is generous of the school board." Nancy said. She sounded so proper when she talked to other adults.

"Well, actually. I fought for two extra. They would only offer one but as it turns out, the fair brings a lot of revenue into town and if the students put on a good demonstration, some of that revenue will go to the school."

"That's very clever of you Allan." Nancy said. David could hear there was a smile in her voice. He sighed and listened on.

"Anyway," Continued Mr. Black, "From looking at David's work, he would have been an asset to the group. It's just too bad he has refused to join."

"David does not need to seek employment. We are doing just fine now. You see. I was offered a promotion at work. I will be scrubbing in on surgeries now and that pays almost double what I was making as a trauma nurse."

"Well, that's wonderful." Mr. Black said. He could hear someone set their cup down on the table. He was happy for his mother's news but not how if effected his excuse to not join Mr. Blacks group.

"Why don't I go up and tell him you're here. I know he would love to join something like this." David jumped up and hurried to his room. He couldn't hear what else was said between the two of them but it took a few minutes for her to come to his room. His hands were sweating when she knocked on the door.

"David, are you awake dear?" His mother's soft voice asked. David was silent for a second. She cracked open the door.

"Yea, mom. I'm up. Just finished getting dressed. You should knock. I could have had my stuff hanging out or something." David mused.

"Oh, son. What a surprise. Unless you grew a second one, it's nothing new to me."

"MOM!" David said laughing and came to the door.

"There is someone here who would like to talk to you." She said.

"Oh, really? Who?" David tried to sound convincing. She lifted one eyebrow and left the room. David rolled his eyes and knew he had been caught. He slowly followed his mother down the stairs. He wiped the sweat off his hands and ran them through his hair before stepping into the kitchen. There, sitting in the spot Amanda usually sits was Mr. Allan Black. He wore a form fitting tee-shirt and tight blue jeans. His hair was parted in the middle today and hung in his face a little.

And here I thought you couldn't get any sexier. David thought as he sat down at his chair at the table.

"Good morning David." Mr. Black said smiling.

"Morning." David said and mock yawned. His mind was running to fast to be tired but a yawn in the morning seemed like the thing to do. Nancy brought David a coffee and he smiled at her. "So what brings a History teacher to my table?" David asked sipping his coffee. Mr. Black smiled and said,

"Perhaps your mothers news first." Nancy smiled at him and then looked at David. David looked at her and lit a cigarette.

"I was accepted in the scrub nurse program." She said nodding and smiling. Her smile was so wide it looked like it might break her face. David mustered up all his acting skills from drama and blurted out,

"Holy shit mom, that's great!" He set the cigarette in the ash tray and reached across to hug his mother. She squeezed him so hard he wished it would make him pass out. It didn't.

"It's just what we needed right now. Now you won't have to worry and interrupt your schooling with a job."

"Ah mom, I would still like to help." David said making a conscience effort not to look at the man at the other side of the table.

"Don't be silly! Mr. Black here has told me all about the fair. I don't want you to miss that." Her face looked like the little girls face from the 'yes there is a Santa Clause' movie. David winced and looked over at Mr. Black. He smiled at David. He looked back over at his mother.

"Mom, it's not a big deal. I could work at the gas station or . . . ."

"I wouldn't hear of it David. You should enjoy your young life. You can get a job when you're an adult and have a family of your own to take care of."

"Yea, but mom . . ." David tried but he knew he was fighting a losing battle.

"Oh, David. Three extra credits would look so good to prospective collages." David rolled his eyes and ashed his cigarette.

"Now we're talking about the Mid-Evil group thing for the fair, right?"

"Yes." Nancy said sipping her coffee. She looked up at the clock. It was 11:00. "I hate to do this but, David, you'll have to finish talking to Mr. Black about this. I gotta head into work for a few hours this afternoon to sign my new contract and stuff." She said and excused herself from the table. Mr. Black stood up as she left. David was frozen in his seat.

ALONE? With him? In the same house that my bedroom is in? David's mind raced as his mother said her good byes and left.

"So what do you think?" Mr. Black asked sitting back down and taking out a package of cigarettes. David stared at him as he held the thing in his teeth and lit it. He even made smoking look sexy.

"About what?" David asked sitting rigid in his chair.

"About the group. It seems your schedule has just been cleared up." He said and smiled.

GOD! What do I do? My mom will kill me if I don't, I'll die from blood loss if I do.

"I don't know, Mr. Black. After school things really aren't my bag." David said taking a long drag from his own cigarette. Mr. Black sighed and twirled his smoke in his fingers.

"David, the fact of the matter is, only 4 students signed up. 2 from grade twelve and one from your class. You would at least make 5."

"But what about all the kids at the sign-up sheet the first day?" David asked.

"They changed their minds one by one. The list is a sorry little page of scratched out names now." Mr. Black said. He exhaled the blue toxin from his lips and David's hair stood on end. Watching him smoke was like a young man's first glance at pornography. The smoke circled around him as though it refused to let go of him. His eyes were so green.

"Why did they do that?" David asked trying to tame the waking beast in his blue jeans.

"I don't know." Mr. Black said rolling the ash off his cigarette. "They didn't give any reasons."

"That's not good." David said and raised his eyebrows. "Can't you do it with the kids you have?"

"I could, but I promised a group of six. They are expecting to give out 18 free credits. I really would like to deliver."

"I bet they would prefer to give out 15." David said and sighed. Mr. Black squinted at David as he did the math in his head.

"15 credits would mean five students, David. Does this mean you'll join?" The anticipation in Mr. Black's eyes almost made David laugh. He suddenly looked young and innocent. Like a kid at Christmas time.

"Yea, I guess." David said and smiled. Mr. Black smiled too. It was the kind of smile that you would expect from someone after a good night in the sack.

"That is excellent news, David. I'm glad you changed your mind."

"Yea, well. You seen my mom. She would have killed me if I would have sent you away without saying yes." David said putting his cigarette out into the tray. He leaned back in his chair and stretched. Mr. Black leaned forward in his seat.

"Do you think you could bring along your collection of books?"

"How do you know about those?" David asked.

"Your mom." He answered and put his smoke out in the tray as well.

"Oh, well, I guess I could."

"Excellent." Mr. Black said and stood up. David watched him stand like it was in slow motion. He pulled his shirt down as he stood. His chest and stomach rippled with his movement. He ran his hand through his hair to pull the bangs out of his eyes. He looked like a modern day Greek hero or something. David stood too. "Well, I should get going. Thank your mom for the coffee will you?" Mr. Black said as he grabbed his leather jacket off the back of the chair he was sitting on.

"Yea, no problem." David answered and walked in front of Mr. Black to the door. He opened it and stepped aside for the man to leave.

"Listen, David. Thanks for joining the group. We can really use you. The other kids are smart, but they don't know this stuff like you do." Mr. Black said as he fixed the collar of his jacket. David stared at the fabulous coat. It hung just below the waste and fit him like a dream. It made his shoulders look amazing.

"Well, I'll do what I can." David said and leaned against the door frame. The sun was shining finally after three days.

"I'm sure you will." Mr. Black said and walked across the street to the wine coloured, 1969 Mustang Fastback. He opened the driver's side door and got inside. The engine sounded like a wild lion. It roared to life as if Mr. Black was the very heart of the beast. He looked over to David and waved. David waved back and watched Mr. Black ride off in his awesome car.

"Wow." David said and turned to go inside. He could see Amanda's front porch from his house. She was standing on the deck staring at him with her mouth open. He smiled and waved her over.

"I can't! I'm babysitting!" She called. David went in and grabbed his cigarettes. He came back out and walked over to where Amanda still stood on the porch.

"Hey." David said sticking his hands in his pockets and smiling.

"What was that?" Amanda said with her mouth still hanging open.

"What was what?" David asked lighting a cigarette and sitting down on the step. Amanda stepped out in front of him.

"What was in that muscle car? Was that Mr. Black?" David smiled and took a drag from his cigarette.

"Oh, that. Yea, that was him. Nice car huh?"

"Nice car? Is that what you have to say? Nice car? Cars like that and pretty girls used to be your weakness David, now, in *that* car was *that* guy. And all you can say is Nice car?" Amanda said looking down the road as if she could still see it.

"Relax Amanda, he was at my place to talk me into joining his Mid-Evil thing." David said trying to imagine what must have been going through Amanda's over active, imaginative mind.

"Oh, well did you join?" She asked looking back at him and then down the street again. David smiled and got up off the step. He stood next to Amanda and looked down the street the same direction she was.

"What are you looking for?" David asked and nudged his friend. Amanda smiled at him and nudged back.

"Nothing, I just can't believe he was at your house. HE was at YOUR house man!" She said and shook her head. David smiled and walked back over to the step. He sat down and patted the stair to invite her to sit down. She did but didn't take her eyes off him.

"What?" David asked and smiled at his friend.

"What was it like? I mean, to have him at your house and stuff." David laughed at her. She acted as though he and his mother had just had tea with the queen of England.

"Weird actually. He smokes. And he called my mom Nancy. He wears a leather jacket kind of like mine and, well, you saw that car." David said throwing his cigarette out onto the side walk.

"What did you talk about?" She asked. Still with the 'Tea with the queen' sounding voice.

"He was here to ask me about the Mid-Evil group thing."

"Oh, right, right, right. And? Did you join?"

"How could I not? The guy came over to my house Mandy. He told my mom about it. You know how she gets about extra education shit." David said looking out on the street.

"So . . . you're gonna be spending extra time with him then, huh?"

"Looks that way."

"Well, that's good David. At least you'll be doing it while you're talking about your favorite thing in the world." Amanda said and put her hand on his back.

"Yea, I guess. Thank god it's not a swim team or something where you have to wear little to no clothing." David joked. Amanda giggled. Just then they heard the baby cry.

"Crap, listen. Come over around 8:00 ok? I'll make sure I've got pizza and my brother said he'd get beer for us if we wanted."

"Cool. Okay. See you at eight." David said and got up from his seat. He walked back to his house and went up to his room. He grabbed the book from the big library and decided it wasn't as good as the cover looked. He tucked it under his arm and headed back out. He walked down to the library and put it on the counter. He took a look around. *This place is so empty on the weekends.*

"Need a new one?" Mr. Relling the owner of the library asked.

"Do you have a new one?" David asked turning to face the tall man. Mr. Relling was like 7 feet tall and looked like Egon from the Ghost Busters.

"We will next week. With that renaissance thing coming to town, we want to be prepared."

"Oh yea, sure Mr. Rellings. I'll be back in next week then." David said and walked away. He had learned early on that getting Mr. Rellings into a conversation meant losing the rest of your day. David walked down to the corner gas station and bought a pack of cigarettes from the guy who always said,

"This is the last time, David. I can't sell to a minor." David would always smile and say 'thank you' and leave. This little Indian guy had been saying that for three years. Since David had started smoking. His father had bought his cigarettes from the same little Indian at the same store when he was alive. David thought the Indian felt sorry for him and that's why he didn't card him at the gas station. David thought about all the funny things his father used to say about the little Indian as he walked home. The little Indian was like the neighborhood therapist. Everyone who ever had anything to talk about would go into the corner gas station and talk to the little Indian. He could hardly speak English, but he always seemed to have some kind of helpful advice. David smiled to himself as he walked through the door of his house. His mother wasn't home yet. He checked the time. 2:00. He went to the fridge and got himself a pop. He walked over to the table and sat down. He looked in his backpack. He knew he had to read chapters 9 and 10 of his WW2 book, so to pass the time; he thought now was a better time than any. He lit a cigarette and opened his book to chapter 9. The boys hid in their little thicket until hunger and thirst called them out. The weather was beginning to grow cold with the coming fall. They knew they would need to find or build shelter before it snowed. They found themselves at a small farm. The people who lived there were two old Jewish women. They were sisters who were left with their fathers property after he died. They agreed to take the two boys in if they would help with the chores they were becoming too old to do. They had apologized that there was only one room they would have to share. The boys said it was fine and they could share a room. They told the two elderly women they would be happy to help out for food and shelter for the winter. The two boys quickly learned their way around the small farm and they became a beloved part of the elderly women's home. The boys did all the outdoor work which included feeding the few chickens, milking the old jersey cow, gathering fire wood to keep the little house warm and hauling water from the powerful river at the edge of the property. When the snow fell the boys were charged with feeding the cow and keeping the snow off the roof. Hans had been experiencing terrible night mares from their run in with the Nazi soldiers but the old women never asked questions about the young boys screams at night. Anthony would hold his young lover when he would wake up crying. He would reassure him that his father had killed the soldiers and that they would never find them at their new home. But even after Anthony's caring words, Hans would still have sleepless nights and if he did sleep, his dreams would be terrifying. One night, when Hans had awoke, screaming and sweating. Anthony did not awake to hold him. He shook the boy and was given no response. He called the old women into the room. They came with their night gowns on and a lantern. Anthony had fallen deathly ill. His fever was very high and when he spoke, he made no sense to Hans. Hans was afraid. The women assured him that his young friend was strong and there for would survive. Hans did the daily chores alone and spent the nights wiping Anthony's brow with a cool cloth. After a few days, Anthony's fever seemed to break. The old woman who was doing the majority of the nursing to Anthony was very confident that he would make a fast recovery. The day that Anthony sat up and ate a bowl of soup was the happiest day in Hans's life. He kissed his friends hands and face. The women only smiled at the heavy affection he showed his dearest love. That night, when Hans came to bed after a long day of chores, Anthony was awake and sitting up waiting for him. Hans helped Anthony clean his body. Anthony stopped his young lovers hand at his midsection. Hans stared at him with a touch of fear behind his eyes.

"I am not one of *them*" Anthony whispered to Hans and slid the young boys hand down on to his swollen erection. Hans kissed Anthony as he did the night the farmer found them together. Anthony moaned and pulled Hans on top of him. They kissed and touched each other all night. They both climaxed into each other's hands as neither of them could bring themselves to make love to each other. The fear and pain they felt from the Nazi soldiers was still too strong to fight. Neither boy slept that night. They held each other and proclaimed their undying love to each other. When the sun reared its face in the morning sky, the old women entered the room. They told the boys they may sleep as they knew they had not slept that night. They assured the boys that their secret was safe with them and that no harm would come to them as long as they lived in their home. The boys thanked them and were soon asleep. Hans slept longer than Anthony. He watched the young man sleep and smiled. He knew what the old women had said was exactly what he needed hear to still the nightmares. He also knew that by spring, the son of the older of the women would arrive their help would no longer be needed. He wondered what he would do once they had to leave. He wondered how he would keep his young, delicate lover safe from the pending doom that may await them off the safe, warm hiding spot they had found.

David shut his book at looked at the time. It was 3:30.

"An hour and a half? God I wish I read slower." He said to himself as he put the book back into his bag. He heard a car pull up outside. He looked out the window and seen his mother coming up the walk. She opened the door and called,

"David, are you here?"

"Yea, I'm in the kitchen mom." He answered and took a sip from his now luke warm pop. She came into the room carrying a few bags of groceries. David helped her unpack the bags then they both sat down at the table.

"So, how did it go with Mr. Black?" She asked as she sipped the iced tea she had gotten herself before she sat down.

"Well, I guess I'm going to do that Mid-Evil fair project." David said.

"Oh, that's wonderful, David."

"Yea, well. You seemed to really want me to so . . ."

"Don't you want to dear? You love that stuff. And Mr. Black seems to really like you. He says you're the best and brightest in your class." She said smiling and looking at him with that endearing mother look she got sometimes.

"It only the first week of school mom. It's easy to be the smartest when we haven't done anything yet."

"You are too modest dear. You have always done well at school. Why does it surprise you when your teachers are impressed?"

"I'm not surprised mom. I just think that 7 hours at school is enough time to hang out with teachers."

"You don't understand it, do you David? Extra projects like this are good for prospective colleges. You do want to go to college, don't you?" David thought about that for a second. School was always so important to his mother.

"Mom, collage is two years away. Or more. I'm not that worried about it yet."

"Well, you should be. It's your future son." She said and sipped her iced tea again. David leaned back in his chair and looked at her.

"I know mom." He said. He found himself saying, 'yes mom' or 'I know mom' a lot just keep her from further questioning. Especially about school.

"Don't you have plans for the future dear?" She asked.

"Well, sure mom." David said and smiled, "I plan on hanging out with Amanda tonight and then going to school next week. Then after that, I guess my evenings will be spent kicking it with a group of kiss asses and Mr. Black."

"Very funny, David. I meant a little farther into the future than that."

"Awe, come on, mom. Do we have to do this now? I mean, let's get through high school first, huh?"

"Oh, David. I guess we don't. But you really should start thinking about what you want to do with your life." Nancy said. She was always so concerned.

"Don't worry about it mom. I'm sure the right thing will come along."

"I hope your right dear." David thought it was a good time to change the subject.

"How was your date with what's his face?"

"Roger? It was nice." Nancy said smiling.

"Well, tell me about him." David said trying desperately not to think of his father.

"Well, there isn't a lot to say sadly. There were a lot of silent moments. We don't really have anything in common except that we both had a partner die and we are both single parents."

"You talked about dad? That's kind of weird." David said lighting a cigarette.

"Well, it just sort of happened. You can only talk about work for so long. We got talking about our kids and then our late spouses."

"Oh, so he had a wife that died?"

"Yes, she died about four years ago. Car accident." She said looking down at her cup.

"I see. And what did you tell him about dad?" David asked rolling his cigarette in the ash tray.

"The truth. He understood." David slammed his hand down on the table. Nancy jumped.

"What's the truth mom? That the cops said it was suicide? Is that what you told him? That dad killed himself while we slept just feet away? Come on mom! What did you tell him?"

"David, please don't yell at me. All I said was that there was an accident and Mike was killed." Nancy said quietly still looking down at her cup. David sighed and his shoulders slumped.

"Sorry mom. I just don't want people to know, that's all."

"We don't even know what really happened that night, David." She said. They talked for some time about Mike Smith. The reminisced about the fun times they used to have when he was sober. They laughed about the times when David was young and used to get Mike into so much trouble with Nancy over silly things that seemed trivial now.

"Anyway," Nancy said after a brief pause in their conversation. "I don't think I'll be seeing him again."

"Why not?" David couldn't believe he asked.

"You're not ready for me to be seeing other people." She said and put her hand on top of his.

"Mom, it's not me that has to be ready." He said rubbing his mother's hand with his thumb.

"You know what I mean. You're afraid I'm trying to replace your father."

"Mom, that would be impossible. He was one of a kind." David said and smiled at his mother. She smiled at him and took the last sip from her cup.

"Besides that, he's really boring." Nancy said and giggled. David shook his head and laughed.

"Well, geeze, mom. Raise your standards then." They both laughed. Nancy glanced at the clock. 5:25.

"When is your date with Amanda?" She asked.

"8:00. It's not really a date mom. It's just me and Amanda."

"Oh, don't be so blind son. That girl is head over heels for you."

"Mom, not really. We're just friends." David said smiling and leaning back in his chair.

"Whatever you say dear."

David had showered and changed into a tight pair of blue jeans and a light blue tee-shirt. He had combed his hair and made himself smell about as good as he could. He came back downstairs where his mother had settled down to a bowl of popcorn and a movie.

"Well, I'm off mom." He said putting on his jacket and slipping his cigarettes into his inside pocket.

"Ok dear. 11:00 tonight ok?" She said. It was a statement more than a request. David nodded.

"Yea, I know." He said and opened the door.

"Have a good time dear."

"Ok, mom." David answered and stepped out the door. It was a little chilly but not enough to be felt through his leather jacket. He walked down the side walk to Amanda's house. The porch light was on when he arrived. He knocked at the door.

"Hi." Amanda said when she opened the door. She was wearing a white tee-shirt and blue jeans.

"Hello." David said as he walked in. He followed her down the stairs to the basement living room.

"The pizza guy beat you here." She said grabbing the pizza from the bar and setting it on the coffee table in front of the couch. David sat down on the right side of the couch where he always sat in Amanda's basement. She sat down next to him and opened the box. She hit play on the c.d. player remote and turned to face him on the couch. He did the same.

"So, what are we gonna do?" He asked taking a bite of his pizza.

"I thought we would talk about the possibility of a date." She said raising her eyebrows and taking a bite of her own slice. David giggled.

"Like a movie and dinner kind of a date?" He asked.

"Yea, like a real date David." She said smiling.

"Ok. When do you wanna do that? We can get out of here now if you want. I can't promise The Keg or anything but I could take you out if you like."

"Not with me David. With someone I know." She said setting her pizza down on the box lid.

"Oh, do you need a chaperone or something?" David asked taking another bite of his pizza.

"Not for me!" Amanda laughed.

"Not for me. I hate blind dates." David said. He had never been on a blind date before but the thought of it creped him out.

"Oh, David. You have to. It would be good for you."

"I have you. What else do I need?" David asked getting up and going over to the bar fridge.

"There is beer in there. Grab me one too." David did as he was told and got two beer from the fridge. He opened them both and handed one to Amanda.

"So, just for shits and giggles, who's this chick?" David asked taking a sip from his beer. Amanda took a sip from hers and set her bottle on the table.

"Well, their name is Todd." David frowned and looked at her. He put his bottle on the table in front of him and turned his body to face hers.

"That's an odd name for a girl." David said trying to stay calm. Amanda rolled her eyes and sighed.

"Yea, it would be." She said and grabbed her beer from the table she took a sip and then held it on her lap. She picked at the label waiting for David to speak.

"You want me to have a date with a dude?" He asked through clenched teeth.

"Don't be mad David. I'm just trying to help."

"I don't think leading a guy on is a good method of help." David said taking a large gulp of beer and holding his bottle with him as well.

"It would be a good way to see if this is just a phase or something. AND, he is really cute."

"So what?" David said. Amanda sighed and shook her head.

"Well, you can fight if forever or you can test the water."

"*Test the water?* What does that mean?" David asked staring at his friend.

"You know, see how you like being in a romantic setting with a guy." David choked on his beer and Amanda giggled.

"Laugh it up princess. That isn't gonna happen."

"Oh, David. Not romantic then. Just ask him some questions about it. Get to know how the other side lives."

"I think reading that book for English class is lesson enough."

"But, it's not real. It's not like hearing about it firsthand."

"Why do you say that? Have you talked to this guy?" David asked. Amanda's face turned red. "Oh, God! It's already all set up isn't it? You'll have to cancel." David said setting his beer on the table and digging out his cigarettes.

"David. I told him you were only curious and might have some questions. He's not expecting anything."

"I can't believe you did this Amanda." David said lighting a cigarette and taking a big drag from it.

"Why? It's no big deal. Besides, he knows you and he would like the opportunity to meet you."

"Oh my God! Amanda! You pointed me out to him?"

"No," Amanda said setting her beer on the table. "He's in your English class." She added.

"And what? He came up to you and said, 'boy I like your friend, how does he feel about sucking dick'?" David asked. Amanda laughed.

"Of course not David. I approached him. I heard he was gay and wanted to learn something's for myself. We have the same spare and for the last two days, we have been spending it together."

"So, how did I come up into the conversation?" David didn't want to know but he had to ask.

"I asked him if there were many homosexuals in our school. He said there we're like three. Him and two other guys he knew about. Then he said something I couldn't believe."

"What's that?"

"Well, he said it wouldn't matter how many fags there were in the school to choose from if you weren't gay." She said and blushed. A little smile spread across her face as David sat speechless at her last comment. "He thinks you're the hottest guy he's ever seen." She added.

"He obviously doesn't have History this semester." David said taking another long sip from his beer bottle.

"Oh, he does. He said that Mr. Black was hot but not the kind of guy he would . . ." Amanda stopped talking and took a sip of her beer. She always drank beer slowly.

"Not the kind of guy he would what?"

"Um . . . Fuck." She answered. David could feel his stomach flip and his face go two shades of red before going white. "What's wrong David? You look like you're going to be sick." He sat silent for a second gathering his thoughts,

Fuck? He wouldn't FUCK Mr. Black. Fuck? It doesn't even sound like a word. Is it word? Fuck . . . Fuck . . . Why does it sound so weird to me? I have heard fuck before. Has this guy Fucked a dude before? Why is Amanda talking to him about fucking Mr. Black? Why is Amanda talking to this guy about fucking at all? Did she ask him if he would fuck me? Is that why I'm hotter to him than Mr. Black is? That's crazy. She wouldn't do that.

"David?" Amanda said. His eyes looked as though he was looking deep into a chasm only he could see. He blinked a few times finally and took a deep breath. He looked at his friend who looked as though she was ready to catch him if he fell or jump out of the way if he was going to throw up.

"He wouldn't *fuck* Mr. Black?" Was all David could ask. He wasn't sure what else to say or ask or anything.

"I guess not. That's what he said."

"Why?" David was so shocked that a real live gay dude wasn't sexually attracted to Mr. Black. He wasn't sure why he cared, it just seemed weird.

"He didn't really say. His only reason was that Mr. Black was old."

"Old? That's hardly a good enough reason." David said taking the he last large gulp from his beer and setting the empty bottle on the table.

"That's what he said. YOU, on the other hand." She said and smiled.

"Oh god!" David said and looked away. He could feel the knot in his stomach grow tighter.

"It's nothing bad David." Amanda said. "He just said that you were a much more interesting prospect." David's head shot around and he stared at her with wide eyes.

"*Prospect?* Like for *Sex?*" David asked. He went for his beer bottle. Amanda smiled when he noticed it was empty and handed him hers. He took it and took a couple big gulps.

"Maybe. But he said it would be cool even to just get to know you."

"Get to know me? Why?"

"Cause he thinks you're hot and he likes you."

"Yea, but . . ." David started but Amanda cut him off.

"Oh, Just meet him you wuss." David blinked at her.

"I'm not a wuss." David said.

"Sure you are. You won't meet him cause he's gay. All this talk and strange feelings about Mr. Black were ok until you had to face it one on one with a real gay person. You're a chicken, David." She said half serious and half playfully. David sighed and looked around the room. There was little he could say that could counter Amanda's argument. He *was* afraid to be faced with it. It was all so new to him and the thought of discussing anything of a sexual nature with a guy that didn't involve tits and pussy was terrifying to him. He looked at Amanda again. She was looking at him with her soft, childlike eyes. He sighed and rolled his eyes. He never could say no to his mother or to her.

"When?" He asked. Amanda practically jumped in her seat. A wide and brilliant smile spread across her face.

"Next Saturday night."

"So soon? Why?" David asked suddenly more afraid than before.

"Better to get it over with BEFORE you spend a bunch of time with Mr. Black, huh?" David ran his hand through his hair.

"Yea, but . . ."

"Never mind David, it will be great!" She said cutting him off again. David sighed and rolled his eyes. "Wanna hear what he said about his first time with a guy?" She asked smiling at him.

"Not really." David answered and put his cigarette out in the ash tray Amanda had dug out for him.

"Come on . . . you'll love it." She said and stuck her bottom lip out like she did all the time when she wanted a definite yes from him. He sighed and closed his eyes.

"*Fine,* what did he say?" He asked through clenched teeth. Amanda leaned close to David and put her hand on his inner leg. He opened his eyes and watched her as she climbed on top of him and put her lips close to his ear. He closed his eyes and took a long deep smell of her hair. He lay back on the couch and she lay on top of him putting a leg on either side of his body. She kissed his neck softly and put her mouth back close to his ear. He ran his hands down her sides and rested them on her hips. He pushed his hardening cock against her and exhaled a deep, sexy, breath.

"Still wanna know what he said?" She whispered and licked the top of his ear. A small moan escaped his throat and he kissed her shoulder.

She trusted her hips against his and she could feel his incredible erection press against her.

"Ok." He whispered and kissed her neck. She whimpered at his kiss and ran her hand down his chest and stomach. She slipped her fingers into the top of his jeans. He smiled and grabbed her backside. She raked her nails along the muscles on his stomach and kissed him. He moved one hand to her hair and rapped his hand in it. He kissed her deeply still pushing himself against her in a mock lovemaking action.

"It was really sexy, what he said." She whispered. David kissed her again and rolled her over so he lay on top of her. He moved his hips in his mock fuck as he kissed her.

"Was it?" He asked. She nodded and pulled at his shirt. He sat up and pulled it over his head. She did the same with hers and tossed it onto the floor. He brought himself back down on top of her and squeezed one breast in his hand as he kissed her. She moaned and pushed her chest against his hand. He moved his mouth down to her free breast and kissed her bra. She smiled and lifted herself so he could rid her of it. He did and took that same breast into his mouth. She moaned and tugged at his hair. He kissed his way down her body to her jeans. He looked up at her. Her eyes were closed and her breathing was heavy. He slowly undid her pants and pulled them off. She sat up and pulled him over to her by the belt loops of his pants. He smiled and followed her lead. She undid his fly and took his pants down. She looked at his erection and her eyes went wide. He quickly kicked his pants aside and kissed her. He knew the sight of him was scary to her and wanted this to be ok, for her. She kissed him back and grabbed at his hips. He slowly lowered himself back down on top of her. She moaned when his warm erect penis touched her. He smiled and continued kissing her.

"Oh, David. Do it." She said in an almost inaudible whisper. He kissed her neck and reached over to his jacket. She kissed his shoulder as he fumbled around in his coat for a condom. He pulled it out of his pocket and came back to kissing her. "Let me do it." She said and took the rubber condom from his sweating hand. He held himself up as she applied the protection. She slowly ran her hands up his muscular frame and into his hair. He lowered himself back on top of her again and kissed her gently. He positioned his hips and looked her in the eyes as he slowly pushed himself inside her. She closed her eyes and tilted her head back. He leaned down and kissed her chin. He slowly started moving himself in and out. She moaned and grabbed his hips.

"Are you ok?" He asked. She looked at him and smiled.

"Oh, fuck me David." She breathed. He kissed her neck and quickened his pace. Her moans grew louder. David could feel her contract around him as her climax was building. He moaned and buried his face in her hair. He moved his hips even faster and he could feel her finger nails cut into his back. He moaned and kissed her neck.

"I love in when you cum." He whispered and kissed her deeply on the mouth. She kissed him and pulled his hair again. He smiled and looked at her. Her eyelids hung on her eyes. Her breathing was a pant now as he brought her to climax again. She turned her head and kissed his arm. He smiled and buried his head in her hair again. He could feel his own climax building now. He arched his back and quickened his pace. She moaned even loader now and raked his back a second time. His breathing became a pleasure pant of his own. She could feel his whole body tense. The sound he made started as a low whimper and then quickly escalated into a passionate, sexy moan as he climaxed. He pushed himself as far as her could inside her. She moaned and clawed his hips. He was immediately aware of his size and backed off. "Sorry." He said quietly. She smiled and ran her hand through his hair. She moved so he could lie down in front of her on his side. He lay facing her. They both breathed heavy into each other's face. David carefully pulled the condom off and tossed it into the trash can next to the couch.

"I never told you what he said." She whispered as they lay naked in her cool basement.

"No you didn't get to that part did you?" He asked smiling. She smiled back and kissed his nose.

"Do you still want to know?" She asked. He brushed a loose hair from her sweaty brow.

"What was it again?" He asked.

"What it was like the first time he was with a guy."

"Oh yea. You said it was really sexy." David said. Amanda giggled.

"What he SAID was really sexy."

"Oh, what did he say then?" He asked.

"He said he came so hard he almost threw up."

"That's not so sexy, Amanda." David said smiling.

"He said that his orgasm with that guy was 10 times stronger than any he ever had with a woman." She said playing with David's nipple.

"10 times stronger than THAT? I don't think so sweet heart." David said referring to the orgasm he had just had. Amanda giggled and sat up to look at the time.

"It's quarter to, David." She said. He rolled and looked at the clock.

"Crap. I hate curfews." He said and sat up. Amanda watched him smiling as he got dressed. He tossed her the shirt she was wearing and she slipped it over her head.

"Promise you'll come to this date?" Amanda asked as David slipped his jacket on and lit a cigarette.

"It's going to be here?" He asked.

"Yea, I thought you would feel more comfortable here." She said and handed him his shoes. He slid them on his feet and stood up.

"Ok. That was weird of you."

"Weird? Why?"

"Well, after a night like tonight, do you really wanna chaperone a date for me?" David teased.

"You're so funny David. I think I will survive one night that the attention isn't on me."

"I don't think he'll be getting the same kind of attention you just got." He said and smiled. Amanda giggled and shook her head. David bent over and kissed her.

"Don't be late getting home." She said and kissed him again.

"No worries. I'll talk to you tomorrow." He said and walked over to the stairs.

"Hey! You want to meet him before Saturday?" Amanda asked before David got to the stairs.

"Let me think about it." David said and headed up the stairs and through the door. It was dark out and cold. He took a long drag from his cigarette and half jogged home. He tossed his smoke out on to the street before walking into the house. It was dark and quiet. The only light on was the one in the upstairs hall way. He quietly went up the stairs and into his room. He looked at the blue numbers on his alarm clock. 10:58. He smiled and walked over to his desk. He hung his coat up on the chair and sat down. He opened his journal.

Sept. 10, Saturday.

He came to my house today. I woke up to find him at my kitchen table. It was so weird. I thought my heart was going to jump out of my chest.

He looked so sexy in his leather coat. AND he smokes to witch was a surprise. And you should see the car he drives. Fucking guy is the composed throng of all my weaknesses. He talked me into the Mid-Evil fair. With mom's help, of course. Extra time with Mr. Black. How torturous of them.

Mom's date with Roger went well last night except he's boring I guess. Too bad for you Roger! Ha ha ha.

My date with Amanda was . . . interesting to say the least. We had sex. That was awesome. But she also dropped an A-Bomb on me of epic proportions. She has set up a date at her house for me and some guy named Todd for next Saturday. She thinks he can answer some questions she thinks I must have. I said I would do it. I don't know what I'm thinking but I couldn't say no. She thinks I should meet him before Saturday. I don't know about that. The whole thing seems weird. I think I might cancel.

Anyway, Thanks for listening.

Chapter 7

Sunday was a pretty slow day over all. David and his mother played their Sunday game of crib like they always did. Amanda called David and they discussed his date. He tried to get out of it but she wouldn't hear it. It was still on no matter what he said. David hated being forced into it but in a way he was a little excited.

A date with a guy might be fun. I might learn a little about this whole Mr. Black thing. Amanda seems to think this guy is a fountain of knowledge. Maybe a couple hour discussions would clear things up a bit. I wonder what he looks like. Amanda says he's really cute. I wonder what really cute is? She said Mr. Black was hot, not cute. She says I'm sexy, not cute. It will be interesting to see what cute is in her eyes.

Nancy had a few things around the house for David to do while she did the laundry. He raked the leaves in the front yard in the afternoon and took the garbage down to the community bin. They used to collect the garbage in front of people's houses until the stray cats made it too much of a problem. Now every neighborhood had one giant can that was emptied every Monday morning. It had a heavy lid so the stray cats couldn't get in. When David got home his mother had dinner on the table. They ate it and talked about the upcoming week and her first days as a scrub nurse. David teased her about all the blood and guts and things she would see. They laughed and finished up. They did the dishes together and watched a bit of T.V. At about 10:00 David was ready for bed. He said good night to his mother and headed up to his room. His entry in his journal was as uneventful as his day. He lay on his bed on his back and stared at his ceiling with a cigarette in hand.

So Monday tomorrow. Back to class and Mr. Black. Wonder what he'll wear? Probably something that you can practically see through. Maybe a pair of tight jeans that his cock is gonna break out of one day. I thought teachers wore those weird business like pants. It's funny he wears jeans. Thank god for them though. He looks amazing in them. Probably even better out of them. Why wouldn't this Todd dude fuck him? Oh, yea. Too old. That's stupid. Mr. Black is young. He looks young anyway. And shaped like a god. I wonder if he works out? He must. There is no way anyone is naturally shaped like that.

David could feel the tug of an erection forming.

So Amanda thinks jacking off would be a good idea.

David sighed and looked down at himself. He was very hard now. He put his cigarette out in the ash tray and lay back on his arm. He closed his eyes and slid his hand down his stomach to till his fingers touched the band of his boxers.

Is it a good idea? I mean, he gets me hard and he drives me crazy but is jacking off in my best interest right now?

David thought as he rubbed the band of his boxers with his fingers. He made a fist and squinted his eye lids.

God! I can't do this. I can't think about him like this. He is gorgeous and all Greek god like yes. He can make me hard as a rock at one look, yes. His voice is enough to make my legs numb, yes. But I can't do this! And if I did. What would it change? I'll have an orgasm to back up the effect of what he can already do on his own.

Although the throbbing of David's erection was intense, he sighed and put both hands behind his head. He closed his eyes and tried to sleep. His mind was swimming with heavy, sexual thoughts of Mr. Allan Black,

What would it feel like to touch your hair? To kiss you gently at first and then stronger and stronger as you got hard. I would touch your hard body and tear you out of your shirt. I would run my hands down your rippled muscles and free you from your poisonous jeans. I would lay you down and push my big, hard cock against you and make you moan.

"Fuck, David! Go to sleep." He said out loud to himself and rolled over on to his side. He thought about the descriptive touches in his WW2 novel and imagined he and Mr. Black as the characters. He squinted his eyes and scolded himself. "Stop it!" he said with clenched teeth. He tried to think about Amanda and this upcoming date with Todd. Soon he fell asleep.

David woke up to the alarm. It was his favorite song so it didn't bother him too badly. He rolled over and grabbed his cigarettes. He took one from the pack and lit it. He lay on his back thinking about the Saturday night he spent with Amanda. He was glad that she never expected anything from him after. She wasn't one of those girls that made things weird or built some kind of relationship out of it. She liked to just have sex with him and that was it. It was the kind of thing that people might call friends with benefits. He smiled at the thought and sat up. The sun was trying to peak its way through the clouds. He yawned and stood up. His unrelenting morning erection was there yet again. He opened his bedroom door a crack and called down the hall.

"Are you in the bathroom mom?" He asked.

"Nope, go ahead." She answered from the bedroom behind him. He collected his clothes for the day and headed to the bathroom. He dropped the clothes on the floor and stood in front of the toilet. His stomach hurt with the need to pee but his erection seemed to fight against the muscles in his bladder. He sighed and turned the water on. He stepped into the shower and let the hot water pound against his chest and face. His hands hung motionless at his sides. He felt like the muscles in his body were going numb by the time he decided to wash. When he was finished, he stepped out of the tub and was finally able to urinate. He got dressed and applied his cologne and deodorant and combed his hair straight back like he always did. He walked to his room and grabbed his book bag and slipped his leather jacket on. He went downstairs to the kitchen where his mother had a coffee ready for him at his seat.

"Good Morning, David." Nancy said smiling at her son.

"Good morning, mom." David replied and lit a cigarette.

"So, when do you think this after school project starts?"

"Um, next week I think. We are supposed to have a test on our mid-evil unit this Friday. The marks on that test are supposed to decide who is in the group, but it sounds like he already has it picked out."

"Well. That's good. And of course my genius son will lead the way." Nancy teased. David smiled and puffed at his cigarette. "You and Mr. Black probably could do it alone with your eyes closed and the lights off." She added. David choked on his coffee and shot his mother a devastated look. "What? You don't think the two of you could handle it yourselves?" David blinked.

"Uh, it's a big project mom and besides, who wants to spend time alone with a teacher?" David asked trying to seem not so devastated. How could he act like this in front of his mom?

"Well, he seems to really like you dear. It wouldn't kill you to like ONE of your teachers would it?"

"Ok, mom." David said. She smiled at him and looked out the window.

"Oh, Amanda is here." She said getting up to get a cup of coffee for her son's friend. David got up and went to the door.

"Hello gorgeous." David said leaning on the door jam. Amanda giggled and pushed passed him.

"You're so weird David." Amanda said walking to the kitchen.

"Hello Amanda. Here's a coffee for you dear." Nancy said pushing out the chair for Amanda. Amanda sat down and thanked Nancy.

"So, what's new this morning?" David asked Amanda who seemed to be out of sorts this morning.

"I think my parents are going to break up." She said. Her voice sounded like that of a forlorn little child who didn't want to wait until Christmas day to open their gifts.

"Oh that's terrible, Amanda. Why do you feel that way?" Nancy asked putting her hand on the table in front of Amanda.

"Well, they have been fighting a lot lately and last night they slept in separate beds."

"Maybe it was just a fight?" David asked taking a sip from his coffee cup.

"It was different this time. They used to figure it all out before they went to bed for the night but, last night, they didn't"

"Have you told your parents how you feel?" Nancy asked.

"No, I don't want to be the cause of more fighting."

"Do you think they would fight if you asked what was happening?"

"Yea, they'll find anything to fight about these days." Amanda explained.

"Hey, if it gets to crazy, you and little Mike can come stay here." David offered. Little Mike was Amanda's baby brother. He was born the night David's father died so Amanda's family named the baby after him.

"Oh, David. That would probably cause more problems." Nancy said then smiled at Amanda, "Of course you could if it got violent. But honey, running away would ultimately make things worse. Even if it was just running to here."

"I know that. And I don't think it would come to hitting or anything." Amanda said. She smiled at David who smiled back at her.

"Anyway, kids. I gotta go. If you need anyone to talk to Amanda, you can always come here and talk to me or David." Nancy said and got up.

"I know that, mom." Amanda answered as Nancy took her cup to the sink and got ready for work. David looked up at the time. It was 8:15.

"We gotta think about going pretty soon too." He said sliding over to the chair next to his friend. They heard Nancy close the door and she waved at them as she hurried to her car.

"It would really suck if my mom and dad split up. I like both my parents. Where would I go? Who would I have to live with?"

"Well, you live here. I mean in the house you're in now." David said.

"Yea, but I'm old enough to choose and I don't wanna hurt their feelings."

"So, use school as an excuse. Whoever leaves would probably head straight to the city. You just stay here cause your already enrolled in school here."

"Yea, I could say that. I like it here, David. But if mom left, she would take Little Mike with her. I would have to go with him." Amanda said. She looked up at the clock and David knew it was probably time to stop talking about it.

"Well, you'll have to decide when the time comes then right?" David asked. Amanda nodded and they both stood up. They got their things together for school and headed out the door. They walked in silence all the way. David felt sorry for his friend but he had no idea what to say to her. They walked to their lockers and got what they needed for the morning. David watched his friends less than bouncy walk as they headed to home room. He wished there was something he could do to cheer her up. Then it hit him.

"Hey Amanda." David whispered across the aisle. Amanda looked at him. "How about you set up a meeting for me and this Todd guy for lunch today or something?" David didn't want to meet Todd earlier than Saturday, but he thought it would give her something else to think about. He was right. Her face lit up and she smiled.

"So you wanna meet him early than?" She asked.

"Sure. What if I wait till Saturday and I don't like him at all?"

"Okay! I have first period with him. I'll ask." She smiled and her back seemed to straighten up a little. David smiled and shook his head.

Like a 7 year old who was just told she's going to the zoo. David thought as he got up and headed out of the room to start his morning. It went by quickly to both his dismay and pleasure. He hated Math, Science and Gym but he wasn't too thrilled to meet Todd. He met Amanda at their lockers.

"So? Where is he?" David asked as he loaded his locker and through on his jacket.

"He's gonna meet us at the table." Amanda said and grabbed David's hand. She practically pulled him out side. When his eyes adjusted to the bright sun light, David could see a tall guy standing at their table.

"Is that him?" David whispered as they walked over.

"Yes." Amanda answered. They arrived at the table and Amanda made the introductions.

"It's great to meet you, David. Amanda has told me a lot about you." Todd said. He had kind of a surfer type voice.

"Has she?" David asked lighting a cigarette. Amanda smiled and sat on the table next to where Todd was standing.

"She has, only the good stuff though." Todd said. David thought it was his attempt at humor.

"I bet that was a short conversation." David answered. He prided himself at being quick on the draw.

"Actually, to be honest, she only told me what I asked. I kind of seeked her out."

"Really? Why?"

"Well, I thought you might be interesting and neat person to get to know." Todd said. David felt weird as he watched Todd's eyes give him the once over.

"So, David. The only thing we didn't come up with was a movie to watch on Saturday. We thought we would let you pick." Amanda said.

"Yes, since we decided on Chinese food and beer, we would like to know what movie you think would go good with it." Todd answered. David thought about it for a second. He thought about Amanda's movies collection and came up with an idea.

"How do you feel about classic horror flicks?" David asked Todd.

"I like them, some of them."

"How about Evil Dead?"

"OH! I even like that one." Amanda chimed in. Todd smiled.

"Evil Dead it is then." Todd said. David wasn't quite sure what to make of Amanda's choice in learning tool. He was about a head and shoulders taller than David. He had dark black hair and brown eyes. He was very slim from what David could tell. He had well chiseled features but not godly like Mr. Black.

"Why don't you guys talk for a while, I have to go help Mr. Steinwinkle in the band room." Amanda said and jumped off the table. David and Todd said 'bye' and both sat down at the table.

"So Amanda tells me you're curious about gay men." Todd said.

Wow, nothing like jumping into it head first. David thought.

"I guess you could say that." David answered taking a long drag from his cigarette.

"Well, what do you want to know?"

"I don't know!" David said suddenly feeling extremely awkward.

"Don't be embarrassed David. Ask anything you want." David thought about it for a minute. He wasn't quite sure if he wanted to know everything about it but he did want to know one thing.

"When did you know? Like for sure?"

"Well, it was grade 6. There was this boy in my class that I was friends with and we were both curious. We had a sleep over and made out and stuff. Nothing too heavy but, he didn't like it. I did. That's when I knew."

"And you've never looked back?" David asked as if maybe there was a chance of a cure or something.

"Nope. I liked it better than girls."

"Why?"

"Well, guys are rougher. I think that's part of it. And I like a guy's plumbing better than a girls. I know what to do with it." David could tell that Todd would be a fountain of knowledge. But it was strange talking to someone other than Amanda about it. "So, why the curiosity at your age? How come nothing before now?" Todd asked. It was a valid question but David wasn't quite sure if he was willing to answer. He thought it might be better to remain as vague as possible.

"Well, I met this guy who seems to do it for me." David said. It seemed pretty vague.

"Okay. Does he know he 'does it for you'?"

"NO! I can hardly believe it let alone tell him . . . or anybody else."

"So, Amanda set up this little thing on Saturday so you could test the water then?" Todd asked in a quieter voice. David could feel his heart beat a little faster.

"I guess so." He answered.

"Well, that's a good start. I never had a girlfriend like that when I was first testing the water."

"Oh, Amanda's not my girlfriend."

"Oh, I thought she was. Sorry." Todd said. The words girlfriend and Amanda had never been put together before. It sounded strange to David. "So who's the guy?" Todd asked. David swallowed hard and looked away. He felt like running away but held his ground.

"I'd rather not say." David answered. Todd smiled.

"That's fair." He said. "Does Amanda know? I think she should at least know."

"She knows. But if she knows what's good for her, she won't say." Todd laughed.

"I wouldn't ask her. I just think that if you guys are as close as you seem, then she is the best person to know. You shouldn't have to go through this alone." Todd said. He put his hand on David back. David shivered and Todd moved it right away. "Sorry." He said and put his hands in front of him on the table.

"No problem." David said and looked at the school doors.

"Yea, it's probably that time, huh?" Todd asked seeing David's anxiousness to leave the conversation. They both got up and headed for the door.

"Look, thanks for meeting me early." David said trying to save what little nit-pick things Todd may say to Amanda when David wasn't around.

"Of course! I'm really looking forward to Saturday." Todd answered.

"Great." David said and walked over to his locker. He was hoping to see Amanda there but she wasn't. He gathered his things for the afternoon and headed to room 19. It had been two days with no Allan Black.

Maybe I got over it on the weekend? Maybe Amanda fixed me up? He thought as he walked into the room. He sat down at his desk and looked around. Mr. Black wasn't there yet. He knew he was a bit early. He got his books ready and waited.

Please GOD! Let this whole thing be over. If I have to sit with that Todd guy and learn to be gay or whatever, I will die. He's kind of good looking for a dude but, what if he expects something? Like kissing or . . . WORSE! David put his head down on his arms. He closed his eyes and wondered what terrible thing he could do to Amanda if this date thing went south. Just then he felt a hand on his back. He looked up. It was Mr. Black.

"Tired again today David?" David sighed at the knowledge that this feeling had not gone away.

"I guess so." David answered.

"Have you considered that you may have a sleeping disorder?"

"It's not that. Just a lot on my mind these days."

"If you would like, we could get together and talk about it after school or something." Mr. Black asked. His emerald green eyes cut into David like razor blades.

"No, it's ok." David answered trying not to get lost in those eyes.

"You know, David, its ok to talk about your problems."

"I know. I'm just not sure it a problem or not." Mr. Black smiled.

"How do you not know?"

"I'm not sure if it really bothers me or if I'm MAKING it a problem." David said. David was surprised with his own answer. It was probably the most honest thing he had said about the whole thing up to date.

"Well, try not to lose sleep over it. Starting next week, I'll need you at peak performance." Mr. Black said patting David's back and walking to the front of the room.

Would it be wrong to tell him I can be at PEAK PROFORMANCE at any given moment? David thought. He laughed to himself and wrote the notes down that Mr. Black scribbled on the board. It was the section of the unit about stoning witches. It was kind of lame but David figured it must be on the test. At the end of class, Mr. Black set a folded piece of paper on David's desk and smiled. David put it in his pocket and hurried to English class.

"What do we have to say about the two old sisters' from chapters 9 and 10?" Mrs. Coldiron asked the class when it had settled down. A bunch of people from the class thought they were the cat's meow being so understanding of Hans and Anthony. The entire class was a discussion of the two sisters and what people thought would happen next. She sent chapters 11 and 12 home for reading but no answer sheets this time. She had decided it was easier to grade the class on their involvement in the discussions opposed to what they wrote down. David packed his things and headed home. The sun was still shining but he could see clouds in the distance. The house was empty when he walked in. His mother wouldn't be home until around six now since her recent promotion. He took his things upstairs and hung his jacket on the back of the folding chair. He sat down and dug the note out of the pocket.

David

I really hope that whatever is bothering you isn't too serious. I would like to help you if I could. I know you probably think that I wouldn't understand, but I seem to have made it out of my teenage years alive so I think I may have learned something. You always have someone to talk to David, I don't have to be just your teacher, I can be a friend too.

Allan.

"Allan? No Black this time." David said allowed. He scratched his head and wondered what to write back. He grabbed a sheet of paper from his binder and his pen and wrote.

Mr. Black,

I really do appreciate your concern. I am glad I could talk to you if I wanted to. I'm just not sure what to say about it. Please understand that I don't mind writing notes back and forth with you but I'm not really a talker. I prefer to write. Thanks for offering me your friendship. I bet I could use it someday.

David.

He read over his note and decided it was pretty good. He really did like it when Mr. Black would write to him. It was like a secret affair or something. He smiled and slid Mr. Blacks note into the drawer of his desk. He dug in his bag for the WW2 novel and went to lay on his bed while he read.

Anthony's illness healed itself very well. The boys were soon doing the chores together again. The months passed and the snow began to melt. The young lovers had still not made love but their nightly activities were becoming more heated. They were free to be themselves here with the two old sisters. The cow was ready to be bread again and the sisters said it would take them about four days to go and get it done. They told the young boys that the one sister's son would be returning with them and it would be time for them to leave. It was a sorrowful good bye as the two sisters left. For the first three days of their absents, the boys did their chores as usual but on the fourth day, they did their chores and completely cleaned the house for two sisters. They left that evening so they would be gone when the sisters and the son returned. The walked all night in the cold until they found an old abandoned barn. They crawled into the hay loft and fashioned a bed from the old straw and bits of cloth they brought with them from the sister's cottage. That night, Hans slept behind Anthony. Anthony could feel Hans run his small calloused hand down his hip and thigh. He shivered and Anthony giggled. He kissed Anthony's neck and shoulders. Anthony could feel Hans grow hard with excitement. He rolled over and kissed his young lover. They held each other and kissed for quite some time. Hans reached down and took Anthony's erection into his hand. Anthony moaned and did the same to Hans. They touched each other like this until Hans rolled over and pushed himself against Anthony. Anthony kissed Hans on the shoulder as he slowly guided himself inside. Hans moaned his enjoyment and pushed against the motion of Anthony's hips. They made love until they were both completely satisfied. Hans lay awake long after Anthony was asleep. He thought of how Anthony had left everything he knew to keep Hans safe. He thought of the night they left Anthony's home and how his father had searched for them. He thought of the night with the Nazi soldiers and how Anthony's father seemed to emerge from the trees like Hercules. He thought of how they ran silently knowing that he would have never survived the fight with them. He thought of how sick Anthony got at the old sisters home. And now, they sleep in a barn, in the cold. When Anthony awoke the next morning, his back was cold where Hans should have been. He rolled over and saw he was alone. Hans had left.

David raised his brows and shut the book.

"So the plot thickens." He said and placed the book back into his bag. He walked downstairs and took some chicken out of the freezer for supper. He popped it into the microwave and put it on defrost. He checked the time. It was 3:30. He went into the living room and turned on the T.V. There wasn't really anything on but it was something to do. About 20 minutes later, the phone rang.

"Hello." David answered lying on his back on the sofa.

"*Hi, how was your visit with Todd?*" It was Amanda on the other end. He had expected a phone call on the subject.

"Well, ok I guess." David said.

"*Just ok? What did you guys talk about?*"

"Well, we talked about dudes. What else would he talk about?"

"*Did you get any useful info on the subject?*" Amanda asked.

"Well, I don't really know how useful it was. More like kind of weird. It's odd talking about this stuff to you let alone some fag."

"*It's homosexual David. Don't be rude.*"

"It doesn't bother me. If I'm gonna be one of these things, it should be up to me what I'll be called."

"*So you think you're actually gay, then?*"

"Who knows, Mandy. I do have a date with a guy." David said and sighed.

"*That just makes you curious David. Besides, you weren't too gay Saturday night.*" Amanda said with a giggle.

"That is true. That was very heterosexual of me wasn't it?" Amanda laughed and the two discussed Todd some more. They decided he would probably be nothing but an outlet for information. It was better that than jump into something that would scare the shit out of David.

"*Anyway, I promised mom I would start dinner. I'll be at your place tomorrow morning, Kay?*"

"Sounds good Mandy. Talk to you tomorrow." They said their good buys and David checked the time. It was nearing five pm. He got up and went out to the kitchen. He made a pot of coffee and popped the chicken into the oven. He dug through the cupboards for a can of vegetables. He decided on green beans. He set the can on the counter and sat down at the table. He heard his mother come in.

"Hi Dave." She called from the door.

"Hi mom. How was work?" He asked as he got up to prepare their coffee cups.

"Well," Nancy said slumping down on her chair, "Its different from what I'm used to, that's for sure." David brought them both a cup of coffee and sat down at the table with his mother.

"Is it harder?" David asked lighting a cigarette.

"Not harder, just different. You really need to be paying attention to everything around you to be a scrub nurse."

"Did you have a surgery today?" David asked. He thought the blood and gore his mother saw everyday was fascinating.

"Yes, two actually. A C-Section and an Appendectomy."

"Awesome. You made a baby."

"Yes I did." Nancy said and giggled at her son. They discussed the procedures while Nancy finished making supper. They talked about David's day while they ate. David made no mention of Todd but did tell his mother he would be at Amanda's place again this Saturday.

"She thinks she can help me get ready for the Mid Evil project." David lied.

"Things seem to go up and down with you two."

"What do you mean?"

"Well, sometimes your friends, then sometimes you're dating. It's hard to keep up son." Nancy said smiling.

"Whatever mom. We are just friends that happen to enjoy each other's company sometimes more than others."

"Are you being safe?" David choked on a bean.

"MOM!"

"What? It's a valid question." Nancy said now laughing at David's reaction.

"Well, yes, ok?" David said quietly.

"You didn't think I thought you were still a virgin did you?"

"Mom. I don't want to talk about this." David said taking another bite of his chicken.

"David, it's completely natural. As long as you guys are being safe . . ."

"OK, mom. Don't worry about me. You have no grandkids on the way." David said. Desperately thinking of a way to change the subject but his mother beat him to it.

"Well, I met someone if you care." She said sipping at her hot coffee.

"You mean, not Roger? Someone else?"

"Yes, Someone else. We are going out this Saturday as well."

"I hope your being safe." David teased. Nancy laughed.

"Don't worry, you don't have any siblings on the way or anything." Nancy teased back. David laughed. They got back on the subject of the Mid Evil project and discussed the fair as they did dishes. They both retired to the living room and watched the news. Nothing happy of course. David thought about Todd and wondered what on earth they would have to talk about. David decided to ask weird questions to try to scare him away from any sexual notions. David looked over to his mother after a while to see her eyes getting heavy.

"Well, I'm gonna turn in." David said getting up from the couch. Nancy looked up at him and then at the clock. It was almost ten pm.

"Good idea. Right behind you I think dear."

"Good night."

"Good night dear." David headed up the stairs and went into his room. He stripped down to his boxers and lay down in bed. He stared up at the ceiling and thought,

I never wrote in my journal today. He looked over at his desk. His journal lay there untouched from where he last set it. He yawned and got up. He sat down on the folding chair and wrote.

Sept. 12 Monday

Well, I met Todd. He's weird I think. Amanda likes him and thinks he can teach me something. Whatever. I have decided to weird him out with funny questions about fags. I really don't want this guy thinking he's getting any.

Mr. Black wrote me another note. Just signed Alan this time. I suppose it's just as sexy as signing Alan Black. He said he wants to be more than my teacher. I wish it meant what it sounds like. He thinks I need a grown up friend or something. I wrote back and told him I was good with that. I don't know why I did it but I did.

Anyway, Thanks for listening.

Chapter 8

The week seemed to fly by. It seemed that it was Friday far too fast. Nancy had worked a lot of late shifts this week so David had to pretty much fend for himself in the evenings. Amanda was consumed with David's pending date with Todd. It seemed to keep her mind off the fighting between her parents at home so David didn't complain. He came down from his bedroom Friday morning to find both Amanda and his mother sitting at the table.

"Good morning." They said in unison. David felt a weird vibe in the room.

"Morning." He answered and sat down at his cup of coffee at the table.

"How was your sleep?" Nancy asked. This was more of a mom and David type of thing to happen.

"Good. Slept like a baby." He said and stared at Amanda. She was wearing a tank top and blue jeans. The shirt was low cut and it showed off the lace in her bra. David raised an eyebrow and lit a cigarette. Amanda smiled and turned to Nancy.

"So, this guy. Is he nice?"

"Not too sure really. My friend at work set it up. I know him but I don't really know him. You know?"

"God girls talk weird." David said taking a long drag from his cigarette.

"Anyway," Nancy said rolling her eyes at her son. "We are supposed to go to the movies and dinner tomorrow night."

"That will be nice." Amanda said sipping her coffee.

"Speaking of nice, I hear you are helping David with the Mid-Evil stuff this Saturday."

"Did he? He doesn't need help with the knowledge. Just helping to get things he might need together. You know how guys can be unorganized and confused." Amanda said giving David a sideways glance. Nancy giggled at David and looked up at the clock.

"Well, Don't work too hard. Try to learn something." She said and got up from her chair. David smiled as Nancy messed his hair as she walked by.

"By mom." David said. Nancy said her good byes and hurried out to her car.

"Mid—Evil project?" Amanda asked. David rolled his eyes and put out his cigarette.

"Would you rather I said, 'oh, I have a date with a guy and Amanda is chaperoning?"

"That would have been awesome." Amanda said laughing.

"Yea, yea. Laugh it up princess. It's not too late to cancel."

"Oh come on. Don't be such a baby. It's one night out of your life. He said he wasn't looking to *do* anything"

"Well, I hope not. It's the only thing that bugs me about it. You should see how that guy looks at me." David said and mock shivered.

"How do you mean?"

"It's like he undresses me with his eyes." Amanda giggled and sipped her coffee. "What? It's true." David answered.

"I think your freaking out David."

"No shit, I'm freaking out. I thought this would be ok but tomorrow is Saturday and I don't know if I can do it." David said in a panicked voice. Amanda smiled and moved closer to David.

"Don't think so much about it. It will be fine. I will be there. What could happen?"

"Yea, yea. Famous last words." Amanda giggled and got up from her chair. She took their cups to the sink and rinsed them out. David grabbed his book bag off the rail and handed Amanda's to her. They walked down the street in silence. David thought about the coming day and tried to look forward to History class. It was the final exam on the war fair unit. He knew he would do well. They walked into the school and walked the busy hall to their lockers. They collected what they needed for the day and headed to homeroom class.

"You could always just think of Mr. Black the whole time." Amanda whispered across the aisle. David shook his head and looked at her.

"Why would I do that?" He asked thinking of the very intense physical reaction he had to the thought of Mr. Black.

"It would make it more enjoyable." Amanda said giggling. David rolled his eyes and smiled.

"You're funny Amanda." The bell rang and they headed to their morning classes. Lunch time arrived and David was itching for a cigarette. He met Amanda at their locker and headed out side. They sat down at the table and David lit a cigarette. He inhaled the blue poison in a heavy breath.

"Dude, you need to calm down." Amanda said. David looked at her and smiled.

"I am calming down. That is what a smoke is for." He took another long exaggerated drag. Amanda shook her head.

"If you hated this idea so much, why didn't you say so."

"I don't hate your idea Amanda. I'm just nervous."

"Why? It's a couple beers with me and Todd."

"It's the reason Amanda. Not the actions. I'm there for the sole purpose of exploring my sexuality. Its bugs me ok." David said and stared out onto the football field.

"So what?" Amanda asked. David was shocked at the question.

"So what? It's hard."

"You talk to me on the phone one minute like its ok. Now your freaking out. The closer Saturday gets the weirder you get."

"It's one thing to talk about it Amanda." There was a long pause. Amanda stared out onto the football field as well. "Why do you care?" David added. Amanda sighed and shook her head.

"I wish I didn't David. But you're my best friend. You're like family to me. What happens to you affects me and vice versa." David sighed this time and thought about that. He remembered Amanda telling him about the almost rape at her grandmother's house and how that made him feel. He looked over at her. She had a very upset look on her face.

"Your right." David said and put his arm around her. "Sorry."

"Really?" Amanda asked looking up into his eyes. David got lost in her eyes for a moment. He liked being there. Nothing else seemed to matter there.

"Really. I'll even be nice to him, ok?" Amanda smiled and kissed his cheek.

"How nice?" She asked in a funny voice. David laughed.

"Not *too* nice." They both giggled and David threw his smoke away. Amanda nibbled at a granola bar she had manifested from her pocket.

"What if he tried to kiss you?" She asked, "Hypothetically speaking of course." David thought for a minute. Normally he would say something about pounding his face in but he thought playing with her for a minute was called for.

"Well, hypothetically speaking." He said. Amanda nodded and waited for his reply. "I would pull his hair and shove my tongue so far down his throat he wouldn't know what hit him." Amanda burst out laughing.

"Nice David." David laughed and shook his head.

"You wouldn't even try it? Just to see how it feels?"

"I don't know Amanda."

"How could you know if your still hanging on to your heterosexuality like it's a commandment or something?"

"I think it is." David said smiling. Amanda shook her head.

"Look, it's the 21st century David. Face the facts."

"What facts?" David wished he hadn't asked.

"Your sexual frustration due to Mr. Black? Your confusion because of it? You're coming date with Todd? It's all facts." She said in a professor like voice.

"Ok. Circumstantial." David said smiling at his friend. Amanda giggled and nudged him with her shoulder.

"David, I'm serious." Amanda said in a quiet voice. David sighed and leaned against her.

"I know you are." He answered and kissed the top of her head. They noticed students walking back into the school. They got up and slowly walked back into the school.

"I want you to really think about how you feel about all this David."

"I have." David said getting his books organized for the afternoon.

"I mean *really* think about it and tell me later today when I call, ok?"

"Ok, Amanda. Come up with questions and I'll answer them as honest as I can. Will that work?"

"That will work." She said smiling and headed off to class. David walked the halls to room 19. Mr. Black was standing at the door.

"Hi David." He said in his seductive voice. David sighed.

"Hi Mr. Black."

"Ready for the test?"

"Of course." David answered. He thought it was a stupid question considering he probably could grade the papers himself.

"Ready for next week? I hear you have some books that might be of interest. Some the library doesn't have." Mr. Black's voice made David almost high. He leaned against the door jamb like Mr. Black was then stood himself back up just as quick.

"Yea, I can bring them." David said and headed into class. Mr. Black smiled and followed. He went to his desk and grabbed the test papers.

"Ok, gang. Test time." He said in a loud voice. David smiled at the groans from some of the other students. Mr. Black started at the other side of the room. Passing each student the test booklet face down on their desk. His hips and shoulders seemed to move in unison. He explained the rules of test writing in his class as he walked. David watched him move around the room. His movements seemed to seduce David. He looked down at the top of his desk.

God save me. I'm losing my mind. Why do I want him so much? This is getting stupid. What did Amanda want me to think about? How I'm feeling right now? I feel horny. I feel like he's doing it to tease me. I can't stand the way he moves. Why is this happening to me? Come on David think? What is so great about Mr. Alan Black? He drives a cool car. So does a million other dudes. He has a great body? Nothing a couple other actors and stuff haven't showed off. His voice sounds like . . . what does his voice sound like? I know it makes me crazy. His voice and his smell. That's not a lot to go on. Amanda isn't going to be satisfied with that.

"Here you go David." Mr. Black's voice broke David's thought pattern and he almost jumped out of his chair. "Sorry. Didn't mean to scare you."

"You didn't." David said looking up at his teachers face. He was so attractive.

"Keep it face down until I say, ok?" Mr. Black asked. David nodded and watched him walk to the front of the class. David moved his eyes down Mr. Blacks frame. His t-shirt hugged his chest and seemed to loosen a little at his stomach. His jeans weren't as tight as usual but David could still make out what they held. He quickly looked back up at Mr. Blacks face. He was explaining the after school project. "We will be starting Monday night. Some of you already know you are joining. Some of you need to get a good mark on this test to make it. You have the rest of class to complete the test. When you're done, put up your hand and I will collect it. Then you can go." There was a couple 'right ons' from the class. "Ok, guys. Go ahead." David could hear test papers flip over. He turned his over and smiled. Attached was a note.

David,

This test might be a bit beneath you. I apologize if it comes across as too easy. I would like to see you for a few minutes after the rest of the class is finished, so take your time.

Alan.

David smiled and pocketed the note. He looked up at Mr. Black. He was leaning back on his chair reading a novel. David looked back down at his paper. The questions were easy and he flew through them fairly quickly. He had finished the test in twenty minutes. He looked around the room. No one had left yet.

Great. I could be here for a while. Wonder what he wants? Me? Ha, ha, ha. You're an idiot Davy boy. But seriously? And what am I supposed to say to Amanda today when she calls? Ok, feelings, feelings . . .

David looked up at Mr. Black. He watched as he repositioned on his chair. The muscles in his stomach and chest rippled with movement. He leaned to one side of his chair and turned a page of his book. He looked up at David. They locked eyes for a second. David's heart raced but he couldn't look away. Mr. Black looked up at the clock. He got up from his desk and walked over. He squatted next to David.

"Are you finished already?" He whispered. David looked into his eyes and nodded. "Let's see." Mr. Black said and took the paper up to his desk. David sighed and put his head down.

Fuck your obvious David. Get a hold of yourself. What would you do if he asked what your problem was? Oh, nothing. I just want you so bad I can taste it. God I'm an idiot. This is the kind of stuff Amanda wants to hear I bet. How stupid this whole thing is getting. And what the fuck! A hard on? Again? Give me a break.

"Looks good David." Mr. Black whispered from in front of David's desk. He was squatted in front like he had done earlier.

"Well, it was easy." David said looking up at Mr. Blacks face again.

"I was afraid of that. Your answers are right on the money."

"I know this stuff, Mr. Black." Mr. Black smiled and stood up. Other students were putting their hands up. He collected their tests and let them leave. It was almost the end of class when the last student left.

"Ok, David." Mr. Black said and pulled a chair up to the front of David's desk. David leaned back in his chair to try to make some distance between them.

"Why did you want me to stay?"

"Well, you're a very bright young man David, and I hate to do this to you, but, I am concerned about the company you have been keeping." David's eyes grew wide.

"What company?" He asked.

"Well, the school I used to work at had a few students this school has now." Alan said. David nodded. "One of those students was Todd Graves." David's heart stopped. Mr. Black continued. "I know you won't do anything stupid, David, but Todd is bad news."

"How do you mean?" David asked trying to stay calm.

"Well, this doesn't leave this room ok?" David nodded again. "He got into some trouble with drugs. I just want to make sure you're not going to waste your clever mind on that kind of stuff." David smiled for a second and then answered.

"A say no to drugs talk, Mr. Black?" He said and half giggled. Mr. Black smiled.

"I was hoping you would react like that. Good, I don't have to worry about it then?"

"Nope. I'm clean." David answered and felt his heart calm to its normal beat.

"That's good news Mr. Smith. Now, you are aware you are the only student from this class joining the project right?"

"I figured. What was with the whole 'get good marks to join the project, gang' stuff about?" David asked, mocking his teacher's voice. Mr. Black laughed.

"Do I really sound like that?" David laughed and shook his head.

"No."

"Formality I'm afraid. Can't have favorites you know." Mr. Black winked at David. David smiled and looked up at the clock. "You're often in a hurry to get out of here David. May I ask why?" Mr. Black asked. David sat quietly for a moment.

Fuck! What do I say?

"I don't care much for school." David said looking at his teacher to see if he bought it.

"Yea, I remember feeling that way."

"Then why are you a teacher?"

"I had a teacher back in the 11th grade that made me change my mind." Mr. Black said getting up and moving the chair back to where he had found it.

"Really? Hot chick or something?" David asked trying to have a guy to guy tone. Mr. Black laughed and shook his head.

"No, unfortunately not. He was an older guy. He made teaching look cool." David thought about it for a second.

"How can teaching look cool?" Mr. Black raised an eyebrow and smiled. He seemed to look off into some distant memory for a second before he answered.

"He could do it." Mr. Black said quietly then added. "He changed my mind about teachers anyway." Just then, the bell rang and David stood up. He collected his books and smiled at Mr. Black.

"Good talk." David said and headed for the door.

"See you Monday David." Mr. Black said. David never looked back. He walked to his English class with his mind racing. He sat down at his desk and stared at the board. There was another test today. He put his books next to his desk and stared at the board.

Ok, did that just happen? What does he mean by 'He could do it'? His voice sounded like mine would 25 years from now talking about him. God! What if the same thing happened with him? He would see right through me then. Holy Fuck! THIS is what Amanda would want to hear. Ok, devil's advocate for a second. Maybe it's not what I think. Maybe he hasn't noticed me checking him out. Even though I am completely obvious. Maybe he just got close to his teacher. Maybe they were friends or something like he wants to be with me. God I hope this isn't gonna blow up in my face.

"Ok, class." Mrs. Coldiron said, "Last test on this book before the last two chapters. Hope we all studied." She added as she handed out the papers. David read through the test and answered the questions in sequence. The bell rang as he finished the last question. He collected his things and headed to his locker. He quickly threw on his jacket and headed out side. It was starting to rain so he hurried home. He took his bag up to his bedroom and threw it against the chair.

"Why am I in such a hurry?" David asked himself out loud. He shook his head and sat down on the bed. He lit a cigarette and stared at the drawers he kept Mr. Blacks letters in. He got up and put the latest one in with the others. He went back to the bed and lay down on his back. He stared at the ceiling.

What if he was curious at my age? What if this teacher of his was as hot as he is? I wonder what he did? He looks like the type that would have hit it head on. Maybe he's waiting to see if I say anything about it. What if I did and I was wrong all along? What if this is just my mind making up shit to fuck me up? He did sound strange when he said 'He could do it.' Like as if they had a thing or something.

David sighed and rolled over to ash his cigarette. He propped himself up against the head board and stared at his cigarette.

Mr. Black gay. That would certainly change things. I wonder if he would be willing to be adventurous like HIS teacher was? I wonder what they did. I wonder if they did anything. Fuck, this is so messed up. Why can't I just have a normal day? Why does this stuff just get weirder every day? Amanda is gonna know something is up.

David sat up and ran his hand through his hair. He sighed and got up off the bed. He put his half smoked cigarette out and headed downstairs. The light on the answering machine was flashing. He pushed play.

Hi Dave, its mom. Listen, I have a 6:00 surgery tonight so I'm going to have dinner with your Aunt Gina in the city. Sorry. You'll have to make something for yourself. I'll try to call later. Love you.

"Well, what's new?" David asked and headed out to the kitchen. He looked in the fridge but didn't see anything appetizing. He grabbed a pop and sat on his dads chair in the living room. He turned on the T.V. and watched some sitcom. The phone rang right at 3:30 on the nose.

"Hello" David said pushing the foot out on the reclining chair.

"Hi, How was your day?" It was Amanda on the other end.

"Not to normal. How was yours?"

"Well fine. What was weird today?"

"I think Mr. Black had a crush on his teacher in grade 11." David blurted out. Amanda was quiet for a second.

"So? And how do you know?"

"He told me. Anyway, this teacher was a dude."

"What!? He told you he had a crush on a guy teacher?"

"No, but that's what it sounded like."

"You're not making any since David."

"Ok, he said he hated school when he was young. So I asked why he became a teacher."

"Well naturally."

"He said it was because of a teacher he had in grade 11."

"Ok, hardly sounds gay David."

"Just listen, he said this teacher made teaching look cool. So I asked how."

"Yea, what did he say?"

"He said, 'He could do it.'" David said mimicking the seductive sound he had heard in Mr. Black's voice hours before.

"THAT'S how he said it?"

"Yea! Weird right?"

"Kind of. What else did he say?" Amanda sounded as though she must have been on the edge of her seat.

"Something about how he changed his mind about teachers."

"Huh, that is a weird day David."

"I know."

"Good thing you have that date with Todd tomorrow."

"Why?" David asked suddenly shocked at Amanda's revelation.

"Well, what if Mr. Black likes you too? It's a little weird but it could happen."

"What does that have to do with Todd?"

"Practice stupid!"

"Practice?! Are you crazy?"

"No, come on. Don't you want to have something under your belt in case you're right about Mr. Black?"

"Practice what, Amanda?"

"It's good logic if you think about it."

"PRACTICE WHAT?"

"Are you really that dumb? If he's been with guys since grade 11, wouldn't you want to have a little knowledge before you do anything with him?"

"Whoa, whoa, whoa, Amanda. Are you talking about sex?"

"No, David, I'm talking about painting." Amanda said sarcastically.

"You can't be serious."

"Why not? Remember that movie we watched were that guy wanted to get a bunch of practice having sex before he finally did it with the girl he really liked?"

"Yea, but . . ."

"This is just like that." David sighed and ran his hand through his hair.

"Amanda, this is a little heavy . . ."

"Oh, David. Start small. Who knows? You might really like it."

"For the love of god, Amanda! We are talking about a guy's dick in my ass!" Amanda burst out laughing.

"I know what we are talking about David. Isn't that what you think about when you think about Mr. Black?"

"No!"

"Well, what do you think about then?" David thought for a minute.

"Well, I think about kissing him."

"That's it? Wow you're easy."

"No that's not it, Amanda. It's hard to talk about it."

"What are you thinking about when you jack off."

"I don't."

"You still haven't? Holy cow David. Ok, so kissing."

"Yea, you know. Like making out type kissing."

"What else?"

"I don't know. Just stuff." David said lighting a cigarette and leaning back in the chair so the foot stuck out again.

"Ok, David. So kissing and other stuff. Don't you wanna be good at the other stuff?"

"I am good at the other stuff, I think."

"So I'm guessing the thought of actually fucking him never entered your mind."

"Well, not entirely."

"So you have thought about it then?"

"Kind of."

"Well, don't leave me hanging here, David. What's kind of?"

"You really get off on this shit, don't you?" David asked. Amanda giggled and answered.

"*Maybe a little. Come on! Give me something.*" Amanda pleaded with a winy voice. David giggled.

"Ok, I *have* thought about being the one DOING the fucking."

"*See, how hard was that?*"

"Fairly, you should have been there."

"*You're a pig David.*" David laughed.

"You asked."

"*Yea, yea. So, that's pretty gay you know.*" Amanda's voice sounded serious.

"I know."

"*Like I said before David. Maybe this date with Todd is a good idea.*"

"I hope your right. I'm not having sex with him or anything though."

"*Whatever, that's none of my business.*"

"Thanks Amanda." David said sarcastically.

"*What? It isn't. Besides that, who said that was even going to happen anyway?*"

"Well, it isn't."

"*So, nothing to worry about then.*"

"Yea, that's easy for you to say. You're not the one doing this."

"*I've been nervous about dates before.*"

"This isn't the same thing."

"*Maybe not. But I'll be here so what could happen, right?*"

"Yea, your right." David said. There was a short pause, then Amanda asked,

"*Why haven't you jacked off yet?*"

"Jesus Amanda."

"*What?*"

"Why does it matter?"

"*Because, it's so unnatural for you.*"

"How do you know?"

"*Come on, David. This is me you're talking to. You tell me everything.*"

"Oh, yea."

"*So, how come?*"

"I feel like it's going against my last binding, heterosexual, jack off to chicks only, rule."

"*You have a jack off to chicks only rule?*"

"Yea, doesn't every guy?" Amanda laughed.

"*Only the ones fighting homosexuality.*"

"Nice Amanda."

"*What? Why else would there be a rule like that?*"

"Just in case you're really drunk or something."

"*HA! Yea right.*"

"I'll tell you what. When I break the rules, you'll be the first to know, ok?"

"*Awesome. That's my boy.*"

"You're so weird Amanda."

"*Look who's talking.*"

"No kidding." David said quietly and put out his cigarette.

"*Anyway, I have a ton of homework. I'll see you tomorrow at 6:00 ok.*"

"Why 6:00? I thought it was 8:00"

"*It is, but I thought you might want a couple hours of 'hang on to the holy shit handles' or something.*"

"Ok. That's a good idea."

"*Ok, talk to you tomorrow then.*"

"OK, bye." David said and hung up the phone. He wasn't too sure what she meant but he knew, beings it was Amanda, it was something helpful. He went into the kitchen and made a sandwich. He sat at the table and ate it. He finished his pop and went up to his room. He sat down at his desk and stared at his journal. He sighed and opened it up.

Sept. 16 Friday,

There is a good chance that Mr. Black may have had the same feelings for his grade 11 teacher that I have for him. It's weird and only speculation but his voice and distant gaze is almost proof enough for me. We start our project Monday night. He is supposed to give times during class. I think I'm his favorite witch is weird. I've never been teachers favorite. Anyway,

My date with Todd tomorrow is a go. Witch Amanda thinks now is good practice in case Mr. Black's gate happens to swing wide open. I don't know what she thinks will happen between this Todd guy and me, but, this is Amanda we're talking about.

Thanks for listening.

Chapter 9

David slept in until well passed 10. He was startled by a knock at his bedroom door.

"What?" He asked in a groggy voice.

"There is a phone call for you." Nancy said from the other side. David took the phone off the receiver on his head board.

"I got it mom." He said. She walked down the stairs and hung up the other end.

"Hello?" David said yawning. The voice on the other end shot him up in the sitting position.

"Hello, David. Sorry I woke you." It was Mr. Black. David looked down at his never fail morning erection and felt himself blush.

"UH, no problem. What can I do for you?"

"Well, nothing really. I was wondering if I might do something for you." David blinked and pinched himself. He winced and closed his eyes.

"Uh, I'm good." David said pushing down on his erection with the side of his arm.

"I don't doubt that David. This is your mother's idea actually."

"My moms idea?" David said looking down at his enormous hard on. It was as if it knew who he was talking to.

"Yea, she thinks you could use a little man to man time."

"With who?" David asked, already knowing the answer.

"Well, with me. If that's ok." Mr. Black sounded like sex to David.

"Doing what?"

"Well, there's a small lake out here at my place and I was thinking about doing some fishing out there before it freezes."

"Fishing? That's a pretty manly thing Mr. Black."

"Well, my dad used to take me so it's kind of a tradition. Want to come?" The question hit David like a bus on the highway. He stared down at his erect penis.

HE didn't just ask 'wanna come'?

"Uh, sure. When?" David answered without thinking.

"Well, tomorrow." David's heart sank. He ran his hand through his hair.

"Tomorrow huh?"

"Yea, I told your mom that was a little short notice but she said you do well with snap decisions. Still want to do it with me?" David's eyes rolled into the back of his head. *What? Come on! Pick your words dude.*

"Uh, yea. Sure, why not?" David answered staring down at his now throbbing erection.

"Great! What's a good time to catch you out of bed?"

"I'll be up whenever you want." David said shaking his head at his dick.

"How about 8? I would like to start earlier, but you probably like to sleep in on the weekends." Mr. Black said. David glowered at his penis.

He could hardly believe the intensity of his erection. This wasn't going away on its own.

"8:00 is perfect. I'll be up." David said and rolled his eyes.

"Perfect! I'll see you tomorrow then."

"Ok, see you tomorrow." David said and hung up the phone. He lay back on his bed and took a few deep breaths. His erection was almost painful. He rested one arm behind his head and other hand on his stomach. He took a few more deep breaths.

Ok, it's your own stupid rule David. This is getting ridiculous. Just do it and get it over with.

He slowly slid his hand down his stomach till his fingers touched the band of his boxers. He stared up at the ceiling.

There's no going back after this. If you cum your gay. Your dads rolling in his grave.

He took another deep breath and closed his eyes. He bit his top lip but didn't move. His penis throbbed waiting for his touch. His heart pounded in his chest. He slid his fingers under the band of his underwear. His body twitched with anticipation. His breathing had already quickened without even doing anything. He moved his hand lower until his grip found its mark. He slowly slid his hand up and down the shaft of his dick. He breathed heavy and felt sweat form on his brow already. He quickened his pace thinking about Alan's hand instead of his. He imagined Alan's powerful kiss and heaving chest. A small moan escaped his throat as he gripped himself harder. His shoulders shook as he moved. His hips matched his hand and he could feel his ecstasy start to form. He pushed his head back into his pillow and moaned again. He imagined doing the same for Alan Black and what his moaning would sound like under his touch. The muscles in his stomach tensed as his orgasm approached. He gripped the pillow with the hand behind his head. With a final hard thrust, David came.

He moaned and slowed his hand. His heart thumped in his chest in time with the throbbing from his orgasm. He moaned again quietly and laid his hand on his stomach. He felt his erection slowly leave and the feeling of having to pee slowly crept up.

"Holy fuck." David whispered and sat up. He took a deep breath and stood up. He grabbed clean clothes and underwear and headed to the bathroom. He urinated and jumped into the shower. He closed his eyes and thought about what just happened.

This is serious. I have NEVER cum like that from jacking off before. That was awesome. Almost better than sex. Amanda is gonna love this.

He washed his body and got out of the shower. He brushed his hair back and got dressed. He went back to his room and grabbed his cigarettes then headed downstairs.

"Are you mad at me, David?" Nancy asked setting a coffee on the table for him. David smiled and sat down.

"Nope. Something like this was bound to happen. You've been looking for a 'big brother' thing or whatever since dad died."

"Well, I thought you would be a little more upset. Thanks for doing this."

"I feel great today mom. No worries." David said and giggled to himself.

Why didn't I do that before?

"I should let you sleep in more often."

"Yea, you should." David said laughing. Nancy shook her head and sipped her coffee. David did the same.

"So, I have to go into the hospital for a few hours before my date tonight. Could you do some laundry for me?"

"Oh, yea. The hot date."

"Oh, David. I thought you didn't want to hear about this stuff?"

"Your right, mom. Laundry. Ok, consider it done." David said and lit a cigarette. Nancy smiled and yawned. "What's going on at the hospital?" David asked seeing that his mother was tired.

"Well, there are no surgeries today so the powers that be thought it was a good idea to hold an afternoon meeting for the surgical staff."

"Awe, that sucks mom. I was hoping we could have our card game today since I'll be gone tomorrow morning."

"Well, we have a little time now. I don't have to leave until noon." Nancy said. David looked up at the clock. That would give them a little over an hour. He got up and went to the china cabinet. He opened the front drawer and pulled out the cards and crib board. They laughed and played until noon. Nancy put things away before she left. David grabbed the laundry basket and collected the dirty clothes and towels from around the house. He carried the lot downstairs and loaded the washing machine. He filled it with soap and turned it on. He turned to go back upstairs when he noticed his dad's old music room door was open. He walked over and stepped in. There was dust on the drum kit and a still full ash tray on the stool. He walked farther into the room. It smelled like old brass instruments and dust. He walked over to the window and slid it open a crack. The outside air poured in like children from the cold. He walked over to the full ash tray and picked it up. He could feel the dust on the outside of it with his fingers. He carried it over to the laundry room garbage can and dumped it out. He cleaned it in the sink and took it back into the room. Soon he was dusting his father's instruments. Everything but his dad's guitar. He swept the floor and wiped down the chairs. He made his way over to the shelf that held his dads music books. On the shelf he saw a wine glass. He cocked his head to one side and picked it up. It had no dust on it and he could still smell the wine inside. He sighed knowing it belonged to his mom.

"Didn't know you still hung out down here, mom." He said thinking back to when his dad died and his mother jumped into a wine bottle. He sighed and took the glass with him out of the room. He shut the door and went into the laundry. He put the wash into the dryer and threw in the second load. He took the glass up to the kitchen and washed the glass. He put it away and searched through the cupboards for booze. He couldn't find any and decided his mother's transgression was a one nighter or something. He sighed and stepped outside with his cigarettes and a cup of coffee. He sat down on the step and lit a cigarette. He watched the cars drive by. Some people waved some didn't even notice he was there. He puffed at his cigarette and sipped at his coffee. He looked at the house across the street. He was always amazed that a house like that was in his neighborhood. It was like a Beverly Hills type house or something. The people that lived there kept to themselves mostly. The father would come outside to get the paper in his house coat every morning. The kids seemed to leave for school before Amanda and David did and the mother seemed to always be hanging cloths on the line. It was like a place from the movies or something. David smiled to himself and got up. He stretched and went back into the house. He took his almost empty coffee cup into the kitchen and set it on the counter. He made himself a sandwich and sat down at the table. He ate it quietly looking out the window.

So, big date with Todd tonight, David. Are you ready for this? Jacking off about Mr. Black was awesome so maybe hanging out with someone who thinks the same will be not too bad. Maybe Amanda is right. Maybe I should try to get a bit of a taste for the physical part of this thing.

"That should be interesting." David said aloud and finished the last of his meal. He wiped the crumbs off onto the floor and looked at the time. It was already 4:30. "Wow, time sure flies when your cleaning that music room." He said out loud and looked down at his clothes.

He decided he should probably change. He went up to his room and found a pair of light coloured blue jeans and a tight black t-shirt. He put them on and went to the bath room. He looked at himself in the full length mirror. He brushed his hair back and put on some cologne. He sighed and headed back to his room. He put on his dads leather jacket and took one last look in the mirror. He raised his eyebrows. "Wow, mom. I do kind of look like dad in this thing." He smiled at the thought and went back downstairs. He went into the kitchen and grabbed a pop. "Fuck, I'm bored." He said and went into the living room. He turned on the T.V. and reclined in his dad's chair. He looked over at the picture of Mike Smith on the book case. "God you would hate my guts right now if you knew what I was about to go do. What I did this morning." He said to the picture and rolled his eyes. He stared at the T.V. not even watching it.

I got to remember to ask what the reasons are that Todd has not to want Mr. Black. He has to think he's sexy. He's gay. I'm just starting this whole fucked up existence and I can see he's sexy. Wonder what kind of weird taste Todd must have if he likes me and not Alan. He's like an older version of me, except I would never be a teacher. He's hot, he drives a hot car, he's a genius in the mid-evil stuff, he smokes. The smoking thing may not be cool but he sure makes it look sexy. He smokes like an action movie actor or something. Man he's hot.

David looked at the little clock above the T.V. "Man I need glasses." He said to himself and got up to get closer to it. It was closing in on 5:30. He ran his hand through his hair and shut the T.V. off. He walked over to the phone and dialed Amanda's number. It rang about three times.

"*Hello*" It was Amanda's older brother, Gabe.

"Hi, I didn't know you were coming out this weekend." David said.

"Oh, hey David. Yea, it was surprise to me too."

"What's going on with you?"

"Not too much, you?"

"Uh, long story." David said and rolled his eyes. Growing up, Gabe was a lot older that Amanda and David and was kind of like a free therapist.

"You too huh?"

"Shit going on with you too?"

"Yea, well. Mom and Dad have decided to go away to work on their shit so they asked me to come out and watch the kids while they are gone."

"Think it will work?"

"Who the fuck knows with those two? They play happy house hold when somebody's looking, then next thing you know their at each other's throats. If you ask me, I think a divorce is just what they need."

"Maybe, but it's hard on Amanda."

"She's a tough kid. Besides, she has you watching her back doesn't she?"

"Yea, she does." David said and smiled.

"Speaking of Amanda, you probably called for her huh?"

"Nice Segway, Gabe. But yea, I did."

"Ok, just a sec." Gabe said giggling. David could hear him call Amanda. He waited a few seconds then Amanda answered.

"Hello?"

"Hey, what's happening?"

"Well, you're holding up production. I was trying to send Gabe to get booze and I just finished getting ready."

"Oh, well. I was board and wanted to come early."

"Awe, your so cute David. Sure. Come over."

"Cool, see you in a sec." David said and hung up. He put his shoes on and headed out.

He knocked at Amanda's door and Gabe answered. David stood staring at him for a second. He was dressed in all black with his long black hair combed straight with a part down the middle. He smiled at David and leaned against the door frame. It had almost been four years since David saw him.

"Hi." Gabe said still leaning on the door frame.

"Hi, Gabe. You look . . . different." David said finding himself oddly attracted to his best friend's big brother.

"You too. You got taller." Gabe said and hugged David. David hugged back and closed his eyes. Gabe felt surprisingly good in his arms. They parted and Gabe kept his hands on David's arms. "You got a lot taller actually. Funny those growth spurts."

"Yea, well. Can't help progress right?" David said and smiled. Gabe moved out of the way and David walked in.

"Amanda's in the can. Wanna beer?" Gabe asked leading the way to the kitchen.

"Sure, yea." David said checking out Gabe from behind. It was strange to David that he hadn't noticed Gabe like this before.

"Sit down. She'll be a while. Little Mike through up in her hair so she's in the shower." Gabe said laughing and bringing two beer to the table.

"That's nasty." David said and sat down with Gabe at the table. They both lit a cigarette.

"So, you and Amanda finally hooked up, huh?"

"Not really. Still just friends." David said sipping at his beer. Gabe raised his eyebrows.

"Huh. I figured you guys would have fallen in love or something."

"Why?"

"I don't know. Just looked like that when you guys were growing up." Gabe said taking a big sip from his beer. David smiled and did the same.

"What about you? Anybody special?"

"Yea, right. No thanks." Gabe said and they both laughed.

"Why not? You're a good looking guy." David said smiling at Gabe.

"I know. Why tie myself down to one person?"

"Wow, you're so put together dude." They both laughed again then Gabe stopped smiling. David looked at him with a puzzled gaze. "What?" David asked.

"What's going on with you?" Gabe asked with a twisted brow. David sighed and shook his head.

"Why do you ask?"

"If anybody knows you two, it's me. I know when something is up."

"Really?" David asked feeling a little put on the spot.

"Look, David. Whatever it is that you and Amanda are into, I can help."

"What do you think it is?"

"Who knows? You tell me. She's been acting weird about tonight. You show up early and seemed a little stunned to see me at the door. It's a little fishy." Gabe said taking another sip from his drink.

"Just weird to see you. I didn't know you were coming. And as far as tonight go's . . ."

"Who's Todd?" Gabe asked cutting David off in mid-sentence. David choked on his beer and Gabe laughed. "Well, don't kill yourself. Who is he?"

"Just a guy." David said clearing the beer out of his throat.

"Yea, that's what Amanda said. Come on, you guys were never liars before."

"He IS just a guy. Amanda thought we would get along so she invited us over for drinks and stuff." David said. He knew that appearing as honest as possible was the only way to get out of explaining the whole thing. Gabe had a gift for getting info from Amanda and him so he knew he had to tread lightly.

"Amanda needs to help you make friends? I find that hard to believe."

"Oh, you know Amanda. She gets these ideas and drags me along."

"Nope, don't know her to do that. Try again." Gabe said. David looked around the room. He strained to hear the shower but didn't know if it was on or not.

"She wants to start a band?" David said. They both laughed knowing Amanda couldn't carry a tune across a barn floor.

"What are you in to, David?" Gabe asked leaning closer to him. David took a deep breath and closed his eyes. "What is it, David?" He asked again seeing David's stress with the conversation.

"It's not drugs or gangs or something dangerous, Gabe. Ok." David said with his eyes still closed. Gabe leaned back in his chair and grabbed his beer.

"Well, that's a shock. You and Amanda, not gang bangers?" Gabe said sarcastically. David opened his eyes and looked at Gabe. He sipped his beer and stared at him. David took another sip from his beer and sat quietly. "Wanna know what I think?" Gabe asked.

"What?"

"I think Todd is gay."

"Why do you say that?" David asked surprised at Gabe's assumption.

"Well, Amanda means well but, this is a bit much." Gabe said.

"What are you talking about?"

"She's playing match maker, isn't she?" Gabe asked sitting back down at the table. David could feel his heart pound in his chest. He sat motionless for a moment. Gabe watched David's body language and smiled. "How long have you known?" He asked quietly. David sighed and took a big sip from his beer.

"A little while." David said and looked down at the table.

"I don't really care, David. I find it interesting that Amanda knows."

"I had to tell her. She's my best friend." David said feeling like his life had just been exposed.

"I get that. Just do me a favor, ok?"

"Sure, what?" David asked.

"Careful what you say around here. Small town and all that." Gabe said and smiled.

"Yea, of course." David said. Just then Amanda walked in.

"Hey, we gotta talk." Amanda said and grabbed David's hand.

"No funny stuff guys. I'll be down with the rum in a bit." Gabe said as he watched them hurry down the stairs. They sat down on the couch.

"How does HE know?" David asked through clenched teeth.

"What? He doesn't know." Amanda said genuinely shocked.

"He sure as hell does."

"I didn't tell him."

"Well, he knows. We just had a little heart to heart at the table."

"I don't know how he knows. Maybe he guessed." Amanda said. They were quiet as they listened to Gabe leave.

"How do you guess something like this?" David asked when the door closed.

"It's Gabe. Who knows?"

"Are you sure he didn't hear us talking or something?"

"No, I was careful only to talk about it when I was alone. Besides, he only got here this morning."

"Well, who else knows?"

"Just us and Todd."

"Well, I'm sure he didn't hear it from him." David said leaning back on the couch.

"Anyway, David. My mom and dad are gone for a while."

"Yea, Gabe told me."

"He thinks they should get a divorce."

"Yea, I know." David said and hugged his friend. They sat there hugging for a while. "Are you ok?" David whispered into her hair.

"Yea, it's just so weird." She whispered back and pulled her head away to look into David's eyes. He smiled at her.

"Not as weird as Gabe knowing about Todd." He said with raised eyebrows.

"He knows about Todd?"

"Yea. AND he knows he's gay."

"That's so weird." Amanda said. She frowned trying to retrace her steps. David looked at her and smiled again. She looked up at him. "What?" She asked.

"Nothing. You're just cute sometimes." David said and moved a wet, stray hair from her face. She blushed and turned her face down. David put his finger under her chin and tilted her head up. He leaned in and kissed her. She kissed back rapping her hands in his hair. His eyes grew wide at her strange forcefulness. He set his hand in the low of her back and continued kissing her. They never heard Gabe come in.

"Gross man." Gabe said laughing. Amanda shot up to a standing position. Her face was beat red and she turned her back to him.

"Damn it, Gabe." She said.

"What? You think when you're an adult you get stupid or something? It's cool." Then he looked at David. "Just wrap it up hey?"

He said. David smiled and shook his head as Gabe went back upstairs. Amanda sat back down on the couch.

"Want a drink?" David asked. Amanda nodded and smiled. "He's right you know." He said as he got up. "You're not a baby anymore Amanda. You're bound to kiss boys by now." He said and headed to the counter were Gabe had set the rum and pop. He poured them both a drink and came back to the couch. He handed Amanda hers and took a sip of his.

"I hate the thought of him thinking we're fucking down here."

"Would you like me to go upstairs and tell him we aren't?" David asked going to stand up. Amanda's hand shot out and sat him back down. There was a look of horror on her face.

"No! I do not." She said. David laughed and rubbed her back. "You're so funny Amanda." He said. She giggled and took a sip of her rum. Her face screwed up with the taste. "Whoa, trying to kill me?" She asked with a cough. David giggled.

"I thought you could use a *stiff* one." Amanda rolled her eyes and laughed.

"How do you turn everything you say into a sexual innuendo?" David shrugged and took a big sip of his drink. "And, is your drink as strong as mine?" David handed her his drink. She took a sip and realized his was even stronger.

"I *do* need a stiff drink." David said smiling as she choked the liquid down.

"No kidding. What time is it anyway?" Amanda asked. David turned to see the clock beside him.

"Almost 7." David said and took another long gulp of his drink.

"Already? Huh. And take it easy David or you'll have all the rum gone before your date gets here."

"That's the idea. Besides, there's two bottles."

"I only paid for one." Amanda said and looked over at the counter. There was two bottles of rum and four two liter bottles of mix. "Why would he do that?" She asked quietly.

"Maybe because he understands the term, Liquid Courage." David said. Amanda looked at him and sighed.

"I really don't know how he knows."

"He's Gabe. He seems to know everything." David joked and took another sip from his glass.

"Are you really nervous?"

"Yea, I am." David said and smiled. He shook his head and sighed. "This whole thing is like a weird dream or something."

"Did coming early help?"

"I don't know. Gabe wasn't the holy shit handle I was expecting." David said. Amanda giggled and then said.

"Yea, I was planning on having sex with you before Todd got here."

"You were?" David said raising his eyebrows. Amanda blushed and nodded.

"I thought, this is a good time to get it one last time." David frowned at her comment.

"Why do you say that?"

"Well, what if you and Todd really hit it off? What if you guys go back to your place and do stuff and you feel the same way he did after his first time?"

"What the hell are you talking about?" David said with a little laugh.

"Well, he said his first time with a guy was ten times better than anytime he had with a girl. He never went back after that." Amanda said and looked down into her glass.

"Amanda, I can't see myself fucking that dude. Ok?" David asked. Amanda nodded but she still looked skeptical. David sighed then said,

"Can I tell you a secret?" Amanda looked at him with bright eyes and smiled.

"Ok."

"Gabe has a better chance with me than Todd does." David said and took a sip from his cup. Amanda tilted her head to one side.

"You're just saying that to make me feel better."

"Nope. I wouldn't do that. Gabe . . . looks different to me than he used to." Amanda broke out into laughter. David smiled and shook his head.

"You think *Gabe* is *hot?*" She asked as she grabbed her sides. David laughed with her.

"Yea. He is." David answered. "In a weird Goth kind of way."

"Wow, I was not expecting that." Amanda said still giggling. David smiled again and took the last sip out of his glass. "Why?" Amanda asked trying to keep a straight face.

"I don't expect you to see it Amanda. He's your brother." David said and went back up to the counter. He looked at the clock while he made a less stiff drink. It was 7:30.

"Yea, but . . . *Gabe?*" Amanda asked again as David came back to the couch. David sat down and made an old man noise.

"Oh, yea." He said.

"Ewe. Don't say it like that." Amanda said. David laughed and sipped his drink.

"Is he hot like Mr. Black?"

"Bite your tongue Amanda. As if." David said. Amanda giggled.

"Kay, just checking."

"Speaking of Mr. Black, I'm going fishing with him tomorrow." Amanda laughed,

"Ha, fuck you, you are."

"I'm serious. He planned it with my mom. They think I need a male figure in my life or something."

"So . . . she picks him?"

"I know, right?" David said rolling his eyes.

"That's really weird. She knew Gabe was coming out. Why not ask him?"

"I don't know. Maybe cause its Gabe." David said sarcastically.

"Good point." Amanda said and sighed. "So the plot thickens." She added.

"It appears so." David said and smiled.

"What's with the smile?" Amanda asked.

"Nothing. Just had a strange experience this morning after I got off the phone with Mr. Black." He said and giggled. Amanda leaned in closer.

"What? What happened?"

"Um, just something." David said in an innocent voice. Amanda rolled her eyes.

"You don't do innocent, David. What happened?"

"Well, I got off the phone with Mr. Black and realized I had a problem that needed my immediate attention."

"You talked to him on the phone?"

"Yea, in the morning. Guess what I have every morning?"

"A cigarette?"

"Come on Amanda. I wake up with a cigarette?" David asked and raised his eyebrows. Amanda's eyes went wide.

"You mean you . . ."

"Yep. Took about 7 minutes." David said taking another sip from his cup. Amanda was on the edge of her seat.

"So, was it different than usual?" She asked. She looked like a reporter getting the latest scoop.

"Oh, yea." David said it the same way he had said it about Gabe.

"Oh, my god. Well?"

"Well what?"

"Details, details." She said almost jumping in her seat.

"I thought masturbation was private." David said laughing at his friend.

"Not with you it isn't." She said. David laughed and shook his head.

"Details . . . Well, it was over so quickly I didn't get a chance to really come up with any good fantasy or anything."

"Who cares about the fantasy, David? I wanna know how good it was." David raised his eyebrows and took a sip from his drink.

"Let's just say, I will never think of that weather lady again." Amanda giggled and sipped her drink. "It was as good as sex Amanda."

"Wow, you must be good at jacking off, cause I'm awesome in the sack."

"Nice Amanda. But yea, it was pretty good."

"So, are you officially gay now or something?" She asked.

"I don't know. I don't feel any different except for that."

"Yea, but you thought about Mr. Black right?"

"Yea, why?"

"Well, if it made you cum so hard, maybe it's a sign?" Just then there was a knock at the door. David sighed and Amanda got up. She answered the door and David could hear Todd's voice. He gulped his drink and went up to the counter to make another. This time it was another stiff one.

"Hi, David." Todd said as Amanda led him into the basement.

"Hi, you a rum drinker?" David asked. Amanda was finishing her drink so David could mix her one.

"Oh, sure. Thanks." Todd said and walked over to David.

"Tell me when." David said and started pouring. Todd took his almost as strong as David. He poured the mix into the three glasses and Amanda led the way to the furniture. She sat on the old rocker leaving the couch for Todd and David.

"So, how about that movie guys?" Amanda asked and put the Evil Dead disk into the machine. It was about half over when David noticed that Amanda had fallen asleep. He looked over at Todd. He was wearing a white shirt and black jeans. He looked down at Todd's glass and noticed it was empty.

"Want another one?" David asked quietly not to disturb Amanda.

"Oh, yea. Thanks David." Todd said and followed David to the counter. David mixed the drinks and handed one to Todd. He took a sip and smiled. "Perfect." He said. David smiled and leaned against the counter. Todd tapped the side of his glass and sat down at the card table. "I have to confess something." Todd said. David took a seat on the low counter and sipped his drink.

"What's that?" He asked satisfied with their safe distance.

"I was a little nervous to come here tonight."

"What? Why?"

"I've been told that people in some small towns trick people like me into pretend dates so they can hand out shit kicking's." David laughed and took a drink from his cup. He thought of the stories that his dad had told him about beating a gay guy half to death once.

"Where did you hear that?" David asked trying to keep on his Ask questions only rule.

"Around. It's not the case, is it?" Todd asked looking up at David sitting on the counter.

"Nope. Not the case."

"That's good. Don't you wanna finish your movie?" Todd asked looking over at the T.V.

"To be honest, I only picked this movie to see what you would say. I know it word for word. If you would rather talk, I'm cool with that." Todd smiled at David and took a sip of his drink.

"You know, for never doing this before, your fairly charming." David swallowed his sip and cleared his throat.

"I am? I don't mean to be."

"That's what's even nicer about it. It's so natural." Todd said getting up and walking over to the counter still keeping his distance. David sighed and took another sip.

"Do I scare you David?" Todd asked in a half whisper.

"Kind of." David said. He had the strangest feeling in the pit of his stomach.

"Well, I'm way over here so you should be ok." Todd said in a bed room voice David had often used on Amanda. David lit a cigarette and stared at Todd.

"What are you doing here, Todd? Why me?" David asked.

"I like you David. Why else would I be here?" Todd said stepping closer and leaning against the counter. David knocked the ashes off his cigarette into the sink.

"What do you expect to happen?" David asked. He could feel the strange ache in his stomach tighten.

"Nothing really. I came to get to know you. If anything happens, it's a bonus." Todd answered. He was still talking in his bedroom voice. David took another puff off his cigarette.

"Happens? Like what?" David asked without thinking. The feeling in his stomach jumped into his throat as Todd walked over and stood between his legs. David stared into his eyes. His heart pounded in his chest. It was more fear than anything else.

"Well, can I kiss you?" Todd asked putting his hands on David's thighs. David looked down at his hands and back up to his face. He dropped the cigarette into the sink and sighed a nervous, fearful breath. "It won't hurt." Todd said moving closer to David. David closed his eyes. His heart was pounding in his ears now. He tried to even out his breathing but it was no use. Then he felt Todd's mouth touch his. His body stiffened and Todd moved away. "Are you ok?" Todd asked in an almost inaudible whisper. David swallowed hard and stared at Todd.

"That was . . ."

"Weird?" Todd finished the sentence for David and smiled. David nodded. Todd moved in again. This time David kissed back. He was surprised how good a kisser Todd was. As they kissed, Todd moved in closer until their bodies touched. David could feel Todd's body against his groin. His breath shook but he didn't push him away. Todd pulled his face away and looked at David. David slowly opened his eyes and stared into Todd's.

"Wow." David whispered and giggled. Todd smiled and kissed David again. David ran his hand along Todd's arm and up to his shoulder. Todd kissed more deeply and pushed against David. David could feel Todd getting hard and his stomach flipped. He ran his hand down Todd's side and stopped at his hip. The other hand griped Todd's other hip. Todd moaned and thrust himself against David. David heaved at the strength of Todd's movement.

"Sorry." Todd whispered between kisses. David pulled Todd in closer and kissed deeper. Todd moaned and went for David's shirt.

"Whoa. One thing at a time ok." David whispered. Todd smiled and slowly moved his hand up David's shirt and felt his muscular stomach and chest heave.

"Wow, your hot, David." Todd whispered and kissed him again. David breathed heavy under Todd's touch. He could feel Todd trace the lines his muscles made in his skin. He pushed his erection against Todd. Todd moaned and pushed back. "Let me fuck you, David." Todd whispered. David pulled his face back and stared at Todd.

"What?" David asked trying to get a grip on the situation. Todd pushed his hard penis against David's.

"Let me fuck you." He said again. David took a deep nervous breath.

"Look, I can hardly believe I'm making out with you let alone doing anything else."

"Well, you seem to enjoy it so far." Todd said and slid his hand down onto David's cock. David sat up arrow straight and pushed Todd's hand away. Todd held David's hands against the cupboard doors and stared at him. He moved his hips in mock sex against David's groin. David fought Todd's hold but he surprisingly strong. "Don't you like that?" Todd asked and kissed David's chin.

"I did." David said struggling against Todd's hold again but it seemed useless.

"Well? What's the problem then?" Todd asked pushing himself against David even harder. David looked up at the ceiling and took a deep breath.

"Please, stop Todd." He said through clenched teeth. Todd laughed and quickened the movement of his hips. David squeezed his legs around Todd and twisted his weight. Todd lost the grip on David's hands and David pushed him away.

"What's your fucking problem?" Todd asked and stared wide eyed at David.

"What? Are you kidding? Did you really think you would get laid? By me?"

"That was the idea." Todd said and grabbed David's arm. He turned him around and bent him over the card table so fast that David couldn't even see it coming. He fought against Todd's body.

"Get off me you Fuck!" David yelled. He could hear Todd laugh and the rocking chair hit the wall.

"What's going on here?!" Amanda yelled and rushed over. Todd backed off and David swung around. He saw that Todd had his pants undone.

"You son of a bitch!" David yelled and hit Todd. Todd hit the floor with a loud thump. He wiped the bit of blood from the corner of his mouth and stood up.

"Don't guys!" Amanda yelled. David looked over to her and then felt Todd's fist connect. Amanda screamed as David hit the floor with Todd on top of him feeding him shot after shot. David tried to swing back but the rum he had earlier seemed to impair his vision. He could hear Amanda calling for Gabe in a frantic scream. He could feel every hit from Todd. He could feel a rib break as Todd gave up on his face. Suddenly he could hear Gabe.

"Get the fuck off him you little fag!" Gabe yelled and threw Todd off of him. David rolled over into the fetal position and hugged his ribs. He could hear Gabe yelling at Todd all the way up the stairs and threw him out the door. Then he felt Amanda's hands gently touch him.

"God David." She cried. He could hear Gabe come back down the stairs.

"Get a bowl of hot water and some rags Amanda." Gabe said. Amanda jumped up and David could feel Gabe pick him up and carry him to the couch.

"Uh, fuck." David breathed as Gabe sat down on the floor next to him.

"What the fuck happened?" Gabe asked in a soft voice.

"I wouldn't . . . I wouldn't . . ." David tried to talk but the pain in his ribs was excruciating. Gabe swore under his breath.

"This dude was here for *you*?" Gabe asked quietly. David tried to move to a more comfortable position. He looked at Gabe and frowned.

"Yea, I thought you knew." David whispered and winced at the pain. Gabe looked up to see Amanda coming down the stairs with the bowl of water.

"I need rags too, babe." Gabe said.

"Oh yea. Are you ok David?" She asked. David nodded.

"Rags, Amanda." Gabe said quietly. Amanda nodded and hurried away. Gabe looked back down at David's beaten body. There was blood all over his clothes.

"How did this happen?" Gabe asked quietly.

"I thought you knew." David said again. Gabe smiled and shook his head.

"I thought Amanda and you had him here for me." David was startled by Gabe's confession. "I thought you two knew about me." Gabe laughed quietly and shook his head again.

"You're . . . your gay?" David asked.

"Since the day I was born." Gabe said and looked up again to see Amanda coming down with rags. "Shhh." He said to David as she neared them. David nodded and looked at Amanda. She handed the rags to Gabe and sat on the floor next to him.

"Maybe we should take him to the hospital?" Amanda said to Gabe. Gabe looked at David and then back to his sister.

"And say what, Amanda? That he was beaten by a sex craved fag?" David laughed and then winced. "Sorry dude." Gabe said and dampened one of the rags.

"What if he's really hurt?" Amanda insisted. Gabe shook his head and got to work on David's face. David winced but sat still. "Maybe you should go to the hospital, David"

"No way. Gabe's right. Besides, my mom works there and she would hear all about it." David said. Gabe stared at the bruising on David's face.

"Nothing on your pretty face looks broken." He said. David shot him a look and Gabe smile.

"But, Gabe." Amanda said. Gabe looked over at her.

"Go upstairs and find my old ice pack ok?" Gabe said. Amanda jumped up and headed up stairs.

"Fuck, I'm stupid." David said rubbing his sore rib cage.

"Why? Cause some dude can't take no for an answer?" Gabe asked rigging the blood out of the rag.

"I asked for it man." David said wincing as he tried to sit up. Gabe helped him and sat down on the couch beside him.

"No you didn't. Don't tell yourself that. No one ever asks for that." Gabe said tossing the bloody rag onto the coffee table next to the bowel of water. David sighed and shook his head.

"We were making out over there and then it got a little weird. Like too heavy for me. I asked him to stop but . . ."

"Yea, that's how it starts. Don't do this to yourself David. We're not all like that." Gabe said and got up to make two drinks. David watched him pour to straight scotch from the liquor cabinet and walk back over. "For medicinal purposes." Gabe said as he handed one of the drinks to David. David smiled and took the drink. He took a big sip from it and winced at the movement.

"Thanks." David said. "Amanda doesn't know huh?" He asked as Gabe sat down beside him.

"Nope. No one around here does. Except you now."

"But, you always had hot girlfriends."

"No, I had hot friends. There's a difference." Gabe said taking a sip from his own cup.

"Weird." David said and sipped at his also. Gabe dug out his cigarettes and lit one for David.

"Thanks." David said and took a long drag. "So, now what happens?" David asked looking over at Gabe.

"Now, you only discuss this shit with me and Amanda. No more learning the hard way, ok?"

"I think I can manage that."

"So? How did it all start?" Gabe asked taking another sip from his glass and setting the cup between his legs.

"It was the first day of school. It was all boring and usual until History class."

"And this Todd caught your eye? He's not too good looking." David laughed and winced.

"No, not him. My history professor, Mr. Black." Gabe raised his eyebrows.

"So, you're into older dudes then?" Gabe said and smiled. David rolled his eyes and took another sip.

"I guess." He answered.

"Look David. It took me years before I could admit it to myself. I tried to be with some of those girls you mentioned, but it made me feel sick."

"Really? They were pretty hot Gabe." David said with disbelief.

"Yea, well. Those are the cards."

"So, what made you try to be with a guy?"

"It was in college. My roommate hit on me one night and got a surprise reaction from me." Gabe said smiling.

"Weird Gabe." David said and laughed. The pain seemed to be calmed by the scotch so he took another big sip.

"Not weird, David. Normal, for me anyway." Gabe said and leaned closer to David. "Under the right circumstances, it's not so bad." He whispered. David looked at him just in time to hear Amanda come down the stairs with the ice pack.

"Got it." She said and handed it to Gabe. Gabe took the ice pack and looked at David.

"Trust me?" He asked. David looked at him funny but nodded. "Amanda, hold his arms so he doesn't punch me." Gabe said. Amanda walked around the couch and held David's arms. "Here we go." Gabe said and carefully lifted David's shirt. The bruising on David's torso was horrifying. Amanda gasped. Gabe looked up at her and saw her face had gone pale. "Are you gonna hit me if I touch you?" Gabe asked David. David shook his head. "Ok, Amanda, go puke."

"Thanks." She said quietly and ran into the bathroom. The two men chuckled as she locked the door behind her.

"What are you gonna do?" David asked as Gabe looked closely at David's chest.

"Find the broken rib and set it." Gabe said and put his cool hand on David's rib cage. David winced as Gabe pushed on every rib. "This is kind of odd." Gabe said smiling.

"Why?" David asked through clenched teeth.

"Well, I get the feeling you're not in a kidding mood so, forget it."

"No, really. A joke would be good right now." David said. Gabe rolled his eyes and went back to work on David.

"Well, I was just thinking that I probably had an easier time getting into your shirt than he did." David giggled and winced. "Sorry. No laughing." Gabe said.

"Your right." David said in a pained voice. "That's why it's funny."

"Well, I'm not looking to get lucky though. I'm being your vet." David laughed and then hit the couch. "Hurts huh?" Gabe asked. David nodded and grabbed Gabe's hand. He moved it to the right side to the epicenter of the pain.

"Over here somewhere." David whispered.

"I know, I was getting a cheap thrill." Gabe said. David laughed again and then yelled out in pain as Gabe set the rib.

"Fuck I hate you!" David yelled. Gabe laughed and sat back on the couch.

"Does it feel better?" Gabe asked as David lay in a heap.

"Kind of." David said. He sat himself up a little and took a couple deep breaths.

"Do me a favor and put your shirt down. My sister is in the other room. Have some decency." Gabe joked. David laughed and put his shirt down. "It's safe to come out Amanda." Gabe called. They could hear the door creak open.

"Are you sure?" Amanda called from down the short hallway.

"Yea." David answered and grabbed his cup off the table. Gabe smiled at him and raised one eyebrow. "What?" David whispered as Amanda walked into the room. Gabe just smiled and shook his head.

"Are you ok?" Amanda asked David as she sat down on the rocking chair.

"Yea, I'm ok." David answered.

"This is all my fault." She said with tears in her eyes.

"This is no one's fault but Todd's." Gabe said lighting both him and David a cigarette.

"I asked him over." Amanda said wiping the tears from her cheek.

"So what? Did you say 'Hay Todd, have fun with my friend David here'?" Gabe asked taking a puff from his cigarette.

"No. but . . ."

"But nothing Babe. This is all on him. Ok?"

"Besides, I'll live." David said trying help Gabe calm Amanda. Amanda smiled at him and sighed.

"Are you sure you're ok?"

"Yes, Amanda." David said shaking his head. Just then the phone rang. Amanda jumped up.

"I got it Amanda. Sit down." Gabe said and headed upstairs. Amanda sat down next to David.

"I'm so sorry." She whispered.

"Don't be, ok. I don't blame you. Neither should you."

"You look terrible David."

"I know."

"Your mom is gonna shit."

"Don't worry about her. I'll deal with her." David said. Just then they heard Gabe come down the stairs.

"You won't have to. That punk called the cops and their at your house now talking to your mom."

"What?" David said and jumped up. He was almost sick from the pain.

"Easy tiger. I'll walk you over there. They want my statement too. Amanda, can you stay here with little Mike?"

"Yea, of course."

"Ok, hot shot. Their waiting for us." David walked up the stairs with Gabe and out the door.

Chapter 10

"That went well" Gabe said as he walked David up to his room. Nancy was filling in paper work for the cops and asked Gabe to get him up to his room.

"Think they bought it?" David asked as Gabe opened the bedroom door.

"What's not to buy? You guys were drinking and things got out of hand. They seen your injuries. That little poke I gave him is nothing compared to your war wounds dude." Gabe said as he helped David sit down on his bed. He reached over and shut the door. "So, what do you sleep in?" Gabe asked shoving his hands in his pockets.

"Why?" David asked.

"Hey, mom said get you ready for bed, that's what I'm gonna do."

"That's weird dude." David said giggling.

"Ok, take off your own shirt then. If you can do that, I'll leave and let you do it alone."

"Ok." David said and stood up he grabbed the bottom of his shirt and got it about half way up his body till the pain made him collapse. Gabe caught him.

"It's ok. You alright?" Gabe asked.

"Dude." David said with tears in his eyes.

"Come here." Gabe said and sat him down. He grabbed the bottom of David's shirt and pulled it over the back of his head. David winced. "Sorry David." Gabe said and pulled the shirt off his arms. "God, you are fucked up David." Gabe said getting a good look at his injuries.

"Thanks. You should see the other guy." David said. Gabe laughed.

"Here, lay down." Gabe said. He helped David lay back on the bed. "Pants now right?" David sighed and nodded. Gabe undid David's jeans and started giggling.

"Now what?" David said trying to look at Gabe.

"I'm totally doing better than that other dude." Gabe said laughing. David laughed and shook his head.

"Just hurry up." David said and took a deep breath. Gabe laughed and pulled David's jeans off along with his socks.

"That's it?" Gabe asked.

"YEA! Yea, that's it." David said. Gabe laughed and pulled the blanket over David. He sat down next to him and lit them both a cigarette. "Thanks Gabe."

"No problem. You ok?"

"Yea, I guess." David said taking a drag from his cigarette. Gabe turned and laid down on his back next to David.

"How did he get the jump on you like that?" Gabe asked putting his arm behind his head and crossing his feet.

"Fuck, it happened so fast." David said taking another drag from his cigarette. Gabe laughed again and David looked at him. "What?" David asked smiling.

"I'm in bed with you David and you're not kicking my ass." Gabe said and laughed again. David laughed and elbowed him in the ribs.

"Hey, hey now. Don't get violent." Gabe said and yawned. They were silent for a while.

"Thanks for doing all this Gabe." David said taking another drag from his cigarette. The ash was long and he looked over Gabe's body at the ash tray. Gabe lay there with his eyes closed. He breathed like he was sleeping. David leaned over Gabe's body and put the smoke out in the ash tray.

"Nice, David." Gabe said with his eyes closed. David giggled.

"I thought you were asleep." Gabe put his hand on David's arm. David stayed where he was and looked at Gabe. "Uh, Gabe." David said leaning against Gabe's chest.

"I'm not holding you here David." Gabe said rubbing David's arm.

"I know."

"Then move." Gabe whispered. David cleared his throat but stayed still. Gabe didn't move. They were both still and quiet. David stared at Gabe's face. His eyes were closed and had no expression on his face. "You gonna move?" Gabe asked. He kept his eyes closed. David slowly moved down and kissed Gabe. Gabe kissed back and ran his hand carefully through David's hair. David finished the kiss and moved away. He lay on his back and took a deep breath.

"Sorry." David whispered. Gabe sighed and opened his eyes.

"Why? I said move. You moved. It was a surprising move but you did it."

"Yea, sorry." David said again.

"For what?" Gabe asked and rolled to face David. David lay shaking with his eyes closed. "Dude. Calm down."

"I can't. That was bad. I'm the same as Todd. I shouldn't have done that . . ." Gabe kissed David to stop his talking. David moaned and kissed back. Gabe's long black hair shrouded David's face. Gabe pulled away then and David kept his eyes closed.

"Want me to stop?" Gabe asked pushing his hair back out of his face. David took a deep breath. "It's ok to say yes." Gabe said. David looked at him and his breathing picked up.

"Gabe." David breathed and stopped speaking.

"Want me to kiss you again?" Gabe asked smiling. David swallowed hard and nodded. Gabe moved in and kissed David gently. David closed his eyes and moaned as Gabe kissed him. Gabe moved closer and gently rested his hand on David's stomach. David tensed up and Gabe moved away. "Whoa, sorry." Gabe breathed. David's smiled and then laughed. "What?" Gabe asked wide eyed.

"Come here." David said and grabbed the back of Gabe's head. He pulled him in and kissed him with a kiss he didn't know was in him. Gabe moaned and slowly moved on top of David. David winced but grabbed Gabe when he tried to move. "It's ok." David said. "It's only pain." Gabe giggled and kissed David.

"I don't want to pop your rib back out." David smiled and ran his hand through Gabe's hair. Gabe closed his eyes and bit his bottom lip.

"I'm scared of you Gabe." David said. Gabe opened his eyes and smiled.

"Why?" He asked in a seduced whisper.

"Cause, your Gabe." Gabe giggled and got off David.

"Why did you move?" David asked.

"Cause your David." Gabe said and ran his hand down David's chest and stomach. David closed his eyes and moaned. "You scare me too." He whispered. David frowned.

"Why?" He asked.

"I don't know. Your just really hot and, I've known you you're whole life. And your Amanda's best friend and . . . I don't know." Gabe giggled and rolled onto his back.

"What?" David said and giggled. Gabe laughed and then sighed.

"Ever felt like you were with somebody a little out of your league?" Gabe asked. David was shocked.

"What? Me?" David said pointing at himself in the chest.

"Yea, I would hate to disappoint you David." Gabe said and smiled. David giggled again and shook his head.

"What? Do you have any idea how exited you just made me? I am not disappointed." Gabe laughed and rolled over to face David.

"Smooth. Really." Gabe said smiling.

"Do I have to prove it?" David asked rolling over and wincing at the pain.

"Don't do that. And don't hurt yourself either. Besides, you're wearing boxers. I can tell." Gabe said. David looked down and laughed.

"Yea, I guess." He blushed and looked back up at Gabe. Gabe smiled and moved closer to David. David smiled and kissed Gabe.

"Can I do something?" Gabe asked.

"What?" David asked looking into Gabe's eyes. Gabe bit his bottom lip and put David's hand on his chest.

"Relax your hand." Gabe said. He was shaking now. David made a fist for a second then relaxed his hand. He slowly moved his hand down Gabe's chest and stomach. He rested his hand on the top of Gabe's jeans. Gabe stared at David. David bit his top lip. Gabe untucked his t-shirt from his pants and David's hand touched bare skin. Gabe could feel the sweat on David's palm. "Are you ok?" Gabe asked. David looked at him and his breath was shaky. Gabe's breathing was heavy but he didn't move. "Your hands are sweating." Gabe said. David giggled and cleared his throat.

"Yea, I know." He said and swallowed hard again. Gabe smiled and put his hand on David's.

"You don't have to go any farther David." Gabe said. David rubbed his thumb on the button of Gabe's jeans. Gabe's breath was shaking.

"You sound as nervous as me." David said giggling. Gabe smiled and licked his lips.

"Well, I don't know what to do with you." Gabe said.

"You know more than I do." David said picking at the button.

"Yea, that's the problem." Gabe said.

"Why?" David asked.

"I would hate to scare you David. Or hurt you." Gabe said.

"My ribs are fine Gabe." David said with sleepy eyes.

"I wasn't talking about your ribs." Gabe said and grabbed David's hand. He pushed it down onto his erection. David's eyes grew wide and he swallowed hard.

"Whoa." David said and shook. Gabe let his hand go but David left it there. Gabe raised an eyebrow.

"Again you surprise me, David." Gabe said. David looked up at him.

"Why?"

"Your still touching my cock." Gabe said and smiled.

"Yea I know." David said and looked down at his hand. Gabe cleared his throat and David looked back up at him.

"David. As much I would love for you to explore your situation a little more, we have a problem." Gabe said not moving.

"What's that?" David asked moving his hand a little further down Gabe's shaft. Gabe closed his eyes and moaned. David smiled and kissed him. Gabe kissed back and pushed his cock against David's hand. David grabbed it and Gabe moaned louder.

"Whoa, whoa David. Stop." Gabe said breathing heavy. David pulled his hand away and looked at him with wide eyes.

"What?" David asked.

"That little problem of ours is downstairs finishing up with the cops. Really think she would be thrilled to walk into this?" Gabe asked. David laughed and looked at the door.

"Yea, maybe not." David said.

"Yea, sorry." Gabe said.

"Why?" David asked. Gabe moved in and kissed David. David closed his eyes and smiled.

"Because I would love to finish this thing right now." Gabe whispered. David sighed and looked over at the desk drawer.

"That's ok. I don't know if I could do it anyway." David said. Gabe looked over at the desk then back to David.

"Oh right. The teacher." Gabe said and smiled. David nodded. "Dude, you got it bad for that guy don't you?" Gabe asked.

"Yea." David said and sighed. He sat up and ran his hand through his hair. "Look Gabe, I . . ."

"Hey! Don't man. I get it. You don't have to apologize to me. Kissing you was awesome." Gabe said and put his hand on David's back.

"Yea, that was pretty cool." David said smiling.

"Maybe another time, huh?" Gabe said running his hand through David's hair. David looked at Gabe. Gabe bit his bottom lip. "Don't look at me like that David or your mother is gonna know everything."

David and Gabe both laughed. Gabe got up and walked to the door. David turned and looked at him.

"Hey, Gabe."

"Yea." Gabe said with his hand on the door handle. David laid himself back on the bed.

"Thanks for everything tonight." David said through clenched teeth as he tried to get more comfortable.

"No problem, David. You don't have to thank me. I would hope there was someone around to do the same for me sometime." Gabe said. He glanced in David's mirror and fixed his hair.

"I'm glad you never grew out of the Goth thing." David said watching Gabe fuss with the part in his long, black hair.

"Why?" Gabe asked turning back toward the door.

"Cause, it's hot."

"I know." Gabe said. David giggled and Gabe smiled. "Hey, I may be running the risk of sounding like a total pedophile here but . . . Please keep tonight between us. I've had to work really hard to keep this from my family." Gabe said with slight embarrassment on his face. David giggled and raised his eyebrows.

"I think it's funny you would say that."

"Why?" Gabe asked still standing at the door.

"Well, what do you think Amanda would do to me if she found out we did that?"

"I don't know." Gabe said smiling.

"Trust me. Telling somebody was the last thing on my mind." David said and yawned. Gabe walked over to the bed and covered David with the blanket. He ran his hand through David's hair and then ran his thumb across David's lips.

"I know that. I just wanted to be sure I said it was a secret. Trying to avoid confusion." Gabe said tracing David's jaw line with his fingers. David took a deep breath and looked at Gabe.

"Can I ask you something?" David said looking into Gabe's dark green eyes.

"Yea." Gabe said sitting on the side of the bed.

"It's kind of weird." David warned. Gabe giggled and looked around.

"I'm good with weird." He said.

"I wanna do a little digging on Mr. Black. I think he might have a history with men."

"Ok. That's not a question David."

"I know, just listen." David said. A nervous quiver left his throat.

"What is it David?" Gabe said looking at the young man beside him.

"You know how you said you didn't want to disappoint me?"

"Yea."

"If I ever had a chance with Mr. Black, I would feel the same way."

"Ok, So, where's this weird question?" Gabe said still puzzled. David sighed and looked up at the ceiling.

"I wanna know what I'm doing." David said. Gabe looked at David still puzzled.

"Ok. What are you asking?"

"Would you, maybe . . . show me." David stumbled over the words as if he was asking out a girl for the first time.

"Show you what?" Gabe asked with a confused giggle. David looked at Gabe. Gabe could see this was a difficult this for David. He gently rested his hand on David's chest. His long black hair fell over his shoulder and tickled David's arm. Gabe tossed his head so the hair was behind him. "Look David." He said and ran his hand through his hair again. "Didn't I tell you to only talk about this shit with me or Amanda?" David nodded. "Ok, then can you be a little more specific?" Gabe said. David giggled and seemed to calm down a little.

"I wanna be good, you know. Like, I wanna know what I'm doing if I get a chance to be with him." David said. Gabe smiled and David could see he understood where this was going.

"So, you want me to be your guinea pig?" Gabe asked. David laughed and winced at the pain in his chest.

"More like a teacher." David said rubbing his rib cage. Gabe ran his hand down David's chest to his stomach and traced the muscles in his abdomen with his thumb. David watched his hand. He could feel his body reacting to Gabe again and he cleared his throat. Gabe looked at him and smiled. He licked his lips and bit his bottom lip.

"I think that's a hell of an idea." Gabe said in a sexy bedroom voice. Just then, they could hear Nancy coming up the stairs. Gabe moved his hand back up to David's chest and smiled. Nancy knocked quietly at the door. "Come on in Mrs. S." Gabe said still looking at David. She slowly cracked open the door and came in.

"Are you ok honey?" She asked. Her face looked as though she had been crying. She came over to the bed and sat down beside Gabe.

"Yea, mom. I think so." David said. Gabe smiled at her and stood up.

"Well, I should get back to Amanda and little Mike."

"Thank you for staying with him." Nancy said and grabbed his hand. Gabe gave her hand a squeeze and smiled at David.

"It was my pleasure." He said and winked. David smiled and looked back at his mom. "I'll see you later, ok David?" Gabe added.

"Yea, ok." David said. Gabe smiled at Nancy and left the room.

"Thank god for Gabe tonight." Nancy said and her eyes filled with tears. David half smiled at his mom.

"Yea, it could have been way worse." David said rubbing his rib cage. Nancy winced at the sight of her son.

"What were you thinking getting in a fight?"

"Mom, I was defending myself and Amanda. The guy couldn't hold his liquor I guess."

"Yea, I heard the whole story twice already." Nancy said and shook her head. David looked up at the ceiling and yawned. Nancy carefully moved a stray hair from David's face. "Want me to call and cancel the fishing trip?" She asked.

"No, no mom. It's late. And I still want to go." David said in a half panic. Nancy frowned at her son.

"Ok, you sure are taking this whole thing really well."

"I've been in fights before mom."

"I'm not talking about that. I'm talking about Mr. Black." David closed his eyes and thought about his question to Gabe. Now he needed all the time he could with Mr. Black to learn about him.

"I think it's a good idea. All I have in the world is you and Amanda. I'm bound to end up growing into a very masculine woman." David said smiling at the flash backs of his time with Gabe. Nancy smiled and shook her head.

"Well, I think Gabe is a good role model. Next to his taste in life style." David frowned and looked at her.

"What do you mean, his taste of life style?"

"Well, his dark cloths and . . ."

"And what?" Nancy looked down at her pants and back to David.

"Well, he's like your dad a little son, that's all."

"What? I doubt that." David said and giggled.

"Well, he's a music major and plays electric guitar. He wants to be a rock star or something. You know what that can lead to."

"Mom, he plays guitar cause the chicks like it." David said protecting Gabe's secret. "And like you said yourself, He's a music *Major*. That means he's educated right?" Nancy nodded and smiled. "Yea, that's nothing like dad. Besides, I've known him my whole life and I trust him."

"Well, do you trust Mr. Black?" The question was so strange David felt like it was spoken in a different language.

Trust Mr. Black? I don't know. Want Mr. Black yes. Trust?

"He's a teacher mom. I guess I trust him." David said trying to answer the best he could.

"Well, if you still want to spend time with him, then I think it's a good idea." Nancy said and sighed. She stared at her son for a while. David's eyes grew heavy and he yawned again. Nancy looked over at the clock. It was 1:00. "It's late David. If you're going to be awake for Mr. Black tomorrow, you better get some sleep."

"Ok, mom." David said and closed his eyes. Nancy kissed his forehead and stood up. "Hey mom." David said with his eye's still closed.

"Yes dear?"

"How was your date?" David asked in a sleepy voice. Nancy smiled and rubbed his forehead with the tips of her fingers.

"It was really good." She said and walked to the door. She looked at David again and smiled. "Good night." She whispered. David was already asleep.

Chapter 11

David was awake at 6:45 with an epic pain in his ribs. He groaned and rubbed the bruises on his chest.

"Wow, that sucks." David said and tried to sit up. The pain kept him down. He reached over to the side table and grabbed his cigarettes. He lit one and took a big drag from it. He lay on his back staring at the ceiling while he smoked.

Fucking Todd. I should kill that guy. I wonder what the fuck he was thinking? Fuck, I'm sore. And Gabe. Did that really happen or did I dream the whole thing? That's the last time I drink straight scotch before bed. It was pretty cool if it wasn't a dream though. Gabe gay. That's weird. And interested in me. That's funny. It was a dream. It had to be.

David reached over and grabbed the ash tray. He noticed two cigarette butts that weren't his in the ash tray and his heart jumped.

"Maybe it wasn't a dream." David said out loud and tapped the ash from his cigarette into the try. He stared at the cigarette butts and thought about the night before. He closed his eyes and tried to remember what Gabe's hands felt like on his body.

Fuck this is weird. Whatever happened to one normal day? Today is gonna be just as weird. A whole day, one on one with Mr. Alan Black. This should be one for the books.

David thought and looked over to the journal on the desk. He rolled to his side and sat up. Pain shot up and down his torso. He winced and stood up. Standing seemed less painful than laying down. He tried to stretch but the pain kept him from doing so. He slowly walked over to the desk and sat down.

"Ouch! Fuck I hate you Todd." He said out loud and hit his fists on the desk. He grabbed the journal and opened it. He flipped to the last entry and noticed it wasn't his. He read.

David,

Do yourself a favor dude and don't write last night down in here. I promise I didn't read too much. Just the last two entries. If you're like me, you read over it to try to recap on a situation. I hope you remember what we did, but let Todd be a memory worth forgetting. That isn't something you want to read over and over. I'm game to be your guinea pig if you find what you're looking for as far as info on Mr. Black go's. Hell, I'm game to do it either way actually. If you want, of course.

Anyway, please don't be mad I snooped. You passed out for a bit but I didn't want to leave you till your mom was done with the cops. I had an awesome time with you. Remember to keep it between us though. And please don't try to kick my ass for writing in this thing. I think you'll thank me for it someday.

Gabe.

David sighed and shut the book. He shook his head and stood up. He looked over at the clock. It was 7:10. He raised his eyebrows and went over to the side table. He put his cigarette out and went over to the closet. He grabbed a pair of jeans and a green t-shirt that had a muscle car picture on it. He grabbed a pair of socks and a pair of underwear from the dresser and headed to the bathroom. He shut the door behind him and looked in the full length mirror.

"Holy god." David whispered as he looked at the bruises on his face and chest. He felt a lump grow in his throat as he thought of the bent over position Todd had had him in. He shook the thought and went to the toilet. He took a pee and then started the shower. He stepped in carefully. The hot water felt good against his skin. He heard the bathroom door crack open.

"Are you ok, David?" His mother asked through the crack in the door.

"Yea, mom. Can you call Amanda?" David asked looking at the shampoo bottle and knew he wouldn't be able to wash his own hair.

"Sure honey, why?" Nancy asked staying out of sight of the tub.

"I need help with my hair I think. I can't lift my arms." David said and winced when he tried again.

"I could help if . . ."

"No way mom. Call please." David said. Nancy giggled and left the room. David let the water message his bruises as he waited. After a few minutes, he heard a knock at the door.

"Help has arrived." It was Gabe's voice on the other side of the door. David laughed and shook his head. Gabe walked in and locked the door behind him.

"Where's Amanda?" David asked trying to see Gabe through the curtain. Gabe walked over to the curtain and opened it. He was wearing a black tank top that fit him like a glove and a pair of black jeans. Gabe looked David up and down and shook his head.

"I bet you're gorgeous without the war wounds." Gabe said and grabbed the shampoo bottle. David rolled his eyes and wet his hair down.

"I asked for Amanda." David said as the water tricked down his body. Gabe watched the water as it snaked down David's frame.

"I know, she was scared to see you like this. She asked me to go." Gabe said and wet his hands in the water. He squeezed the shampoo into his hands and massaged it into David's hair. David closed his eyes while Gabe worked.

"You wrote in my journal." David said as Gabe washed his hair.

"Are you mad?" Gabe asked taking his time. David shrugged and sighed.

"No. I think it adds character to the thing." Gabe laughed and rinsed his hands in the water. David stepped back into the shower and Gabe rinsed his hair. David stood in the water while Gabe got the conditioner ready.

"Ok, let's make that beautiful head of hair soft shall we?" Gabe asked. David smiled and stepped out of the water. Gabe massaged the conditioner into David's hair. David started to laugh. "What?" Gabe asked with a confused look on his face.

"I half expected you to get in here with me when you came in." Gabe giggled but kept working on David's hair.

"I thought about it." Gabe confessed. He rinsed his hands in the water and David stepped back into it.

"Why did you change your mind?" David asked as Gabe worked. Gabe sighed and looked at David's injured body.

"You should heal before I break you." Gabe said. David laughed and splashed water into Gabe's face. Gabe smiled and stood back from the tub. He closed the curtain and waited for David to finish washing. When David shut the water off, Gabe grabbed the towel and held it out for David. David stepped out of the shower and grabbed the towel. He dried the most of his body that he could. Gabe dried his hair and back for him. "You know something, David?" Gabe asked as he put the towel down and handed David his underwear.

"What?" David asked as he pulled the boxers on.

"You're a natural tease I think." Gabe said and handed David his pants. David smiled and pulled the jeans on. He did up the button and fly and stood there with no shirt on.

"Why do you say that?" David asked as he put on his deodorant and cologne. Gabe walked up behind David as he stared at himself in the mirror. He rested his hands on David's hips and bit his bottom lip.

"Trust me. I don't think you even try." He said and kissed David's shoulder. David smiled and turned around. He was about a forehead shorter than Gabe but he could look him right in the eye. David stared at Gabe for a second and then kissed him. Gabe moaned and pulled David's hips against his. David giggled and finished the kiss. Gabe pulled away and shook his head. "You are so hot." Gabe said and smiled. David shook his head and raised his eyebrows. He turned to look at himself in the full length mirror again.

"Have you seen this? I am not too hot right now." David said and winced at the sight. Gabe pursed his lips and grabbed David's shirt from the counter. He pulled it over David's head and helped him push his arms through.

"You really shocked me when I answered the door yesterday." Gabe said as he opened the drawer and pulled out a brush. He walked up behind David and started brushing his hair.

"Why?" David asked as he watched Gabe brush.

"Well, four years ago you were just Amanda's friend David. But yesterday when I answered that door . . ." Gabe stopped talking and shook his head.

"What?" David asked looking at Gabe in the mirror. Gabe looked into the reflection of David's eyes.

"David, if I would have known I had even the slightest chance at that moment, I would have took you up to my room right then." David laughed and shook his head. Gabe laughed to and finished brushing. David remembered the way Gabe looked at the door. He did have a funny look on his face, and the way he leaned on the door frame was almost as though he caught himself from falling.

"Come to think of it." David said turning to face Gabe. "I think I noticed that." Gabe laughed and put the brush back. David took another look at Gabe's work and nodded. He opened the door and stepped out. Gabe gathered the laundry and followed him to his room. David walked over to the chair and grabbed his coat. Gabe walked over and helped him pull it onto his shoulders.

"At least he won't see your body. Your face doesn't look that bad." Gabe said. David looked in the mirror. His right eye was bruised and the corner of his bottom lip was split and a little swollen. He raised one eyebrow and looked at Gabe.

"I look like shit Gabe." He said. Gabe laughed. There was a knock at his bedroom door.

"Yea?" David said toward the door.

"Mr. Black is here David." Nancy said.

"Ok. Be right down." David said and took a deep breath.

"I can't wait to see this guy." Gabe said and giggled. David rolled his eyes and went to the door. "Hey, wait." Gabe said and grabbed David's arm. David stopped and looked at Gabe. Gabe kissed David and grabbed his back side. David giggled and frowned. "For luck." Gabe said and grabbed the door handle.

"You're such a tool." David whispered. Gabe laughed and followed David down the stairs. They turned the corner and saw Mr. Black at the table. He was drinking coffee and smoking a cigarette. He was wearing a skin tight t-shirt and light coloured blue jeans. He had his hair parted in the middle. Gabe secretly nudged David. "Hi." David said. Mr. Black stared at him for a second.

"It's not so bad." Mr. Black said looking at David's face.

"You should see the rest of him." Gabe said. David elbowed Gabe as he walked by and sat at the table.

"Come and sit dear." Nancy said. David slowly walked to the table and sat down next to Gabe. Nancy got them both a coffee and sat down at the end of the table.

"We don't have to do this today." Mr. Black said still staring at David's face.

"No, it's cool. I wanna go." David said taking a sip of his coffee. Gabe smiled and leaned back in his chair.

"So, your David's history teacher?" Gabe asked trying to change the subject.

"Yes, I am." Mr. Black said smiling at Gabe, "And you are?" Mr. Black said offering his hand.

"Oh, yea. I'm Gabriel Moore. I'm the neighbor." Gabe said and shook Mr. Blacks hand.

"Well, nice to meet you Gabriel."

"Oh, call me Gabe. I'm saving Gabriel for the priest that reads my last rights." Gabe said. Everyone laughed.

"Well, Gabe. It's nice to meet you." Mr. Black said and looked back at David. David hadn't taken his eyes off Mr. Black since he sat down.

"Are you sure you want to do this?" Mr. Black asked. David could feel Gabe touch his leg with his.

"Oh, yea." David said and cleared his throat. Gabe laughed and sipped his coffee. David kept his leg still and Gabe never moved his.

"Well, we should get going then. It's supposed to be hot today so we should stop and pick up something to drink on the way." Mr. Black said. Nancy smiled and stood up.

"I made some fruit salad for you two." She said and went to the fridge. Mr. Black stood up and took his cup to the sink. He grabbed the plate from Nancy.

"Thank you. That's very kind."

"Oh please. I can't expect you to feed that bottomless pit for the whole day." She said they both laughed. Gabe and David looked at each other and raised an eyebrow. Gabe smiled and mouthed 'hot' To David. David blushed and nodded. Gabe giggled then mouthed 'Like, fucking hot." David giggled and punched him playfully in the leg.

"Well, shall we?" Mr. Black said walking back out to the table.

"Yea, let's go." David said and stood up.

"Have fun guys." Nancy said as they left the room. Gabe got up as well and walked them to the door. He followed them out.

"What are you fishing for?" Gabe asked as they walked to the wine coloured, 1969 Mustang Fastback.

"Perch mostly." Mr. Black said as they reached the car.

"Hot car." Gabe said, mostly to David, but Mr. Black answered.

"Yea, it gets me back and forth." He said. Gabe shook his head and smiled. Mr. Black took Gabe to the front of the car and lifted the hood. They chatted about the engine for a while. David stared at Mr. Black while he talked about his car. Gabe looked up at David and winked. David rolled his eyes and shook his head. Mr. Black closed the hood and shook Gabe's hand.

"Well, it was a pleasure sir. Enjoy your day." Gabe said and winked at David again.

"Will do." Mr. Black said and walked to the driver's side door. David opened his door and got in. Mr. Black did the same. He started the engine and they both waved at Gabe. Gabe waved back and they drove off. "Nice guy." Mr. Black said. David smiled and nodded. His heart pounded in his chest as Mr. Black changed gears in the car.

"Yea, he's cool." David said trying to stay in the conversation and out of la-la horny land.

"Known him long?" Mr. Black asked as they turned on to 50th street.

"My whole life." David answered. Mr. Black pulled up to the gas station and parked the car.

"What kind of chips do you like?" He asked. David shrugged and looked at Mr. Black. He was like a bill board for sex and David smiled.

"Uh, I prefer pretzels actually." David said.

"Ok, pretzels it is. And pop?"

"Anything but root beer." David answered. Mr. Black smiled and got out of the car. David watched him as he went into the store. He leaned his head back against the seat and sighed.

Quit acting like such a bitch. Talk to him like Gabe was. That was a lesson if I ever saw one. Gabe knows Mr. Black makes me as nervous as hell. Just talk to him like he's just another guy. Quit being so tongue tied. He is trying to do something nice for me, or mom. One or the other. How can I expect to learn anything about him if I sit here like a nervous little girl?

Mr. Black opened the door and through two bags of chips and a case of Coke into the back seat. He sat down in the car and shut the door.

"Look, David. I know this is weird for you or something. But I'm not trying to creep you out. I just want to spend some time with you." He said. He sat quietly without starting the car. David sighed.

"I know. I just never really spent time with anybody since dad . . . I mean, sorry." David said stumbling over his words.

"I just want you to enjoy yourself David. Your mom said you could use some man to man time or whatever." David giggled and thought of his mom.

"Yea, that sounds like her." David said and leaned against the arm rest.

"She means well, David. I am sure of that. Mothers have a way of showing they care. It's different for all of them." He said and started the car.

"Well, she's been looking for a man for me to hang out with for a while." David said as Mr. Black pulled the car out of the parking lot.

"She mentioned that. She thought your Uncle Carl would be good but I heard that didn't go over well." David rolled his eyes.

"You guys sure talk a lot, huh?"

"Don't get the wrong idea, David. She's not sabotaging you or anything. It was more of a heads up for me I think." He said and smiled. David smiled and remembered the fight with Carl.

"Wants you to know what you're getting yourself into huh?" David asked. Mr. Black laughed and David bit his lip at the sound. He had the sexiest laugh he ever heard.

"I wouldn't put it like that." Mr. Black said as he turned onto the highway. "Scare easy?" He asked. David frowned,

"No, why?" David asked. Just then Mr. Black punched the gas and car took off down the high way. David watched him as he changed gears. Mr. Black looked over at David then back to the road. David laughed and shook his head.

"What?" Mr. Black asked as he slowed the car back down to highway speed.

"Nice to see a guy doesn't grow out of some things." David said and looked out the wind shield. Mr. Black laughed and shook his head.

"Yea, I guess that's not the role model your mother was looking for." He joked as he pulled out to pass a minivan.

"HA!" David scoffed, "She lets me hang out with Gabe, so you're a saint." He added.

"What's wrong with Gabe? He seems like a good guy."

"Yea, he is. She doesn't like his black clothes and his electric guitar." David answered.

"Nothing wrong with electric guitar." Mr. Black said as he slowed the car to turn off the highway. David smirked and looked at him.

"Don't tell me you play." David said hoping to hell he didn't.

"Sure, I piss with it a little." He said as he drove slowly down the gravel road.

Just another sexy thing you do. God help me.

"Of course you do." David said and shook his head. Mr. Black frowned and looked at David.

"Why? You think teachers have their noses in text books and grading papers all the time?" He asked smiling.

"Its nothing. I'm sure you have a life outside the institution." David said looking out the window. Mr. Black laughed and shook his head.

"You really dislike school, don't you?" David looked over at him.

"It just takes up the best years of your life, completely consumes your days and nights, and calls for early mornings. What's to dislike?" David said sarcastically. Mr. Black laughed again. "Then of course, there are teachers." David added gesturing to Mr. Black.

"I'm cool, aren't I? I mean, I got the car and the looks." Mr. Black joked back. David giggled and shook his head.

That you do have. He thought.

"Yea, well there are exceptions to every rule I guess." David said looking back out the window.

"Here we are." Mr. Black said and turned into a thickly treed driveway. David looked out the window at the scenery. It was quite impressive. Every so often, David could see the edge of a deep ravine through the trees. They pulled up to a big log house. Mr. Black parked the car next to a red Camaro.

"What? You have two hot cars?" David asked and opened the door. Mr. Black smiled and got out of the car. They walked to ward the Cherry red Camarro.

"Six actually. The other four are in the shop." Mr. Black said and gestured to the massive shop to the west of the property. David shook his head and looked inside the car. It had black leather interior and was a standard transmission.

"Wow." David said.

"I like to fix them up. This little baby was my latest project." He said running his hand over the roof of the car. "I saw it in a junk yard trashed to hell. I couldn't leave her there." He said. David shook his head again and smiled.

"It sure is nice. What year is it?" He asked trying to put Gabe's lesson into practice.

"Well," Mr. Black said and giggled. "Originally she's an 87. But the body was so trashed that when I rebuilt her, she took on more of a 79 look." He said and smiled at his car. David raised his eyebrows.

"Cool Mr. Black." He said.

"Please, call me Alan." He said. David blinked and took a deep breath. Hearing that was like hearing 'Take me know right over my car'. He smiled and nodded.

"Well, shall we?" Alan asked.

"Yea, good idea." David said and they both walked back to the Mustang. Alan got the stuff out of the back of the car and handed the bag with the chips in it to David. David took the bag and followed Alan down the hill to the lake. There was a boat tied to the little dock and two lawn chairs sitting at the end of it.

"So, we can take out the boat or we can sit on the dock. Take your pick." Alan said as they reached the dock.

"The dock is good for me." David said looking at the fiberglass Lund. It looked like it could go fast.

"In that case," Alan said and reached into the boat and took out a cooler. He set it between the chairs and put the pop inside to cool. "Grab a rod there David." He said as he packed the ice around the bottles in the cooler. David grabbed two rods from the boat and handed the nicer of the two to Alan.

"I'm guessing that's yours." David said as Alan took the rod.

"They both are but I do prefer this one." He said and grabbed the tackle box from the boat. He rigged up both rods with a pickerel rig and cast out for David.

"I probably could have done that." David said as he took the rod from Alan.

"Well," Alan said casting out his own line and tightening the line. "Have you paid any attention to the way you have been moving today?" He asked as he sat down on the lawn chair next to David. David rolled his eyes and looked out onto the water.

"Yea, I guess I'm not hiding it well, huh?" He asked and smiled.

"Not really." Alan said and laughed. "So, what really happened?" He asked as he leaned back in his chair and stared out at the lake. David sighed and leaned back in his chair as well.

"Didn't mom tell you?" He asked and shut his eyes. The sun was warm on his face and it felt nice.

"Sure, she told me what the cops were told." Alan said. David smiled and shook his head.

"We were drinking and it got a little rowdy." David said still enjoying the sun on his face. Alan looked over at him and raised an eyebrow.

"You don't strike me as the fighting type." He said. David looked over at him. His sandy coloured hair shown in the sun light and his light green eyes reflected the lake water like emeralds.

"No?" David asked trying not to hesitate.

"Not really. You're a really quiet, keep to yourself kind of guy. Fighters are cocky and arrogant." Alan said smiling at David. David's heart jumped and he looked away.

"I guess rum has a strange effect on me." He said. Alan laughed and looked back out onto the lake.

"Yea, I think you're probably not the only one." He said. David looked back at him from the corner of his eye. He sat leaned back on his lawn chair with his legs wide open. He was looking out onto the lake. David bit his bottom lip as he stared at Alan. Then, Alan moved. He seemed to thrust his hips up to slid himself down the chair a little. David closed his eyes again and swallowed hard.

Holy God. He thought and looked back out onto the lake.

"So, looking forward to the project?" Alan said after a while and opened up the cooler. David looked over at him. The muscle in his arm bulged as he dug around for a pop. He handed one to David and then dug one out for himself.

"Yea, it should be cool." David said opening his pop. He and Alan took a sip at the same time.

"I hope so. It would be great for the school if that funding goes through." Alan said. He recapped his pop and set it down on the dock beside him. David did the same and looked at Alan.

"The funding, right." David said. He leaned back on his chair again and retightened his line.

"Yea, sorry. No shop talk today." Alan said and looked at David.

"It's ok. We do have school in common." David said.

"Yea, but that sucks." Alan said. They both laughed and looked back out onto the lake.

"That's a first for me." David said.

"What? Hearing a teacher say school sucks?"

"Yea." David said and laughed again. Alan smiled and shook his head.

"I like to teach. I don't like the job."

"That makes sense." David said. They discussed the institution of school for an hour. Mostly laughing and coming up with ways to change the system. Then Alan changed the subject.

"I'm hungry. Are you hungry?" He asked.

"I could eat." David said. They looked at the bags of pretzels. Alan sighed and looked at the fruit plate.

"Wanna go into town and eat?" He asked. David laughed and got the drift.

"None of it looks very good huh?" He asked.

"Well, we've been fishing all morning and haven't caught anything. I kind of want a burger." He said and sighed.

"Fishing to burger? You're random." David said with a smirk. Alan laughed and reeled in his line. David did the same and helped Alan pack the fishing stuff back into the boat. Alan grabbed the cooler and David grabbed the chip bag. They walked back up the hill to the house.

"Just leave it all here. I'll grab it when I get home." Alan said and set the cooler on the step. David set the bag on top and went to the car with Alan. They both got in and Alan started the engine. He pulled out of the drive way and headed down the little gravel road. "Sorry we didn't catch anything." Alan said as David looked out the window at the trees.

"Why? We would have to fillet them and stuff if we caught any." David said. Alan laughed and shook his head.

"So it's the *act* of fishing you like." He said.

"Yea, I'm not a fish lover really. My dad took me out a couple times a year. We never caught much either. But we talked a lot. Really the only time we did that." David said and looked over at Alan.

"That's too bad."

"Not really," David said with a smirk, "We didn't have much to talk about the rest of the year anyway." Alan smiled.

"Well, we should make fishing a habit then, you and me." He said. David smiled and nodded.

"That would be cool." David said and looked back out the window. They traveled in silence till the high way. Then Alan turned the opposite way than town. "Where are we going?" David asked looking back at Mr. Black.

"Well, I thought we would go to that Big Rig truck stop place instead of back to town. It suddenly hit me that you probably don't want the other kids in the school seeing you have lunch with me." He said and smiled. David laughed and shook his head.

"Yea, I hadn't thought of that."

"That's why I'm driving." Alan said and gunned the gas pedal like before. He couldn't get it up as fast as before due to traffic and David laughed. "What?" Alan asked smiling at David's laughter.

"You have a problem with speed." David said and looked at him. Alan looked back at him with mock shock.

"It's not a problem. More of an obsession." He said and winked. David sort of coughed and giggled at the same time. Alan laughed.

"You know, speed kills." David said. Alan laughed again and nodded.

"Only if you lose control." He said. David laughed and shook his head. "Wanna listen to some tunes?" He asked and reached for the stereo.

"As long as it isn't old guy music." David said. Alan rolled his eyes and pressed play on the C.D. player. Alice Cooper started to sing Feeding my Frankenstein.

"How's that for old guy music?" Alan asked and tapped the steering wheel along with the song. David took a deep breath and leaned his head back.

I love you lord. He thought. David realized there wasn't a thing he disliked about Alan Black.

"This is a good song." David finally said and Alan smiled.

"What were you expecting?"

"I don't know, easy rock or something gay like that." David said and smiled at the word. Alan looked at David and laughed. "Maybe golden oldies." He added. Alan laughed again and shook his head.

"How old do you think I am?" Alan asked. David looked at him and thought about it.

"I don't really know." He said.

"Take a guess." Alan said and looked between David and the road a few times. David cocked his head to one side and answered.

"40." He said. Alan laughed.

"Wow, thank you for that. Remind me to punch my hair dresser." He said. David laughed and shrugged.

"Older or younger than 40?" David asked. Alan smirked and shook his head.

"Younger." He said and smiled.

"Ok, 35." David said. Alan smiled and looked at David.

"Well, that's closer." He said and looked back at the road.

"How old are you?" David asked, now genuinely curious.

"39" He said and laughed. David laughed and shook his head.

"40 was closer."

"Yea well, tell that to yourself when *your* 39." Alan said and slowed to turn into the truck stop. They both got out of the car and went inside. They picked a table by the window and both ordered coffee to drink.

"So, can I ask you something Alan?" David said looking across the table at the gorgeous teacher he was now on a first name basis with.

"I'm an open book" He said.

"Why such a liking to me?" He asked. It came out so fast in was like a hot knife through butter.

"Well, you remind me of me at your age." He said and leaned back in his chair. The muscles in his chest and stomach rippled with the movement.

"Oh, why?" David asked. It was digging time. He wanted something to go on before he saw Gabe or Amanda again.

"Well, I don't know about you but, when I was your age I had a real hard time fitting in. I had friends and stuff but they were all dumb." David laughed at Alan's choice of description. "I felt more comfortable with adults. Their conversations were more interesting to me or something."

"I get that." David said keeping the conversation going. The waitress came to the table then and took their orders. They both ordered the big rig burger and fries.

"Anyway," Alan said taking a sip of his coffee. "Like you, school seemed pointless and easy to me."

"I hear that." David said smirking and taking a sip from his coffee.

"Well, I was gonna drop out."

"Really?" David asked. He was genuinely surprised.

"Yea, really. I hated it. The teachers were jerks and my friends were so busy partying and having sex with everything that moved that I thought . . . I don't know, I was too smart or something for school anymore." Alan said. David felt like he was on the edge of his seat. His chance to ask the best digging question was upon him.

"What happened?" It came out of his mouth like the national anthem. It was like right out of the bible or something.

"Well, remember that teacher I was telling you about?"

"Yea." David said.

"Well, that's what changed my mind."

"What was so great about him?"

"He was awesome. He just seemed to know how to talk to me. He took a liking to me right away. Sort of the same deal as we have. He was older than I am now but he was still cool." Alan said and sipped his coffee again.

"I doubt it's the same." David blurted out and instantly hated himself for it.

"Why?" Alan asked. David sighed and looked around.

"Did your mom talk him into hanging out with you?" David asked trying to divert what he was really thinking.

"Well, no. I did it on my own." Alan said. The waitress walked over with the coffee pot and filled both cups back up.

"Why?" David asked. Alan smiled and took a deep breath.

"He was different than other teachers." He said and sipped his coffee. David could feel his heart pound.

"Different how?" He asked. Alan smiled.

"Why the twenty questions? Since when do you talk so much?" He asked and giggled at David. David leaned back in his chair and smiled.

"Just trying to figure you out, that's all." David said. Alan smiled and shook his head.

"There was a time in my life, David, that I wasn't too sure who or what I was going to be. He was . . . helpful." Alan said. David sat quietly for a second. The waitress brought their food over and they ate with minimal small talk. David was surprised at how hungry he was. He finished his entire burger and half his fries. He pushed the plate to the side and sipped his coffee again. Alan did the same at almost the same time. "So, now its your turn David." Alan said and leaned back in his chair.

"My turn for what?" He asked.

"Tell me something about *your*self." He answered.

"Um, like what?"

"Tell me about Amanda." Alan said sipped his freshly refilled coffee.

"Amanda." David said and raised his eyebrows. "Well, we grew up together." David said.

"Ok, she's Gabe's little sister, right?"

"Yea, much younger. He's almost your age I think. Anyway, We met cause she fell off her bike in front of my house the summer before kinder garden."

"Oh," Alan said giggling. "Love at first sight or something?" David laughed.

"Hardly. I thought she was a big whiner. But, she was my age and our parents insisted we played together."

"And what about now?"

"Well, now, now I would die for her and vice versa." David said and smiled.

"Hence the fight last night?"

"No, that was just me and Todd." David said.

"Oh, Todd." Alan said and raised his eyebrows. David remembered back to the warning Alan had given to him about Todd.

"Yea, well. Please don't say I told you so."

"I wouldn't do that." Alan said and smiled. "So, Amanda. She your girlfriend or something?"

"No, just a friend." David said and sipped his coffee.

"She looks at you like there is something more than that."

"Yea, well. We have a little history I guess." Alan raised his eyebrows and smiled.

"A physical history?" He asked. David laughed and nodded. "I don't want to sound like an old guy but, you guys are safe, right?" David looked at Alan and laughed.

"Yes, dad." He said. Alan laughed and shook his head. He looked at his watch and back to David.

"Smoke time?" He asked.

"Oh yea, I gotta piss first." David answered and stood up.

"Good idea." Alan said and got up too. David took a deep breath and headed to the bathroom. He walked in to see the one and only stall was out of order. He walked over to the urinal and pulled his penis out. Alan walked in and stood beside him. David took a deep breath. He could hear Alan peeing. "Stage fright?" Alan asked with a giggle. David laughed and nodded.

"Looks like." he said. Alan leaned over the urinal and looked down. David held his breath and could feel sweat building on his brow.

"Why?" Alan asked and zipped up. David looked down at his exposed penis with wide eyes. Finally the pee came. Alan finished washing his hands and waited for David. When David finished he washed his hands and dried them. Alan opened the door and giggled.

"What?" David asked as they made their way through the truck stop to the door.

"With something like that, I find it hard to believe you suffer from stage fright." Alan said and went outside. David's heart pounded.

Oh my God. He just complimented my dick. He thought as he followed Alan out.

"Thanks, I think." David said as he dug out his cigarettes. Alan laughed and lit one himself.

"Do you know where stage fright comes from?" Alan asked as David puffed on his cigarette. He stood silent and let Alan speak. "It's the fear of being up-staged."

"Ok." David said.

"I don't think you have that problem." Alan said and flicked the ash off his cigarette on the ground. David blushed and looked down.

"Sorry, didn't mean to embarrass you. I can see why she likes you so much." Alan apologized. David laughed and answered.

"I'm not embarrassed, Alan." He said.

"Ok, then why the shyness?"

"I don't know. Not a lot of guys have complemented my dick in the past." Alan laughed and shook his head.

"The difference between boys and men David is being sexually comfortable." David looked up at him and frowned.

"What?" He asked. Alan took another puff from his cigarette and leaned on his car.

"Guys your age are so scared of being labeled gay or something. When you get older, you learn that knowing the competition is half the battle." David laughed and shook his head.

"Now I've heard it all." Alan laughed and put out his cigarette. David did the same and got into the car with Alan.

"It's true you know . . . kind of." Alan said and started the car. David leaned his head back against the seat and thought.

Alan Black just had a discussion with me about my dick. How do I feel? "So what now?" Alan asked breaking into David's thought.

"Well, aren't you sick of me yet?" David asked smiling. Alan laughed and shook his head.

"Nope, sick of me yet?" He asked in return.

"Nope." David said looking Alan up and down quickly and wondering if was possible to get sick of him.

"Well, you play guitar?" Alan asked.

"A little." David said wondering where this was going.

"Wanna jam for a while then? It's been a while since I played with company." David thought about it. He hadn't played the guitar since his dad died.

"Why not?" David asked and smiled. Alan smiled to and headed down the highway back to his place. As they drove, they compared songs they both knew how to play and had compiled a fairly long list by the time Alan turned into the drive way. David fallowed Alan into the house. It was bright considering the trees outside. The door opened up into the kitchen. David could see pots and pans hanging from the ceiling over an island stove. The cupboards were red oak and the counter was a black marble. "My mom would kill for this kitchen." David said as they walked through to the basement stairs.

"Really? Think she's that violent?" Alan joked as he turned on the stairs light and walked down. David laughed and followed. They landed in a large room with a bar in it. There was a collection of old records hanging on the wall and beneath them on fancy stands were two Stratocaster guitars.

"Whoa." David said as he admired the two six string electric guitars as if they were art in a museum. Alan smiled and went over to the bar.

"Pop or, if you don't tell your mom, beer." Alan said holding up one of each. David turned around and looked at him.

"Beer." He said and smiled. Alan nodded and got two beer out of the little fridge. David tried to take his jacket off but the reminder of last night's brawl shot through him like a bullet. Alan was beside him in a flash. He set the two beers on the stools and asked.

"Are you ok?" David looked at him and smiled.

"Honestly? No." He said and smirked. Alan smiled and grabbed the collar of David's leather coat.

"Here, let me help." Alan said and slowly pulled David out of his jacket.

"Thanks." David said as Alan handed him his beer.

"Witch one do you like?" Alan asked gesturing to the guitars.

"I have a choice?" David asked almost sounding like a 10 year old at a candy store. Alan laughed and sat down on one of the stools. David sat down.

"The black one." David said. Alan handed David the black one and grabbed the wood coloured one for himself.

"Let's rock." Alan said.

Chapter 12

It was 7:30 when Alan and David pulled up at David's house.

"I had a great time, David." Alan said. David smiled and sighed.

"Me too." He said.

"Say hi to your mom for me." Alan said as David grabbed the handle of the door.

"Sure." David said.

"Hey, David." Alan said as David got out of the car. David looked into the open window at Alan.

"Yea."

"Ever handled a stick?" David blinked and swallowed hard.

"What?" David asked. His heart pounded in his ears. Alan grabbed the gear shift and looked up at David.

"Ever drove a standard?" David breathed a long breath and closed his eyes.

"Yea, a little." David said with a half laugh in his voice.

"Wanna learn?" Alan asked. David raised his eyebrows and nodded.

"Yea, that would be cool."

"Ok, if it's ok with you, that's what we do next time."

"Sounds sweet." David said and walked around the front of the car to Alan's window. "Thanks, for all this stuff." David said. Alan smirked and nodded.

"No problem, I enjoy it." Alan said. David smiled and did a half solute and headed for the door. "Hey, David." Alan called. David turned around to look at Alan.

"Yea?" David asked.

"What did you think I meant when I asked you if you could drive a stick?" David shook his head and smiled.

"Nothing, never mind." Alan laughed and waved. He drove off and turned the corner. David walked into the house and shut the door.

"Have a good time dear?" Nancy called from the kitchen. David walked in and sat down in his chair.

"Yea, yea I did. Good call mom." He said and lit a cigarette. Nancy smiled and looked at her son.

"So, what did you do?" She asked in a nosey voice. David smiled.

"Well, we fished all morning but didn't catch anything."

"That's too bad."

"Oh well, that was ok. We didn't want to filet any anyway." David said and puffed his cigarette. Nancy giggled. "So, we got hungry and had lunch at the truck stop."

"Oh, that was nice of him."

"Actually we both threw 10 on the table. I wouldn't let him pay for the whole thing." David said. Nancy smiled. "Then we went back to his place and jammed."

"Jammed? Like music?"

"Yea, he's really good at guitar. And he has these two Strads that kick ass. It was awesome." David said and took another drag from his cigarette.

"I thought you didn't play anymore." Nancy said with a raised eyebrow. David sighed and shrugged. "It's nice to hear you're playing again son." Nancy said and smiled.

"Yea well, who can say no to a cherry black Stratocaster?" David asked smiling.

"You sound just like your dad." Nancy said laughing. David laughed and shook his head. "Are you going to spend time like this with Mr. Black often?" She asked. She had a hint of hope in her voice.

"Yea, actually." David said thinking about Alan and his offer to drive his car.

"Oh good." Nancy said sounding relieved. David laughed and shook his head. "Oh, by the way, Amanda called. I told her you would call back when you got home."

"Ok. Thanks mom." David said and got up. He went up to his room and laid down on his bed. He reached over and grabbed the phone. He dialed Amanda's number and listened to the rings.

"*Hello*" It was Gabe. David smiled.

"Hi." David said.

"*Oh, hi. How did it go?*" Gabe asked. David sighed and lay his head back on the pillow and stared up at the ceiling.

"Good, but I should tell Amanda about it first. She's gonna get jealous that we talk so much." David said. Gabe giggled.

"*Well, Amanda went to the store to get munchies. So you're stuck with me.*"

"Ok. It was weird and awesome at the same time."

"*How so?*"

"Well, I think he may have had a thing for a teacher of his back in school that may have turned physical."

"Really? Why do you say that?"

"Well, he was vague with the details, like trying not to say too much or something."

"It's possible. What else?"

"Well, he plays guitar." David said. Gabe cleared his throat.

"That's hot dude."

"You should watch him play. God to be that guitar." David said and sighed. Gabe laughed.

"You're a case David." He said and laughed. David laughed and sighed again.

"He also complimented my dick." David said. Gabe coughed on whatever he was drinking and David giggled.

"He what?"

"Yea, we were in the bathroom at the truck stop and I freaked. I couldn't piss. The stall was out of order and we both had to use the urinals."

"ok."

"Anyway, I had stage fright."

"Figures. I can see that." Gabe said joking.

"Yea, yea. Wanna hear this or what?"

"Yea, sorry go on."

"Well, he commented on the stage fright and looked over the urinal at my dick. He said I shouldn't suffer from stage fright because of what I had."

"No way."

"Yea, he said stage fright comes from the fear of being up-staged and I don't have to worry about that."

"He pretty much told you that you got a big dick, David."

"I know."

"*That's a pretty good sign if he's checking you out.*"

"Is it? He also said that the difference between boys and men was sexual knowledge or some shit. He said half the battle was knowing the competition."

"*Wow, good line.*" Gabe said. David laughed and winced at the pain. "*Are you ok?*" Gabe asked hearing David's discomfort through the phone.

"Yea, it's worse when I'm laying down." David said.

"*You're laying down?*" Gabe asked in a quiet bedroom sounding voice. David laughed again and shook his head.

"Yea, I am." David said. He mocked Gabe's horny sounding voice. Gabe giggled and then cleared his throat.

"*As much as I would love to see were that conversation would go, Amanda's back.*"

"Ok." David said and smiled. "You turn me on." He said to tease Gabe.

"*I know.*" He said and laughed. "*Here's Amanda.*"

"*Hello*"

"Hi. So that was fun." David said.

"*I wanna hear everything.*" David recapped the same way he did for Gabe. Amanda was convinced that at some time in Mr. Black's life, he must have been with a guy.

"It's as confusing as it is exciting." David said.

"*No doubt. But he's a teacher David. Cant he get in trouble or something?*"

"Yea. I thought about that too."

"*Well, we don't have anything concrete yet, right?*"

"No, I guess not."

"*You're going driving or something with him next time?*"

"Yea. Why?"

"*Well, why not be more straight forward with your questions?*"

"How do you mean?"

"*I don't know. Tell him Todd hit on you and that's what started the fight. Maybe he'll open up to you about some curiosity he had once or something to help you understand.*"

"Yea, I could do that. He already doesn't buy the story we told the cops."

"*That's cause he's smart.*" David giggled.

"That he is." He said and turned to look at the clock. It was 9:18. He yawned and it hurt his ribs.

"*You sound tired.*" Amanda said quietly.

"Yea." David answered.

"*Ok, I'll let you go. I'll see you tomorrow, ok?*"

"Ok. See ya." He said and hung up the phone. He put it back on the receiver and got up. He walked over to his desk and opened his journal. He sat down on the folding chair and wrote,

> Sept. 18, Sunday
>
> Well, Gabe is gay and an awesome kisser. Todd's a dick and handed me a beating that I should remember for a while, and to top it all off, Alan Black is a wicked guitar player. It's been a while since I wrote but so much has happened, it almost seems easier to sum it up. I think Gabe is gonna be who I take any being gay advice from. Amanda doesn't know it, but Gabe is gay. Which is good for me because

apparently I'm his type. We made out last night after my ass handing. It was awesome. And he's willing to show me the ropes in case I ever get a chance to be with Mr. Black. Who has asked me today to call him Alan. I learned a little about him. He's 39 and collects old cars. And he makes playing the guitar look like porn. He has a collection of old albums witch is cool and likes the good old hard rock. He's after my heart I tell you.

Anyway, He's gonna take me out driving one of these old cars the next time we have our little man to man play date. Mom is happy we get along. She's been working on this for some time.

But, I guess that's all till tomorrow. The mid-evil project starts tomorrow night. That should be interesting.

Thanks for listening.

David woke with the alarm the next morning and groaned at the pain in his sides. He had slept in his shirt because he couldn't get his arms up to take it off. He sat up and rubbed his sides.

"Fuck you *are* a dick Todd." He said and stood up. He sighed and shook his head. There was a knock at his door. He frowned, "Yea?" He said looking at the door.

"It's Amanda, can I come in?" David smiled and went to the door. He opened it and let her in. He closed the door behind her and yawned.

"Why are you here so early?"

"Well, Gabe said you need help with your shirt and washing your hair." She said and sighed.

"Amanda, you get sick at the thought of what I must look like under this shirt. How will you help?" She sighed again and shrugged.

"Can't I try to help? I feel partially responsible."

"Ok, but don't puke on me or something." David said. Amanda smiled and dug through David's closet for jeans and a t-shirt. He watched her riffle through his dresser for clean socks and underwear.

"Ok, let's go." She said and led him to the bathroom. Nancy was just walking out.

"Good morning." Nancy said as they walked into the bathroom.

"Good morning mom." David and Amanda said in unison. Nancy smiled and shook her head.

"Think you got this handled?" Nancy asked Amanda.

"I think so." Amanda said and shoved David into the bathroom. He laughed and shook his head. Amanda fallowed him in and shut the door behind her. "So, go pee." She said and went to the tub. David did as he was told and peed while Amanda got the shower ready. He dropped his boxers to the floor and stepped out of them. "What's the best way to do this?" Amanda asked grabbing the bottom of David's shirt.

"Well, ever watched hockey?" He asked. She nodded. "Pull it up the back and over my head." He said.

"Like when they fight?" She asked.

"Just like that." He said. Amanda pulled the shirt up David's back and over his head. He pulled his head out and she pulled the shirt down his arms. "Easy huh?" He asked. Amanda's face turned white as she looked at David's torso.

"Oh god, David." She whispered. The bruises were black and red. There was an outline of green around the outside of the bruising.

"Some art work, huh?" David asked looking at himself in the mirror. Amanda winced and closed her eyes.

"Come on." She said quietly and led him to the tub. He stepped in and left the curtain open.

"It would be easier if you got in." David said. Amanda looked at him and smiled.

"You would like that wouldn't you?" She asked. David laughed and stood under the hot water.

"Your short, Amanda. It would be easier to wash my hair if you got in. And less messy on the floor." Amanda looked at the water coming out of the tub from the splashing shower. She closed the curtain and got undressed. She stepped in with David and looked at the bruises again.

"It must really hurt." She said and put her cool hands on his injured torso. David smiled and put his hand on hers. She looked up at him with tears in her eyes.

"Don't cry Amanda." David said and hugged her. She cried against his sore chest as he held her.

"I'm so sorry." She sobbed. David rubbed her back.

"This isn't your fault. Don't blame yourself Amanda." He said and kissed the top of her head. She nodded and stepped back.

"What's first?" She asked shivering. David smiled and stepped around her to put her under the hot water. He grabbed the bar of soap and started to lather it up. She took it from him and lathered up her hands. She set it down and carefully washed his chest and stomach. She worked her way across his genitals and down each leg. Then she stood up and had him turn around. He did and she did the same on his back. She stepped out of the water so he could rinse off. She got the shampoo ready and waited. He stepped out of the water and to face her. She massaged the shampoo into his hair. He stared into her eyes while she worked. She had to step on her tip toes to rinse the soap off her hands. She smiled at him as he backed into the water to let her rinse his hair. "This is kind of fun." She said quietly.

"Five minutes ago you were crying. Now it's kind of fun?" David said giggling at Amanda.

"Well, I feel like you're always taking care of *me.* It's nice to go the other way." David thought back to the time Amanda had broken both her elbows falling off the monkey bars at school in grade three. He had done all her writing and carried her books for her every day. And the summer between grade six and seven when she broke her leg and her elbows still weren't strong enough to use the crutches. He had fashioned a chair in the leaf wagon for her. He pulled her everywhere she wanted to go.

"I think you have it a little easier than I did." David joked. Amanda laughed as she got the conditioner ready for his hair. She massaged it in and smiled at him.

"Was it really that bad? I mean doing stuff for me when I was hurt?" She asked. David smiled and shook his head.

"No, it was kind of fun." David confessed. They both laughed as she rinsed the conditioner out of his hair.

"Anything else you do in here?" She asked. David's face curled into a wicked smile. Amanda blushed and shook her head. David laughed.

"No, that's it." He said. He turned and shut the water off. He let Amanda dry off with the towel first. He took the towel from her and started drying what he could. Amanda put on her bra and panties while David struggled with the towel. He winced at the pain in caused him. "Fuck I hate that dude." David said. Amanda sighed and looked down.

"I am so sorry David." She said. David dropped the towel and went to her. He held her in his arms.

"It's ok, Amanda." He said quietly. She sighed again and nodded her head. She pulled away and collected the towel. She dried his hair and his back. She helped him dress and brush his hair. David brushed his teeth while Amanda fixed her hair. He put on his deodorant and cologne.

"All done?" She asked. David smiled and nodded and they left the room. They went to his room so he could collect his books, jacket and cigarettes then headed downstairs. Nancy had two coffees on the table for them.

"How you feeling?" She asked as David slowly sat down at his chair.

"Like a pile of shit." He breathed. Nancy winced and looked at her son with great worry.

"You could stay home today, if you like." She offered. David raised his eyebrows and looked at his mom. He thought of Alan and the project after school. He thought about spending the whole day at home with nothing to do.

"Naw, that's ok mom. I'll go."

"If it gets too bad he could always just come home, right?" Amanda asked Nancy.

"Of course." She said and smiled at the two teenagers at her table. They sipped their coffee in silence until Nancy had to leave. "Please call me if you need anything." She said and kissed David's forehead.

"And pull you out of surgery? No way." He said smiling. Nancy smiled at her son and mouthed 'bye' to Amanda. Amanda did a girly wave and Nancy left. David looked up at the clock. It was 8:00.

"Why don't you stay home?" Amanda asked.

"What? Are you kidding? Mom spent the entire day yesterday cleaning, so there's nothing for me to do here. And I kind of want to see Alan."

"You're on a first name basis with Mr. Black?" She said giggling. David rolled his eyes.

"Away from school I am." David said. He had remembered Alan reminding him when they jammed the night before to call him Mr. Black so we didn't confuse the masses."

"Well, you could always spend it at my house. I'm sure Gabe wouldn't mind." Amanda said sipping her coffee. David thought about that for a second.

I am in way too much pain to spend a day with Gabe. He smiled at the thought.

"No, he's got his hands full with little Mike. Its ok Amanda, I'll leave if it gets too bad." He said trying to reassure his friend. Amanda smiled and seemed satisfied. They finished their coffees and got ready to leave. It was a beautiful morning and David smiled at the shining sun.

"It's nice out, huh?" Amanda said. David nodded and winced at his book bag. Amanda frowned.

"What's wrong?"

"My bag hurts my ribs." He said trying to readjust it. Amanda pulled it off his back and threw it over her shoulder. David laughed and tried to take it back.

"Don't even try it David. You've done it for me." Amanda said. David rolled his eyes and let her win. They got to the school and Amanda kept the bag till they got to their lockers. David got his books ready and they headed to home room. They sat through attendance and went their separate ways for their morning classes.

At lunch time they met at their lockers and headed out side. They sat at their usual spot at the smoking table.

"Do you think Todd is here today?" Amanda asked as David puffed at his lunch time cigarette.

"I haven't seen him." David said.

"Me neither. He's in my English class and I didn't see him."

"Well then, today is looking up then isn't it?" David asked smiling.

"Do you think he went to jail?"

"Not unless my mom pressed charges."

"You didn't ask?" Amanda was stunned.

"I didn't think about it." David said puffing on his cigarette again. Just then they saw Mr. Black come from the school doors they used to go outside. David smiled and Amanda blushed. Mr. Black walked over to them with a cigarette in hand.

"You made it. I thought your mom would try to talk you into missing today." He said as he lit his cigarette. He said hi to Amanda and looked back at David.

"She tried." David said looking at the magnificent creature that was Mr. Alan Black.

"He's being stubborn." Amanda piped up and Alan laughed.

"I see." He said and shook his head.

"I would have been bored at home." David said trying to defend himself.

"I thought you hated school." Alan said winking at Amanda. Amanda blushed and giggled. David shook his head and looked back at Mr. Black.

"I do, but I hate sitting around at home with nothing to do even worse."

"Well, it's good to see you here." Mr. Black said and smiled. David smiled back and butt out his cigarette. "I got to get back in. See you in half hour." Mr. Black said and turned to go. David and Amanda both said bye and watched him walk back into the school.

"Man, he is so good looking." Amanda said. David smirked and looked at his friend.

"Yea, he is."

"So, what do you think about the talk you guys had? Given it any more thought?"

"Of course I did, Amanda. It's just that, I hate the mystery." David said shifting in his seat to get more comfortable.

"I know. That's my problem too. It seems the info you dug up could go either way." David nodded and looked out onto the football field. They discussed the different ways that Mr. Black high school teacher could have been 'helpful' in some kind of mysterious way. The bell rang as they spoke and they went in. They collected their things from their lockers and went their separate ways. David walked slowly to room 19 for History class. His ribs seemed to hurt worse today than before. He stepped into the room to see Mr. Black at his giant oak desk.

"Hi." David said as he went to his desk and sat down.

"Sore today?" Mr. Black asked from his desk. David nodded and took out his history binder. "It's just notes today." He added.

"Have you heard what's going on with Todd?" David asked opening to a blank page in his binder and digging out a pen.

"Not a lot. Home arrest I guess." Mr. Black answered quietly as the other students filed into the room. Mr. Black smiled at David and stood up. He was wearing a dress shirt and dress pants that made him look like James Bond. David smiled and shook his head.

Even when you dress like the rest of the teachers around here, you're still a babe.

"Ok, class. The fun is over. Today we start on Jack the Ripper." The class cheered and got right down to business. "It's actually quite boring. Quit being such History loving geeks." Mr. Black said and smiled. The class laughed. Including David witch made him wince. Mr. Black noticed and winced too. He got to work with the notes on the board. He wrote all class witch was typical for Mr. Black. He liked to get all the notes for the whole section done on the first day to save them from having to waste time on notes every day. At the end of class David was almost nauseous from the pain in his ribs and he sat in his desk long after the other students left.

"Come on, David. I'll take you home." Mr. Black said to the pale white face sitting in front of him. David sighed and nodded. He gathered his things and walked to his locker with Alan by his side. "I'll find out what you need for English and call you, ok." Alan said as David loaded his bag and put on his jacket.

"Ok." David said. Alan took David's bag and had him follow him to the office. He signed David out and they went to his car.

"I'll call and let your mom know." He said as he started the Mustang.

"Thanks, Alan." David said. Alan smiled and patted David's arm that rested on the arm rest. David shivered under his touch but Alan didn't notice.

"It's really no problem."

"I really hate that Todd guy." David said and they both giggled.

"I bet. Listen," Alan said as they turned onto David's street. "If you miss tonight, that would be ok." Alan said looking at David.

"I wouldn't miss it if my head was chopped off." David said smiling at Mr. Black. Alan shook his head and smiled.

"You look like shit, David."

"I know."

"Try and rest then, before tonight." Alan said as they pulled up in front of David's house. Alan grabbed David's bag and carried it to the house for him. David unlocked the door and stepped in. Alan followed and set the bag at the foot of the stairs.

"Thanks, Alan." David said as he kicked off his shoes.

"Quit thanking me. I can't believe you made it as long as you did." Alan said laughing. David smiled and leaned against the stair railing. "Try to rest up a bit. I'll call you later with your English stuff, ok?" Alan said putting his hand on David's shoulder. David nodded taking in the scent of Alan's cologne. "Ok, I'll see you later then." Alan said and turned to go.

"Hey, Alan." David said. Alan turned to face him.

"Yea?"

"What did your teacher do to help you?" He asked. Alan smiled and shook his head.

"It's a long story, David." He said.

"Oh, ok." David said trying to stand up straight to stretch his back.

"Maybe I'll tell you someday." He said and opened the door. David smiled and shut the door behind Alan. He rubbed his sore rib cage and went over to the couch to lay down. He took a few deep breaths to try to calm the pain. He closed his eyes and tried to sleep. Then the phone rang. David frowned and grabbed the phone.

"Hello?" He said in a groggy sounding voice.

"*Was that a 1969 Mustang Fastback I saw at your house?*" It was Gabe. David smiled and sighed.

"Yea."

"*What's going on?*" Gabe asked. He sounded genuinely concerned.

"Oh, apparently I look like shit and should spend the rest of the day resting."

"*Sounds cushy.*"

"Yea, sure." David said laughing.

"*How ARE you feeling anyway?*"

"Like I got hit by a bus. I can't believe Todd is as tough as he is."

"*You were never a fighter, David.*" Gabe said in a soothing voice.

"Yea, but . . . he's gay." Gabe laughed.

"*If I remember correctly, you weren't exactly a bill board for the heterosexual community Saturday night.*"

"No, I guess not." David said with a hint of laughter in his voice.

"*But I know what you mean. He didn't really look like he had it in him.*"

"No, it didn't."

"*So, he got six months house arrest and can't come within 100 yards of you. Does that make you feel any better?*"

"Not really. I'd like to give him the beating of his life." Gabe laughed at David's comment.

"*I bet you would. But at least you won't be seeing him around.*"

"Yea, well. That won't last forever."

"*It will last till you heal at least.*" Gabe said. David smiled and nodded.

"What are you up to today?"

"*Well, mom and dad will be home tomorrow I guess so I'm cleaning house today.*"

"Oh, that sucks." Gabe giggled.

"*Why do you say that?*"

"Well, that means you'll leave." David said. Gabe sighed and was quiet for a while.

"*I'm coming back for the fair.*" Gabe said.

"You are? Why?" David asked.

"*Cause I wanna see what comes out of this little project of yours.*"

"Oh, well it's just the torture stuff."

"*I know.*" Gabe said in his bedroom voice. David laughed and then winced at the pain.

"You're so weird."

"*You like it.*"

"Yea well, that's still to be determined." They both laughed.

"*I gotta go to work soon anyway. Its good mom and dad are coming home.*"

"Did they work anything out?"

"*Yea, they figured out who gets what in the divorce.*" David blinked with shock.

"Wow, Amanda's not gonna be happy with that."

"*It gets worse. Their selling the house.*"

"What?!" David sat straight up and then fell back in pain. Gabe heard the heavy thump and the gasp from David.

"*Whoa, calm down. There's a bright side.*"

"What? How? I can't live without you and Amanda!" David yelled. He felt tears form in his eyes.

"*You won't have to.*" Gabe said in a quiet voice.

"What?" David asked in a sorrowful voice.

"*I'm gonna buy the house and move Amanda in.*" David blinked at Gabe's plan.

"Your parents will never go for that."

"*It's Amanda's choice.*"

"She'll never leave little Mike."

"*I already talked to her about it.*" David was shocked again.

"She never said anything to me."

"*I told her not to.*" Gabe said. David was quiet for a second. He couldn't believe what he was hearing.

"Why?"

"I told her that I wanted to tell you."

"Why?"

"Because, I was actually going to tell you tonight." David frowned.

"When? I have that mid-evil thing tonight."

"I know." Gabe said in a mysterious voice.

"Then what did you plan to do? Show up there and tell me this then?"

"No." Gabe answered in the same strange voice.

"Then what?" David asked wondering what all the mystery was about.

"I was going to come see you after."

"At like ten o-clock at night?" Gabe laughed and David started to piece it together. "You pig." David said laughing. Gabe laughed again.

"I'm just kidding. She is still a little shaken up by the news and I told her you had enough shit on your plate right now so I would tell you when you got home from school."

"Oh, well a late night visit would have been cool too." David said laughing. Gabe laughed again.

"I could . . . if you wanted me to."

"I do, but I hurt like a bitch and I'm afraid I wouldn't be much fun."

"That's what I was thinking." Gabe said and they both laughed.

"Does it hurt?" David asked when the laughing subsided. Gabe sighed,

"Yea, they first couple times. But it gets better."

"Todd told Amanda he came so hard he almost puked the first time." Gabe laughed and shook his head.

"He's either full of shit or the dude he was with was pretty small."

"Oh. So what about the other way."

"You mean, doing the fucking? Not receiving?"

"Yea." Gabe sighed again.

"*That doesn't hurt at all.*" Gabe said laughing. David laughed.

"Yea, but what does it feel like?"

"*Well,*" Gabe sighed. "*It's different than a chick, that's for sure.*"

"Oh, like how?" Gabe giggled.

"*Aren't you supposed to be resting?*"

"You promised you would answer this stuff for me."

"*I know, but it's hard to explain.*"

"Can you try?" Gabe sighed and thought for a minute.

"*Well, it's tighter. And depending on how you do it, you have more stuff to look out for.*" David could only surmise that he meant testicles.

"Tighter huh?" David asked. Gabe giggled.

"*Yea.*"

"That doesn't sound so bad." David said. Gabe giggled again.

"*No it doesn't.*" David yawned and Gabe sighed.

"Fuck, I'm sore." David said through his yawn.

"*Well, why don't you sleep for a while and we'll talk about this later.*"

"Ok." David said.

"*Ok, by David.*"

"Bye." David said and hung up the phone. He closed his eyes and sighed.

Tighter than Amanda? That would be interesting. He thought to himself as he drifted off to sleep.

Chapter 13

David was stirred from his sleep by the phone ringing. He grabbed the receiver.

"Hello?" He said in a groggy voice.

"*Hi David. Did you get any sleep?*" It was Alan.

"Yea, what time is it?"

"*Its six.*" David raised his eyebrows and looked at the clock. It was 6:03.

"Wow, I slept all after noon."

"*Well, that's good. How do you feel?*"

"Like I slept all afternoon." David answered and laughed. Alan laughed too.

"*I meant your ribs.*"

"They hurt, but I'm still alive."

"*Ok, still want to come out tonight?*"

"Yea. I dug out some pretty awesome books for it too."

"*Oh, great, David. Would you like me to pick you up?*"

"I think I can manage."

"*How many books do you have to bring?*"

"Nine." David answered and giggled. Alan sighed.

"*I'll pick you up at quarter to seven, you can't carry that stuff to the library with your ribs the way they are.*"

"If you insist." David said and grabbed a cigarette from his pack.

"*I do.*" Alan said. It sounded to David as though he also lit a smoke.

"Hey, did you talk to Mrs. Coldiron?"

"*Oh yea I did. She said considering your health, she would be kind and not assign anything for you.*" David raised his eyebrows.

"Wow, she loves homework."

"*Yea well, I think she has the hots for me so . . .*" David laughed and took a drag from his cigarette.

"That's just wrong, Alan." David said. Alan laughed.

"*Why? I'm a handsome guy.*"

"Maybe, but she's like a walking cadaver." Alan burst out laughing. David joined him.

"*David!*" Alan said through his seductive laugh. "*That's hardly fair.*"

"What? It's true. She's like 150 years old." David said laughing.

"*I don't think she's that old.*" Alan said. David smiled.

"She's at LEAST 40." Alan laughed again.

"*Uh huh. Very good.*" Alan said. David laughed and took another drag from his cigarette. "*Why did you ask about my teacher earlier?*" Alan asked when the laughing and kidding subsided. David cleared his throat.

"Just curious."

"*Oh, I see. It's kind of private. I don't mean to keep it from you.*" Alan said apologetically. David's heart thumped.

"I get that." He said trying not to sound as though his heart would leap out of his chest.

"*I was going through some shit in my life, and he helped me through it. It taught me a lot about myself.*" David listened quietly trying to keep his breathing steady. Alan continued, "*He was very knowledge in the crap that was going on with me, so he took it upon himself to help.*"

"That was nice of him." David said still keeping tabs on his breathing.

"*Yea, it was.*" Alan said in the same distant voice he had used in the truck stop.

"Do you still talk to him?" David asked trying to keep Alan talking.

"*Not as much as I would like to.*"

"Why don't you call him?"

"*I don't know.*" Alan answered. David felt a smile creep across his face. He thought to himself, *there's only one reason why I wouldn't call.*

"If you guys were so close, what's the big deal?" David asked. Alan was silent for a while.

"*It's a little complicated.*" Alan said. David almost fell off the couch. *You fucked him, didn't you?* David thought.

"Well, I hope you sort it out." David said trying to sound serious.

"*Maybe someday. I should go though and get my shit together here. See you at 6:45?*"

"Yea, I'll be ready." David said. They said their good buys and David sat silent staring at the phone for a while. Then he dialed Amanda's number.

"*Hello?*" It was Amanda.

"Alan fucked that teacher of his I think." Amanda laughed.

"*Why do you say that?*"

"I just got off the phone with him. We got talking about that teacher and apparently their history is *complicated*."

"*Really? Why?*"

"He didn't say, but you should have heard his voice Amanda."

"*What did it sound like?*"

"Like I do talking about him." David answered and stood up. He walked to the kitchen with the phone on his ear.

"*Wow, and you're pretty weird when you talk about him.*"

"I know. It's the same deal with Alan." David said as he dug some left over lasagna out of the fridge and popped it into the microwave.

"*Do you really think he's gay?*"

"No, I don't think he's gay. But he has certainly been with a guy. I can almost be absolutely sure about that."

"*Ok, so do you think he knows how you feel?*"

"I don't know, I'm accidentally obvious all the time. I try not to be but . . . well you've seen him." David said staring at the plate go round and round in the microwave.

"*And I've seen you around him. He can't be stupid enough not to notice.*" She said and giggled. David smiled.

"I know. I wish I was cooler about it."

"*I don't, I think it's sexy the way you react to him.*" David laughed.

"What?"

"*It is. It's like you're powerless against your own body.*"

"Well, that's true." David said and rolled his eyes.

"*Are you going to your mid-evil thing tonight?*"

"Yea, Alan's gonna pick me up at quarter to seven and I haven't even eaten yet."

"*Well, you do that and I'll talk to you tomorrow then.*"

"Ok, bye Amanda."

"*Bye bye.*" She said and they both hung up. David put the phone down on the counter and took his dinner out of the microwave. He took it to the table and ate it quickly. He washed up the bit of dishes that was in the sink and went up to the bathroom. He took a piss and then brushed his hair. He looked at the green bruise on his eye.

"Man that's nasty." David said and poked at it with his finger. He winced at the ache it caused and shook his head. He brushed his teeth and washed his face. He smiled at himself in the mirror and left the room. He stopped at his room and collected the nine books he promised Mr. Black. He winced at the pain in his ribs as he carried the heavy books down the stairs. He set the books down by the door. He looked at the time. Mr. Black would be there any minute. He slipped his feet into his shoes and carried his books outside. He set them down on the step and lit a cigarette. He sat down and watched the cars go by while he smoked. When he was almost finished his cigarette, a red Camarro pulled up at the end of his side walk. He smiled and put out his cigarette. Alan got out of the car and walked up the side walk to David.

"Hi." Alan said smiling at David.

"Hey, no Mustang tonight?" Alan looked back at the car.

"Don't think she's classy enough for you?"

"Oh, she'll do." David said and they both laughed. Alan picked up the books and heaved.

"You carried these down the stairs?" He asked as they walked to the car.

"Yea." David said with a little laugh.

"Their heavy." Alan said and set them in the back of the car. They both got in and Alan started the engine.

"It doesn't sound as hot as the Mustang." David said.

"That's cause this one has turbo. Hear that whistle?" Alan asked as he stepped on the gas a couple times. David nodded and smiled. "She's hot enough." Alan added and put it in gear.

"You said you had four other ones in the shop." David said offering up conversation.

"Yea, there's a 1970 Oldsmobile Tornado in there. And two Corvettes. One is an 89 and the other is a 76. The 76 is a Shelby." Alan said and smiled. He turned on to the street that the library was on.

"What's the last one?" David asked looking at Alan. Alan smiled and looked back at David.

"That one is rare. It's a right hand drive import. Ever heard of a Lotus Elise?"

"Yea, on Grand Terismo." David said recalling his favorite car on his video game.

"Well, she's one of the first ever built. She's in rough shape but I plan on buying the kit for her someday." Alan said pulling up to park in front of the big doors of the library.

"That's cool." David said. Alan smiled and got out of the car. He got the books out of the back as David got out of the car. They walked into the library together and picked the biggest table in the place. Alan set out David's books and went back out to get his things. David sat down on one of the wooden chairs at the table. He looked around at the empty library.

"Kind of beautiful when its empty. Huh?" Alan said setting his bag and briefcase down on the floor. David looked at him and smiled.

"Yea, it is." David answered and looked around again at the 200 year old building. The town had restored it to as original as possible. The wood work was amazing and the windows were still the original stained glass.

"I was thinking of a show and tell kind of thing." Alan said as he took out some paper and pens.

"What do you mean?" David asked looking back at Alan.

"Well," Alan said picking up his brief case and setting it on the table. "You know how a lot of the weapons work, right?" David nodded. "Ok, then. Since you aren't the public speaker of the year." Alan said and smiled. David rolled his eyes. "I was thinking, as the other kids explain the weapons and torture devises, you could demonstrate."

"How?" David asked. Alan sat down on the chair across from David and leaned on the table.

"What if I told you I could get my hands on some of the old tools?" Alan asked and moved his eyebrows up and down. David giggled.

"Ok, like what?"

"Well, I already own a couple different swards, and I can get a guillotine." Alan said. David's eyes grew wide.

"Cool." David breathed. Alan laughed and leaned back on his chair.

"I have been making some calls and I think . . ." Alan said and stopped talking. He took out a paper from the stack and set it in front of David. David looked down at the paper and his breath caught in his throat.

"An Iron Maiden?" David said like a kid at Christmas. He picked up the paper and stared at the photo of the ancient machine. Alan smiled and nodded.

"My buddy back home knows a guy that has one. He said we could use it if we went and got it." David looked up at Alan and then back down at the paper with wide eyes.

"I've never actually seen one." David said. Alan was still smiling.

"Not a lot of people have. It's your favorite right?"

"Yea." David said still staring at the paper. They could hear the door open and saw a two of the other students come in. Alan stood up and thanked them for coming.

"Joe isn't gonna show." The girl said.

"Oh, how come?" Alan asked sitting back down.

"Well, he said he wasn't as interested as he thought he was." The girl said. Alan sighed and raised an eyebrow.

"Well, at least you guys are here." He said gesturing to the three of them. They chatted about Alan's idea for the presentation for a half hour.

"It doesn't look like Page is going to make it either." Alan said looking at the clock. "Let's not waste any more time waiting then." He said and handed out paper to David, Samantha and Ron. Both Samantha and Ron where grade 12 students. They thought it was cool that David knew as much as he did about the weapons. They wrote down the list of tools and weapons they could get their hands on. They all took three or four different books on the weapons they were to study.

"So, David. You know how to use these things?" Ron asked as they looked over the books.

"I know how they work, yea." David said steeling a glance every so often at the picture of the Iron Maiden.

"Think you can do this acting thing Mr. Black is asking for?" Alan smiled at David.

"Yea, anything is better than talking." David said and smiled. They discussed the way they would present the items. They had decided that Samantha and Ron would take turns explaining each tool and David would demonstrate how it is used.

"The Iron Maiden I will present." Alan said looking at David. Everyone agreed as some of the parts of the machine were hard to pronounce. They finished at 9:00 and Samantha and Ron left. Alan and David gathered up all the books and got ready to leave.

"Think they're an item?" David asked as they reloaded Alan's car.

"Oh yea." Alan said and they both giggled. They turned all the lights off and Alan locked the door behind them. They got into the car and headed to David's house.

"So, when are you going to get the Maiden?" David asked still thinking about the photo he had seen.

"I thought we would go next weekend." Alan said smiling.

"I can come?" David asked excitedly. Alan laughed and nodded.

"Sure, if it's ok with your mom. It's a long drive so it will be an overnight thing." David could feel his heart jump into his head. He swallowed hard and looked at Alan. He was paying attention to his turn on to David's street.

"Would we stay at your friends place?" David asked trying not to sound like Alan had just propositioned him.

"I will call and see. We will probably hotel it if that's alright." David's eyes rolled into his head. He shook it off and smiled at Alan.

"Yea, whatever is easiest." David said. His heart pounded in his chest and his palms sweat like he had just been caught stealing.

"I'll let you know what the plan is when I know. Ok?" Alan said as he pulled up to David's house. They both got out of the car and Alan went to get David's books.

"Hey, keep them. It's easier than hauling them back and forth." David said. Alan set the books back down and looked at David.

"Are you sure?"

"Well, yea. Are we gonna use them every project night?"

"I would like to."

"Then keep them till we're done." David said. Alan smiled and nodded. He walked with David to the door. David opened it and stepped in.

"Well, that went well, David. Stay home tomorrow if you feel like you did today, ok?" David nodded. "Say hi to your mom." Alan said and turned to go. David watched him leave.

God, you're sexy. David thought as he watched Alan get into his car and drive away. He shut the door and went into the kitchen. There was a message on the machine. He pushed play. *Hi honey. I'll be working late so don't wait up. I hope your project night went well. The school called and told me you went home. I hope your feeling alright. I'll call at 10 ok. Love you.* David smiled and erased the tape. He went to the kitchen and grabbed a pop from the fridge. He looked at the clock. It was 9:30. He yawned and headed up to his room. He took his jacket off and hung it on the folding chair. He set his pop down after taking a big sip and opened his journal.

Sept 19, Monday.

Well, the project is gonna be sweet. Alan is gonna let me play with an Iron Maiden. Speaking of that, we have to go get it. Far away. He wants to get a hotel while we are gone. I'm not too sure what to think but I plan to be ready for anything. I think I might get Gabe over here again and learn what I can as far as being with a dude is concerned. I think Alan may have a little experience in the subject so I better know something just in case.

Todd got a 100 yard restraining order and 6 months house arrest for what he did. I don't know if that's justice but it will have to do.

Amanda's parents are splitting up and selling the house. Gabe is gonna try to buy it and keep Amanda with him. I think having BOTH Amanda and Gabe next door all the time is gonna be a juggling act from hell, but hey, that seems to be the way my life is going these days.

Anyway, thanks for listening.

David closed his journal and took another sip from his pop. He got up and went to his bed. He set the can down on the night stand and lit a cigarette. He lay on his back staring at the ceiling.

A road trip with Alan. Why am I so nervous? Don't I want to get with him? I guess it's like staring down a fantasy or something. Maybe Gabe would know why I feel the way I do. He seems to have a handle on this whole thing. And him being next door all the time is gonna be weird. I'm surprised at how much I like him. Fuck he's like super-hot all of a sudden. Fuck my life is weird. Just then the phone rang. David put out his cigarette and picked it up.

"Hello."

"*Hi Hun. How are you feeling?*" It was Nancy.

"About the same." David said rolling back over onto his back.

"*Oh sweet heart. Did you get any rest this afternoon when you came home?*"

"Yea, actually, I slept till six."

"*Oh, that's good. With a nap that long, do you think you'll sleep tonight?*"

"Oh, I think so. Get this mom. I get to fuck with an Iron Maiden for the Mid-Evil project."

"*Oh really? Which one is that?*"

"It's the standup coffin with the spikes in it. You know, the one that makes your stomach turn."

"*Oh, that one. You are strange.*" Nancy said. David could imagine her shivering and putting her hand over her mouth like she did the first time he had shown her a picture or it.

"Yea, Mr. Black can get one and he wants me to go with him to pick it up next weekend."

"*Oh, that sounds like fun. Where is it?*"

"His buddy has a handle on one. I guess it's pretty far. He said it would take two days."

"*Oh, like a holiday.*" Nancy said. She seemed pretty cool with the whole thing.

"Yea, can I go?" David asked shocked at his mother's willingness to send him away with a strange man.

"*Well, why not? Do you want to go?*"

"Hell yea." David said. Nancy giggled. "Mr. Black said he would call you and give you the details."

"*Well, its fine with me dear. You should get out of town for a while. Given what has happened.*" David sighed.

"Well, thanks mom."

"*Of course dear. I'll make sure you have spending money for the trip. But I have to get going. I'll see you tomorrow ok.*"

"Ok. Mom. Bye."

"*Bye, love you dear.*"

"Love you too mom." David said and hung up the phone. He lay back and smiled at himself. He closed his eyes and quickly drifted off.

"You fell asleep in your cloths." A whispering voice said waking David from his sleep. He opened his eyes and saw Gabe lying next to him. David smiled and rolled over to face him. He yawned and stared at Gabe.

"What time is it?" He asked squinting. Gabe looked over David at the alarm clock.

"Its 1:30." He answered still whispering. David raised his eyebrows and smiled.

"What are you doing here?" David asked and ran a hand through his hair.

"I was thinking about what you were asking me and thought you might be up for a talk." Gabe said and rolled over on to his back. David did the same and they both stared at the ceiling.

"Ok, in the middle of the night?" David asked giggling. Gabe smiled and nodded.

"In the middle of the night." He said and put his arms behind him so he could rest his head on them.

"Well, that was nice of you." David said smiling and resting his hands on his stomach.

"I aim to please."

"I bet you do." David said and they both laughed.

"How was your evening?"

"Interesting. Alan has asked me to go for a two day trip to pick up an Iron Maiden."

"Wow, that's sexy." Gabe said and David smiled.

"Yea, he mentioned hotel and I think I passed out for a second." David said. Gabe turned his head and looked at him.

"What?"

"Well, my eyes like, rolled back for a second. It was weird." Gabe smiled and shook his head.

"David, you need to calm down dude." David frowned and looked at Gabe. Gabe laughed and looked at the ceiling again. "Why do you think that shit happens?"

"I don't know."

"Cause you want him as bad as you do. If I was to guess, I would say just the thought of him makes you crazy right." David nodded. "You need to try to think of something else when you're around him."

"Like what?"

"Who knows anything? But you can't be sporting wood and be ready to cum every time you see him." Gabe said and smiled. David sighed and shook his head. "Look, I've been where you are, David. It sucks I know but if you think you may have the slightest chance with this dude, you don't want to blow it by psyching yourself out."

"I can't seem to help it." David said and looked at Gabe. Gabe rolled over and faced David. He propped his head up on his hand. His hair was long enough to touch the bed and David smiled at his masculine beauty.

"You need to, David." Gabe said. David nodded and sighed.

"It doesn't happen all the time."

"I know, only when he mentions the possibility of sex or even just being alone with him, right?"

"Yea, how do you know all this?"

"Like I said. I've known a guy that did the same thing. I got with him eventually, but that's not the point."

"Does anyone ever deny you?" David asked rolling to face Gabe. Gabe laughed and nodded.

"Not every hot dude is gay you know."

"I know. God this is so fucked up."

"Why?"

"I can't get my dad out of my head."

"That is fucked up." Gabe said with a sadistic look on his face. David rolled his eyes.

"Not like that, you weirdo." David said. They both laughed. "I mean, I remember something he told me once and I can't shake it."

"What was it?"

"He told me about a time him and a bunch of his drugged up buddies beat some guy half to death just cause he was gay. He seemed pretty proud of it too. I just think it's strange that this would happen to me when . . ."

"You had a dad who lynched fags?" Gabe finished the sentence for him. David nodded and sighed.

"Look, my dad is a lot like your dad when it comes down to that shit, David. That's why nobody knows about me. I couldn't add fuel to an already blazing fire. My dad would have blamed my mom and they would have more to fight about. I keep it to myself and their the better for it. It's not like your dad is around to see it."

"I know, but you're different than me, Gabe."

"How is that?"

"You got your life all figured out. You can deal with this shit better than me." Gabe laughed and tossed his head back.

"Yea, I'm a poster child for normality. David, I had a fucked up time with it too when I first started to accept it. I think everybody does. I still get worried about my dad finding out or someone hating me just because I like guys."

"You do?"

"Yea, fuck. I don't think that ever goes away."

"But how do you keep it all together?"

"You still like girls, right?" Gabe asked. David nodded. "Well, do you act like a lunatic around them?" David laughed.

"No."

"Same thing, man. Just cooler plumbing." Gabe said and rolled back over onto his back. David looked at him for a while.

"What was your first time like?" Gabe sighed and cleared his throat.

"I was scared out of my mind but really horny at the same time." Gabe said and rested his hands on his stomach. "The guy was my roommate. I thought he was like, the sexiest thing I ever saw in my life. Something like you and Mr. Black." David nodded and listened to Gabe's story. "It was just after Christmas holidays. Everybody was getting ready for the second semester. We were having a couple drinks and talking about our families back home. It was all pretty normal conversation. Then all of a sudden, he just kissed me."

"Whoa." David said and giggled.

"Yea, you're telling me. I was shocked of course. But not as shocked as he was when I didn't pull away."

"Then what happened."

"Well, "Gabe said and rolled to face David again. "We stared at each other for a while not even blinking. I don't think we even breathed." David smiled and nodded. Gabe continued, "He asked me if I liked it. I said yes. He was pretty surprised. Anyway, I jumped on him and stuck my tongue down his throat. That pretty much sealed the deal."

"So you guys had sex then?"

"Not right away. I was scared and he was, let's just say, eager to teach." David smirked. "We did all kinds of things till I practically begged to fuck him."

"You what?" David said with surprise in his voice. Gabe laughed and nodded.

"Just wait till the first time a guy gives you head and see how far you'll go after that." David's eyes grew wide. Gabe giggled and rolled back over to stare at the ceiling. David did the same and exhaled a deep breath.

"That's cool." David said. Gabe laughed and shook his head.

"Anything a chick can do to you, David, I can guarantee you could do to a guy even better."

"Why?"

"Cause you're a guy. You know what feels good." Gabe said. David turned and looked at Gabe. Gabe looked over at David. "What?"

"It's nothing. I just feel like a clumsy virgin all over again." David said and sighed.

"You are a clumsy virgin, David. Most dudes are. Cause you know, virgin literally means never been entered by a man."

"I knew that, but . . ."

"I know what you mean. Don't worry, if you like it, it all comes pretty naturally."

"It does?"

"Well, did fucking Amanda need an instruction manual?" David blushed and shook his head. "Did she say you were good?"

"Yea." David said and looked up at the ceiling.

"She isn't lying either. She told me all about it. I couldn't sleep for a week." Gabe said. David laughed.

"What? Why?" Gabe sighed and cleared his throat again.

"She was fairly . . . candid about the whole thing."

"So?" David asked. Gabe laughed and shook his head.

"She told me over the phone. Every . . . little . . . detail. I was hard as a rock just thinking about it after that." David laughed and held his painful ribs.

"What?" David asked is disbelief.

"Yup, the way she explained you in the bedroom was like listening to the invention of sex."

"No way."

"Yes way. Or she exaggerated. One of the two." David and Gabe both laughed. David winced at the swollen reminder of Saturday night in his chest. Gabe winced and moved closer to David he sat up and lifted David's shirt. "Looks bad, dude." Gabe said gently touching the bruising.

"I think it's out again." David said. Gabe felt the spot he had fixed before. He nodded.

"I think your right." He said and squinted at David. "Want me to fix it again?"

"God, if you think it will help." David said and shut his eyes. He felt Gabe's hand find the spot he had popped into place before. He held his breath waiting for Gabe to administer the painful push for the second time. Instead he felt Gabe's kiss. He hissed back and expelled the air from his lungs. That's when Gabe pushed. "Uh, FUCK!" David yelled and heaved a breath.

"Sorry." Gabe said. David looked up at him. His hair shrouded his face and reminded David of some kind of mid-evil wizard or something.

"That sucked dude." David said. His voice cracked with pain.

"I know." Gabe said but staid where he was. David stared into his eyes.

"You know something?" David asked as the throbbing in his chest subsided to a dull roar.

"What?" Gabe asked in his quiet sexy voice.

"You're like, really hot." David said. Gabe smirked and shook his head.

"It's the hair right?"

"Yea, I think so." David said and giggled. Gabe laughed and tossed his head. His hair settled on his back like black silk. "It's definitely the hair." David added.

"I would love to fuck you, David." Gabe said with a nervous smile. David took a shaky breath that hurt his ribs. Gabe sighed and moved to the side of the bed. He sat there with his back to David. He reached for his cigarettes and lit one. David lay there puzzled for a while.

"Why don't you?" David asked. The question shocked both of them and Gabe spun his head around to look at David. David had wide eyes and Gabe realized it was as just as a surprise to David as it was to him.

"Uh," Gabe said with a surprised sort of half laugh.

"Sorry, I don't know where that came from." David said blinking as though he had been momentarily possessed. Gabe's face cracked into a half smile and David giggled.

"That's a uh . . . interesting burst of truth there David." Gabe said and laughed.

"Why? You don't think I would believe that you wouldn't do it if I pressed the issue enough?" Gabe shrugged.

"Kissing and touching is one thing, David, but to go all the way is . . . You just have to be sure, ok?" Gabe said.

"You went all the way the first time."

"No, no I didn't. I had my fair share of practice runs before Chad."

"Oh," David said. Gabe bit his lip and shook his head.

"I'm not saying no, David." Gabe said. David had shock on his face again and Gabe smiled. "Just, do me a favor before you go choosing your first time ok?"

"Ok, what?" David said still shocked at the whole conversation.

"Heal, for one thing." David smiled and nodded. "And make damn sure Mr. Black isn't going to do it." The statement surprised David.

"Huh?" Gabe laughed and shook his head.

"Wouldn't you rather your first time be with him?"

"I never thought about it."

"Do you think Amanda went out and practiced before she gave it up to you?"

"No." David said and finally understood what Gabe meant.

"Dude, I would do you right now if I was the one that triggered this in you. But I think you should see what the story is on Mr. Black first. I don't mind being second on the list." Gabe said. Then added "I am on the list, right?" David laughed and lay back down.

"Yea. You're on the list."

"Awesome." Gabe said and smiled. "But I better go before you start begging for me to do god knows what to your poor frail body." David laughed and nodded.

"Thanks for the talk, Gabe."

"Yea, of course." Gabe said and stood up. He quietly opened the bed room door and turned back toward David. "Try a line on him and see what happens."

"Like what?"

"He's gonna let you drive that car right?"

"Yea."

"Ask him if you look as hot as he does driving it. See what he says."

"Ok. What if he says no?"

"He won't. It's the way he answers that I'm more interested in." Gabe said and stepped out.

"See you, Gabe."

"Chow." Gabe said and disappeared into the dark. David shook his head and closed his eyes. He was asleep in minutes.

Chapter 14

The sun on David's face woke him the next day. He squinted and looked at the clock. It was 11:30.

"Shit!" David said and jumped out of bed. Pain shot through him like a bullet and he fell to the floor with a hard thunk. He could hear someone run up the stairs and push open the door.

"What happened?" It was Gabe. He picked David up off the floor and sat him down on the bed.

"What are you doing here?" David asked reeling in pain.

"Your mom asked me to come stay with you today. She decided to keep you home for a few days till you heal up a bit. I brought little Mike over with me this morning when she left for work. Are you ok?" David coughed and winced.

"I thought I slept in and I jumped out of bed and then you were here." David said Rubbing his rib cage.

"Come on. Well get you in the tub and I'll make coffee ok?" David nodded and followed Gabe to the bathroom. David peed while Gabe filled the tub with water.

"A bath?" David asked.

"The hot water will feel good. Come on, get your clothes off." David rolled his eyes at Gabe's sadistic look. Gabe helped him get his clothes off and lay down in the tub. "Want a smoke?" Gabe asked.

"Yea, that would be good." David said as he let the hot water cover him like a warm blanket of healing. Gabe left the room and returned in a few minutes with a lit cigarette and an ash tray. "Thanks." David said and took a drag from the smoke.

"Ok, you lay here, all naked . . . and healing . . ." Gabe said and David rolled his eyes. "I'll go make coffee. Are you hungry?" David shook his head no and Gabe left the room. David lay in the hot water. It felt good against his sore body. He laid his head back and stared at the battle between the steam from the tub, and the blue smoke from his cigarette. He finished his cigarette and butt it out in the tray. He laid his head back again and closed his eyes.

A couple days off huh? It could be worse I guess. I could be at school. I wonder what Alan is wearing today. Probably something that looks like a million bucks. David thought and sighed. The water seemed to massage his ribs and David moaned. It did feel good. The water seemed to be doing its job.

So, work a line on Alan. That should be murder. He thought to himself. *Hey, Alan. How do I look? As hot as you? No that's dumb. So, do I look as good as you do driving this thing? Oh sure, David, I never thought you could look so good holding my stick.* David laughed to himself and shook his head.

"Hey, Gabe!" David called. He listened for Gabe to come up the stairs. He peaked his head in the door.

"You rang?" He asked in a voice that mimicked Lurch from the Adams Family. David laughed.

"I was thinking about that line to use on Alan."

"Yea, and?" Gabe asked coming in and sitting on the lid of the toilet.

"I think it sounds dumb." Gabe laughed and shook his head.

"Why? It's classic."

"Well listen, do I look as hot as you do driving this thing?"

"Don't say 'driving this thing'" Gabe said laughing. "Say something like, 'What do you think? Hot or what?'" Of course you'll be referring to yourself.

"It sounds better when you say it." David said and laughed.

"That's cause you're not confident enough. It will come." Gabe said and stood up. "Ready to get out?" David sighed.

"Yea, I think so." Gabe put his arms under David arm pits and helped him up. David stepped out of the tub and Gabe pulled the plug. David dried his legs and arms. Gabe took over to do his back and gently dry his chest.

"You are sexy, David Smith." Gabe said as he pat dried his chest.

"Yea, I know." David said sarcastically. Gabe laughed and helped David into the robe he had found for him. They went down stairs to the kitchen where David seen little Mike playing in his play pen and two cups of hot coffee on the table. "You're gonna make a good wife someday." David said to Gabe.

"Fuck you." Gabe said and laughed. David laughed and sat down at the table. He sipped at the coffee and looked out the window. They talked about David's pending trip with Mr. Black and all the possible lines he could use on him to get a feel for weather or not he was 'Fair Game' as Gabe called it.

The next few days were about the same. Gabe took care of David and Little Mike. They talked about the guys Gabe had been with and the coming trip of David's. Amanda would come over every day to visit David after school and then relieve Gabe of little Mike when she left. Nancy came and went as work beckoned. Mr. Black kept David updated on what he was missing at school every evening with a phone call. Alan had talked to Nancy about the trip and it was a go. They were to leave right after school on Friday. David felt better every day and was sure he would live through the week end with Mr. Black no matter what happened.

On Friday morning, David awoke to find Gabe lying next to him.

"Good morning." Gabe said and smiled.

"How will I go on when you're done playing nurse maid?" David asked and smiled.

"I was wondering the same thing about myself."

"Why?" David asked as he had the first successful stretch since his fight with Todd a week ago.

"I'm gonna miss that gorgeous morning wood you always have." Gabe said and smiled.

"Fuck, whatever. Like you don't get it." David said and sat up. Gabe laughed and handed him his cigarettes and lighter.

"Not like you do. That's epic man." Gabe said. David looked down at his swollen penis. He rolled his eyes and lit his cigarette.

"Whatever." David said and laughed again. Gabe smiled and sat up.

"So, big trip today. Are you ready?" David lifted one eyebrow and looked down at his erection again.

"Looks like it." Gabe laughed and shook his head.

"You're my hero man." He said. They both laughed and David stood up. He stretched his back again and grunted. "Still hurt?"

"Yea, but not as bad as it did." He said and went to the bathroom. He peed and got ready for a shower. Gabe came in after him and shut the door.

"Think you can do it yourself today?" He asked as David stepped into the tub and turned the water on. He lifted his arms carefully above his head.

"Maybe. Wanna spot me anyway?" He asked. Gabe smiled as David shut the curtain. Gabe undressed and got in with him. David looked at Gabe's naked body with wide eyes.

"I figured," Gabe said moving David out of the water and wetting his silk black hair under the water. "I have seen you naked every day this week. I thought I should return the favor." David's eyes were still wide. He carefully studied Gabe's body. His hair hung down his back like satin sheets. His broad chest and shoulders slowly shrunk down to his ripped stomach. His hips were as defined as his jaw line was. David stopped at his penis. It was about the same size as his but seemed thicker. David took a deep breath and looked back up at Gabe's face. "Well? How does a naked guy make you feel?" He asked with a straight face. David raised his eyebrows and shook his head.

"Well, I don't know." David said and moved Gabe out of the way and wet his own hair. Gabe smiled and applied shampoo to his hair. He handed the bottle to David and he did the same. Gabe watched David wince as he rinsed the shampoo out but let him do it himself anyway. David moved and applied conditioner as he watched Gabe rinse now.

"You know, I've never showered with a guy before." Gabe said as he moved to let David rinse out the conditioner and apply his own. David laughed as he rinsed.

"Me neither." He said.

"It's kind of cool." Gabe said as David moved and watched Gabe rinse the conditioner out of his hair. He watched the water wonder down his body, over his penis and finally down his legs.

"Yea, it is." David said and grabbed Gabe by the hips. He pulled him in and kissed him. Gabe kissed back wrapping his arms around David's shoulders. David could feel Gabe's erection forming against his own. They stood there kissing for quite some time. They were both fully exited when Gabe pulled away and looked David up and down.

"Wow." Gabe said resting his eyes on David's erection. David giggled and shook his head. David looked at Gabe. Gabe was bigger than David as he expected. He took a deep breath and looked back up at Gabe's face. "So, now how do you feel?" Gabe asked still standing in the water. David raised his eyebrows and took another deep breath.

"Horny." David answered. Gabe smiled and pushed David against the wall. HE pressed his body against David's and kissed him again. David moaned and Ran his hands down Gabe's wet back. Gabe took David's erection into his hand and David gasped. Gabe giggled and continued kissing him. David's hands gripped Gabe's hips while he massaged David's penis. David moaned again and put the back of his head against the shower wall. Gabe looked at David's face. His eyes where closed and his breathing was heavy.

"Wow." Gabe whispered and David looked at him. Gabe smiled and shook his head. David grabbed the hand that Gabe touched him with and squeezed it to tighten his grip. Gabe smiled and kissed David again. David slowly ran his fingers around Gabe's hips to the front and took Gabe into his hand. Gabe moaned and kissed deeper. David massaged Gabe in time with Gabe's movements. "Holy fuck, David." Gabe breathed as they kissed. David smiled and kept working. He could feel Gabe's body tighten as he moved. David moaned and kissed Gabe's shoulder. He could feel his orgasm building. Gabe knew it and tightened his grip a little more. "Me too, David." He whispered as David's body shook. Their breathing was equally heavy but David's orgasm came first. Gabe grabbed David's shoulder and kept his eyes closed as his orgasm came soon after. David kissed Gabe and whimpered. Gabe slowed the kiss and pressed his body against David's. David could feel the water had gotten cold.

"Gabe." David said between Gabe's light, after sex kissing. Gabe pulled away and looked at David. He looked worried and David smiled. "That was awesome." David said. Gabe smiled and kissed David again.

"Yea, it was." He said and pulled away. He turned around and shut the water off. They both stepped out of the shower and dried off. Gabe put his cloths back on as David brushed his teeth and hair.

"Did you plan that?" David asked as he applied his cologne and deodorant. Gabe laughed and shook his head.

"No, actually. I was just going to shower with you so you could see me naked." David laughed and shook his head. He watched Gabe brush his long black hair before they left the room and went to go find David something to wear. Gabe sat on the bed while David dressed.

"Where's little Mike?" He asked having the realization that Gabe hadn't gone down to check on him or anything.

"Mom's home today. I'm flying solo."

"Oh." David said as he did up the fly on his jeans.

"So, how do you feel now?" Gabe asked as David finished dressing and pulled on his leather coat. David raised his eyebrows and took a deep breath.

"Like I should have done that a long time ago." David said as he sat down beside Gabe and lit a cigarette. Gabe did the same and smiled.

"Good, I was scared I scarred you for life or something." David laughed and shook his head.

"Are you kidding?" David asked as if they did this all the time.

"No, I had this thought yesterday that, since your fight with what's his face, I've been hitting on you and getting all the free peep shows in the world." Gabe said. David laughed and Gabe continued. "It had occurred to me that the only naked dude you probably ever saw up close was your dad." David nodded in agreement. The shower room was closed off stalls so there wasn't a lot to see. David's dad, on the other hand, went skinny dipping every spring and drug every one along. "Then I thought, 'fuck Gabe, get naked and let him see."

"That's what you thought?" David asked and laughed.

"Well yea, I mean, it's one thing to think about it, but to see it, well . . ." Gabe smiled and raised his eyebrows.

"Yea, I get it." David said and ashed his cigarette into the ash tray.

"Well, I think you look amazing. Especially when you come." Gabe said and smiled. David smiled and raised his eyebrows.

"Dido." He said. Gabe laughed and shook his head.

"Dido? That's very Swayze of you."

"Sorry, I mean . . ." David stuttered and Gabe laughed.

"I know what you mean, and thank you."

"You're welcome. So now what?" David asked.

"What do you mean, now what?"

"Well, now what do we do?"

"We go drink coffee." Gabe said and stood up pulling David to his feet with him. They went downstairs and Gabe got coffees for both of them. They talked about the mid-evil project and the Iron Maiden trip. They had decided to play a game of cards when the phone rang. Gabe got the crib board ready while David answered.

"Hello."

"Oh good, your awake. How do you feel today?" It was Nancy. David smiled at the question and looked at Gabe. Gabe made a kiss form

on his lips and tipped his head at David. David shook his head and answered.

"A lot better today, mom. Really good."

"*Oh that's great dear. Are you all packed yet?*"

"No, I was gonna pack after lunch."

"*Ok, try not to forget anything ok. There is money in an envelope on the fridge for you.*"

"Ok, you won't be home before I go?"

"*No, I'm sorry dear. I really tried but the 12:30 surgery got pushed to 2:00*"

"No problem mom. I think I can lock up and stuff myself." David said sarcastically.

"*I know. Is Gabe with you?*" Nancy asked. David looked back over at Gabe again. He licked his lips and ran his hand slowly across his groin. David laughed.

"Yea, he's here." He answered.

"*Ok, I guess I'll see you when you get back ok.*"

"Ok, mom. Love you."

"*I love you too dear.*" She said and hung up. David looked over at Gabe and shook his head.

"You're a dick." David said and laughed.

"Yup." Gabe said laughing and they got to their card game. Their hands seemed to be evenly matched the first couple games but David was victorious over all. They had sandwiches and coffee for lunch and Gabe ran to the store to buy David some cigarettes while he packed. He packed his journal last and took his bag downstairs. Gabe got home with four packs of cigarettes and a bottle of rum.

"What's this for?" David asked as Gabe handed him the bottle.

"Well, I was thinking. You might get thirsty in that hotel room tonight." He said and smiled. David shook his head and set it in his bag with his cigarettes. "Got everything you need?" Gabe asked in a weird voice.

"Yes, why?" David asked looking at Gabe funny as they walked back out to the kitchen.

"No reason." Gabe said and smiled. David shook his head and looked at the time. It was 3:15.

"Holy shit. He's gonna be here pretty soon." David said and lit a cigarette.

"Yup." Gabe said and lit one for himself.

"Two days and one night." David said quietly.

"Yup." Gabe answered again. They smoked in silence as David stared at the clock. "You know, David." Gabe said, "He is really hot."

"Yea, I know." David said looking out the window.

"Like, really, really hot."

"I know, what's your point?" David asked. Gabe smiled.

"I'm just worried about performance." David frowned and looked back at Gabe.

"What the hell is wrong with my performance?" Gabe laughed and shook his head.

"Nothing. I'm pretty hot, right?"

"Yea." David said still a puzzled look on his brow.

"Yea, ok. I'm thinking about stamina."

"Stamina?"

"Yea, my advice. In case anything happens tonight, with him." Gabe said pointing out the window at the wine coloured Mustang Fastback. "Knock off the easy one first." David blushed and went to the door. "I'm serious man."

"Shut up." David whispered through clenched teeth as he opened the door.

“Hi David.” Alan said. He was wearing his sexy leather jacket and Blue jeans.

“Hi.” David answered and stepped aside to let Alan in.

“Hi.” Gabe said standing in the kitchen door way.

“Oh, Gabe right?” Alan asked and out stretched his hand. Gabe shook it and nodded. David grabbed his bag and shot Gabe a quick smile.

“Have a good time.” Gabe said and winked at David. David rolled his eyes and mouthed ‘thanks’. He followed Alan out to the car. Alan opened the trunk and David set his bag inside.

“Lock it up hey?” David called to Gabe. Gabe waved and David got into the car.

“He always at your place?” Alan asked as he put the car in gear and drove off.

“Yea, he nursed me back to health.” David said smiling.

“Well, remind me to thank him.” Alan said. David nodded and laughed. Alan pulled out on to the highway and pulled over.

“Why are we stopping?” David asked. Alan took off his seat belt and smiled at David.

“I worked all day, you drive.” He said and got out of the car. David got out of the car and they passed each other at the front. “Don’t hurt her.” Alan said as they switched sides.

“Wouldn’t dream of it.” David said and climbed in. They both did up their seat belts and David took a deep breath.

“You have done this before right?” Alan asked before David put the car in first gear. David looked at him and smiled.

“Wait and see.” He said and pulled out on the road. He got up to highway speed without a glitch. Alan smiled. David came up behind a truck and camper that was driving a little below the speed limit. He checked to see if the way was clear. Alan watched him as he gunned the gas pedal and passed. He smiled again at the boy at the wheel.

"Good job" Alan said and pissed around with the C.D. player.

"Well, I may have done this a few more times than I said." David said with a giggle. Alan smiled and pressed play. David listened as The Shortest Straw by Metallica filled the car. "Metallica?" David asked surprised.

"Yea, it's a weakness." Alan said and drummed along on the arm rest with his fingers.

"You're so weird."

"Why? Not a Metallica fan? I can change it." Alan said.

"No, no. It's just that, you're a teacher. You surprise me sometimes." Alan laughed and David smiled.

"I'm a man first, David. *Then* a teacher." David laughed and nodded. He gripped the steering wheel while Gabe's line ran through his head. He took a deep breath and asked.

"So, do I look as good driving this thing as you do?" David asked and looked back and forth between Alan and the road ahead of him. Alan smiled and took a long look at David. His dark brown hair fell to his shoulders. His leather jacket hung on him like a heavy metal shroud. He had one hand on the gear shift and one on the top of the steering wheel. His light coloured blue jeans were painted on him. His legs were spread open with one foot on the gas pedal and the other resting close to the door.

"Well, I don't know if you look as good as I do, but you certainly look like you belong there." Alan said. David smiled wondering what Gabe would get out of that. "Why do you ask?" The question was strange. Like hearing another language for the first time.

"Just wondering." David said as he listened to Metallica play. Alan raised an eyebrow and shook his head.

"And you say I'm weird."

"Hey, I'm a man first, Alan. *Then* I'm weird." David mocked and they both laughed. David drove to the hum of the stereo and smiled thinking of his morning with Gabe.

"So, it's a long drive. Are you the type that drives in silence? Cause if I can help it, I try to talk to *my* passengers while I drive." Alan said disturbing David's day dream.

"It's your car, it's your rules." David said steeling a look at Alan.

"Ok. So the Iron Maiden. What's the attraction?"

"Where should I start?" David said with a smirk. "I think the idea of a coffin that kills is . . . poetic."

"Poetic? How?" Alan asked looking through his C.D. collection he had brought along.

"Well, you're alive when they put you in that thing. When they close it on you, you slowly bleed to death through like, 200 or so holes punctured into your body. When you die, they haul your corps out and burn it. You never get a real coffin. It's . . . Edgar Allan Poe." David said. Alan shook his head and raised his eyebrows.

"Well, it's a cool device but, I don't think it wards as much consideration as you have given it."

"Why not. I feel the same way about the guillotine." David said keeping a straight face. Alan looked up at him with a weird smirk.

"What? A poetic guillotine?" David laughed and Alan shook his head.

"I'm just kidding. The guillotine is cool but doesn't even hold a candle to the Maiden." David said giggling.

"You're a serial killer aren't you?" Alan asked then laughed.

"Hey," David said looking over at Alan, "Don't tell anybody Kay?" Alan laughed again and kept looking through his C.D's. "Are you looking for something specific?" David asked as Alan skimmed through as if on some kind of mission.

"Yea, actually." Alan said and then smiled, "Here it is." He said and changed C.D's. David waited. Suddenly the car filled with electric cellos.

"Apocolyptica?" David asked with wide eyes.

"You know them?" Alan asked.

"Yea, there awesome. The things they can do with a cello, uh." David said and closed his eyes for a second. He opened them to look at Alan.

"Have you noticed the same weird thing I have noticed?" Alan asked. David racked his brain wondering where the conversation had gone.

"That depends." David said tapping the steering wheel along with the music. "I've noticed a lot of weird things." Alan laughed at David's answer.

"How is it that we can have a 28 year age difference and be almost exactly the same?" The question was strange to David.

"I doubt we are *exactly* the same." David said.

"Well, of course there are differences. Fingerprints, shoe size, education and I am clearly the better looking . . . but otherwise, we're like Abbot and Costello." David laughed and shook his head.

"There is no way you're the better looking." David joked back. Alan laughed and lit a cigarette. He handed it to David and then lit one for himself.

"What I meant, on a serious note, was you remind me a lot of myself."

"Like when you were young?" David asked rolling down the window a crack to let the smoke escape.

"Yes. Exactly." Alan said reaching into the back seat and getting two pop from a grocery bag.

"Is that a bad thing?" David asked taking one open pop from Alan and taking a sip. He set the bottle in the cup holder and flicked the ash of his cigarette out the window.

"No, I just think it's strange." Alan said ashing his out the window on his side. David wondered *how* much they had in common. "So, I was going to ask. How bad were the injuries to your ribs?"

"Well, my rib is broken and I have a hell of a lot of bruising still. But I should live."

"Wanna tell me what *really* happened?" Alan asked. David stole another look at Alan. He took a drag from his cigarette while he waited for David's answer. David sighed and looked back out on to the high way.

"Todd and I had different ideas on what a good time should be." David answered. His heart thumped in his chest waiting for Alan's response.

"What did he do?" Alan asked. David took another deep breath and read a services sign on the side of the road.

"It's . . . complicated." David said and drove in silence.

"Hey, sorry for digging. I was just curious as to what merit's a fight these days between friends."

"Todd's not my friend. And don't apologize." David said feeling bad for making Alan feel uncomfortable. It was one thing for David to be uncomfortable around Alan, but for him to be uncomfortable around David was weird.

"Ok," Alan said. They were quiet for a while. David drove thinking about what the harm was in telling Alan what happened. A few minutes passed before David said,

"He wanted to have sex with me." Alan was quiet. David never looked at him. He kept his eyes on the road not sure he wanted Alan to say anything. Alan cleared his throat and spoke,

"So, he propositioned you and you hit him?"

"No, there was no propositioning." David answered trying to stay as vague as possible.

"Oh." Alan said and looked out the wind shield.

"It's no big deal. He should live a long happy life." David said thinking about the dull pain in his ribs.

"It is a big deal, David. Something like that can change a person."

"I'm sure he'll be fine."

"I meant you." Alan said. David thought back to Alan's warning about Todd again and sighed.

"I should be ok." David said and tried to smile convincingly at Alan. Alan smiled back.

"I'm sure you will." He said and thankfully tried to change the subject. "Thank goodness for Gabe though." David laughed and shook his head. "What's so funny? I heard he was there when it happened."

"He was." David said remembering his morning shower and smiled.

"He's been taking care of you this week, right?"

"Yea, he's been cool." David said. Alan smiled and nodded.

"Well, that's good. It's important to have friends you can count on. He's a bit older than you, isn't he?"

"Yea, he's 26 or 27 now."

"Oh, he looks younger than that."

"I'll tell him you said that." David said and thought about how Gabe would react that Alan had thought anything of him. Alan laughed and shook his head.

"Well, you seem to get along pretty good." David smiled at the thought of Gabe's face when he came for David just hours before his trip with Alan.

"Yup. Your worst nightmare when we're together." David joked. Alan laughed and shook his head. He looked up at the coming signs.

"You wanna turn left up here." He said. David did as he was told and turned toward the Oregon border. He got the car back up to high way speed and got himself comfortable again. Another sign flew by them that said *Oregon 126 miles.* David raised his eyebrows.

"Are we going to Oregon?"

"Yup, Portland actually." Alan said. They talked about school and made fun of the other teachers. Alan filled David in on the interesting dirt that the students never get to hear. It was getting dark when David pulled into Portland. Alan looked at his watch. "So you wanna see it now or wait till tomorrow?" Alan asked with a devious smile.

"We can see it now?" David asked as though he was just told he could meet a real live angel.

"We can if you want." Alan said. They decided Alan would drive through the city. David pulled into a gas station on the south side of the city. Alan quickly refilled the car and they were on their way. They drove to the other side of the city. Alan took out his cell phone and dialed a number.

"Hi, we're here . . . . Uh I think so . . . . We decided to get a hotel instead . . . . we can yea . . . . Ok we'll see you there." He hung up and smiled at David. David waited quietly as Alan pulled into the parking lot of a brand new ware house.

"Now what?" David asked.

"Now we wait for Charlie." Alan said and got out of the car. David did the same and stretched. We rubbed his sides.

"Can I see?" Alan asked lighting a cigarette. David raised an eyebrow.

"It's not as bad as it was." David said and took off his jacket. Alan walked toward him as he lifted his shirt. The bruise was not as big as it was but it was still dark. The green circle around the outside was a wider ring.

"Wow, looks painful." Alan said and touched David's bruise. David could feel his heart jump and closed his eyes. He could feel Alan touch the broken rib and push it gently. He ran his fingers around David's bruise and then stepped away. David opened his eyes and put his shirt down. He smiled at Alan and put his jacket back on. "That's terrible." Alan said shaking his head.

"It was worse a week ago." David said taking a drag from his cigarette. He could still feel Alan's hand touching him. He shivered but Alan didn't notice. They both looked as a car pulled up to the ware house. It was a brand new Jaguar.

"That's Charlie." Alan said and walked toward the car. He shook hands with the guy that got out of the car. He introduced David and they chatted about the trip while they finished their cigarettes.

"Shall we?" Charlie asked and took the keys to the ware house out of his pocket. Alan smiled at David. David stared at the door as it opened. Charlie went in first and Alan let David go ahead of him. They walked over to a long line of light switches. Charlie turned on two of the switches and the ware house lit up. David looked around. There were a lot of things covered with dust sheets. There were a few things that looked like they must have been cars. He followed the two older men to the far side of the building. Charlie walked over to a six and a half foot dust sheet and smiled. "You wanna do it?" He asked David. David's eyes grew wide and he looked at Alan.

"Go ahead. She's under there." Alan said and smiled. David took a deep breath and Charlie stepped back to stand with Alan. "He's never seen one." Alan whispered to his friend.

"This is the kid with the obsession with the Maiden?" Charlie whispered back.

"In the flesh." Alan answered and then they fell silent and watched David put one hand on the dust sheet. He took another deep breath and in a single movement, he yarded the cloth off of the Iron Maiden. It pulled from the iron coffin like silk. David stared at the ancient machine. His eyes traveled from the top slowly to the bottom as if it were the first time he had seen a naked woman. David sighed and looked at Charlie.

"Can I touch her?" He asked. His voice cracked and Alan laughed.

"Fill your boots, son." Charlie said. David stepped closer and put his hands on the cold iron. He closed his eyes and ran his hand along the side to the latch that had locked and squeezed the life out of her victims. He felt Alan's hand on his shoulder. He turned his head to look at his teacher.

"Open it." Alan whispered in his ear. David's fingers worked the lock as if he had used it a thousand times. Alan smiled and stepped back as David opened it as wide as the door would go.

"So, will she do?" Charlie asked David. David looked at him with shock.

"Are you kidding?" Alan laughed at David's answer.

"You didn't think you were getting the real thing, huh?" Alan asked as David ran his hands along the blood rusted iron spikes. David swallowed hard and looked at Alan.

"This is the coolest this I ever touched." He said. Alan laughed and shook his head. Charlie was laughing to as he walked over,

"You mean to tell me a good looking kid like you never touched a woman?" David looked at him and smiled.

"I have. This is still cooler." David said and looked back at the 200 spikes of this beautiful machine of death.

"Well, you weren't kidding Alan my boy, he is obsessed." The two men laughed but David ignored them. He turned to face the spot her victims had stood. He stepped in and ran his hand along the long iron spine in the back.

"Have fun David, Charlie and I have to go over the paper work to ship this thing. You can't just through something like this into the back of a pick-up and expect to make it through the city." Alan said. David nodded and turned around and leaned against the spine. He put his feet into position and set his hands on the place where shackles would have been.

"Hey Alan." David called. Alan looked back from where he and Charlie looked through paper work. "I'm standing in an Iron Maiden." David said. Alan smiled and winked at him. David closed his eyes and leaned the back of his head against the spine. He thought about his morning with Gabe.

This might be even cooler than that was. I can't believe I'm actually standing in this thing. I wonder how many people died in here? David opened his eyes to see Alan and Charlie staring at him.

"Would you like some time alone?" Alan asked and giggled. David laughed and stepped out.

"Do you have the cleansing list?" David asked Charlie. Charlie raised his eyebrows at David then looked at Alan.

"You weren't kidding. He does know his Maiden, doesn't he?" Alan smiled and nodded. Alan dug in the paper work and pulled out an ancient paper that was protected with a plastic page cover. He handed it to David. David looked at it with wide eyes.

"Well, am I your new favorite teacher or what?" Alan asked. David looked up at him and shook his head.

"Alan . . . the things I can't find the words for." David said. Charlie and Alan both laughed again as David read over the names of the men and women that had had their last moment in the Iron Maiden that stood behind him.

"Come have dinner with my wife and I Alan." Charlie said. Alan looked at David.

"Think you could pull yourself away from her and have dinner?" David smiled and looked back at the Maiden.

"I don't know." David said and laughed.

"She's all yours for a month young lad." Charlie said and smiled. David handed the list back to Alan and shut the heavy door on the Iron Maiden.

"This is like a dream." David whispered to Alan as they walked to the door of the ware house.

"Well, I'm glad I could see that." Alan whispered back.

"See what?"

"You laying your eyes on that thing for the first time." David giggled and looked at Alan.

"I almost cried." David whispered as Charlie opened the door for them and they stepped out into the street lights. Alan giggled and shook his head.

"So dinner?" Charlie asked as he set the alarm and locked up the ware house.

"What do you think?" Alan asked David. David shrugged.

"You're the boss." He said. Alan smiled.

"You're on Charlie."

"Oh good, she was already expecting you." Charlie said. The two men laughed.

"We will follow you." Alan said. The men walked to their cars and got in. Alan and David had just shut their doors when David started to laugh. "What?" Alan asked as he started the car.

"That was so awesome, Alan!" Alan laughed at David's excitement.

"Well, glad you think so."

"Oh God! I can't believe that even happened." David said with a beaming smile on his face.

"Well, it happened." Alan said as he pulled out of the parking lot to follow Charlie's car. They drove through the city a little way before pulling into a new housing division.

"Wow, nice places." David said looking out the window.

"Yea, they are." Alan said and looked around at the big houses. They followed Charlie to the big brick house at the end of the street.

"Whoa." David said as they pulled through the gates and parked in front of the miniature castle that was Charlie's home. Alan laughed and shut the car off. He got out and David followed. An older woman was standing on the front deck.

"Alan Black!" She called with a big smile. She ran down the cobble stone walk and jumped into his arms. He caught her and hugged her as he spun around in a circle. He put her down and she looked at his face. "How long has it been?" She asked smiling at him.

"Uh, 10 years." Alan guessed and turned to face David.

"Paula, this is David." He said and motioned for David to come over. Paula took David's hand in hers.

"This is David? How do you do? We have heard a lot about you this past week."

"Hi." David said and smiled. Charlie came over.

"Won't you stay the night?" Paula asked.

"No, no. I wouldn't dream of putting you out." Alan said as they all walked up the stairs to the house. David looked around as they stepped in. The grand entrance way was made of marble and there was a huge stair case separating the room. A butler hurried over to them and took their coats. He hurried away from them and they walked into a room that, to David, was heaven. There were four silver knights lining the far wall. Above each was a sword and shield that hung on the wall. There was leather chairs that made a semi-circle around the large fire place at the right side of the room. They walked over to the chairs and all sat down.

"Fancy a drink Alan?" Charlie asked.

"Oh, absolutely." Alan said and turned to David. "Want one?" He asked with raised eyebrows. David looked around the room and leaned toward Alan. Alan leaned close to hear David.

"I'm not sure what to ask for." David whispered. Alan laughed and looked over to Charlie.

"What you got back there?" Charlie looked around behind the bar.

"Whatever you want I think." He said and laughed. Alan looked back at David and smiled.

"Well?" David thought for a second.

"What are you gonna have?"

"Scotch." Alan said. David sighed thinking of Gabe and nodded.

"Sounds good." Alan smiled then turned back to face Charlie.

"He's drinking with us." He said. Charlie smiled and poured the expensive looking Scotch into three crystal whiskey glasses. He poured red wine into a wine glass for Paula and set all the drinks on a serving tray. He brought the drinks over and handed them out starting with Paula. He took his own drink and set the tray on the little table next to the fire place and sat down on the chair next to his wife.

"So, are you still teaching History? Paula asked Alan.

"Yea, that's what we needed the Iron Maiden for . . ." Alan explained the mid-evil project and the fair starting on Halloween. Charlie and Paula smiled as Alan spoke. ". . . David here is the expert. I couldn't bring myself to come here without him." Alan said finishing his story. David raised his eyebrows.

"The expert?" Paula asked smiling at David.

"Well, I know a bit about her I guess." David said and sipped at his Scotch. Charlie laughed and said,

"A bit?" Charlie looked at his wife. "You should have seen it dear, this kid knew where to put his hands and feet."

"You got into it?" She asked surprised. David looked at Alan. Alan smiled and nodded as if it was safe to say whatever he wanted. David looked back at Paula.

"Why not?" He asked. Alan and Charlie laughed.

"It's a terribly horrifying thing." She said. David smiled and looked at Alan again. Alan laughed remembering David's spout of poetic justice during their drive.

"What?" Charlie asked.

"David has a spot in his heart for that thing. It's weird." David and Alan laughed. They discussed the shipping procedures. It turned out that the Iron Maiden would be shipped on the train. Alan still had to make arrangements with a trucking company to get it to the train station. Soon after, a butler came in and cleared his throat. Everyone stopped talking and looked at him.

"Dinner is served." He said and left the room.

"Oh, good. I'm starving." Charlie said and took his wife's arm. David stood up and looked at Alan.

"You doing ok?" Alan whispered as they followed Charlie and Paula to the dining room.

"This place is like the movies. Do they really live this way?" David whispered back. Alan giggled as they walked into the room. It was lit by a giant crystal chandelier. The long table was set with four places on the end closest to the entrance. Charlie sat at the end and Paula sat to his right. David and Alan sat to left of the table next to each other. David looked down at all the cutlery around his plate.

"Work your way in from the outside." Alan whispered as a butler filled the wine glasses in front of them with red wine.

"So, grade 11 huh?" Charlie asked as the butler's put out the first course in front of everyone. David looked down at the escargot and back at Charlie.

"Yes sir." He said and looked back down at his plate.

"They taste better than they look." Charlie said. Alan and Paula laughed. Alan picked up a long skinny fork with two prongs. David copied and stuck one of the snails on the fork. He looked at it and sighed.

"It's not bad David. Don't be afraid to try new things." Alan said and popped one into his mouth. David slowly put the fork to his mouth and put the snail in his mouth. He raised his eyebrows when he found he liked it.

"Not bad, huh son?" Charlie asked. David smiled and nodded. They chatted about Alan's new job at David's school while they ate. David sipped at his wine when he finished his escargot and looked at Alan. He talked quite comfortably with Charlie and Paula. He seemed to fit right in to their crazy life style. The butler brought out the next course. It was a T-bone steak, a baked potato and long green beans.

"There, David. Normal food." Charlie said and cut into his meat. David laughed and ate his meal. When they finished, Paula asked,

"Are you interested in dessert?" Alan looked at David. David felt like his insides would explode if he ate another bite.

"Uh, no thank you ma'am." David said as politely as he could.

"None for me either, Paula." Alan said. Charlie patted his wife's hand.

"Shall we?" Charlie asked. Alan patted David's leg and David shot straight up in his chair. The only one to notice was Paula. Alan and Charlie left to go back out into the den. David followed.

"David." Paula said quietly. David stopped and turned to face her. She walked up to him and took his hands into hers. David looked her in the eyes and waited for her to speak. "You and Alan are getting pretty close, aren't you?" She asked. David raised his eyebrows.

"Well, my mom thinks I need a good role model. She picked Alan." David said. She smiled and led him to the doors of the den.

"How do you feel about that?" She asked as they stopped outside the door. David smiled at her.

"I like him." David said and sighed. Paula smiled and rolled her eyes.

"Any fool can see that." She said. He looked at her with a puzzled gaze. "He is a good man, David. He will be good to you if you let him." She said and opened the door for him. David looked at her strange then looked at Alan. He smiled at David and waved him in. David looked back at Paula. She smiled at him. "I'm glad we could meet you. I'm glad he could meet you." She said and walked away. David walked in the room and went to Alan.

"You ok?" Alan asked. Charlie had gone to the bar to mix everyone a drink.

"Uh, yea. I think so." David said looking back at the door. Alan looked at the door and smiled.

"Paula is a special lady. She can see things about some people they can't even see in themselves." Alan whispered to David and smiled. David raised his eyebrows and sat down next to Alan.

"You're telling me." He said. Alan looked at David with a puzzled gaze. Charlie came over then with the drinks.

"When you heading back?" Charlie asked Alan as he sat down across from them.

"Well, tomorrow after we get David's girlfriend on the train." David laughed and shook his head.

"So soon?" Charlie asked with a frown.

"Well, it would be kidnapping if I don't get David home." Alan said laughing. Charlie smiled at David.

"I guess. It's uncanny isn't it?" Charlie asked looking at David.

"What?" Alan asked. He too looked at David and David shifted uncomfortably in his chair.

"He is so much like you were." Charlie said.

"Not in as much trouble though." Alan said and smiled. Charlie smiled and sipped his drink. Alan still looked at David. "So, what do you think?"

"About what?" David asked taking a big sip from his drink. Alan raised his eyebrows at how easily David swallowed such strong Scotch.

"This place?"

"It's, awesome." David said.

Chapter 15

David yawned as Alan pulled up to the hotel they had decided to stay in. They both carried their own bag into the room. There was two queen sized beds and a 26 inch T.V. on the small dresser. Alan and David both tossed their bags next to a bed each.

"Well, that was a day, huh?" Alan asked as he kicked off his shoes and lay back on his bed. David did the same and sighed.

"Yea."

"I hope Charlie and Paula didn't make you too uncomfortable." Alan said rolling on his bed to face David. David did the same and stared at Alan. He was propped up on one arm with his feet crossed.

"Uh, well Paula's weird." David said. Alan giggled and nodded.

"I thought so too at your age."

"So are you related to these people or something?" David asked. Alan smiled.

"I thought you would have figured out who Charlie was at least." David thought for a second and his eyes grew wide.

"That's the teacher you never want to talk about?" David asked. Alan laughed and nodded.

"That's the one." Alan said and stood up. He took his cigarettes out of his jacket pocket and through them on the bed. He took off his jacket and gently set it on the dresser.

"That's a good idea." David said and did the same. They both lit a cigarette and sat on the edges of their beds facing each other.

"What did Paula say to you after dinner?" Alan asked. David squinted his eyes at him.

"If I tell you will you tell me what the big deal is about Charlie?" Alan crinkled up his nose and sighed.

"Deal."

"Well, she said you were a good man and you would take good care of me if I let you." David said then took a drag from his cigarette. He stared at Alan and waited for his end of the deal. Alan sighed and stood up. He walked to the window and looked out at the darkness. David watched him and realized that it may not have been a fair trade. "You know what, Alan. Never mind." David said and dug in his bag for the rum. He looked through and found the bottle and pulled it out. Alan looked at him and a crooked smile crossed his face.

"What are you doing with that?" He asked and stepped away from the window. David stood up and set it on the night stand between the two beds.

"I feel like I kicked a nerve. The rum is a piece offering." He said and went to the bathroom. He grabbed two cups from the counter and brought them out. Alan was still standing where he had been when David walked away.

"It's ok, David." Alan said and took a cup from David. "We need mix." He said and went out to the car. David watched Alan dig around in the Mustang through the window. Alan hauled out the grocery bag and then went around to the trunk. The lid of the trunk kept Alan hidden from David's view. David sighed and turned to pour the rum into the two cups. He decided it was smart to not make them too strong since they each had two straight scotch and half a glass of wine under their belts. The door opened and Alan walked in carrying the bag in his teeth and a guitar case in each hand. David hurried over and took the bag from Alan's mouth.

"You brought them?" David asked wondering what they would plug them into.

"You bet. Gotta go get the amp." Alan said and went back out to the car. He brought the amp in and set it on the floor. David handed Alan his drink and helped him unpack the guitars. They plugged them in and Alan sat on the funny little chair across from David. David strung a few cords and stared at Alan. He took a sip of his drink and ran his hand along the wood finish of his guitar. David stopped strumming and sighed.

"Are you ok?" He asked leaning his arm over the cherry red guitar.

"You know something? That guy is like . . ." Alan stopped talking and started to play Knocking on Heavens door. David sighed again and joined in. Alan sang as they played. David shut his eyes and listened. When the song was over Alan sighed and took a sip of his drink. "He's just Charlie." Alan said and Smiled at David. David took a big sip from his drink and set it down on the side table.

"We don't have to talk about it, Alan."

"I know." Alan said and started to play Rocket Queen. David played along and listened to Alan sing again. The song filled the room and when they were finished, there was a knock on the door. "Shit." Alan said with a giggle and got up to answer it. There was a guy at the door. He looked like he was in his 20's. "Sorry, too loud?" Alan asked. The guy laughed.

"Dude, you guys rock! Know any Arrow Smith?" Alan laughed and invited the guy in.

"Hi." David said.

"Hi, I'm Jake." The guy said. David shook Jakes hand first and then Alan did.

"Hi, Jake. I'm Alan and this little guitar genius is David." David giggled and took a sip from his drink. Alan made a drink for their guest. "So, Arrow smith, huh?" Alan asked. Jake thanked Alan for the drink and sat down on the other little chair in the room.

"I know one." David said. He started to play Living on the Edge. Alan smiled and joined in. Jake sang along with Alan and drank his drink. When the song was done, Jake took the last sip from his cup.

"Thanks a lot guys." Jake said and stood up.

"We aren't bothering you are we?" Alan asked looking at the time. It was 10:15.

"Are you kidding? Carry on." Jake said and opened the door. He said bye and left. Alan and David laughed.

"We have fans." Alan said and got up. He walked over to the bottle. "One more before bed?" David looked over at his empty glass.

"Sure." David said. Alan mixed them both a drink and sat back down in his chair.

"Think the rest of our neighbors mind?"

"I don't know." David said and laughed. They decided to pack up the guitars. Alan used the bathroom first then David did. He came out to see Alan lying on his back on his bed making smoke circles with his cigarette. David lifted his shirt and looked at himself in the big mirror on the wall next to the dresser. He shook his head and laid on his bed the same as Alan. He lit a cigarette and stared up at the ceiling.

"Did you know he would try that?" Alan asked. David sighed and felt his heart speed up.

"No." David said. It wasn't a lie. He and Amanda both thought he was a decent enough guy.

"I never would have thought he would do something like that." Alan said. They both still stared at the ceiling. David watched the smoke from his cigarette circle on the ceiling. Alan took a sip from his cup and rolled over face David. David noticed to move and turned his head to look at him. "So, are you scarred for life or anything?" Alan asked smiling. David laughed and rolled to face Alan.

"I think we're safe." He said and took a sip from his cup. Alan smiled at him and sighed.

"Are you glad you came?"

"Yea, I am." David said. He stared into Alan's eyes for a while. Alan smiled and looked away. David all of a sudden felt awkward. He tapped his ash into the ash tray and took another long sip of his rum. Alan yawned and looked back at David.

"You look at me funny." Alan said and took a sip from his drink. David coughed and raised his eyebrows.

"I do?" He asked trying to sound innocent. Alan sighed and put his cigarette out.

"Yea, like your trying to read my mind or something." David laughed and took the last drag from his cigarette before putting it out.

"Last time I checked. I couldn't read minds." David said and rolled back over on to his back. Alan did the same and stared up at the ceiling.

"Afraid of the dark?" Alan asked. Alan's voice sounded like seduction.

"Nope." David said. Alan reached up and shut the lamp off. The moon light flooded the room.

"What are you looking for when you look at people like that? I saw you do it to Paula and Charlie too."

"Just trying to figure them out." David said and crossed his feet. Alan laughed.

"Good luck with that."

"I figured." David said and smiled. Alan got up and took off his jeans. David took a deep breath while he watched. Alan took off his shirt next and climbed under the covers. David swallowed hard and closed his eyes. The sight of Alan's bare chest etched into his mind.

God, help me. David thought.

"I don't know about you but sleeping in jeans is hard on the junk." David smiled and stood up. He undressed down to his boxers. Alan lay on his back with his eyes closed. David climbed into bed and stared back up at the ceiling. He closed his eyes and all he could see was Alan's half naked body. He could feel his groin twitch.

No, No, NO! Not now. He begged his body in silence.

"So, is he gay or was he just drunk?" Alan asked out of nowhere. David's eyes shot open and he turned to look at Alan. He was still on his back with his eyes closed. David looked back up at the ceiling and a shaky breath escaped his throat. Alan heard it and looked at David. David looked back at him but lay silent. "You don't have to tell me." Alan said still staring at David. David sighed and nodded.

"Yea, he's gay." David said and looked back up at the ceiling. Alan smiled and looked up at the ceiling above his bed as well.

"You didn't have to tell me that." Alan said. David lay quiet. He racked his brain for something to say but came up with nothing. Alan sighed. "You know. You probably reacted like anyone else your age would." David looked at him and laughed. Alan looked at him and frowned with a smile. "What?"

"I doubt that." David said. Alan laughed and shook his head.

"Why do you say that?"

"Well," David said and sighed. "I probably should have known, that's all. Seen it coming you know?" Alan raised an eyebrow and stared at David.

"How can you see something like that coming?" David sighed and remembered the make out session with Todd.

"I don't know, gut instinct or something." David answered.

"Well, those don't pop up for every situation." Alan said and rolled back over.

"So I have learned."

"How do you feel about it now?"

"Not too sure. It was a learning experience that's for sure." David said and closed his eyes. Alan smiled and closed his eyes two. There was silence in the room for a while. David brought back the picture of Alan in his boxers and smiled. He could feel his groin react again but he let it do its thing this time. It wasn't long before he was fully erect. He sighed and stared at the ceiling.

"Good night, David." Alan said in a sleepy voice. David smiled.

"Good night." He answered and closed his eyes.

David woke the next morning to find Alan was gone. He sat up and looked around. There was a note on the bed side table. He picked it up and read.

> Good morning sleeping beauty.
>
> Just went to find a coffee and talk to the trucking company about shipping your lady. I'll be back as soon as I'm done.
>
> Alan.

David shook his head and smiled. He grabbed his bag and went into the bathroom. He went pee and then jumped into the shower. He washed his hair and body and got out. He quickly dried himself and dug in his bag for something clean to wear. He found a clean pair of boxers and pulled them on. He found socks and pulled them on. He pulled out the pair of jeans. They unrolled and a tube of K-Y jelly and a note hit the floor. David frowned and picked up the note.

Just in Case.

"Fucking Gabe." David said out loud and laughed. He tossed the lubricant back into his bag and pulled on the jeans. He did them up and reached into the bag for a shirt. He pulled out a white t-shirt and put it on. He didn't recognize the form fitting shirt that left little to the imagination. There was another note taped to the front of the shirt.

Bet you look awesome in this.

David smiled and put the note in his bag. He looked at the shirt in the mirror. It did look pretty good on him. He brushed his hair and teeth and then applied his deodorant and cologne. He took one last look in the mirror and stepped out of the room with his bag in hand. As he stepped out of the bathroom, Alan came back into the room.

"Oh, hey." David said setting his bag by the bed. Alan looked at him and raised his eyebrows.

"Nice shirt." He said. David smiled and silently thanked Gabe. Alan handed him a coffee and sat down on the little chair he had used the night before. David noticed that the guitar and amplifier were already loaded into the car. "Well, we have hit a snag." He said as David sat in the other little chair.

"What's that?" He asked.

"We have to wait for the shipping permit."

"How long does that take?" David asked sipping his hot coffee.

"Well, we'll have it this afternoon but we have to be at the train station when your lady is loaded." David smiled.

"So?"

"Well, she gets loaded tomorrow." Alan answered. David raised his eyebrows and sipped his coffee again. "We'll have to stay in Portland for another night. That ok?"

"Yea. I'll just call my mom and let her know." David said. Alan smiled and handed him his cell phone. David dialed the number and waited for her to answer. He got the answering machine so he left a message. "Hi mom. We can't leave Portland till tomorrow so we'll be gone another night. If you get worried call Alan's cell." He said and hung up. "She has your cell number right?" David asked. Alan laughed and nodded.

"Yes I gave it to her just in case." Alan said and sipped his coffee. David smiled and thought about Gabe's 'just in case' note.

"So, how will we kill time then?" David asked lighting a cigarette. Alan did the same and thought for a second.

"We could go horseback riding." Alan said. David laughed.

"No, seriously."

"I'm serious. My buddy Carman has a horse ranch just outside the city." David raised his eyebrows.

"Ok." David said and sighed.

"Do you ride?" Alan asked as David grabbed his bag and left the room.

"Well, I have." David said. Alan loaded David's bag and got in the car. David did the same.

"Like, you have once or twice or you have like you've driven a stick a few times?" Alan asked remembering David's modesty about driving. David laughed as Alan started the car. "Well?" Alan asked.

David remembered back when Amanda used to take him out to her uncles horse and sheep ranch for a week every summer.

"Like . . . it's been a while." David said. Alan laughed and pulled out of the parking lot. David looked out the window at the down town scene that was Portland. Alan tapped his fingers on the steering wheel to music only he could hear. David looked over at him and smiled. Alan noticed.

"You're doing it again." Alan said.

"Doing what?"

"Trying to read my mind." Alan said and laughed. David shook his head.

"Just wondering what you're thinking about." David said staring at Alan's face. Alan sighed and looked back at David. He had stopped at a red light.

"I'm thinking about Charlie." He said and looked back out to the light. David watched the traffic go by taking their turn.

"What about Charlie?" David asked still watching the traffic. The light soon turned green and Alan drove on.

"Just wondering why he did all this for me." Alan said as he drove. David looked at Alan.

"I thought you guys were like, really close or something."

"We were. Remember I said we hadn't spoken for a while?"

"Yea."

"Well, the reason was . . ." Alan paused briefly, "that's not important. I just feel like he's sucking up or something." David raised his eyebrows.

"Lucky us." David said trying to lighten the mood. It seemed to work. Alan was smiling. They drove to the edge of the city and Alan turned into a driveway. "Wow, you weren't kidding. It is right on the edge of town." Alan laughed.

"Portland has grown since I've been out here. I would have probably missed it if I hadn't already talked to Carman this morning." David shook his head.

"Why didn't you just say you already planned to come out?"

"Well, I didn't plan to ride. We'll go if you want to." Alan said and stopped in front of the garage. The house was massive and almost as nice as Charlie and Paula's place.

"Are all your friends rich?" David asked as they got out of the car. Alan laughed.

"Well, these ones are." David shook his head and looked up at the house. Alan tossed David his bag. David looked down at it and back up at Alan. "Carman, we don't say no to." He said and smiled. David picked up his bag. Alan handed him a guitar case to carry in to.

"Does, *Carman* play?" David asked. Alan smiled and shook his head.

"No, but he sings just like Axel Rose." They walked up to the house and Alan yelled. "DEAD MAN WALKEN!" David laughed and waited to see what would come from the house. The door opened a nice looking man about Alan's age was standing in the door.

"You didn't trade me in for a younger model did you?" The man asked and came down the stairs. They both laughed and Alan hugged the man.

"Carman, this is David."

"Hi there." Carman said and shook David's hand. David said hi and Carman gave him a once over. David stood very still and looked at Alan. And put his hand over his mouth to conceal his laughter. "Huh. Not what I pictured." Carman said to Alan. Alan laughed. Carman started walking to the house and Alan moved close to David.

"He's harmless. He only bites if you ask him too." He said. Carman laughed.

"You're a dick Alan." They both laughed and David followed them into the house. The first this David noticed was a pool table where a dining room table should have been.

"What is this?" Alan asked setting his bag and guitar case to the side. He took David's bag and case and set it next to his.

"What? This?" Carman asked putting hands on the pool table. Alan laughed and nodded. "Well, when Jan left, I thought I would redecorate. I figured, Fuck 'em if he can't take a joke." Carman said. Alan laughed. David looked back and forth from Alan and Carman then the words 'Fuck 'em if *he* can't take a joke'.

Alan has a gay friend? David thought to himself.

"So, how do you put up with this guy every day?" Carman asked David gesturing to Alan. Alan smiled at David.

"Well, I sit quietly and let him do all the talking." David answered and smiled. Alan and Carman both laughed.

"A sharp one huh?" Carman said to Alan.

"Well, of course." Alan said and they made their way over to the living room. In there was the dining room table and a bar. "More redecorating?" Alan asked. David giggled looking around the room.

"Yup, you like?" Carman asked and sat down at the table. Alan and David joined him. David looked around the room and shook his head. Alan smiled at him and Carman winked at Alan. Alan gave him some kind of dirty look and they both laughed.

"Sorry, David. Carman is *my* Amanda." Alan said and laughed again.

"Hey, whatever floats your boat." David said and leaned back in his chair. Carman laughed and slapped the table.

"I love him already, Alan. Where did you find him?"

"He's in my grade 11 history class."

"Little old for high school aren't you?" Carman asked Alan. This time David laughed while Alan shook his head and smiled at his friend.

"Nice." Alan said. David laughed again and looked at Carman. He was actually quite attractive. He had short blonde hair he wore a little messy. He had a chiseled jaw line like Alan. He looked as though he was probably fairly well built.

"So, David. The Iron Maiden huh?" Carman asked leaning against the chair.

"Yea." David answered and looked at Alan. Alan smirked at him with the sexiest smirk David had ever seen him do. David looked down and sighed. Alan giggled and looked at Carman.

"Thanks a lot by the way." Alan said.

"Hey, when I heard you wanted her, I couldn't refuse. I called up Charlie right away and told him to hand her right over." David's eyes grew wide and he stared at Carman.

"The Maiden belongs to you?" David asked in a half whisper. Alan giggled.

"She sure does." Carman said and winked at Alan again. Alan shook his head and looked at David.

"Where did you get it?" David asked in a more steady sounding voice.

"Family air loom." Carman answered.

"Your family is the original owners?" David asked. Carman smiled and nodded.

"Pretty cool huh?" Alan asked David. David nodded and stared at Carman. Alan giggled again. "You're in trouble Car." Alan said and sat back in his chair. Carman looked at David's almost sexy stare.

"Well, wanna see the rest?" Carman asked David. David blinked and looked at Alan. Alan closed his eyes and suppressed a laugh.

"There's more?" David asked. Carman got up.

"Come on then." Carman said and Alan and David rose up.

"Prepare yourself." Alan whispered to David. David looked at Alan as they walked to the basement stairs. Alan smiled at him and let him go ahead down the stairs. David followed Carman down the stairs. Carman turned the lights on and got out of David's way. David looked wide eyed around the huge room. There was a collection of silver and red knights to one side. There were two Iron Maidens against the far wall. One was open and one was closed. There were hundreds of swords, axes and daggers hung on the walls. There was a guillotine in the middle of the room and two perfectly intact sets of war horse armor on fake horses. David let out a shaky breath and took a step forward. Alan stepped beside David. "Go . . . touch." He said and smiled. David looked at Carman.

"Hey, you break it, it's broken." He said. David walked over to the Iron Maidens first and ran his hand down the cold iron seems like he had done the night before. Alan stood next to Carman and watched as David caressed the machine he referred to as David's Lady.

"Thank you Carman." Alan said quietly.

"Hey, no problem, of course." Carman said and studied his friend. Alan looked at him.

"What?" Alan asked. Carman smiled.

"Why this kid, Alan?"

"What do you mean?" Alan asked looking back at David. He had made his way to the war horses and was inspecting the armor.

"You never took one of your kids on like this. Why this kid?"

"I don't know. He reminds me of myself." Carman raised his eyebrows and looked at David.

"He's a good looking kid." Carman said. Alan smiled and nodded.

"Well, what do you think?" Alan asked loud enough for David to hear. David looked at Alan and smiled.

"Would I be gay if I cried?" David asked and looked back at the armor. Carman and Alan laughed.

"Tears hurt the metal. Be careful." Carman said. David laughed and walked over to the guillotine. "That sucker is armed." Carman warned. David looked at him and raised an eyebrow. Carman giggled and left the room. Alan walked over to David.

"It would not be gay if you cried." He said and smiled. David laughed.

"This is the coolest weekend I have had in a long time." David said looking into Alan's eyes. Alan smiled and looked at the guillotine.

"He's gonna go find something for you to chop in half you know." David's eyes grew wide and Alan laughed. Just then, Carman came into the room with a watermelon in each hand. "Ok, two things." David giggled as Carman walked over.

"Know how it works?" He asked as he set one melon in the head slot.

"David could probably show *you* how it works." Alan said. Carman smiled.

"Really? Well, do show." Carman said and stepped aside. David smiled and walked over to the release handle. He pulled the pin and closed his eyes. "it's a melon kid, what's with the dark eyes?" David laughed and opened his eyes. He pulled the release handle and the blade came down. It cut through the melon like a bullet through a gun. Alan smiled at the look on David's face.

"Cool." David said. Carman clapped and had David reload the blade. He put the other melon on and let David pull the pin and chop the next one. Carman stood in front of the head bucket and smiled.

"I hope you guys like watermelon." They all laughed. David and Carman cleaned the blade while Alan picked up the melon pieces. David took one last look around before they headed upstairs. Carman took them to the back porch to sit on the deck furniture. "Well, what did you think of that David?" Carman asked as he handed Alan and David each a beer.

"That was awesome." David said and sipped his beer.

"Well, I gotta tell ya. When Alan called me and told me about you, I thought, wow. A kid like we were. I went out and picket up those melons special for you to mutilate." Alan laughed at Carman's confession.

"You talk about me a lot?" David asked winking at Alan. Alan laughed and shook his head. Carman laughed and kicked Alan under the table.

"Alan here has been looking for just the right kid for years now." Carman said. Alan looked down at his beer as Carman spoke.

"For what?" David asked. He looked at Alan but Alan didn't look up.

"Well, he's been working on those Mid-Evil fair ass wholes for years but couldn't get them to help fund a school. They gave him an ultimatum, find a kid that knows his or her shit about turn of the century war fair, and we will send funding to school of your choice." David looked at Alan. Alan looked up and smiled at David. "Those dicks have never liked a kid he has found yet. Trust me, David. You're like a gift from god." Alan smiled and shook his head.

"Now, Carman." Alan said.

"What? It's true. You can finally stick it to those cock suckers." David laughed and looked at Alan. Alan shook his head and changed the subject.

"Talked to Paul?" Alan asked. Carman smiled and shook his head.

“Nope. He’s too good for us anymore.” Carman said and stuck his bottom lip out. David giggled and looked back at Alan. Carman watched David watch Alan and smiled.

“That’s too bad. We could have used a drum player tonight.” Alan said and took a sip from his bottle.

“That’s right. You brought Susan and Gloria didn’t you?” David spit his beer across the table. Alan and Carman burst out laughing. David laughed too and looked at Alan.

“Susan and Gloria?” He asked. Alan smiled at him and shrugged.

“They needed names.” Alan said. Carman laughed and shook his head. Alan and Carman told David stories of when they were young and in school. Neither one mentioned Charlie.

Chapter 16

Carman left to go on a liquor run while David and Alan got the guitars ready in Carmen's music room.

"So, you're using me?" David asked smiling. Alan looked at him and sighed.

"It's not as bad as it sounds." Alan answered setting the wood finished guitar known as Susan against one of the stools. David laughed and shook his head.

"It's cool. I just like to stay in the loop, that's all."

"Well, what Carman said is true. But I'm not using you. I like spending time with you."

"You do?" David asked. Alan smiled and nodded. They finished getting ready and both sat down on a stool. "Can I ask you something?"

"Sure." Alan said resting his elbows on the bar behind him. David looked at the way his body seemed to scream sex and sighed.

"Is Carman gay?" Alan smiled.

"As queer as a three dollar bill." He answered and looked into David's eyes.

"Well, that explains a lot." David said. Alan laughed and tilted his head back. David watched the blood pump in his jugular and the muscles in his neck flex as he brought his head back to face David again.

"He's harmless."

"I don't doubt that." David said looking around the room.

"I'm only telling you that because of Todd. I don't want you to be scared of Carman."

"I'm not. I'm not scared of Todd either. Just the wrong place at the wrong time." David said and sipped the last of the beer out of the bottle. He handed the bottle to Alan and he set it on the bar behind him.

"Well, that's good." Alan said. Just then they heard Carman come in.

"DEAD MAN WALKEN!" He called from the door. Alan smiled and shook his head.

"What's with that anyway?" David asked. Alan laughed and looked at David.

"Well, we used to yell that when we came into the house just in case one of us was getting laid." David raised his eyebrows. Alan laughed. Carman came into the room with a bottle of rum and a case of pop.

"So, what did I miss?" He asked as he set the stuff behind the bar.

"We were just discussing getting laid." Alan said and spun around on his stool to face Carman.

"Damn it! I always miss the good conversations." He said and David laughed. Alan patted the stool next to him.

"Come on David. The bar tender is in." David laughed and came to sit next to Alan.

"What are you having?" Carman asked David as he tossed a towel over his shoulder. Alan laughed and shook his head. David ordered a rum and so did Alan. Carman mixed three drinks and ran around the bar to sit next to David. "Come here often?" He asked. Alan burst out laughing and patted David on the back.

"Play a long or you'll never live it down." David thought for a second and said.

"Has that line ever worked?" Carman looked at Alan. Alan laughed.

"Alright, hard ball huh?" Carman asked. David shrugged and took a sip of his drink.

"Try one on him." Alan whispered to David. David looked at Alan and smiled.

"So," David said and looked at Carman with the sexiest look he could muster up with out laughing. Carman squirmed in his chair and Alan giggled quietly. "How do you feel about giant . . . Italian . . . Sausage?" David asked. Carman closed his eyes and tried to keep a straight face. Alan burst out laughing and David took a sip of his drink, never cracking a smile. Carman let a shaky breath escape from his throat. He looked over at Alan.

"Don't look at me for help, you started it." Alan said and took a sip of his drink. David stared at Carman waiting for an answer. Carman took a sip of his drink and looked into David's eyes. David stared back straight faced.

"I like mine young." Carman said. Alan burst out laughing and Carman smiled. David did not crack. He raised his eyebrows and said,

"Careful old man," He said, then leaned in and whispered in Carman's ear but still stayed loud enough for Alan to hear. "I would give you a heart attack." Carman and Alan both laughed now. David smiled and took another sip from his glass.

"We have met our match Alan." Carman said looking around David to look at Alan.

"You play this stupid game too?" David asked. Alan smiled.

"Are you kidding? Alan's the champion." Carman said.

"Really?" David asked and looked at Alan. "Let's go then." David said. Alan rolled his eyes and looked at Carman.

"Hey, you wouldn't save me." Carman said and smiled. Alan looked back at David and sighed. David raised his eyebrows and waited. Alan stared into David's eyes for a few minutes then asked,

"Are you a betting man?" Carman giggled but David didn't look away.

"That depends on the wager." David answered. Alan's face was stone.

"Huh, you a god fearing man?" Alan asked staring deep into David's eyes. David could feel his heart pounding in his chest.

"Not overly." David answered. Alan moved his fist up and put it in front of his mouth. He squinted his eyes and parted his lips. David kept a straight face but his insides where screaming. Alan rubbed his lip with his thumb.

"Ever pray?" Alan asked in the sexiest bedroom voice David had ever heard. David cleared his throat and Carman giggled.

"No." David answered never breaking the show down. Alan looked David up and down and David could feel his body react so violently he thought he might fall off his chair.

"Well then, I bet I could make you." Alan said in that same sexy voice. David squirmed in his seat and Carman giggled again.

"He's gonna crack Alan." He said quietly but neither Alan nor David moved.

"Really?" David asked in the same bedroom voice Alan was using. Alan leaned forward with a seductive look in his eyes and put his lips close to David's ear. David cleared his throat again and waited. Alan breathed on his neck and whispered,

"Say oh God or I'll stick my tongue so far down your throat you'll choke on it." He pulled away. Carman waited. He hadn't heard what Alan had said but guessed it was good because David whispered,

"Holy God." Alan and Carman laughed and David took a sip of his drink.

"You ok?" Alan asked quietly as Carman picked up Alan's guitar and handed it to him. David smiled and cleared his throat again.

"You are the master." David said and moved to the stool next to the cherry red Stratocaster known as Gloria. Alan smiled and looked at Carman.

"What you singing?"

"What you playing?" Carman asked and winked at David. David smiled and looked at Alan. Alan opened up with Welcome to the Jungle by Gun's and Roses. David smiled and joined in. When Carman started singing, David was shocked. Alan smiled and continued playing. Carman danced in his chair while he sang. Alan let David have the guitar solo and Carman raised his eyebrows. They ended the song and Carman yelled, "Holy shit kid!" David and Alan both laughed. They were just about ready to play their next song when there was a knock at the door.

"Must not be anyone who knows the rules." Carman said and got up to go answer it. As soon as he left the room Alan said,

"Fuck David. I'm sorry. I wasn't thinking about Todd. It hit me when you never laughed at what I said." David laughed and shook his head.

"Alan. Amanda, Gabe and I used to play that game all the time. I didn't crack cause I'm that good at it."

"Are you sure?" Alan asked. David laughed again.

"I may have flipped if you actually kissed me." David said. Alan laughed and shook his head. Carman came back into the room with an envelope in his hand.

"Well, she ships safely tomorrow Mr. Smith." Carman said handing the envelope to David. David took it and shot a puzzled look at Allan.

"Carman thought it would be funny to put the permit in your name." Allan said strumming his guitar.

"Funny? It fricking awesome." David said staring at the envelope. Allan laughed and look at Carman.

"Now what are you singing?" Carman sighed and looked at David.

"That depends. What you playing kid?" David raised his eyebrows and put the envelope down on the stool beside him. He looked at Allan and smiled. He started to pick the beginning of November Rain. Alan smiled and played the guitar chords. David and Alan stared at each other as they played. David closed his eyes as Carman sang. The song seemed over to fast when Carman was cheering again. They played every Gun's and Roses song they knew. When Carman's throat was too sore to keep singing they put it all away and headed to their rooms. David got the room in the basement. He set his bag inside and walked out into Carman's collection room. He walked over to the Iron Maiden and stepped inside. He leaned against the iron spine and shut his eyes.

"You know, there is a bed." Carman said as he entered the room. David looked at him and laughed.

"Yea, I know." David said and stepped out. He followed Carman into the utility room. Carman took the hot water pilot light cover off then checked his pockets.

"Got a light?" Carman asked. David reached in his pocket and pulled out his lighter. He handed it to Carman. Carman lit the pilot light and handed David his lighter back. They walked out of the room into the room that held Carman's mid-evil war fair collection. "What did he say to you at the bar?" Carman asked. David looked at Carman and smiled.

"He said 'say oh God or I'll stick my tongue down your throat till you choke on it'" Carman giggled and shook his head.

"Fucking Alan. Good luck." Carman said and laughed.

"Good luck with what?" David asked. Carman led David to some chairs by a table where it looked like Carman was refinishing some old swords. They sat down.

"I have known Alan since I was in diapers." Carman said and David smiled. "He may be a teacher or whatever to you but, to me he's a guardian angel and a hero."

"Why?" David asked picturing Alan in his boxers again. Carman smiled.

"He has stuck with me through everything. If it's a best friend you're looking for, David. You found it." Carman said and looked down and smiled. David sighed and shook his head.

"I didn't look for him. He just sort of happened." Carman laughed and nodded.

"Yea, that sounds like Alan."

"What was he like? I mean, he always says he was like me but I'm not sure I know what he means."

"Well, Alan was the kind of kid that seemed to find trouble quite easy. He was facing jail time when Charlie came along." Carman said then seemed suddenly pissed off with himself for saying that name. David sighed. He had to know.

"Yea, what is with that guy?" Davis asked. Carman looked at David and shook his head.

"I think that is Alan's story to tell." He said and stood up. David did the same. "Still got your shipping info?" Carman asked changing the subject. David raised his eyebrows.

"Yea, I do." David said and smiled.

"Good, you can't get her home without it."

"I know. Thanks a lot for letting us use her" David said and smiled. He looked over at the other two Iron Maidens at the side of the room. Carman smiled.

"You really got a thing for her, don't you?" Carman asked watching David stare at the Iron Maiden.

"Oh yea." David said in a horny sounding voice. Carman laughed and shook his head. David looked back at Carman and laughed to.

"Well, I better hit the hay. I wanted to shower but the pilot light was out. Just about time for a new water heater I think."

"Yea, ok. Well, thanks again Carman." David said and put his hands in his pockets and headed for his room.

"Hey David." Carman said stopping at the stairs. David turned around and looked at him. "You can talk to him about anything you know. Doesn't matter what it is." David smiled and looked down.

"I know. Good night."

"Good night." Carman said and headed up stairs. David took one last look at the Iron Maidens and walked into his room. The bed was a queen size. It was a black sleigh bed. There were two dressers in the room but only one with a mirror. David took his clothes off and inspected his bruising. It was slowly getting better but he figured he had a lot of healing left to do. He climbed into the soft warm bed and lay staring at the ceiling.

Jail time? So Alan was a bad ass. That figures. And that thing he said. I wonder if he would have done it I didn't say oh god? I should ask him what he would have done if I said do it. Ha! He would have broke I bet. Other than Carman, he probably played that game with straight dudes. Damn it! Should have been thinking. Oh well, if I'm lucky, there will be a next time. I can't believe I've made it through this weekend. What did I expect though? Drop dead from being horny? I wonder if Paula knows. She sure acted strange after dinner. Well, in a perfect world, I won't ever have to know. David thought about the Iron Maiden and how cool it was going to be to oversee the loading and shipment of her. It wasn't long before he fell asleep.

David was stirred awake by a knock at the door. He opened his eyes and listened. He could still feel a bit of the rum he had drank the night before and sighed. There was another knock.

"Yea." David said in a groggy voice. He could hear Alan giggle.

"Are you decent?" Alan asked from the other side of the door. David rolled over on to his back and could feel the tight tug of a morning erection. HE rolled his eyes and sat up.

"I'm never decent." He answered. Alan giggled again and opened the door. He was dressed in a tight black shirt and light coloured blue jeans.

"Good morning." He said and stood at the foot of the bed.

"What time is it?" David asked squinting at him.

"6:30" Alan answered. David fell back onto the bed. Alan laughed and shook his head.

"Wow, I don't think I can move at 6:30." David said smiling and Alan's snickering.

"Can you move at 6:30 for Your Lady? She's got to be on the train by 9:30 and she isn't loaded on a truck yet." David smiled again and sat up.

"Ok, I can move at 6:30." Alan smiled.

"I put a towel in the bathroom for you." He said and left the room. David yawned and swung his legs over the side of the bed. He carried his bag to the basement bathroom and got ready for the day. He went back into the room, made the bed and then headed upstairs. Carman and Alan were standing in the kitchen drinking coffee. Carman handed one to David.

"Thanks." David said and sipped the coffee.

"Got all the paper work?" Alan asked. David reached into his inside jacket pocket and pulled out the envelope. He fanned his face with it and the two older men laughed.

"You haven't opened it?" Carman asked. David raised his eyebrows.

"I didn't know I could." He said.

"Well go ahead." Alan said and smiled. David set his coffee cup on the counter and opened the envelope. The first thing he saw was a bill of sale. It had his name on it. He frowned and read the paper. Carman giggled.

"Why is the bill of sale in my name?" David asked still reading the paper.

"Well, that was my idea. I thought I would help Alan out with those cock suckers from that festival and let them think you own the Maiden. If that's not enough to convince them to fund Alan's school, nothing is. But you have to promise to sell it back." Alan smiled and Carman laughed.

"What did I buy it for?" David asked looking up at Alan.

"Time." Alan said and smiled. David felt a shock go through his body.

How do you do that to me? He wondered, but he smiled. He looked through the other papers and signed the papers that needed a signature. When Alan and David finished their coffees it was time to go. David thanked Carman again and headed out to the car. He got in and watched Alan with Carman. They stood at the door and talked for a few minutes. Alan looked back at the car once and smiled. David smiled back and waited. Carman reached out and hugged Alan. Alan stood there hugging is friend for a while. David thought it looked sexy. When Alan came to the car and opened the door, Carman yelled to him,

"Invite me to the wedding! I could be his matron of honor!" Alan laughed and got in the car. He waved as they drove off.

"Matron of honor?" David asked and giggled. Alan laughed and shook his head.

"Yea well, that's Carman for you." he said and drove to the ware house. Charlie's car was already there. Alan took a deep breath and got out of the car. David followed. They went into the building to find Charlie tying the Iron Maiden onto a motorized lifting apparatus.

"Good morning boys." Charlie said as the little machine squealed with the weight of lifting the large Iron coffin.

"Good morning" They said in unison.

"All ready to take her to the fair?" Charlie asked as the little apparatus followed easily behind him.

"You bet. David has all the paper work." Alan said as they pulled the Maiden out of the building on to the parking lot.

"Now we wait for the truck." Charlie said and smiled at David. David looked down the street both ways.

"How was Carman?" Charlie asked Alan. Alan smiled.

"He was Carman." He answered. David giggled but continued watching for a truck.

"How is he doing since the break up?" Charlie asked.

"He seemed fine. Why don't you call him and ask him yourself?" Alan said lighting a cigarette. David looked over at the two men.

"He never seems to want to talk." Charlie said.

"Well, you sort of fell off the face of the earth. Can you blame him?"

"I suppose not." Charlie said and sighed. Alan looked at David and tilted his head as if he could see something behind him. David turned around to see a truck pulling into the parking lot. David smiled and watched the truck pull up to the Iron Maiden. The truck driver got out of the truck and looked at the Maiden.

"Can't say I ever hauled something like this before." He said in a gruff voice. Alan shook the man's hand and thanked him for coming. He smiled at David. The man looked at his clip board and looked up.

"Which one of you is David Smith?"

"I am." David said and took the paper work out of his jacket. He handed it to the truck driver. The little fat man looked over the paper and took one piece out. He stuck it to the clip board and smiled at David.

"Well, young man. Shall we get your toy to the train station?" David giggled and nodded. Alan and Charlie both smiled. They watched as the man loaded the Maiden and strapped it down. He climbed out of the back of the truck and looked at David. "Wanna check it?" David nodded and looked at Alan. Alan followed David into the back of the truck. David looked at the closing mechanism of the maiden and the spine.

"What are you looking for?" Alan asked whispering.

"I wanna make sure he didn't bang her around. These are the spots that would get the most damage." David whispered back. Alan smiled and watched David inspect his lady.

"Satisfied?" Alan asked as David stepped away.

"I think so." David answered and they got out of the truck.

"Ok, you'll have to bring the rest of your shipping information to the train station before I unload." The truck driver said. Alan and David thanked him and he got into his truck and drove off.

"Well, thanks again." Alan said to Charlie and shook his hand.

"No problem Alan." He said and turned to David.

"Don't let him boss you around, ok?" Charlie said smiling. Alan laughed and shook his head.

"I never do." David said and shook the old man's hand.

"Have a safe trip." Charlie said.

"We will." Alan said and walked with David to the car. They got in and Charlie waved. Alan waved and drove off toward the train station.

"Well, that's over with." Alan said to David and smiled. David looked at Alan.

"I can't *stand* it, Alan." David said still staring at Alan. Alan blinked and looked at David.

"What?" Alan asked. David shook his head and sighed.

"I really don't want to pry or whatever, but, what is the deal with you and that *guy?*" Alan looked out the windshield and didn't say anything for a few minutes. He looked back over at David and smiled.

"It's a long story." Alan said.

"It's a long drive." David said back. Alan smiled.

"Ok, David. You win." Alan said and pulled over. David looked at Alan with a confused gaze. Alan turned in his seat to face David. David stayed quiet and listened. Alan cleared his throat and looked down at the gear shift. "I was about 17. Carman had just told me he was gay. I was cool with it or whatever, you know?" David nodded. Alan continued. "Anyway, Carman went out for a date with this dude from a different school one night and got raped." David shivered thinking of Todd and how close that was to being his story. Alan went on, "About two days later I found the guy that did it." Alan said and looked up at David. David looked into Alan's eyes. "What I did to him, David was horrible." Alan said and looked back down. David sighed and looked out the window. "Anyway, the cops arrested me and I was sitting in jail. Charlie came and bailed me out. He got me a lawyer and the whole thing. I got off with a year of house arrest and a record that would stay with me forever." Alan said and looked back at David. David stared at Alan while he spoke. "Charlie schooled me at home for the rest of grade 11 and most of grade 12." Alan said and smiled. "Carman was there every day. He felt like he owed me or something. Well, Carman started seeing some guy that he wouldn't tell me about." Alan looked at David and sighed. "It was Charlie, I found out from a reliable source." David raised his eyebrows.

"Really?" David asked. Alan nodded and leaned back in his seat.

"I was so mad. I still don't know why. I think it had to do with Paula or . . ." Alan trailed off and looked out the window. He leaned his head back against the chair and closed his eyes.

"Or what?" David asked. The story was so incredible that David couldn't bear to have him stop now. Alan turned his head to look at David.

"Carman told me once he liked me. I guess I was jealous or something." Alan said and put the car back into gear and headed down the road. David stared at him as if he had just confessed to murder. "I don't know what it was, but I left home and left them both behind.

I went to school and became a teacher so I could help kids. What Charlie did for me was awesome. Him being with Carman, well, I never got over it." Alan said and smiled at David. David heaved a long sigh and raised his eyebrows.

"Huh." David said and looked out the window. Alan laughed.

"Huh? That's what you have to say?" David looked at him and laughed.

"I don't know *what* to say, Alan. It's not what I thought." David said.

"What did you think?" Alan asked as they turned the corner. David could see the train station.

"Something else." David said. Alan shook his head. He pulled up to the loading area where the truck driver waited for them. "We're here." David whispered to the Iron Maiden.

"Are you gonna be ok? You're talking to a truck." Alan said and laughed. David laughed and got out of the car. They walked over to the truck driver. He smiled at David.

"It's on the train guys. Without a hitch." The driver said and introduced them to the conductor. He looked over David's paper work and took his copy. He told them they would arrive in Winnemucca by 10 pm. Alan and David thanked the two men and got back into the car.

"How long did it take us to get here?" Alan asked.

"Uh, about four hours." David answered and smiled. Alan looked at David,

"You made it all the way across the state of Oregon in four hours?" David laughed. Alan shook his head and drove off onto the main street. He pulled into a coffee shop drive through and ordered two coffees. He handed David his and put his own in the cup holder. "Four hours." Alan said under his breath and David laughed.

"Hey, it's a good car. Use it." David said. Alan smiled.

"You're lucky we didn't get pulled over."

"You were sitting right next to me." David said in self-defense. Alan laughed and shook his head.

"Well, I knew you were speeding, I just didn't know you were going *that* fast." David and Alan both laughed. Alan stopped at a gas station and filled the car. He had filled it when they got to the city but he didn't want to risk it. They chatted about the fair and the project for the first hour of the trip. They fell silent for a while and David broke the silence.

"What would you have done if I didn't say oh god?" David asked. Alan looked at David and laughed.

"I don't know."

"Do you think you would have broke?"

"Oh, I don't know. I may have." Alan said. David felt a flip in his stomach. He stared at Alan while he drove.

"If I was you, I would have played chicken." David said. The flipping in his stomach got more intense.

Cut it out nerves! He thought.

"What do you mean?"

"Well, if it was me, and you didn't say oh god or whatever, I would move in for that kiss and see what you do." Alan and David both laughed.

"I'll have to remember that." Alan said. David's body was certainly playing against him today. He closed his eyes and took a deep breath. "You said you had a guess or something about what the story was with Charlie. What was it?" Alan asked. David opened his eyes and sighed. "Wow, is it that bad?" Alan asked. David laughed and shrugged.

"That depends." David said.

"On what?"

"On what you consider bad." David said and looked at Alan. Alan raised his eyebrows and looked at David.

"Ok, try me." Alan said. David's stomach flipped with the thought of telling Alan what he thought.

"Well, I didn't think Carman was with him." David said. Alan thought about it for a second. Then the light seemed to come on. Alan looked at David with a shocked expression and David laughed.

"You thought I was?" Alan asked. David looked out the window and said nothing. The outside scenery rushed passed Mr. Blacks wine coloured car. David could see the shadow of the vehicle in the grass that lined the road. Alan looked at David. He smiled at the young man then said, "I wouldn't consider that bad." David looked back at Alan.

"You wouldn't?"

"No." Alan said. They were silent for the next hour. David read the signs that slowly decreased in distance to Nevada. He thought about Gabe.

I bet he's waiting for me. Playing it cool but dyeing to know what happened. I wonder if mom told him why we staid an extra night. If she didn't, I can just imagine what he must think. This weekend has been incredibly awesome. The only thing that would have made it better would have been a good make out session with Alan. He looked over at Alan. He was sitting quietly, tapping the steering wheel to the music playing in the car. His side profile was so sexy to David. His jaw was cut so strong and loose strands of his sandy hair fell to the corner of his eye. His mouth looked like it could strike the fear of god into you with even the lightest kiss. David could feel his body react to his thoughts and he turned back toward the window.

Wow, I love the way I react to him. I wonder what he would think if he knew. I wonder if he would let me act on impulse. That would be one hell of a night. David thought and smiled. He could feel the tightness of his erection. He imagined Alan's kiss and what it would sound like when he moaned under David's touch. Alan's voice cut into his fantasy,

"What did you think of Carman?" David looked over at him. He now had one hand resting on his inner thigh. David closed his eyes for a second to regroup his thoughts.

"He's a pretty funny guy." David answered. Alan smiled.

"Yea, he's good shit."

"How often do you see him?"

"Well, not often enough. I do talk to him on the phone two or three times a week though. We try to keep each other in the loop as much as possible."

"Does he ever come to see you?"

"Oh, sure he does. The last visit was last June when I first got my Dad's place. He came and helped me build that shop." Alan said. David remembered the shop at Alan's house that held all the old cars.

"That was your dad's place?"

"Yea, remember I told you he used to take me fishing down at the lake? That was the lake."

"I thought you grew up in Portland?" David asked.

"I did. Not all families stay together, David." Alan said and looked at David. David stared at the eyes of his teacher. He wanted so badly to just be able to lean over and kiss him. His mind swam with the idea. "But it's no big deal. My parents were never meant to be together." Alan added with a laugh.

"They didn't get along very good I take it."

"Not really. Their dreams for the future were too different and it made living together pretty difficult."

"That's too bad." David said still thinking about kissing Alan.

"Not really. If they hadn't separated, I probably would have killed one of them." They both laughed. David loved it when Alan laughed. The sound was so wonderful to David.

"I felt like that sometimes when my dad was still alive."

"How did he die?" Alan asked. David sighed and shook his head. Alan could see he struck a nerve with David. "You don't have to tell me." He added. David looked out the windshield and then back at Alan.

"He killed himself." David said and looked back out the windshield. Alan shifted in his seat and David caught it in the corner of his eye. He smiled at the up word thrust of Alan's hips.

"I'm sorry." Alan said. David looked over at him. He stared out at the road ahead of him. David sighed.

"It's ok. He was a drunk and a drug user. It was bound to happen."

"He overdosed then?"

"Yea. I think it was on purpose, but mom thinks otherwise." David confessed. David knew about the problems that plagued his home before his father died. Neither one of his parents had been perfectly faithful. His dad's band was going nowhere and his mother was the sole provider for the house. They would get drunk every night and fight. Then his dad would get mad and leave. He would either find himself in the arms of another woman or in a fist fight with some dude at the bar.

"That's too bad David. Maybe she wants to believe he didn't because she has you." Alan said answering the on purpose or not comment.

"Maybe." David said replaying the night through his head that he found his father dead on the bathroom floor.

"Were you two close?" Alan asked. David thought about the question. He recalled only being in trouble with his dad a handful of times. He remembered the hours of guitar lessons and talks about girls. He remembered driving his dad's firebird for the first time and all the times after. He remembered how proud his dad was when he got his driver's license. He also remembered how proud he was when David said he had given his virginity to Amanda.

"Yea, we were close." David answered. "I was the one that found him too." David answered.

"That's horrible." Alan said looking back and forth from the outside road to David.

"It was."

"How do you deal?" Alan asked. David smiled. He hadn't dealt with it at all. This was the first time he talked about it other than with Amanda.

"I hang out with you." David answered. Alan giggled.

"Really. I was being serious."

"Me too. I have not thought about it. Mom was looking for a man for me to hang out with like I used to with my dad. She thinks losing him has made me antisocial or something."

"Has it?"

"I guess." David answered and laughed. Alan smiled and shook his head.

"You're a tough kid David."

"Tell that to Todd." David answered rubbing the dull ache in his ribs that seemed to act up when he mentioned Todd's name.

"He'll get his, David. They always do." Alan said. David thought back to the story Alan told him about Carman's bad date. He remembered that Alan hadn't fully disclosed what he had done to the guy.

"What did you do to that guy that raped Carman?" Alan stared out the windshield at the road in front of him for a while.

"Well, nothing very nice." Alan answered.

"You don't like to talk about any of that situation, do you?" David asked remembering how hard it was to get the original information out of him to begin with.

"Not really. I guess we have that in common too, huh?" Alan asked and winked at David.

"Why do you say that?" David asked. Alan laughed and shook his head.

"Sometimes I get the feeling you're not telling me everything either."

"Oh." David said and looked back down at the hand that rested on Alan's thigh. He could feel his heart pound in his chest. He took a deep breath and closed his eyes.

"Like whatever you're thinking right now. Would you ever tell me?" Alan asked. David shot his eyes open and stared at Alan.

"Nope." David answered and Alan laughed.

"See. Neither one of us ever tells the whole story." They both laughed. David looked at the services sign outside the window.

"Wanna eat?" David asked trying to change the subject from his sexual interest in Alan.

"Yup." Alan said and slowed the car to turn into the road side restaurant. He pulled up to the eatery and shut off the car. They both got out at the same time and went into the diner. They discussed the mid-evil project over their meal. They finished eating and stepped outside for a cigarette. "Did you have a good weekend?" Alan asked as they both leaned against the car smoking.

"Yea. I had an awesome time." David answered remembering the thought of the one thing that would have made it better.

"That's good, so did I." Alan said.

"What are we gonna do while we wait for the train to arrive?"

"Well, I have a few arrangements to make for Your Lady when we get back to town. But if you didn't want to go home right away, we could find something to do."

"It's up to you. It makes no difference to me. My mom is probably wanting to hear what happened and I do need to get clean clothes."

"Ok, well. I will drop you off at home then and go deal with storage for Your Lady. Then I'll pick you up later to go pick her up."

"How do you deal with stuff like this on a Sunday?" David asked. Alan smiled and raised his eyebrows.

"Yee of little faith. I am amazing." Alan answered and put out his cigarette. David smiled.

I bet you are. David thought as he did the same and got back into the car with Alan. It wasn't long before they entered Nevada. David read the oncoming signs and seen that home was a little over an hour away.

"What time is it?" David asked looking over at Alan's watch. Alan checked the time.

"Well, I'm almost making as good of time as you did. It's 1:30." David mock yawned and stretched.

"Man, if I was driving, we would be home by now." Alan laughed and shook his head.

"Well, if you didn't get hungry, we would only be a half hour away."

"Nice excuse." David said and they both laughed. David stared at Alan as he drove. The stereo played quietly in the background. It was Alan's Queen C.D. playing now. He smiled as Alan tapped the steering wheel.

"Do I get to know that thought?" Alan asked looking over at David.

"Nope, not that one either." David said.

"You remind me of Carman when you do that." Alan said. David's eyes grew wide.

"Why?"

"He used to do that too. Keep his thoughts to himself. I used to hate it. I always told him what I was thinking."

"Well, you share, and I'll share." David said not willing to tell the whole truth about his thoughts of Alan.

"Ok, I'm thinking about shampoo." Alan said. David laughed and tossed his head back against the seat.

"Why?" He asked.

"Well, it's weird." Alan said and looked at David.

"Ok, weird is good." David said. Alan cleared his throat and seemed to try to prepare himself for his reason. David felt as though he was on the edge of his seat waiting.

"I noticed the smell of your hair last night at Carman's place. At the bar?" Alan answered. David recalled the closeness of Alan's face and remembered the feeling of his breath on his shoulder.

"Ok." David said.

"Well, I like how it smells." David could feel his heart jump in his chest again. "I was wondering what kind of shampoo you use." Alan finished and looked back at David. David smiled and cleared his throat trying to choke back urge to say, *smell it again and guess.*

"Vidal Sassoon." David answered. Alan smiled and nodded.

"Now, what are you thinking about?" Alan asked pulling out David's end of the deal. David sighed and cleared his throat again.

"Carman's bar." David answered. Alan laughed and shook his head.

"Yea, that was a bad call. I'm sorry. I really wasn't thinking about what happened last week with Todd."

"Actually, I wasn't as freaked out as you think." David said feeling his heart pound with the thought of Alan's swagger at the bar. He remembered how the way Alan sounded made him feel.

"That's not the point." Alan said looking out the windshield.

"Then, what is the point?" David asked in a more bedroom sounding voice then he had meant to use.

"The more I get to know you, the less the point makes sense actually." David decided not to press the issue. Alan drove in silence looking as though he wished the subject never came up.

"Well, it was a pretty cool night." David said trying to sooth Alan. Alan smiled and seemed to look off into the far distance out the windshield.

"Yes it was." Alan said quietly.

Chapter 17

Alan waved at David as he drove away. David walked into the house and his mother was waiting in the kitchen for him.

"How was the trip?" She asked smiling as she got up and hugged her son. David hugged her with a strong hold and sat down at the table with her.

"Oh, it was awesome mom." David said.

"Well, how did it go? What did you do?"

"Well, the Iron Maiden was frigging sweet. Alan and I have to go pick it up at 10 tonight."

"Oh, why so late?"

"That's when the train gets in I guess." David said and went to the kitchen to get a cup of coffee. He made one for himself and his mother.

"You guys must have done other things." Nancy said as David handed a cup to her. He sat back down on his chair and sipped his coffee.

"Yea, we did actually. When we got there it was late and after seeing the Maiden, we had supper at Alan's old teacher's place. He's like mega rich."

"That sounds nice."

"Yea, it was. Their house was like a castle or something." David said and Nancy smiled. "Then we slept in a hotel the first night. Alan brought Susan and Gloria with him, so that kept us occupied till we went to sleep."

"Who is Susan and Gloria?" Nancy asked frowning at her son. David laughed and shook his head.

"Alan's guitars."

"Oh, I see."

"Anyway, Saturday we found out that we couldn't move the Maiden until today. Did you get my message?" David asked remembering he didn't hear back from her.

"Yes I did. I called back and had to leave a massage but Alan called last night and filled me in." Nancy said.

"Well, anyway. Alan got all the crap ready for shipping and then we went and hung out with his buddy Carman."

"Oh, and how was that?" David thought back to the bar again and smiled.

"It was pretty cool. I guess the Maiden belongs to Carman. He has two of her sisters and a shit load of other stuff. He even has war pony armor." David explained.

"I bet *you* were in your glory then."

"Oh yea. It was so cool mom. It's the kind of basement I'm gonna have." Nancy giggled and sipped her coffee.

"So did you stay there last night then?"

"Yea, we played guitar and Carman sang. He is awesome! He could fill in for Axel Rose if he wanted."

"Who is Axel Rose?"

"Gun's and Roses mom. Come on, I'm embarrassed for you." David said. Nancy and David laughed. He told her about how the guys had put everything in his name and she smiled as he explained. "How was your weekend?" David finally asked.

"Well, I worked yesterday. That's why I wasn't here when you called. And between Amanda and Gabe, the phone hasn't stopped ringing." She said and laughed. David smiled. He missed his friends and wanted to see them. Nancy could see it in his face and smiled. "Why don't you go see them until dinner?" She said. David jumped up and kissed his mom's forehead.

"What time?" David asked heading for the door.

"6:30." She said and giggled at her son. He nodded and went out the door. He walked quickly to Amanda's door. He knocked and waited. Gabe answered. He smiled and stepped outside. He quickly kissed David and then let him in. David laughed and shook his head.

"Hi." David said. Gabe bit his bottom lip and stared at the shirt David was wearing.

"That does look good on you." Gabe said. David laughed.

"Yea, it was noticed."

"Really? Tell me all about it." Gabe said and pulled David down to the basement. Amanda was on the computer in the corner. She turned around and looked at him.

"David! Your back!" She said excitedly and jumped out of her chair and into his arms. David giggled and held his friend.

"Yea, I survived a whole weekend with Alan." He said and smiled. Amanda blushed and pulled David to the couch.

"We have been placing bets on what happened." Gabe said as he came over with a pop for everyone. David told the whole story about his weekend. Amanda giggled at the story about the bar at Carman's house. Gabe smiled and stared at David as he spoke. Every once in a while, Gabe would catch David's gaze and hold it for a while. David would smile and wonder what he was thinking about. Amanda asked a million questions about how Alan made David feel with each different sexy thing David told them Alan did. They talked about the things Alan said at the bar the most and the shampoo conversation. Gabe giggled when they discussed the shampoo conversation. David figured it was because he was thinking about the morning before he left.

"Yea, that's nice smelling shampoo." Gabe had said and got a giggle out of David. Amanda seemed to be oblivious to the two men's flirting. She was so engrossed in David's story that she seemed to forget Gabe was even there. David, on the other hand, was very aware that Gabe was there. He liked the way Gabe looked at him and wished Amanda would look away long enough for David to return the favor. He enjoyed sleeping with Amanda, but after this weekend, he wanted Gabe. He wanted to feel Gabe touch him again and he knew Gabe could see it.

At 6:30, David said his good byes and went home. He ate dinner with his mother and they chatted about the surgeries she had over the weekend.

"Oh, Mr. Black called and said that all the arrangements are made and he will be here at nine to pick you up." Nancy said as she cleared the table. David got up to help her.

"Mom, he's only Mr. Black at school." David said. Nancy smiled and shook her head.

"I am surprised at you, son." She said as she got the sink ready to do the dishes.

"Why?" David asked as he dug a dish towel out of the drawer and waited for his first dish to dry.

"I just never thought you would connect with another man like you did with your dad."

"Well, there was never Alan before was there?" David asked and smiled. Nancy laughed and started the dishes.

"No, I guess not." She said. They chatted a little about Mike while they washed the dishes. David could see that talking about his dad was becoming easier for his mother. They laughed at the good times and never brought up the bad. When they finished the dishes, David went upstairs and changed his clothes. He sat on his bed staring at the phone. He wanted to call Gabe and tell him how bad he needed him as soon as possible. But he figured Amanda would think it was strange that he called to talk to Gabe right after he had just spent the last couple of hours with him. He sighed and unpacked his bag. He set his journal on the desk and smiled.

"Have I got a lot to write tonight." He said out loud and then left to take his cloths to the basement. He changed the laundry over for his mom and went back upstairs. His mother was watching the evening news in the living room. "Laundry is in." He said as he sat down in his dad's chair.

"Oh thank you dear." Nancy said and smiled.

"So the bruising is getting better." David said as he stared at the weather lady.

"That's good. How does that rib feel?"

"Not as bad as it did last week. I think I may survive." Nancy giggled as David never took his eyes off the weather girl. Nancy had always thought it was cute that David had such a crush on her.

"She's too old for you, son." She said with a teasing smile. David looked at her and laughed.

"That just means she could teach me something." David answered. Nancy laughed and shook her head.

“You need a psychiatrist.” She said. David rolled his eyes and looked back at the T.V.

“You have no idea, mom.” He said as he thought about the morning in the shower with Gabe and the few minutes of intense arousal at the bar at Carman’s house. They watched the news and talked about the coming week of school and work. She told that the teachers were satisfied with the work he had sent back and forth with Amanda. They watched a few of his mother’s favorite sitcoms until there was a knock at the door. David answered it. It was Alan.

“Hi.” Alan said and stepped in.

“Hi.” David said and smiled. Nancy came into view.

“Hello Nancy.” Alan said and smiled. Nancy said hello and Alan told her not to expect David until after 11. They said their good byes and Nancy watched them as they headed to off.

“So, she’s gonna stay right here in town.” Alan said as they drove away.

“That’s awesome. Where?”

“At the library. There is a storage room that only has three keys.” Alan said and held a key in front of David. “One for me, one for Mr. Relling and one for you.” He said and handed David the brass key. David took it and felt Alan’s fingers against his. He shivered a little and put the key in his pocket.

“That’s awesome.” David said and Alan smiled.

“There is a guy that’s going to meet us there and bring Your Lady home.” Alan said and smiled again at David. David could feel his body begging for him reach out and touch Alan, anywhere.

“Fuck, that’s awesome.” David said ignoring his body’s request.

“I told you I’m amazing.”

"Yes you did." David said and closed his eyes for a second to fight the urges his body was so willing to experience in Alan's presents. Alan looked at David and shook his head.

"Fighting excitement or something?" Alan asked. David shot a shocked look at Alan.

"What?" David managed to ask.

"Well, it seems whenever we talk about Your Lady, you act funny."

"Oh, well . . ." David sighed and cleared his throat. "It's a pretty exciting thing." He said and giggled a little at Alan's uncalled for modesty.

Don't you know how sexy you are? David thought.

"Yea, it kind of is." Alan said smiling. They talked about the Iron Maiden until they got to the train station. David dealt with the paper work once the train arrived, and the loading dock guys unloaded the Iron death machine. Alan spoke with the truck driver as David looked over his Lady. "Did she make it?" Alan asked coming up behind David. David looked at Alan and smiled.

"She is beautiful." David said and let the truck driver take over. He was a lot more careful than the first driver that had loaded it in Portland. He also let David check on the tie job before they headed off. Alan and David led the way and the truck driver followed.

"Almost have her home. How does that make you feel?" Alan asked. Without even thinking, David answered.

"Like having sex." Alan burst out laughing and David giggled at his reaction.

"Wow, that happy, huh?" Alan asked still giggling at David comment. David laughed and shook his head. "I guess that's understandable." Alan added. David looked at him with a confused gaze. "I mean, she is pretty sexy." David shivered at the word sexy. He liked how it sounded coming from Alan.

"Yup, she is." David said looking in the side mirror at the truck behind them.

"Speaking of having sex," Alan said. David shot a look at Alan that would have gave him whiplash if it were a fraction faster. "Have you seen Amanda yet since you've been home?" David laughed at Alan's question. "What?" Alan asked looking at David.

"Why would you associate Amanda with sex?"

"I just remember you mentioning it when we went fishing." Alan said. David laughed again.

"You think about me and Amanda having sex?" Alan burst out laughing again.

"NO!" He said through his laughing. "I do not." David laughed and shook his head.

"Yea, I saw her." He answered. Alan composed himself and looked at David.

"And, is she as excited about this as you are?" David thought about Alan's question and remembered the talk at Amanda's and Gabe's heavy gaze.

"Actually, Amanda doesn't like this kind of stuff. Gabe was more interested than she was."

"Oh, yea he looks like the type that would." Alan said. David thought about Gabe's long black hair and the black trench coat that made him look like the devil himself.

"Yea, he's looking forward to seeing it."

"Well, you wanna call him and invite him to the library?" Alan asked handing his cell phone to David.

"I can do that?" David asked taking the phone from Alan. This time he purposely touched Alan's fingers. He didn't seem to notice.

"Well, tonight. But try not to make a habit of it." Alan said and winked. David smiled and dialed the phone.

"*Hello.*" It was Amanda.

"Hey, ask Gabe if he wants to see the Iron Maiden." David said.

"*Ewe, who would want to see that?*"

"Just ask, Mandy." David said and giggled. Alan smiled at David. There was a pause on the other line.

"*Satan speaking.*" It was Gabe. David felt his stomach jump and he giggled.

"Hey, wanna see something cool?" David asked. Gabe giggled and David could feel himself blush. Alan looked at David puzzled.

"*I sure do.*" Gabe said in his seductive voice. David giggled and cleared his throat.

"Come to the library in like, 20 minutes." David said trying not to sound as though what Gabe said had such an effect on him."

"*Ooo, kinky.*" Gabe said and giggled. David rolled his eyes.

"Are you gonna come or what?"

"*He's sitting right next to you isn't he?*" Gabe asked in that same seductive voice. David looked at Alan.

"Yes." David answered than looked away and asked, "Will you come?"

"*Yup, maybe even before you do this time.*" David blushed and closed his eyes. Alan looked at him again with that same confused look. "*I'll be there.*" Gabe added.

"Ok, see you in 20 minutes then." David said and hung up the phone before Gabe could do any worse.

"Well, we will have company then?" Alan asked and put the phone back on the case at his hip.

"Yea, looks like it." David said and cleared his throat again.

"Well, good." Alan said looking at David again. David looked at Alan and raised his eyebrows. Alan laughed and looked back out the windshield.

"What?" David asked not really wanting to hear the answer. Alan raised an eyebrow and looked back at David.

"Nothing." Alan said and smiled. David sighed and looked at the side mirror at the truck again. Alan cleared his throat and said.

"So, tell me about Gabe." David closed his eyes and leaned his head back.

"Well, he is Amanda's older brother." He answered and looked at Alan.

"I knew that already." Alan said.

"He is older than us."

"Yes, I knew that too."

"He's a guitar player." David said trying to be as compliant to Alan's questions as he could.

"And he is gay." Alan said. David's eyes went wide and his heart pounded in his chest. "Did you think after all the years I spent growing up with Carman I wouldn't know a gay guy when I saw one? It practically resonates from him." Alan said. David looked through the windshield and sat silent.

"It's that obvious?" David asked hoping it wasn't so with him.

"Sure. Can't you tell when eyes move over your body David?" The question caught David so off guard he thought he would pass out. "I can." Alan added and laughed. David could feel his heart pound in his chest and he felt short of breath. Alan noticed and put his hand on the hand that David gripped the armrest with. David looked at Alan's hand and thought he would die. "Don't worry, David. He was looking at me." Alan said trying to sooth David's nerves. David looked at Alan.

"He was?" David asked with the most pitiful voice. He cleared his throat to try to fix it. "I didn't notice." He added. The clearing seemed to help. Alan smiled and put his hand back on the gear shift.

"This stuff really bothers you, doesn't it?" Alan asked looking back and forth between David and the dark road. David stared at Alan not knowing what to say. "Don't worry, it won't be weird." Alan said and slowed the car to turn into town. David looked back at the Truck and watched it turn to follow. "Are you ok?" Alan asked looking at David's pale white face. David looked at him and smiled.

"Yea, I'm ok."

"You don't look like it." Alan said slowly driving down Main Street. David held his gaze on Alan and answered.

"I guess you caught me off guard with that one."

"Well, that's a first. I should have used that at Carman's place." He said and giggled.

"No, the thing you used there was pretty good." David said and felt the color return to his face. Alan smiled and pulled up to the library. They got out of the car together and Alan guided the truck back to the door. The truck driver got out and unloaded the Iron Maiden. Alan thanked him and signed some papers. The truck driver left and Alan and David stood staring at the machine. It was still on the mechanical devise Charlie had put it on earlier in the day. David looked down the road and watched Gabe's big black Hearse pull up.

"He drives a Hearse?" Alan asked as Gabe got out of the car.

"Cool huh?" David asked and watched Gabe walk over. His long black trench coat hung on him like a black shroud. It matched his long, silky, black hair perfectly. He tossed his cigarette away and smiled at David. Then he saw the Iron Maiden and stopped.

"Wow." Gabe said.

"I think that was David's reaction." Alan said as they all stood staring at the machine.

"That's awesome, David." Gabe said and David smiled.

"Almost as awesome as that car you drive." Alan said turning to look at the Hearse again. Gabe laughed and looked at Alan.

"It gets me from A to B." Gabe said and Alan laughed.

"What year is it?"

"85." Gabe said. David turned to watch Gabe talk to Alan. Alan smiled and knew why he watched his friend like he did.

"Well, it is certainly nice to look at." Alan said. Gabe smiled.

"I know." He said and looked at David.

"Well, let's get it open." Gabe said. David laughed and looked at Alan.

"That's the second thing David thought to do too." Alan said as he slowly walked the machine into the building and into the storage room. It was completely empty. "They cleaned it out so there was no reason for anyone to go in." Alan said to David as the three of them untied the ropes that held it to the machine. Alan carefully moved the lifting apparatus from underneath of it and set it aside. "Well, better open it." Alan said and smiled at David. Gabe smiled at Alan. They watched David carefully open the Iron Maiden and get inside.

"Sexy." Gabe said and Alan giggled. David smiled and got out.

"Get in." He said and Gabe did. Gabe also knew where to put his hands and feet.

"Did you get the list?" He asked as he stood in David's Lady with his eyes closed. Alan laughed and shook his head.

"Do you guys always repeat each other's days like this?" Gabe opened his eyes and smiled at Alan.

"He asked for the list too, huh?" Alan nodded and handed the list to Gabe. David looked at Alan. Alan seemed to study Gabe and David found it oddly attractive.

"I can't believe you did this." David said to Alan. Alan looked at David and smiled.

"Are you kidding? She is the star of the show. And with you at her side come Halloween, it's gonna be something of beauty." Gabe smiled as Alan and David talked but never looked up from the page.

"Well, I don't know about that. As far as beauty goes, I think she stands alone."

"Don't be so modest. You heard Gabe, you make it look sexy." David looked at Gabe and Gabe laughed. Alan smiled and shook his head.

"It's true David, you do." Gabe said and stepped out. David went over to the Iron Maiden and ran his hand down the spine again. Gabe handed the list to Alan and smiled. "This is a huge deal for him." Gabe whispered.

"I know." Alan whispered back but never took his eyes off David. Gabe smiled and looked back at the young, sexy guy that inspected every inch of his Lady. "I probably could have left him in it the whole weekend." Alan added. Gabe looked at him and giggled.

"I can believe that."

"Think the novelty will wear off?" Gabe snorted at the comment and Alan laughed. David looked back at them.

"Are you guys talking about me?" He asked and closed the coffin door.

"Of course." Gabe answered and Alan smiled. David rolled his eyes and latched the door. Gabe giggled and looked back at Alan. "He is so easy to bug."

"Not really, you should see him when he has to keep a straight face."

"Yea, I heard all about it." Gabe said and looked back at David. David refused to turn to face them and Gabe laughed.

"Yea well, I was more surprised than he was I bet." Alan said and smiled.

"Somehow I doubt that." Gabe said and David turned around.

"Well, should we go?" David asked trying to stop the conversation. Alan and Gabe laughed and followed David out of the room. Alan shut off the light and locked the door behind them. They all walked out of the library and Alan locked those doors too.

"Can I drive you home?" Gabe asked David. Alan smiled and lit a cigarette.

"Uh, yea. I guess." David answered and looked at Alan.

"Hey, get some sleep tonight. You have school tomorrow." Alan said and smiled again.

"Will do." David said and followed Gabe to his car. David looked back at Alan and waved. Alan waved back and got into his car. David sat down in Gabe's car and watched Gabe stare at Alan's tail lights. As soon as they were out of sight he turned and looked at David.

"Ok, wanna fuck?" Gabe asked. He had the most serious look on his face hat David had ever seen on him before. He stayed silent for a few seconds processing the question.

"Fuck?" David asked as if the word was foreign.

"Yea, fuck." Gabe said and held David's gaze. David swallowed hard and blushed. "Try to, at least." Gabe added noticing David's sudden fear. David smiled at him and shook his head.

"Yea, I do." David said and Gabe smiled. He turned on the engine and drove to his house. "Here?" David asked looking at the house that Amanda slept in.

"No, I just need to get something." Gabe said and got out of the car. David waited trying to gather his thoughts.

Holy shit. Can I do this? What did he need to get? What if I chicken out? Will he be mad? How can this be happening? How can I sit here and wait like this? Just then, Gabe came back out to the car.

"Gabe, I . . ."

"I know. Relax." Gabe said and pulled out of the drive way. They drove to a secluded road and Gabe pulled over.

"Holy fuck." David said as Gabe turned to face him. Gabe laughed and shook his head.

"You don't have to be ready for sex, David. I just wanted to get you alone for a second." David looked at Gabe with a puzzled gaze and waited for him to speak. "Did you get a good feel about where he stands on his sexuality?"

"I don't know." David asked and looked down at his hands.

"David, you *need* to know this stuff. Watching you look at him is like watching porn." David laughed and looked back up at Gabe. Gabe smiled and reached into his pocket. He pulled out a guitar pick and a folded piece of paper. He handed them to David.

"What's this?" David asked and opened the paper. It was the guitar score for David's favorite song. "Think about You by Gun's and Roses?" David asked and looked up at Gabe.

"Yea, I heard you didn't know it so I got it off the net for you." Gabe said and smiled.

"Thanks." David said and looked at the pick.

"That was Axel Rose's first guitar pick."

"What?!" David said staring at the old pick.

"Yea, I got it from an action. I want you to have it." Gabe said and lit a cigarette. David looked at Gabe and then back at the pick.

"Fuck, that's awesome." David whispered and stared at the pick.

"*Now* do you wanna fuck?" Gabe asked and smiled. David looked at him and sighed.

"You're hopeless." David said and leaned in and kissed Gabe. Gabe set the cigarette in the ash tray and leaned his seat all the way back.

"Come here." He whispered. David put the song and the pick in his pocket and took his jacket off. He climbed over the shifter and straddled Gabe's lap. Gabe smiled and David kissed him. Gabe ran his hands down David's spine to the low of his back. David ran his hand through Gabe's long hair and Gabe moaned. "Fuck, I want you." Gabe whispered as David kissed his neck.

"I know." David whispered and kissed Gabe's mouth again. Gabe pushed his hard penis against David. David's eyes rolled back and he whimpered. "Get in the back." David whispered and Gabe giggled. David climbed into the back and Gabe followed. Gabe lay on top of David shrouding him with his hair and long coat. David pushed Gabe's coat off his shoulders. Gabe sat up and took it off along with his shirt. David did the same with his shirt. They kissed again with a little more vigor this time. David rapped his hand in Gabe's hair and Gabe moaned. He kissed David hungrily and went for the fly of David's jeans. David didn't hesitate. He helped Gabe get his tight jeans off and moaned as Gabe kissed his stomach. He pulled Gabe's hair again and Gabe playfully bit him. David closed his eyes and bucked his hips against Gabe. Gabe kissed his way down and took David's swollen penis into his mouth. David moaned so loud that Gabe stopped and looked at him. "Don't stop Gabe." David scolded and Gabe smiled. He messaged David's penis with his tongue inside his mouth. David moaned and pulled Gabe's hair. David could feel his body shake as Gabe worked. He moaned louder the deeper Gabe took him. Soon Gabe kissed his way back up David's body and lay on top of him again.

"Fuck your noisy . . ." Gabe said then added, "I love it." David giggled and helped Gabe out of his pants. Gabe lay back on top of David. He moved his hips and rubbed his erection against David's still kissing him. David backed his hips against Gabe again and Gabe smiled. "Fuck me David." He whispered and David stared at him. David pushed Gabe off of him and laid Gabe on his stomach. He lay on top of Gabe kissing the side of his neck and slowly pushed himself inside. Gabe moaned and David caught his breath.

"Holy fuck." David said as he slowly moved his hips pushing himself in and out. Gabe moaned and clenched his fists on his coat. David's breath shook as he moved.

"Oh god, David." Gabe moaned and pushed his ass against David's thrusting hips. David sped up and closed his eyes.

"Fuck . . . Gabe." David said through his passionate moaning and Gabe's body tightened under David. David smiled and moved faster. Gabe moaned louder and grabbed David's arm.

"Pull out." He whispered and David did as he was told. Gabe quickly rolled over under David and pulled him down on top of him. David kissed Gabe and Gabe moaned. David could feel Gabe cum and the warm semen felt so good to him. David moaned and continued kissing Gabe. Gabe's body shook underneath him. "Your turn" he whispered and reached into his jacket pocket for something. He rolled David onto his back and squirted a strange liquid on his hands. He kissed David as he rubbed it on David's erection. David moaned as Gabe touched him. Gabe smiled and kissed his way back down David's body. David watched Gabe as he made his way down to his throbbing penis. He wasted little time getting David back into his mouth. He ran his hand up David's stomach to his chest. David moaned and trusted his hips against Gabe. Gabe sucked harder and David moaned louder. He could feel his orgasm build. He pulled Gabe's hair and closed his eyes. Gabe pulled away as David's orgasm came and pushed a finger up David's ass. David moaned so loud it was almost a scream. Gabe moved his finger in and out as David came. David lay shaking when Gabe pulled his finger out and lay next to him. He stared at David and smiled.

"Kiss me." David whispered never opening his eyes. Gabe raised his eyebrows and kissed David. David pulled Gabe back on top of him while they kissed. Gabe giggled and David smiled.

"So, are you ok?" Gabe asked staring down at David and playing with his hair. David opened his eyes and looked at Gabe. He giggled and ran a hand through Gabe's hair.

"Are you kidding?" David asked. Gabe smiled and kissed him. David held Gabe and kissed back. "That was incredible." David whispered into Gabe's ear. Gabe smiled and kissed David's neck.

"Told you I would cum first." Gabe whispered and looked back down at David. David giggled and shook his head. "You actually have incredible stamina for your first time." He added.

"I do?" David asked looking up into Gabe's sleepy eyes.

"Yea, I figured you would cum at penetration. I did my first time."

"You did?" David asked amazed. Gabe giggled and nodded.

"Yea."

"Imagine what next time will be like." David said and kissed Gabe. Gabe laughed and rolled off of David.

"I can't wait." Gabe said staring up at the roof of the back of his car. David smiled and shook his head.

"Well you have to. I'm exhausted." David said closing his eyes. Gabe laughed and pulled his cigarettes out of his jacket. He lit one for himself and one for David. They lay on their backs smoking.

"I think you're the best I've ever had." Gabe said turning to look at David. David looked at him.

"Really?" He asked a little shocked.

"Yea, certainly the biggest." Gabe said and sat up. "I won't walk right for a week." He said and pulled his boxers on. David giggled and sat up.

"Sorry." David said and started to get dressed as well.

"Fuck, David. Don't apologize for *that.* It's a good thing." Gabe said pulling his shirt and pants on. David smiled and finished dressing. They climbed back up to the front seat and finished their cigarettes. "I guess I gotta take you home now huh?" Gabe said looking at David and smiling.

"Afraid so. Can you survive without me?" David asked giggling. Gabe started the car and laughed.

"I don't know." He said teasing back. He turned the car around and headed toward the lights of town. "So, have a preference yet?" Gabe asked as he slowly drove toward home. David laughed and raised his eyebrows.

"Let's do it again and I'll tell you." He answered.

"Fair enough."

"So, I didn't suck?" David asked a little amazed at Gabe's earlier comment. Gabe smiled.

"No, I did . . . and you liked it." Gabe said. David giggled and looked out the windshield. Gabe turned down the road to home and David sighed. "One of those nights, huh?" Gabe asked.

"What do you mean?" David asked as Gabe stopped about a block from home.

"The kind that you wished wouldn't end." He said staring out the windshield toward home. David smiled and nodded. Gabe put the car in park and leaned over to kiss David. David kissed Gabe and ran his hand through his hair. "You like my hair, don't you?" Gabe asked when he finished the kiss.

"Yea, I do." David said staring at Gabe. Gabe smiled and drove the car up to David's house.

"If you hate me tomorrow, tell me ok." Gabe said not looking at David. David laughed and asked.

"Why would I hate you?"

"It happens sometimes the morning after the first time." He said and still wouldn't look at David. David stared at him.

"Gabe." David said. Gabe turned to face David. David kissed him again and pulled his hair. Gabe moaned and answered back with a rake of fingernails down David's back. "I doubt I'll hate you." He said and grabbed his jacket. He checked to be sure the pick and the song were still in the pockets and opened the door.

"You just kissed me in front of your house." Gabe said and giggled.

"You kissed me in your door way earlier." David said and got out of the car. David walked around to the driver's side window and Gabe rolled it all the way down.

"Need a hand in the shower tomorrow morning?" Gabe asked smiling at David. David laughed and leaned in the window.

"Do you?" He asked and kissed Gabe again. Gabe smiled and shook his head. David walked over to the house and quietly opened the door. He watched Gabe park in his driveway and get out of his car. Gabe looked over at David and smiled. He waved and walked into the house. David did the same and went upstairs. He got into the shower and cleaned up. He thought about Gabe as he showered.

What a night. I can't believe I've been missing THAT all along. I wonder if I'm as good at giving head as he is? David smiled at the thought and got out of the shower. He walked into his room and over to his desk.

Sept. 25, Sunday.

The trip with Alan was awesome. We got the Maiden home to the library. It is the coolest thing I ever saw. We stayed with a friend of Alan's that's gay. He's was pretty cool. Alan and him seem pretty close. Apparently Alan beat the shit out of some guy that raped him when they were young. And the teacher Alan wouldn't talk about before was apparently having an affair with Carman. Alan said it pissed him off and made him jealous. I wonder what that means. Anyway, Alan and Carman play this game where they try to make the other one crack by being as crude as possible with each other. Alan tried it on me and I thought I would die. I couldn't believe what he said. He said he would stick his tongue down my throat till I choked on it if I didn't say 'oh god'. Of course I did say it but I wondered later if he would have done it if I hadn't said anything. Should have been quicker on the draw with that one.

Gabe . . . Gabe and I had sex. It was totally AWESOME! He asked me to fuck him and he sucked me off. I have never felt anything like that before. It was fricking amazing. It felt so good to be inside him. Then he rolled over and he came on me. Well between us I guess. That was so cool. It felt so warm and

I gotta say, it was nice to do that for him. When I came he stuck his finger up my ass. THAT was cool. I have never cum so hard in my life! He wants to do it again. So do I, I think. He says I'm really good at it. I know he is. Anyway, thanks for listening.

Chapter 18

David's bedroom door flew open and Amanda jumped onto his bed.

"It's official! Their splitting up and Gabe is buying the house." She said. David opened his eyes and squinted at her.

"What time is it?" He asked still half asleep.

"Didn't you hear me?" She asked crossing her arms.

"I heard you, but what time is it?" He asked waking up a little. She sighed and looked at the clock.

"6:30" She said. David groaned and pulled her down beside him. She giggled and cuddled up with him.

"Ok, what happened?" He asked closing his eyes and breathing in her hair.

"They announced it this morning. Gabe got up and left."

"Where did he go?"

"Well, I caught him outside and he said he had a lawyer to talk to about the house."

"So he is gonna buy it?"

"I guess so." Amanda said and looked up at David. He still had his eyes closed. "I'm gonna stay, and live with him." She added. David tightened his arms around her and sighed. She smiled and tucked her head in his chest. "You smell good this morning." She said smelling his hair.

"Yea, I showered last night when I got home."

"Did Gabe like your torture thing?"

"Gabe liked my torture thing." David said and giggled.

"You guys are weird."

"Why?" David asked and looked at her. She looked up at him.

"Cause, you guys like that weird stuff. I don't get it." David smiled and shook his head.

"It's cool stuff, Mandy." David said and stretched. Amanda moved out of the way and let David sit up. "Why are you here so early?" He asked looking at the clock and seeing the insane early time.

"I had to tell you about my parents." She said and smiled at him. He shook his head and got out of bed. She watched him dress and giggled.

"What?" He said as he did up the fly in his jeans.

"Nothing, you're just so sexy sometimes." David half smirked and pulled a shirt on over his head.

"So are you, but I don't laugh about it." He said and kissed her quickly on the cheek. She giggled again and blushed. He left the room and went to the bathroom. He peed and then moved to the mirror. He brushed his hair and teeth and applied his cologne and deodorant. He stepped out of the bathroom and went back to his room.

"Are you ready to go back?" Amanda asked as David put on his leather jacket that Gabe's cologne still clung to.

"I think so." David said smelling the jacket and smiling to himself.

"Well, I hear that the after school project guys miss having you around."

"Do they?" David asked. Amanda nodded and smiled. David shook his head and grabbed his book bag. They walked down to the kitchen together.

"She got you out of bed I see." Nancy said putting coffee's down for both of them.

"Yea, she did." David said and sat down at the table.

"So, Nancy. Are you going to go see that thing they brought back with them?" Amanda asked.

"Oh, I think I'll wait for the fair." Nancy answered and sipped her coffee. David giggled knowing his mother had about as much interest in the Iron Maiden as Amanda did.

"Yea, me too I think." Amanda said and smiled at David. David shook his head and looked out the window.

"What kind of law office is open this early in the morning?" David asked Amanda. Amanda looked at him with a puzzled gaze. "You said Gabe went to see a lawyer."

"Oh, he is a friend of his in the city I guess. He was going to see him at home." Amanda answered and sipped her coffee.

"It's really too bad about your parents Amanda, but it will be nice to see you stick around." Nancy said in her overly maternal voice.

"Yea, well. I guess you can't kick a dead horse or whatever, right?" Amanda asked. David looked at her and smiled.

"What time did you get in last night, David?" Nancy asked. David thought about the night with Gabe and shivered.

"Late, like midnight or something."

"Wow, that is late."

"Yea well, I had to show it off to Gabe and the time got away on us I guess." David answered and looked back out the window.

"What did he think?" Nancy asked.

"He loved it, of course." Amanda answered. David smiled and raised his eyebrows. He lit a cigarette and looked over at Amanda.

"Well, I suppose there is some kind of attraction to something like that." Nancy said and sipped her coffee again.

"What's not to like?" David asked. Amanda and Nancy looked at each other as if he had lost his mind. "She's sexy and romantic." He added and laughed. Nancy and Amanda both shook their heads and sipped at their coffee. David shook his head and puffed his cigarette. Nancy looked up at the clock. It was 7:15.

"Well, I gotta go kids." She said and stood up. She took her cup to the sink and made her way to the door.

"Have a good day mom." David said as she left the house. She waved at them through the window as she walked by and got into her car and left.

"So, Alan Black is even sexier away from school, huh?" Amanda asked.

"He's sexy all the time, Amanda." Amanda giggled and stared at David.

"Did you have a lot of private time with him?"

"Yea, it was crazy, man." David said thinking about Alan in his boxers again. It had been a detail he left out of the recap the afternoon before.

"So, do you like him more then?"

"Yea, I think so." David said thinking about his night with Gabe and now knowing what it would feel like with Alan.

"How often were you hard?" She asked and then giggled. David looked at her and laughed.

"Like, most of the time."

"So, you probably really needed to jack off last night then?" David laughed and nodded.

"Amanda, sometimes you surprise me."

"Why?"

"Cause you know me all too well." He said and finished his coffee. Amanda giggled and watched him get a new cup of coffee. They talked more about David's trip and how horny Alan made him. When it was time to leave, they collected their things and headed out the door to school. Amanda playfully picked on David as they walked. He laughed at her digs and shook his head. They got their books from their lockers and headed to home room. They sat through attendance and went to their morning classes. David met Amanda at their lockers and headed outside to the smoking table for lunch break. When they sat down and David had his cigarette lit, he saw a black Hearse pull up to the school. His stomach flipped as he watched Gabe get out of the car.

"Gabe is here." Amanda said and waved at him. Gabe smiled and came over to them. He looked at David and David took a deep breath. Gabe looked into David's eyes for a second and David seemed to whimper a little. Gabe smiled and looked at Amanda. She hadn't noticed David's reaction.

"So, Kyle said I have a big enough down payment and there should be no problem with me buying the house." Gabe said. Amanda squealed and jumped into his arms. Gabe hugged her and looked over her shoulder at David as he held her. David smiled and Gabe smiled back. He looked David up and down and mouthed 'Are you ok today?' David nodded and mouthed 'better than ok'. Gabe smiled and let Amanda go. She looked up at him and had the widest grin on her face.

"So we can stay then?"

"We can stay." Gabe said and she hugged him again. David giggled at Amanda's excitement.

"When do you get position?" David asked.

"As soon as all the paper work goes through. Mom is gonna stay for a while until she finds a place in the city for her and Little Mike. Dad is off apartment hunting right now."

"Where is he gonna go?" Amanda asked.

"To the city too. He works there so it makes sense." Gabe said and looked at David. David smiled and bit his bottom lip. Gabe smiled back and then looked at his sister. "You can have my room now if you want it."

"Oh, that's so cool!" Amanda said and practically jumped up and down. Gabe and David both laughed. "I'm so happy Gabe!" She said and jumped back into his arms. Gabe looked over her shoulder again at David. David sighed and licked his teeth at Gabe. Gabe closed his eyes and shook his head. 'You're in trouble.' He mouthed a David laughed.

"Well," Gabe said and let Amanda go again. "I better go. I'll see you later ok?" He asked Amanda and she nodded still smiling. He looked at David and smiled.

"See you later?" David asked and raised an eyebrow at Gabe.

"You bet." Gabe said and turned to leave. His long trench coat swayed with his walk and David sighed.

"Isn't that awesome?!" Amanda asked David and giggled.

"Yea. It's great Amanda." David said and smiled at his friend. He could hear the thundering engine of Gabe's car roar to life and shut his eyes.

"It's so cool that Gabe is buying the house." She said and looked back at her brother's car. She waved and he gunned the gas to answer. He pulled away and Amanda looked back at David. "I was so scared I would have to move." She said and hugged David. David held her and smiled.

"Well, I'm glad you're not." He said to his best friend. Amanda squeezed him as tight as she could manage. David giggled and squeezed back.

"I love you David." She said smiling with her eyes closed. David raised his eyebrows and looked down at her.

"You what?" He asked quietly. Amanda seemed to go stone still in David's arms for a second. She pulled away far enough to look up at him. Her face was beat red but she repeated her words.

"I love you." She said and stared at him. David cleared his throat and held his breath for a second.

"You do?" He asked. She smiled and nodded. "Why?" He asked. Amanda giggled and reached her head up to kiss him. He kissed her and held her tight. Amanda leaned back with her eyes still closed.

"Because I do." She said and smiled at him. David smirked and shook his head.

"Well, that's new." He said and she looked at him. She had a puzzling look on her face that was both shock and disappointment.

"I tell you I love you and you say *that's new?*" She asked. David sighed and sat back down.

"I wasn't expecting that." He said staring at her. Amanda sighed and sat down next to him.

"Why not?" She asked putting her head on his shoulder.

"Weird timing I guess." David answered and kissed the top of her head. Amanda giggled.

"I know, sorry." She said and kissed him on the cheek. David smiled and looked at her. "Don't say anything ok. Figure this other stuff out for right now. I don't want you to say anything you don't mean." Amanda said and smiled at him. David raised his eyebrows.

"Ok, Amanda. But I can figure this stuff out and still say, I love you too." Amanda giggled and turned red. "What? You didn't think I cared for you like that?" He asked. Amanda shook her head. "You *are* dumber than I thought." David teased and Amanda giggled.

"I thought you would say something like, 'Amanda, I love you like a friend.' or something like that."

"Well I do. But I also love you like a lover. Or a girl friend or whatever you wanna call it."

"A *girl friend?*" Amanda asked with a wrinkled up nose. David laughed and nodded. "I don't wanna be your girlfriend David. I just want to be in love with you." She added. David raised his eyebrows and laughed.

"Ok, but then you can't get mad at me if I fuck Alan or something." He whispered. Amanda burst out laughing and shook her head.

"I cross my heart. If you have sex with Alan, or any other guy, I would be happy for you. But you're off the market for other girls." She said. David laughed.

"It's a deal Amanda." He said. She kissed him again and then asked.

"Any rules for me?" David thought about it for a second and said,

"You can sleep with girls whenever you want, but you're off the market for guys." Amanda laughed and nodded. They both laughed and watched as people started to go into the school.

"Looks like its time." Amanda said and grabbed David's hand. David held Amanda's hand as they walked to their lockers. They collected their books for the afternoon classes and Amanda turned to go.

"What, no kiss?" David teased. Amanda's face went red and she quickly kissed him and hurried off. David laughed. He knew how much Amanda hated public displays of affection. He shook his head and walked down to room 19. He walked in and went right over to Mr. Black.

"Check this out." He said and handed Alan the pick and the music score for Think about You.

"Oh man. We gotta play this. And where have I seen this pick before?"

"Oh, maybe in the sexy hands of Axel Rose." David answered. Alan giggled and raised his eyebrows.

"Really?"

"Yup." David said as Alan handed the pick and music score back to him.

"Where did you get it?" Alan asked as David walked over to his desk and sat down.

"Your boyfriend." David answered and laughed. Alan shook his head and watched the other students come in.

"Gabe?" Alan asked whispering. David nodded and Alan laughed. "My boyfriend. You're such a dick." He said quietly. David laughed and Alan went to the front of the class.

"Ok, Gang. Last week we read about the victims of our friend Jack. Anybody do the assigned work sheets?" Mr. Black automatically went to David's desk to get his without David even putting up his hand. David handed it to him and he went around collecting the finished ones. "Ok, everybody that didn't do it, I want it tomorrow." He said and continued with the lesson. He talked about the investigation its self and the problems the detective ran into thinking it was an educated man. The class had a lot of questions, as they always did but David just stared at Alan as he spoke. Once in a while Alan would look at him and David would find himself lost in Alan's eyes. He could feel his body reacting to the movements his body would make as he talked.

God I could fuck you right now. David thought as the class neared its end. Mr. Black had no homework for the students who had the work sheets finished. The bell rang and the class cleared out. David waited for everyone to leave and he stood up.

"So, where did Gabe get it?" Alan asked as David put his jacket back on and picked up his books.

"At an auction." David answered.

"He gave you this last night?"

"Yup. He thought I would like it." David said remembering Gabe's moans from the night before.

"Was he right?"

"Fuck yea." David said and laughed. Alan laughed too and shook his head. David headed out of the class room and down to his English class. Mrs. Coldiron smiled when she saw him.

"Nice to see you're feeling better David." She said. David thanked her and sat down at his desk. The bruise on his eye was hardly noticeable and his lip was completely healed. "So, we know that after Han's left and Anthony looked for him for all those years, there was never any other lover in Anthony's life. How do we feel about Han's new wife?" She asked the class. A flood of hands raised and she went through the answers one at a time. David listened to the class's discussion and was glad that the book was finally over. She announced at the end that their new book would be the coactive works of Edgar Allan Poe. David smiled and thought about the Iron Maiden. He could hardly wait to see it again. He knew there was the project group that night and looked at the clock. Just as he did the bell rang and he was almost the first person up. He went to his locker and got out the books he would need and put them in his bag. He could feel someone breathing on his shoulder. He spun around to see Gabe.

"What are you doing here?" David asked and shut the locker.

"Wanna see something cool?" Gabe asked and David laughed. He followed Gabe out to his car and got in. Gabe got in and started the engine.

"What is it?" David asked.

"Shhh." Gabe said and drove off. They drove to the highway and Gabe turned toward the city.

"Where are we going?" David asked. Gabe smiled and looked at David.

"For a drive."

"Where?" David was very persistent.

"I want to show you something. Is that ok?" Gabe asked. David smiled and shook his head. "So, do you hate me today?" Gabe asked as he drove.

"Not at all." David said lighting a cigarette for both himself and Gabe.

"Thanks." Gabe said taking the cigarette. "I'm glad you don't because you're about to fall in love with me." Gabe said. David laughed and shook his head.

"Sorry, no can do. Your sister beat you to it." David said. Gabe laughed and looked at David.

"She said it?"

"You knew she would?" David asked.

"Yea, I said it was a bad idea because of your little . . . indecision on your sexuality. She said she didn't care about that. She would love you anyway and said she wouldn't tell you not to be with guys. I wouldn't have done what we did last night if she hadn't said that." David giggled and looked at Gabe.

"Yea, last night." David said in a very seductive voice.

"You're so gay." Gabe said and laughed. David laughed too. "How is Alan today?"

"Hot."

"Of course. Show off your present?" Gabe asked referring to the pick and guitar score.

"Yea. He thinks it's sweet. He wants to play it with me."

"Tell him you'll let him for sexual favors." Gabe said. David laughed and ashed his cigarette out the window. "I'm serious."

"I know you are." David said and Gabe laughed. They chatted about Alan until they hit the city. Gabe drove right through and pulled into the pawn shop parking lot.

"How much money you got?" Gabe asked as he shut off the car.

"Uh, 120 bucks I think." David said.

"On you?" Gabe asked.

"Yea, why?" David asked. Gabe smiled and said.

"Come with me." He got out of the car and David followed him to the doors of the store. "Now, don't scream, ok." Gabe said putting his hand on the door of the store.

"Aren't I supposed to fall in love with you or something?"

"That too, but don't scream." Gabe said. David agreed with a puzzled look on his face and Gabe opened the door. David stepped in and the only thing he saw was the red flames that stung the jet black paint of his dads Stratocaster guitar he had pawned when David was young. It was the guitar David learned on. David stared at the thing and didn't even breathe. Gabe staid quiet and watched David as his eyes never left the guitar. Gabe looked at the girl behind the counter and said, "Get it down for him sweet heart." The girl blushed and took the stool over to the guitar. David didn't move. She carefully took it down and handed it to David. He slowly took the guitar and stared at it. Gabe reached into David's back pocket for his wallet and went up to the counter. David stood there with the guitar in his hands. Tears filled his eyes.

"What's up with him?" The girl asked looking at David.

"That was his dad's guitar. It's been gone for like 10 years." He answered quietly.

"He's been looking for it for that long?"

"No only about 2 years. Since his dad died."

"Awe, that's so sad." The girl said. Gabe looked back at the girl and smiled.

"How much?" He asked. The girl stared at David and watched as a single tear trickled down his cheek. He still hadn't moved.

"Take it." She said looking back at Gabe.

"What?" Gabe said shocked.

"It's my dad's store and he has a similar story. He'll understand and would have just given it to him."

"Wow, thanks babe." Gabe said and winked at the girl. She blushed and nodded. Gabe walked back over to David and put his wallet back into his pants. David's fingers had found the spot where the paint had chipped when he dropped it down the stairs. "Let's take her home, David." Gabe said quietly and put his hand on David's shoulder. David looked at him and swallowed. He looked as though he would explode. "Ok, wait till we get to the car." Gabe whispered and opened the door for David. David got to the car and set the guitar in the back. He sat down on the passenger seat next to Gabe. Gabe looked at him.

"Get out of here." David said staring out the windshield.

"Ok." Gabe said and pulled away. Gabe looked over at David who still hadn't moved. He raised his eyebrows and waited for David to say something. David seemed to take his first breath since he seen the guitar.

"How did you find it?" David asked quietly.

"I had to wait for Kyle this morning. I like to see what kind of axes they have in that place and seen it." Gabe answered waiting for

David to have a less pained look. "Are you ok?" Gabe asked pulling out onto the highway. David looked at Gabe. Gabe raised his eyebrows and smiled.

"I might be sick." David said.

"Not in the car David." Gabe said and David laughed. He looked back at the guitar and then at Gabe.

"You know, I'm gonna have to thank you properly for this." David said. Gabe laughed and nodded.

"I was hoping you would say that." David laughed and quickly kissed Gabe. Gabe smiled and continued driving. David looked back at the guitar then back to Gabe.

"How much did it cost?" David asked going for his wallet.

"Nothing actually. The girl at the store thought I was so hot, she gave it to me." David raised his eyebrows and checked his wallet anyway.

"*You* paid for it?" He asked.

"No, I told you. She gave it to me. I guess her dad had the same kind of thing happen to him and he would have just given it to you anyway. So she did."

"No way." David said and looked back at the guitar again. Gabe smiled and ran his hand through David's hair.

"In love with me yet?" Gabe asked in a seductive voice. David laughed and looked at him.

"I hope you're not serious." David said leaning close enough to Gabe he could have kissed him. Gabe laughed and stared out the windshield. David looked back at the guitar and Gabe sighed.

"I'm glad you're not missing that thing anymore." Gabe said as David sat back down in his seat properly and tossed his cigarette out the window.

"How did you know I was?"

"Amanda." Gabe answered. David rolled his eyes and nodded.

"Of course." David said.

"So, do you love her too?" Gabe asked looking at David again.

"Yea, I always have." David answered.

"And what about the way she feels about you and guys. Gonna still explore that?" Gabe asked and cleared his throat.

"Until she tells me I can't." David answered and Gabe smiled.

"Are you going to tell her about us?"

"I don't think so. You've worked so hard to make sure your family doesn't know. And I don't think fucking her brother was what she had in mind when she said *guys*." David said. Gabe laughed and nodded his head.

"Yea, you're probably right." Gabe said. They talked about the guitar for the rest of the drive. Gabe pulled in at his house and waited for David to get the guitar out of the back. "Gonna name her?" Gabe asked. David looked at the guitar and smiled.

"Yea, Abby." David said.

"Good name." Gabe said and walked with David back to his house. Amanda was waiting on the front steps for them.

"Well, you bought a guitar." She said and stood up. David turned the guitar so Amanda could see the red flames. She gasped. "Oh my God David." She said and stared at the guitar.

"Gabe found her at the Guitar Pawn Shop." David said and looked at Gabe.

"Wow Gabe. That's amazing." Amanda said. Gabe smiled and put his hand on David's shoulder.

"Go serenade her and I'll see you later." He whispered. Amanda giggled and David smiled.

"Bye Gabe." Amanda said and followed David into the house. They both dropped their book bags on the floor and went down stairs.

David plugged the guitar into his dad's old amp while Amanda put out a stool for him and a little chair for her. He sat down and looked at her.

"So," He said and strummed the guitar. "It seems to be in tune. What do you want to hear?" He asked and pulled the pick out of his pocket. Amanda smiled and sighed.

"Um, can you play that song where you have to whistle in the front?" David smiled and played Patients by Gun's and Rose's for her. He sang along with the music and Amanda swayed in her chair with her eyes closed. He stared at her while he played the solo. She swayed along with his playing and he smiled. When the song was over, Amanda clapped. "I forgot how good you were." She said and smiled. David laughed and looked down at the guitar. He flipped the pick along the back of his fingers.

"Anything else?" She thought for a second and requested Billy Jean by Michele Jackson.

"If you tell anyone I can play that song, I'll disown you." David said. Amanda crossed her heart with her fingers and smiled. He played and sang her song for her. She sang along on the chorus but let David sing the rest. She clapped at the end again and David laughed.

"I love it when you play." She said and got up and kissed him. David smiled when she sat back down.

"Now what?" He asked.

"Anything you want." She said. David played a few of his favorites and Amanda clapped at the end of each. After his fourth song, he saw his mom in the door way. He looked up at her and smiled. Nancy had tears in her eyes. Amanda got up and took Nancy's hand. She led her to the leather chair in the corner. David turned on his stool and looked at her.

"Hey." David said quietly to his mom.

"Hi" She said and smiled through her tears. "Is that . . . ?" David nodded and she gasped. "Oh David." She said and the tears rolled. David smiled and played Knocking on Heavens Door for her. She closed her eyes and listened to her son. Amanda smiled and watched David play through his own tears. She had remembered the story about how Mike had played that song, on *that* guitar, at him and Nancy's wedding. David sang it like he wrote it and her heart pounded in her chest. Nancy cried when the song was over and hugged her son. David hugged her tightly and Amanda clapped.

"God your good David." Amanda whispered. David smiled at her and looked at his mom.

"Better than your dad." She said and wiped the tears from her face.

"I don't know about that." David said and laughed. Nancy giggled and looked at Amanda.

"Your brother called." She said and David's stomach fluttered.

"He did? Do I have to go home?" She asked.

"Well, he said you're gonna want to hear this first hand." Nancy said. Amanda said her good byes and kissed David quickly before she left. Nancy raised her eyebrows but said nothing. She sat down on the little chair Amanda had sat on and looked at her son. He smiled at her and ran his hand along the neck of his dad's guitar. "You look good with that thing." She said.

"I know." David answered and Nancy smiled.

"Ok, play Copper Head Road." She said and David laughed. David played the song for his mom and she sang along. When the song was over she looked around the room. "It's strange to have music play in here again."

"Yea, I know." David said stroking the neck of his guitar again.

"So, Amanda hey?" She asked smiling. David smiled at her and shook his head.

"It's always been Amanda, mom." He said and pulled the guitar score out of his pocket.

"What's that?" Nancy asked.

"Think about You." David answered and Nancy smiled.

"Gun's and Rose's right?"

"Very good mom." David said and looked over the music. Nancy smiled and got up.

"Dinner is in an hour." She said and left the room. David practiced the song until he could play it without the music. His mother called him up for supper and he joined her in the kitchen. "Sounds good." She said as they ate. David thanked her and looked at the time. It was 7:30. He raised his eyebrows and thought about the project at the library.

"I think I'm going to take the camera with me tonight." David said thinking about the Iron Maiden waiting in the storage room for him.

"That's a great idea." Nancy said. They finished their dinner and Nancy dug out the camera while David did the dishes. She set it on the table for him and found an extra set of batteries.

"Thanks mom." David said as he dried his hands. He picked up the camera and

Re-taught himself how it worked. Nancy dried the dishes while David played with the camera. Just then, the phone rang. David answered it.

"Hello?"

"*Hey, am I picking you up?*" It was Alan. David smiled and sat down at the table.

"Sure." David said.

"*Ok, you wanna go early and move Your Lady out of the storage room to show her off?*"

"Yea, good idea." David said and looked at the camera again. "I'm bringing my mom's camera with me." David added.

"*That's a great idea, David.*" Alan said.

"I know. When you coming?"

"*Well, actually, I'm on my way right now. We moved the time to 8:30. If we're going early, we better go now.*" Alan said. David looked at the time. It was almost eight.

"Ok. I'll see you in a couple minutes then."

"*I can almost see you already.*"

"You're on your cell phone aren't you?"

"*Yep. I'll be there in 30 seconds.*" Alan said and David laughed.

"Ok" David said and hung up the phone. He got up and looked at his mom. "Well, I'm out of here."

"Ok, have a good time." Nancy said as David left the room. He put his shoes on and stepped outside. It was chilly but seeing Alan's car pull up seemed to warm him up. He walked over to the car and got in.

"Guess what?" David said as soon as he shut the door. Alan laughed.

"What?" He asked as he drove away.

"Your boyfriend found my dad's olds guitar at a pawn shop and we went and picked it up after school today." Alan shook his head at David's boyfriend comment.

"Really? This is a good thing I take it."

"Oh yea. And I have learned to play Think about You." David said in an excited sounding voice.

"So when do we play?"

"This weekend if you want."

"Ok. Sunday afternoon?" Alan asked as he turned the corner.

"Cool." David said and looked down the street at the library. They pulled up and hurried out of the car. Alan took the camera from David as he unlocked the storage room door. They both sighed when the light went on and they could see the Iron Maiden. "Hello beautiful." David said and stepped in. Alan laughed and went in with him.

"So, we gonna take her out or leave her in here?" David thought about it for a second.

"I wonder if loading her up and unloading her from that machine is hard on her." David said looking at Alan.

"Ok, let's leave her be then." He said and turned the camera on. He had David stand beside it and then inside of it for pictures.

"So, what's the plan for tonight?" David asked as they put out the books on the table closest to the open storage room door.

"Well, I think it's a lot of going over what people will say and . . ." Alan stopped talking and went behind the counter. He picked up a box that was filled with swords, throwing stars, and two small maces. David shook his head and smiled at Alan. "Oh, there's more." Alan said and pulled out a shield, a javelin and a bow with a leather wither filled with arrows.

"Wow, cool." David said and looked over the things Alan had gathered.

"We need to see you work this stuff." Alan said and leaned on the counter. David pulled out the Long Sword from the box and held it in front of him. "Well, let's see." Alan said. David stood back away from the tables and thought back to his fencing lessons. He closed his eyes and tossed the sword behind him with his right hand and caught it with his left hand. He swung the sword round his head and pointed at Alan. Alan smiled and nodded. "Awesome." He said and David smiled.

"Now what?" David asked and Alan dug in the box. Just then, Samantha and Ron walked in.

"Hi guys." Alan said. David turned with the sword in his had to face the two students.

"So, the prodigal son returns." Ron said and shook David's hand. David smiled and shrugged.

"We heard what happened. Are you ok?" Samantha asked setting her bag by the table.

"That depends on what you heard." David said looking at Alan. Alan shrugged and looked at Samantha.

"Well, we heard you got in a fight protecting your girlfriend from some sicko perv." She answered. David smiled and shook his head.

"That's what happened." Alan said and stepped toward David. "But, it's over now, and David here has something to show you." Alan smiled at David and David smiled back.

"Come with me, guys." David said and led them to the storage room. They looked inside and both gasped. Alan and David laughed.

"Is it real?" Ron asked.

"Of course it is." Samantha said and smiled at David and Alan. David walked into the room and opened the big Iron door. Ron walked forward and inspected the spine and the hinges and every little thing David had inspected when he first seen it.

"This is incredible." Ron said stepping away from the machine. Samantha looked the machine over as well and was just as amazed.

"I think she's a hit." Alan whispered to David.

"Of course she is." David said and smiled. When Samantha walked away, David stepped into the Iron Maiden. He placed his hands and feet in the appropriate places and closed his eyes.

"Wow, that's awesome." Ron said and Samantha agreed.

"He makes it look good doesn't he?" Alan asked and the two students nodded.

"He has *got* to do that at the fair." Samantha said. David opened his eyes and looked at Alan. Alan smiled and nodded.

"What do you think, David? Could you show Your Lady off like that at the fair?"

"His lady?" Ron asked. Alan laughed.

"Well, look at him. The maker himself didn't love her as much as David does." Samantha said. Alan and David both smiled.

"So what was with the sword when we came in?" Ron asked as they left the room and David locked the Iron Maiden safely away.

"Yea, show us your stuff David." Samantha said and pulled a chair away from the table to watch. Ron and Alan did the same.

"Ok." David said and picked the sword back up. He did the same show he had done for Alan and they all clapped.

"Throwing stars!" Ron yelled. Alan laughed and looked around.

"We gotta find a target." Samantha said and they all searched the library. They found an old box and some hunks of wood. They put together a target for David and sat back down.

"Don't miss." Alan said looking at the shelf of books propping up the makeshift target. David rolled his eyes and aimed at the target. Alan, Ron and Samantha all stared without blinking at David. He closed his eyes and let the first star go.

"Holy shit!" Ron said and Alan laughed.

"Do it again, David." Alan said quietly. David aimed again and shut his eyes. Samantha squeaked when the star hit right next to the first one.

"That's impossible! How do you do it?" Ron asked getting up and standing next to David.

"Well, I just aim and throw."

"No way dude. You close your eyes." Ron said amazed with David's ability.

"I aim first. Then I close my eyes for effect." David whispered. Alan laughed and shook his head.

"The crowds will love it." Alan said and handed David a mace to demonstrate. David demonstrated every weapon Alan had other than the bow. It was 10 and David was tired.

"Well guys." Alan said as Samantha also yawned. "You know what David can do. Get writing your overviews."

"I think David's demonstrations speak for themselves." Ron said through clenched teeth trying to pull out the throwing stars David had used earlier. David giggled and walked over to Ron.

"Slight counter clock wise turn. Then pull." David said. Rod did as David said and the stars came out as easy as thumb tacks. Alan laughed and shook his head.

"Let's do our homework guys. We don't want David making us look bad out there." Alan said and smiled. Samantha and Ron thanked David for the demonstrations and left with a collection of books to study. As soon as they were gone, David sat down in a chair and hugged his ribs. "Are you ok?" Alan asked as he rushed to David's side and placed a hand on his back.

"Just too much moving around I guess." David answered and sat up straight again.

"You were amazing today." Alan said as he backed away and let David stand. David smiled at him and nodded.

"Thanks." David said. Alan and David packed up the rest of the weapons and David collected his camera. They stepped out into the cool night air and both lit a cigarette. Alan locked the library door and walked over to his car. They both got in and Alan wheeled his window down. David did the same and they sat in the car smoking.

"About what Carman had said about me needing a kid to do this . . ." Alan started but David cut him off.

"Alan, this has been the coolest week of my life. I like to do this stuff. If you're getting something out of it that's cool but really, I couldn't have ever dreamed of seeing all this stuff in the same room. Let alone getting to be the one that uses it all."

"Well, I still wish there wasn't an underlying agenda." Alan said and flicked his cigarette out the window. David shook his head and sighed.

"Wanna make it up to me?" David asked. Alan laughed and nodded. "Ok, tell me what you did to that guy that hurt Carman." David said and looked at Alan. Alan sighed and looked at David. David handed his cigarette to Alan and Alan smiled. He took a drag from it and blew the smoke out the window.

"Why do you want to know?" Alan asked handing the cigarette back to David and lighting one of his own.

"Don't through that one away." David said and giggled. Alan smiled and looked down at the lighter he held in his hands. David sighed and cleared his throat. "I want to know because whatever it was, it was bad enough to make *you* act like that." Alan sighed and looked at David.

"I really don't want to talk about it. I know I probably should . . ." Alan paused and looked back down at his lighter. "But not today." He finished saying and started the car. David sighed and shook his head.

"Well, you better do something about it. I hate seeing you act like it just happened yesterday." Alan smiled and nodded. He pulled the car out of the parking lot and headed towards David's house.

"Ok, what else could I do to make it up to you then?" David burst out laughing at the question. Alan looked at David with a puzzled gaze.

"Sorry, I just really don't want to answer that. I know I should . . ." David said and paused for effect. "But not today." He finished. Alan laughed and shook his head.

"Nice David."

"I'm sorry, I couldn't resist." David said and tossed his cigarette out the window. Alan pulled up in front of David's house and looked at David. David's smile vanished at the first sight of the seriousness on Alan's face.

"I gave him a taste of his own medicine." Alan said and looked out the windshield. David repositioned himself in the seat he was in and cleared his throat.

"Oh." David said and sighed. He put his hand on Alan's arm and Alan looked at him.

"It was terrible, David. I'm not proud of it. But after what he did to Carman . . ." Alan stopped talking and looked away again. David squeezed Alan's arm then let him go.

"I get it." David said and smiled at Alan.

"You do?" Alan asked frowning at David.

"I think so. Anger does strange things to people." David said and looked at the house. There were no lights on and David looked back at Alan. "I would invite you in for a drink or something but it looks like mom is asleep and it's a school night." David said and giggled. Alan laughed and nodded.

"Thanks David. You shouldn't have to listen to crap like this from me. I'm supposed to be here for *you*."

"Fuck, give me a break Alan. I will be 18 in February and I'm in grade 11. Do you think that's from failing?" David asked. Alan shook his head to answer no. "No, I was in the pen for a year for possession. I heard worse crap in there than you could dish out in a life time."

"I didn't know that." Alan said quietly. David raised his eyebrow and clicked his teeth.

"It's not exactly the thing that's told around the camp fire." David said. Alan nodded and looked into David's eyes. They stared at each other for quite some time before David's body begged him to either kiss him or look away. David looked away. Alan blinked his eyes and shook his head. "I should go." David said and opened the door. Alan grabbed David's arm to stop him. David looked back at Alan.

"Is there something I don't know?" Alan asked and David closed his eyes.

"Probably." He answered and opened them to look at Alan. Alan smiled and let go of David's arm. David stayed where he was and Alan looked at him with shock.

"I thought you would pull yourself out of the car and leave." David smiled and shook his head.

"Alan, I am full of surprises." He said but this time he did get out of the car. He walked around to the driver's side door and Alan wheeled down the window.

"I think we need to get all our shit out of the way someday." Alan said and David leaned on the window. He sighed and looked at Alan.

"Is today that day?" David asked and squinted his eyes. Alan laughed and shook his head.

"No, not today." Alan said. David smiled and patted the car. He walked up to the house and waved as he unlocked the door. Alan waved back and left. David went up to his room and leaned against the shut door.

"Holy shit." He breathed and went over to his desk.

Sept. 25 Monday continued . . .

I think Alan has been with a dude but not the way I thought. I think he raped the guy that raped Carman but I can't be sure. I told him about my 11 months in the pen. Then I think we had some kind of moment that Alan most definitely noticed! He wants to get all our shit off our chests and throw it all on the table. I don't think I can do that. I want him so badly but I am so freaked that it would scare him off or something. I need to talk to Gabe about this. Sorry for the add on.

Chapter 19

David woke up with a massive migraine. He groaned and rolled over to look at the clock. It was 4:30 am. He closed his eyes and held his head in his hands. He took a few deep breaths and tried to go back to sleep. When that failed, he got up and went to the medicine cabinet for some medication. He looked through the cupboard and found Advil for migraines. He took two out of the bottle and popped them into his mouth. He could always swallow pills with no water but he seemed especially thirsty. He walked into his room and grabbed his robe and went down to the kitchen. He poured a glass of water and stood at the sink drinking it. He could hear a strange noise coming from outside and peered out the window. He couldn't see anything so he went to the door and stepped outside. He could hear Amanda's parents yelling at each other. He rolled his eyes and turned to go in until he heard Amanda and Gabe's voices chime in. He shut the door and slowly walked toward Amanda's house. He could hear only Gabe and Amanda's dad arguing now. He stopped at the end of the drive way and looked in the kitchen window. He could see Gabe and his father standing within striking distance of each other. Amanda stood behind Gabe and Amanda's mother behind her husband. All of a sudden, Gabe's dad punched him straight in the jaw. Amanda screamed and her mother held her husband back from hitting him again. David ran up to the house and flew in the door. He ran into the kitchen and ploughed into Amanda's dad knocking him back into the table.

"David!" Amanda yelled and pulled him off her Dad.

"Steve!" Amanda's mother yelled and helped him up off the table. David looked at Gabe and Gabe was on the floor knocked out cold.

"Get out!" Amanda yelled at her parents. David looked around and saw that they were drinking. Amanda's mother went toward the stairs. "What are you doing?" Amanda asked her standing in her way.

"I am not leaving without my son!" She yelled. David stood between Amanda and her mom. "Who do you think you are?" She asked David and tried to push passed him. David pushed her away.

"You're drunk. Little Mike stays here. Go sober up." David said in a low steady voice. He looked over at Gabe and seen he was starting to come around. He tried to get up and David reached down and touched his shoulder. "Stay down." David said to him. Gabe glowered at his father.

"Is this the guy? Huh?" Steve slurred and pointed a finger at David. David raised his eyebrows and stared the intoxicated man. "Sure you are . . . Your Mike's boy aren't you?" He asked stepping closer to David. He could feel Amanda tense up behind him. "Boy, he would love to see this." Steve said stumbling but moving ever closer to David. David stared at him and shook his head. "Don't shake your head at me you trader!" Steve said and pushed David. Amanda squeaked with fear behind David.

"Stop it dad!" She screamed.

"Stop it? Stop it? Did you know your boyfriend turned your brother gay?" Steve said. David raised his eyebrows again and looked at Gabe. He was just getting to his feet when David threw a punch. Steve hit the floor like a sack of potatoes and Amanda's mother screamed.

"Shut up mom! He's fine. Get him out of here." Gabe said and picked his dad up.

"Get your disgusting hands off me." Steve said and followed his wife out of the house. Amanda ran around David and hugged Gabe.

"Oh my god Gabe." She said crying. David stood staring at Gabe. Gabe squinted his eyes at him and shook his head.

"Go check on Mike for me babe." Gabe said to Amanda. Amanda looked at him and then at David. She smiled at her brother and walked over to David. She rubbed David's arm as she walked by him.

"What happened?" David asked. Gabe moved over to David and looked at him.

"They heard me telling Amanda I was gay." Gabe said and looked down. David walked over to Gabe and wrapped his arms around him. Gabe hugged back and sighed. "I told her I was interested in you and was asking if my being with you was a problem." David raised his eyebrows.

"Why would you do that?" David asked. Gabe looked at him and smiled.

"She already knew something was up with us. She pretty much guessed the whole thing." Gabe said and sat down on the chair. David sat down next to him and sighed. "She doesn't know what we've done. She just knows there is a mutual attraction." David nodded and looked down at the floor. Gabe looked at David's attire and smiled. "You came over in your house coat?" David looked down and laughed. He explained to Gabe what he was doing outside in the first place and Amanda walked into the room. They both looked up at her.

"I changed him. He's sleeping now." She said and sat down next to David. She held his hand and looked at him. "Thank you for coming over." Amanda said and hugged him. David held Amanda and looked at Gabe over her shoulder. Gabe smiled and rubbed his sisters back.

"It was fate." David said and smiled. Amanda looked at him and frowned.

"Why?"

"I only came over cause I was up with a migraine. I heard the fighting. Now the headache is gone." Amanda smiled and leaned against David's chest. He looked at Gabe again and Gabe smiled.

"Are you ok?" David asked Gabe. Gabe leaned back in his chair and nodded. They sat silently every so often David or Gabe lighting a cigarette. David could feel that Amanda had fallen asleep. He tapped Gabe's leg and pointed at Amanda. Gabe smiled and picked her up off David. She snuggled into his chest.

"Am I sleeping?" She asked in a quiet voice.

"Yes you are." Gabe said as he moved Amanda over to the couch.

"I think you would be better for David to learn on than Todd ever was." She said and rolled over. Gabe smiled at her and looked at David. David giggled and shook his head.

"Good idea." Gabe whispered in her ear. Amanda smiled and nodded.

"I know." She said and fell back into a deeper sleep.

"What a start for your day." Gabe said walking back out to the kitchen and sitting next to David. David smiled and shrugged his shoulders.

"I could think of better ways to start my day I suppose."

"Like a good morning kiss from a really sexy guy?" Gabe asked smiling at David. David smiled back and leaned into Gabe. Gabe kissed him and smiled. "Better?" Gabe asked in a whisper.

"Much." David answered. He looked over at the clock. It was 5:49.

"You could take the day off and get some sleep." Gabe said. David laughed and shook his head.

"No, you should keep Amanda home though."

"I planned on it." Gabe said.

"I gotta get my Alan Black fix for the day anyway." David said and stood up. Gabe got up with him and giggled.

"How did it go last night anyway?"

"The project meeting was good but after was weird." David said. He explained the whole story to Gabe about the strange moment in the car and Alan's reaction. Gabe raised his eyebrows and leaned against the wall.

"Sounds like a pure, unadulterated, moment you guys had. I wonder if he wants to lay it all out on the table because it caught him off guard. I mean, its pretty easy to get lost in your eyes David Smith." David smiled at Gabe and shook his head. "Or he's battling with a morals issue."

"What do you mean?"

"He's your teacher dude." Gabe said and ran his hand through his hair. David watched as his hand pulled through it like a fine toothed comb. It wrapped around his fingers and fell to the side. David smiled and stepped toward Gabe. Gabe put his hand down and David moved so close that their bodies almost touched.

"I should go." David whispered staring into Gabe's eyes. Gabe smiled and pulled David right up against him by the hips.

"Yea, you should." Gabe whispered with his mouth so close that if David even blinked, their lips would touch. David stood motionless for a moment then kissed Gabe. Gabe moaned and pulled David's hair. David bit Gabe's bottom lip and Gabe giggled. "I thought you were leaving?" He asked kissing David again and raking his fingernails down David's back. David tossed his head back and moaned.

"I am." He whispered and ran his hands down Gabe's body to his hips. He pulled Gabe hard against him and locked him in a hungry kiss. Gabe moaned and dug his nails into David's back as they kissed.

"You better go now if you're going." Gabe whispered to David. David smiled and nodded.

"You're probably right." David said and let Gabe's hips go. Gabe took a deep breath and closed his eyes.

"You're such a tease." Gabe said smiling and walked David to the door. David laughed and kissed Gabe at the door.

"I don't mean to be." He said and ran his hand slowly across the front of Gabe's jeans. Gabe closed his eyes and smiled.

"Yea, you do." He said and gave David one last kiss good bye. David went home and upstairs to the shower. He got ready for his day and went down to the kitchen with his mom.

"Where did you go at 4 in the morning?" Nancy asked as he came into the room. David sat down at the table and told his mom the story of Gabe being gay and the big fight he walked in on. He left the parts out that involved him and Gabe as it seemed that was the way it was still going to be for a while. Nancy listened in disbelief. "My god. Those poor kids." She said shaking her head.

"Yea I know." David said thinking about how hard Steve would have had to hit Gabe to knock him out. "There sure is a lot going on over there." David said sipping the last of his coffee.

"You must be tired." Nancy said and pushed a stray hair from David's face. David yawned and nodded.

"I am. But its ok mom." David said and smiled at her. They chatted about the neighbors until both Nancy and David had to leave.

The next few weeks were fairly quiet. Alan and David played guitar every Sunday. Amanda was so shaken about her father attack on Gabe that there was very little time away from her for David or Gabe. Especially to be alone. David continued to have incredibly intense erections caused by Alan Black and the same went for Gabe about David. But with the trouble with Amanda and all the things going on with the separation, Neither David or Gabe could use each other as an outlet for these strong physical reactions they both had.

David woke up on the last Friday before the fair. It was October 27 and the countdown had started in town. It seemed everyone wanted to see the project that David, Alan, Samantha and Ron had put together. He lit a cigarette and lay on his back. He cursed his morning erection and got out of bed. He took his cigarette to the bathroom with him and looked in the mirror. The bruises on his chest were almost a distant memory. He used the toilet and got into the shower. He stared at the wall in the tub as the water beat against his naked body.

Man, I am grouchy this morning. David thought as he washed his hair and body. He got out of the shower and dried off. He brushed his hair and teeth and applied his deodorant and cologne. He went back to his room and got dressed. He gathered his things for the day and headed downstairs.

"Good morning." Gabe said to David as he walked into the room. David stopped and looked at Gabe with wide eyes. He hadn't been at David's house in the morning since the fight with Todd.

"Hi." David said and sat down at the table. Gabe smiled and got up to get David a coffee. "Where is Amanda?" David asked. It was been strange to see Gabe without Amanda around since that night at their house.

"Having a shower and getting ready for school." Gabe said setting a cup in front of David. David smiled and took a sip. "I bet she won't take her time coming over so you better get over here and make it count while you can." Gabe said. David jumped up and straddled Gabe's lap. Gabe giggled and kissed David. David wrapped his hand in Gabe's hair and pulled. Gabe moaned and pushed himself against David. They kissed for some time until they were both fully erect. "I wonder how much more time we have." Gabe said as David pulled Gabe's head back and kissed his neck. David snapped his head up and looked at the time.

"When did you get here?"

"About ten minutes ago." Gabe said. David groaned knowing Amanda did not take long to get ready. Gabe giggled and kissed David's Adam's apple. David closed his eyes and let him kiss. When Gabe stopped, David got off of him and found his seat again. "We gotta get more time together, David." Gabe said looking down at his throbbing erection.

"No shit." David said readjusting his pants so his own erection wasn't so uncomfortable. Gabe bit his bottom lip. David shook his head and smiled. They could see Amanda coming up the walk. Gabe sighed and ran his hand through his hair. They could hear her come in the house.

"Hi guys!" She called from the door.

"Hi." They called in unison. She walked in with Little Mike on her hip. Since the fight with Gabe and Amanda's parent's, they had never come back. All Gabe knew was that they were staying with cousins in Florida and wouldn't be back for a while.

"How are you?" Amanda asked David as she sat down at the table.

"Grouchy this morning actually." David answered. Gabe smiled but said nothing.

"Awe, that's too bad. Where's mom?"

"Work. Early surgery Monday." David answered and smiled at Little Mike. Mike giggled and clapped his hands. Everyone at the table laughed at him. They spent the morning playing with Little Mike. David and Gabe stole glances at each other when Amanda wasn't looking. When it was time to leave, Gabe took Little Mike home and Amanda and David headed to school. They chatted about what would happen if her parent's Steve and Sandra never came home. Amanda was convinced that Gabe would be a good brother and finish raising Little Mike and get her the rest of the way through school. They got to their lockers and gathered their things for the day. The morning went by fast and David was ready for a cigarette. He met Amanda at their lockers and headed out side. When David lit his cigarette, Amanda spoke.

"Are you sleeping with Gabe?" She asked. David burst out laughing and shook his head. He recalled the last few weeks and how clingy she had been.

"When would we have time for that?" David asked looking at Amanda's face. She looked tired.

"You guys have lots of time." Amanda said sitting down on the picnic table and setting her feet on the seat. David stood in front of her.

"When, Amanda? Have you seen us do it?" He asked.

"No." Amanda said with a giggle. "That doesn't mean you guys aren't."

"We couldn't Amanda; you seem to need all the attention in the world lately." David said sounding cruller than he meant to be. Amanda blinked and looked down. David could see the comment had hurt her.

"Oh, I see." She said and sighed. David stepped closer to her.

"Look, Amanda. I didn't mean it bad. I get what you're going through."

"You don't have sex with me either David." She said. He could see tears fill in her eyes.

"I didn't know you wanted to." David said putting a hand on her leg. She smiled and nodded.

"Well, I do." She said and looked down at David's hand. David raised his eyebrows and sighed.

"Well, that's good because I would like to have sex with you."

"You would?" Amanda asked looking back up at him.

"Yea." David said and giggled. Amanda giggled too and seemed to be in a better mood. "Why would you think I was sleeping with Gabe?" He asked.

"Well, it's the way you guys look at each other sometimes. It's like I walk in at the wrong time or something." Amanda explained. David giggled and took another drag from his cigarette.

"I see." David said. Amanda looked at him and rolled her eyes.

"Sorry for being in the way."

"You're not in the way." David said and hugged her. She hugged back and took in the smell of him.

"You always smell so good." She said with her eyes closed. David kissed the top of her head and smelled her hair.

"You always smell like berries." He said and Amanda laughed. They finished their lunch hour talking about Alan and how sexy Amanda thought he looked in her History class. David thought it was cool that they both thought the same way about what guys were hot or not. Watching movies with her was a lot more fun now being able to truly voice his opinion on the guys. When it was time, they made their separate ways and David went to room 19 for History. He walked in and seen Alan and was shocked. He had been wearing teacher looking cloths for weeks now but today he wore tight jeans and an awesome fitting t-shirt.

Thank you lord. David thought as he gave Alan the once over then sat down at his desk. Alan smiled at him and walked over to his desk.

"Ready for tonight?" He asked looking as sexy as ever. David sighed and nodded.

"Yup." He answered and Alan smiled.

"Are you satisfied with the write ups that Ron and Samantha have done?"

"I think so. Ron is getting pretty good at the pronunciations and Samantha, well, she's book smart thank god." David said and Alan laughed.

"I think it will go well." Alan said and went back to the front of the class. There was to be a test on their Jack the Ripper unit that had taken a week longer than Mr. Black had expected. The test took David the whole class mostly because he spent a lot of it looking at Alan. His hair had grown a little so now the stray strands fell right into his eyes. David watched him run his hand through his hair to keep it back. He smiled at the sexiness of it. He liked the way Alan's arms flexed when he moved them. Especially when he fixed his hair or played his guitar. David thought back to the last Sunday they had spent together. Alan had tried to talk David into singing along with him but David wouldn't do it. He liked to hear Alan sing. He was like a guitar ballad genius stuck in a teacher's life. His body was that of a sexy rock star as well. When class was over, David winked at Alan without thinking before he left. "Careful, I gotta work. I don't need to stand up here with a hard on all day." Alan joked. David stopped in the door way and turned around.

"Why not?" David asked and felt the pit of his stomach tighten. Alan laughed and shook his head.

"Get out of here or you'll be late." He said. David smiled and did as he was told. He liked that he could talk to Alan the way he did. Since their trip to Portland together, things with them had really changed. They joked and laughed a lot more. The uncomfortable moments were becoming a lot more frequent though. David felt himself staring into Alan's eyes a little deeper than he meant a lot more and Alan said things that would make David aroused instantly. He shook the thought and went to English class. The Edgar Allan Poe unit was winding to a close as well and David was not looking forward to Romeo and Juliet. After English class, David collected his things at his locker and headed home. He walked in the door and dropped his bag. He headed to the phone to call Gabe as he had done every day since the fight with Steve and Sandra. He dialed the number and waited for him to answer.

"*I could set a watch by your call I bet.*" Gabe said. David giggled and lay down on the couch.

"Alan wore those tight jeans today." David said lighting a cigarette and setting the ash tray on his stomach.

"*I love those jeans.*" Gabe said in his seductive voice. David giggled again.

"Me too."

"*Any weird moments today?*"

"I winked at him and he told me to be careful cause he didn't want to teach his next class with a hard on."

"*What did you say?*" Gabe asked giggling.

"I asked why not?" Gabe and David both laughed.

"*Some morning huh?*"

"Yea, Amanda knew something was up. She called me on it at lunch time."

"*And . . . what did you tell her?*"

"I asked how the hell we would have time to sleep together when she was around 24-7"

"*Wow, that's pretty harsh.*" Gabe said.

"Yea, I made up for it. She wants to fuck." David said. Gabe laughed and David could hear him light his own cigarette.

"*Nice.*"

"How about you? How was your day?"

"*Little Mike. That's about it. I certainly wasn't propositioned today.*" Gabe answered and David smiled.

"Wanna fuck?" David asked. Gabe giggled.

"*Wow, David. I think that's the first time you ever asked me a stupid question.*" David and Gabe laughed. "*Of course I do.*" Gabe added.

"I know. Me too."

"*Well, you should come over here on your lunch break when Mike is sleeping.*"

"I would, but we talked about this before. Amanda would come." David said taking a drag from his cigarette and flicking the ash into the tray.

"*Yea I know. It's getting to the point where I may have to have a talk with her.*"

"Don't do that Gabe. I'll come see you tomorrow night."

"*Amanda will be here.*" Gabe said and sighed.

"She'll be sleeping when I show up." David said in a very seductive voice.

"*Ahh, a tee-pee creep?*" Gabe asked. David giggled.

"That's the idea."

"*When?*"

"I'll surprise you." David said and took another drag from his cigarette. He could hear Gabe giggle again.

"*You are SUCH a tease.*"

"I know."

"*Do you? I don't think you really know.*" Gabe said. David laughed and shook his head.

"Well, I think I've learned from the best."

"*Me or Alan?*"

"Both of you." David answered and they both laughed.

"*Well, I better feed this kid. Got your project thing tonight?*"

"Yea I do. I should eat and stuff. I guess we're going early today cause Samantha has to work at 8:00."

"*When are you leaving?*"

"5:30"

"*Wanna come make out for an hour then?*"

"Yes." David said and put out his cigarette. Gabe laughed.

"*Ok, I'll talk to you tomorrow.*"

"Ok, bye." David said and hung up the phone. He went into the kitchen and got a pop out of the fridge. He sat down at the table and did his math homework. When he was almost done, the phone rang.

"Hello."

"*Hi, do you have graph paper?*" It was Alan. David laughed and dug in his book bag.

"Maybe, why?"

"*We need some to plan out the lay out of the presentation tonight and I left the school without grabbing any.*" Alan said. David could tell he was smoking. David pulled out his binder and found a new pack of graph paper.

"Yup, I have some." David said.

"*Oh good. Are we still alright to do this early?*"

"I think it's funny that you run everything by me." David said leaning back in his chair and looking out the window.

"*Well, I think it's funny how you look at me sometimes.*" Alan said back and David rolled his eyes.

"Ok." David said and smiled. "When will you be here?"

"*4:30. I wanna go eat first.*" Alan said. David looked up at the time. It was almost three.

"Sounds good." David said and looked down at his math homework. "Remember your grade 11 Algebra?" He asked. Alan laughed.

"*I remember I hated it.*"

"Yea, I thought you would say that." David said and sighed.

"*Is it something I could help with on Sunday?*"

"But we play guitar on Sunday."

"*Aren't you old enough to alter your routine a little?*" Alan asked and David laughed.

"Yea, I guess." He said and shut his text books.

"*Ok, then. I will see you around 4:30 then.*"

"I'm buying."

"*You wish.*" Alan said and hung up. David smiled and set the phone down. He put his books back in his bag and set it by the door. He went up the stairs and to his room. He looked at himself in the mirror and decided he should change. He took out a pair of baggy hip hugger jeans and a black t-shirt that hung fairly loose on him.

"Do your worst, Alan." He said looking at how concealed any erection would be. The pants were fairly baggy and the shirt hung down past his waist. He went to the bathroom and brushed his hair and teeth. He gave himself an extra squirt of cologne and left the room. He went down to the basement and sat down with his guitar. He played a few songs to pass the time. He had gotten really good at playing Think about You and wanted to play it for Gabe. Gabe never played with David before and he thought it was about time. He wanted to watch Gabe play. He thought about how sexy Alan looked when he played guitar and shivered. "Whoa." He said out loud. The shiver was fairly violent and surprised David. He shook his head and headed back upstairs to the kitchen. He watched his mom pull up. She waved as she came by the window.

"Hi mom. I thought you worked tonight?"

"I do, but not until 9 and I feel like I haven't showered in days." She said as she walked into the room.

"When is Alan coming to get you?"

"Like, any minute." David said.

"So early?" She asked as she put her purse down on the counter and got a pop from the fridge.

"We are having the meeting at 5:30 today cause Samantha has to work. So we thought we would go and eat first." David said leaning on the counter.

"That's a good idea." She said and took a sip of her pop.

"So, is tonight that brain surgery?" David asked smiling. Nancy giggled and nodded.

"That's the one." She said.

"I wanna sit in the gallery one time." David said. Nancy raised her eyebrows.

"Well, I will see what I can do." She said and smiled. David could hear Alan's car pull up. He closed his eyes for a second then grabbed his graph paper and headed for the door. "Have fun." Nancy called. David waved and went out to Alan's car. Alan smiled at David when he got in.

"I thought she worked tonight?" Alan asked. David looked at him with a puzzled gaze as he handed him the graph paper.

"How often *do* you guys talk?" He asked as Alan pulled away. Alan shook his head and smiled. "She does, she came home to shower." David said and yawned.

"Tiered today?" Alan asked.

"Math does it to me."

"Yea, I know the feeling."

"Where are we eating?" David asked. Alan shrugged.

"My house." He said and giggled. David looked at him and raised an eyebrow.

"Ok." David said with questioning in his voice. Alan laughed and turned onto the highway toward his house.

"How's Amanda and Gabe?" Alan asked as he drove. David sighed and smiled.

"Well, Amanda is horny and Gabe . . . is Gabe." He answered. Alan laughed.

"Well, that's enough info." David laughed and shook his head. "You're weird today." Alan added. David looked at him and giggled.

"Why?" David asked.

"You just are."

"Weird day I guess." David answered thinking back to his make out session with Gabe and then the hard on comment from Alan earlier.

"Well, it's about to get worse." Alan said as he turned off the highway on to the gravel road he lived on. David looked at Alan with a puzzled gaze again.

"What's going on?" David asked. Alan laughed but said nothing. "And you say I'm acting weird today." David added and Alan smiled. He turned his car into the driveway. David could see a red pickup truck parked in front of Alan's house with a guillotine strapped in the back. Beside it was Ron's car. David itched his forehead as Alan parked.

"Well, get out." Alan said and laughed. David got out of the car and looked at the truck.

"DEAD MAN WALKEN!" David heard come from behind him. He spun around to see Carman, Samantha and Ron standing next to

Alan's fire pit. David laughed and looked at Alan. Alan laughed and walked over to stand next to David.

"I thought we would celebrate tonight." He said and led David to the fire. David hugged Carman and they both laughed. Ron handed David a beer and smiled.

"What are you doing here?" David asked Carman.

"You were in need of a guillotine, I delivered." Carman said and smiled at Alan. Alan laughed and got a beer from Samantha.

"That's awesome." David said and sipped his beer. Alan walked over to Carman and whispered something in his ear. Carman raised his eyebrows and smiled at David.

"Really?" He asked and Alan nodded. David looked at them both with a puzzled gaze. Ron spoke next.

"I think we need some tunes." Carman looked at him and then back at David and then to Alan.

"What do you think guys?" He asked. Alan looked at David and tilted his head toward the house. David nodded and they walked into the house together. When Alan closed the door, David stopped him.

"What did you say to Carman?" David asked. Alan looked into David's eyes and smiled.

"Nothing." He said and headed back toward the basement. David shook his head and followed.

"It wasn't nothing." David said as they went down the stairs. Alan giggled as he handed David Susan and Gloria and picked up the big amp.

"It was nothing." Alan said and walked passed David. David closed his eyes and took in the scent of Alan's cologne. Alan turned and looked at David. "Are you coming or what?" David laughed and followed Alan up the stairs. "What's so funny?"

"Nothing." David said and Alan rolled his eyes.

"It's something." Alan said as they got to the door. David shrugged and Alan shook his head.

"Hard ball, huh?" Alan asked as he opened the door.

"You tell me your's . . . I'll tell you mine." David said as they stepped out. Alan laughed and they headed toward the camp fire. Carman rang his hands together and elbowed Ron in the side.

"You're in for a treat dude." He said to Ron.

"You play guitar too?" Ron asked David.

"Oh, I fool around with it." David said and pulled the pick out of his pocket he got from Gabe.

"Yea right." Carman said and laughed. Alan and David set up the amp and guitars and both sat down on a cooler. David watched Alan as he started to strum Think About You. David smiled and played along. Carman sang and Ron and Samantha danced along. David stared at Alan and Alan stared back. They played without looking away. At the end of the song, Carman, Ron and Samantha all clapped and cheered. Alan laughed and looked up at Carman.

"Now what?" Alan asked.

"Whatever you want." Carman said and Alan looked back at David.

"What do you want to play?" Alan asked David. David looked into Alan's light green eyes and sighed.

"How about Love Hurts." David said and Alan laughed. David led into the song and Alan followed. This time David didn't dare look at Alan. His body had already reacted enough. They played and Ron sang along. David thought his voice was too deep for the song but it still sounded pretty good. At the end of the song, Carman clapped and Samantha kissed Ron quickly on the cheek. He blushed and Alan and David laughed.

"Do you know Knocking on Heaven's Door?" Samantha asked and Alan looked at David knowing the significant of that song. David cleared his throat and looked at Alan.

"Yea, I know that one." David said and put his fingers on the first cord.

"Will you sing it?" Alan asked quietly and every one waited for David to answer. David stared at Alan and started to play. Alan joined in and David sang. Alan smiled and shut his eyes while he listened. Carman sat down in front of David on a log and stared at him while he sang. Ron and Samantha did the same. Alan opened his eyes to see David staring at him again. He could see tears in David's eyes but he never faltered as he sang. When the song was over, Alan staid locked in David's gaze. Everyone was quiet and then out of nowhere, Carman cheered. Soon everyone even Alan was clapping. David smiled and sipped his beer.

"Wow." Carman said and shook his head.

"No shit." Ron said and patted David's back. Alan just stared at him. David looked down at the guitar and started to play Welcome to the Jungle. Alan played along but Carman sang this one. Ron sang along and Samantha tapped her foot on the ground to the beat. The next few songs David picked were as upbeat as he could manage.

"Ok, Can I request another one?" Samantha asked and David looked at her.

"Sure." He said. She smiled and asked for Momma I'm Coming Home.

"Ozzy?" Ron asked and David laughed.

"I know it. Do you?" He asked Alan.

"It's been a while but I think I can manage." Alan said.

"I want you to sing it." Samantha said to David and sat in the seat Carman had used for Knocking on Heaven's Door.

"Yea, sing it for us David." Carman said and got himself another beer. David sighed and looked at Alan.

"Ready?" David asked. Alan nodded and David played. David sang the most of the song and Alan joined him with the chorus. At the end Alan and David laughed and Alan set his guitar aside. David did the same and they both got off their coolers and dug inside for another beer.

"Is there anything you can't do?" Carman asked David. David looked at Alan for a second then back at Carman.

"Yea, there is." He said ad went over to talk to Ron And Samantha. Carman raised his eyebrows at Alan and Alan shrugged.

"You were right earlier. He can sing." Carman said as David walked away.

"I was guessing." Alan said and the two men laughed. The group talked about the coming fair and David's ability to use every weapon he can get his hands on. David remained modest but the rest of them knew his abilities.

"You should see him with a sword." Alan said to Carman.

"Ok." Carman said and headed to his truck. Alan laughed and looked at David.

"Sorry." Alan said and smiled. David laughed and shook his head as he saw Carman returning with a Long Sword. He handed it to David and winked. David rolled his eyes and every one stood back. David laughed and closed his eyes. He tossed the sword behind him with his right hand and caught it in his left. He swung the sword above his head and put the blade against his forehead. He stood like that for a second and then started an epic sword play dance. He ended it, still with his eyes closed, pointing the sword at Alan. He opened his eyes and stared down the blade at his teacher.

"Wow." Carman said and clapped. Ron and Samantha clapped and David lowered the sword. Alan smiled and David laughed.

"You didn't do that whole deal at the library." Ron said and David shrugged.

"I was saving it for Carman." He said and Alan and Carman laughed.

"You gotta do the whole thing at the fair." Samantha said and Ron agreed. David looked at Alan.

"I think you should." Alan said and looked at Carman.

"Fuck yea. That's the coolest this I've seen all day." Carman said and everyone laughed. Samantha made the mistake of asking what the coolest this he saw yesterday was. "My cock." Carman answered with a straight face and David and Alan laughed. Ron giggled when Samantha wasn't looking which made Carman laugh.

"Well, let's get the girls inside before they get hurt." Alan said to David. David nodded and picked up both guitars. Alan carried the amp and they went to the house. They put everything back and when David turned to go back out, Alan stopped him with a hand on his shoulder. David's heart jumped but he turned around.

"What?" David asked fighting the frog in his throat.

"You shouldn't keep your mouth shut when you play that guitar David. You have an amazing singing voice." Alan said and sighed.

"I don't sing in front of people much." David answered feeling his heart calm down.

"Why did you then?" Alan asked. David wasn't sure how to answer and the pit of his stomach attacked him when he gave Alan his answer.

"You asked me to." David said and then cleared his throat. Alan blinked and raised his eyebrows.

"Oh." Alan said still looking stunned. David sighed and looked away. "What's wrong with you David?" Alan asked.

"Nothing." David said trying to fight the urge to lean in and kiss Alan. Alan sighed and looked up the stairs.

"Wanna go outside?" He asked. David nodded and Alan led the way. They went outside and Carman came to Alan and David walked over to Ron and Samantha.

"That took long enough." Carman said looking into the eyes of his friend.

"Something's up with him but he aint talking." Alan said getting a beer and taking a long sip. Carman looked over at David and watched as David would look over at Alan as he spoke to Ron and Samantha. Carman looked back at Alan and laughed. "What?" Alan asked looking at Carman with a puzzled look.

"Wow, Alan. I'm embarrassed for you." Carman said and took a sip from his beer.

"Why? What did I miss?" Alan asked. Carman laughed and shook his head. He leaned in and whispered in Alan's ear.

"That kid wants you probably worse than I do." He said and pulled away. Alan blinked and looked at David. He was laughing at a joke Ron told. He looked back at Carman.

"Your fucking crazy." He said quietly and shook his head.

"Alan, I know it when I see it." Carman said and sighed. "You don't help with your long stares and that shit out at my place." Carman added.

"What long stares?" Alan asked and Carman looked at him with a cocked eyebrow.

"Yea, what long stares?" Carman asked sarcastically and took another sip from his beer. Alan sighed and looked at David again.

"Should I talk to him about it?" Carman choked on his beer and said,

"Fuck No!" Ron, Samantha and David looked over and Alan laughed. The three of them rolled their eyes and got back to talking.

"Why not?" Alan asked quietly. Carman shook his head and sighed.

"How long have you been hanging out with this kid?"

"About a month or so."

"That's why." Carman tapped Alan's beer with his. Alan shook his head and looked back at David.

"You're probably right." Alan said and sipped his beer.

"I'm always right." Carman said and nudged his friend. Alan smiled and looked at his watch.

"Hey Sam!" He called and Samantha looked at him. "It's 7:30" Alan said.

"Thank you." Samantha said and said her good byes to David. She walked over and told Carman how nice it was to meet him. She said by to Alan and followed Ron to the car. Ron waved as he got into the car. Carman, Alan and David waved back and watched him drive away.

"Ok." Carman said and threw the beer bottle over his shoulder. Alan and David laughed. "Rum time?" He asked. Alan looked at David.

"Curfew?" Alan asked and David laughed.

"It doesn't count when I'm out with you, Alan. You know that." David said and tossed his own bottle behind him. Carman laughed and headed to the truck to get the rum. Alan and David pulled out the long garden hose and put out the fire. When they were finished, David gathered the empty bottles and Alan grabbed the coolers. They took their lot into the house to see Carman standing behind the island in the kitchen with a towel thrown over his right shoulder.

"Looks like the bar tender is in." Alan said and David laughed. Alan grabbed three stools and set then in front of the island. David sat down and Alan sat next to him. They ordered a rum and Carman poured three. He came around his pretend bar and sat next to David.

"You a betting man?" He asked David and David burst out laughing. Alan laughed to and shook his head at Carman.

"Yes, Yes I am." David said and composed himself. Alan laughed and Carman giggled.

"Now what do I say?" He asked and David laughed. Alan shook his head again and sipped his drink.

"Tell Carman about Gabe." Alan said. David looked at him and raised his eyebrows.

"Why?" David asked.

"Cause it changes the subject." Carman said and Alan shot him a glare. David noticed it and giggled.

"Lovers coral?" David asked and Alan laughed. Carman smiled and sipped his drink.

"Who *is* Gabe, now that you bring him up?" Carman asked. David looked at Carman and sighed.

"He's Alan's boyfriend." David answered and Alan laughed. Carman looked at Alan.

"So the plot thickens." He said and David laughed.

"No, he's a buddy of mine who's gay. You'd like him." David said and Alan laughed.

"Oh would I?" Carman asked and raised his eyebrows.

"He drives a Hearse." Alan said and Carman smiled.

"Kinky." He said and David and Alan laughed. They chatted about Gabe and the fair project. There were a few times David noticed Alan look at Carman funny but ignored it. At midnight, Alan looked at David.

"Well, where you wanna sleep?" Alan asked and David laughed. Carman giggled and raised an eyebrow at Alan. Alan rolled his eyes.

"The couch is good." David said and stood up. Alan led him to the couch and said good night. David lay down and stared up at the ceiling. He could hear Carman laugh and Alan swear at him. That just seemed to make Carman laugh louder. He closed his eyes and sighed. Sleep had almost taken him when he felt a hand on his arm. His eyes shot open and he looked up. It was Carman.

"You awake?" Carman asked and David rolled his eyes.

"Now I am." He said and sat up. Carman sat on the arm chair across from him.

"Can I talk to you about something?" Carman asked quietly.

"If it's about Alan, save it. I don't wanna talk about it." David said and lit a cigarette. Carman raised his eyebrows.

"A little touchy aren't we?" He asked and David raised an eyebrow.

"You woke me up. What did you expect?" David asked and then giggled at the pathetic look on Carman's face. He cleared his throat and rolled his eyes. "What is it?" David finally asked and blew a long stream of blue smoke out of his mouth toward the floor.

"I just wanted to know how things were going." Carman said and leaned back on the chair. David laughed and shook his head.

"Fine." David answered and rested his arms on his legs. He looked down at the black rug on the floor.

"You like him, don't you?" Carman asked. David sighed and felt like he had just been asked to kill someone. He said nothing. "I get it, trust me, I do." Carman said. David still stared at the floor letting his cigarette burn away. "I also know what it's like to spend any time with him. He's the worst tease in the world." Carman said and David looked up at him. Carman smiled and sighed. "It only gets worse, buddy, trust me." Carman said and David looked back down.

"How could it?" David asked quietly and took a drag off his cigarette. Carman handed him an ash tray and David set it on the spot on the floor he was staring at. He flicked the ash off his cigarette but never looked back at Carman.

"It just does." Carman said and moved to sit on the front of the chair. "I think he knows how hot he is." Carman whispered and David laughed. He looked up at Carman and nodded his head.

"You might be right." David said and leaned back on the couch. Carman smiled and bit his bottom lip.

"Don't freak out, but, you're fucking hot." Carman said and David laughed.

"So they tell me." David said and reached down for the ash tray. He put it on his leg and rolled his cigarette against the side. Carman smiled and cleared his throat. David looked at him and sighed. "What?" David asked.

"Nothing." Carman said and stood up. David shook his head and looked back at his cigarette. Carman walked toward the bed room door where he was going to sleep and stopped in the hallway. He looked back at David. "He's delicate, so be careful with him." Carman said and David shot a surprised look at him. Carman giggled and went into his room and shut the door. David put his cigarette out and lay back down. He closed his eyes and sighed.

"God help me." He said and fell asleep.

Chapter 20

David awoke the next morning to the sound of Alan laughing and the smell of coffee. He sat up and looked around the room. There was a fire place on the opposite side of the room than he was on. There was a chair to the left, the same chair Carman had sat in the night before. There was a side table next to the couch that David's cigarettes were on. He grabbed the pack and took out a cigarette. He found his lighter in his pants pocket and lit the smoke. He leaned his head back against the couch, closed his eyes and took a drag from his cigarette.

I wonder if Carman was drunk enough last night to forget what we talked about. If he wasn't, I hope he hasn't talked to Alan about it. Things are weird enough around him with him knowing how I feel. Just then he heard Alan laugh again. He smiled and took another drag from his cigarette. He could hear someone come into the room. He kept his eyes closed and listened. He could feel something warm on his chin. It crept up his face to his nose. He could smell coffee. He smiled and opened his eyes. He could see Alan standing over him from the back of the couch holding the coffee cup under his nose.

"Good morning." Alan whispered in David's ear. David took the cup.

"Good morning." David answered and Alan smiled.

"It's alive!" He called into the kitchen and David laughed. He could hear Carman say something about sleeping beauty. "How was your sleep?" Alan asked as he came around the couch and sat next to David. David looked at him and took another drag from his cigarette.

"Dark." David answered. Alan frowned at him.

"Dark?" He asked. David giggled and looked up at the ceiling.

"Yea, my eyes were closed. So, it was dark." Alan laughed at David's comment and took a sip of the coffee he had brought out for himself. "What's Carman doing?" David asked still looking up at the ceiling.

"He is fixing my computer." Alan said.

"Oh, you don't wanna learn how to do that?"

"Nope, Carman told me to fuck off." Alan said and sipped his coffee. David laughed and shook his head.

"Nice." He said and reached behind Alan to flick the ash off his cigarette into the ash tray. Alan leaned forward so David could reach.

"When do you want to go home?" Alan asked. David sighed and shrugged.

"Whenever." David said. Alan smiled and stood up.

"Let's go." Alan said and David raised his eyebrow.

"Now?" David asked.

"Yea, let's go." Alan said. David stood up and laughed.

"I knew you would get sick of me before I got sick of you."

"I'm not sick of you. I wanna go for a drive and I want you to come." Alan said and handed David his coat. David raised his eyebrows and took the coat. He pulled it on and followed Alan to the kitchen.

He could see Carman sitting at Alan's computer typing in some kind of program code.

"Hey Carman," David said and ran his hand through his hair. Carman turned and looked at him.

"Is he allowed to use the computers at the school?" Carman asked referring to Alan. Alan laughed and shook his head. David smiled and nodded. "God help us." Carman said and went back to his work. David and Alan laughed as they both took their last big gulps of their coffees and went outside to Alan's car. They both got in and Alan started the car. He drove down the driveway and turned toward the high way.

"What time is it?" David asked. Alan smiled.

"Does it matter?" Alan asked looking at his watch. David smiled and shrugged.

"I guess not. I just hate silent awkward drives."

"Awkward?" Alan asked. David sighed and looked out his window. Alan stared at him for a second. He looked tired and a little stressed out. "Can we have that lay it all out on the table conversation now?" Alan asked. David looked at him in disbelief.

"Now? Why?"

"Why not." Alan said and slowed as they reached the high way. "Which way?" Alan asked. David sighed and pointed left toward town. Alan turned the wheel and took off down the high way. "Ok, let's hear it." Alan said as he sped down the road.

"Hear what?" David asked looking out the windshield.

"Why you've been acting so strange."

"Have I?" David asked feeling the pit of his stomach tighten and his heart beat faster. Alan rolled his eyes but didn't look at David. David could tell he was either pissed off or really upset. "Are you ok?" David asked as Alan brought the car to an even faster speed.

"Are you?" Alan asked and looked at David. David blinked at the tone of Alan's voice.

"Well, I'm not the one trying to kill us." David said glancing at the speedometer. Alan looked down and David could feel the car slow down. Alan sighed and pulled into a side road. They drove down it about half a mile before Alan pulled over and stopped. David looked at him. He still stared out the windshield. He was clenching the steering wheel as if it was his only grip to reality. "Ok. What are we doing?" David asked. He could feel the palms of his hands sweating.

"Do I stare at you?" Alan asked still looking out the windshield. David looked out the windshield and then back at Alan.

"What do you mean?" David asked shifting nervously in his seat. Alan sighed and looked at him.

"Do I stare at you?" Alan asked again. David cleared his throat and raised his eyebrows.

"You're staring at me now." David said. Alan blinked and looked back out the windshield. David itched his forehead then ran his hand through his hair. "Look, Alan. I don't know what's wrong with you, but, I haven't notice you staring at me." David said. He recalled playing the guitar the night before and the long stare Alan had held with him as he sang but he thought soothing his teacher was the best thing for now. Alan sighed and loosened his grip on the steering wheel.

"Are you sure?" Alan asked. David shifted in his seat again and squinted at Alan.

"Yea, I'm sure."

"Ok then." Alan said and put the car back in gear. David looked at Alan with a puzzled gaze.

"That's it?" David asked. Alan looked at him and then back out the windshield.

"That's it." Alan said and turned the car around to head back toward the high way. David sighed and felt the pit of his stomach loosen. He watched Alan as he drove. When they reached the high way, Alan stopped the car and looked at David. "Sorry." He said staring into David's eyes.

"For what?" David asked. He felt like Alan was looking right into his soul and instead of the pit of his stomach reacting, it was his groin.

"For that back there. I was worried I may be weirding you out or something. Carman said I stared at you. I am just trying to figure out, that's all."

"Well, that's ok." David said still feeling the tightening in his pants. Alan smiled and pulled out on to the highway. He drove toward town and David's freedom of home.

"Can I ask you something?" Alan asked after a short while. David looked at him and took in a deep breath.

"If I was to say no, would you still ask?"

"Probably." Alan answered. David rolled his eyes and the pit of his stomach reacted again.

"Ok then." David said. Alan looked over at him and then the road.

"I know being a guy, this is a strange question but, am I a tease?" Alan asked. David giggled and looked out the window. He raised an eyebrow and thought this was a better time than any to get a real feel for Alan's sexuality.

"Well, maybe." David said trying to say something that meant yes but wasn't as obvious.

"Really?" Alan asked looking back and forth between David and the road again. David laughed now and shook his head. Alan slowed to turn into town.

“I wouldn’t worry about it. Being a tease is a good thing isn’t it?” David asked as Alan headed toward David’s house.

“I don’t know.” Alan said quietly and seemed to wince. David’s hands were sweating again. He watched Alan and he seemed to be struggling with some inner monster that wasn’t going to let him win. David sighed and looked out the windshield. He could see his house now and wasn’t as glad to be getting out of Alan’s car as he was now. “Three days till the fair. You gonna be ready?” Alan asked changing the subject. David was happy for that.

“Oh yea. I’m ready.” David said looking at Amanda’s house as Alan slowed down to stop in front of his.

“Well, good. I’m looking forward to it.” Alan said as he put the car in park. David thanked him and got out of the car. He walked around to the driver’s side and Alan wheeled down the window. “I guess I’ll see you tomorrow huh?” Alan said. David smiled and looked into Alan’s eyes.

“Don’t always listen to everything Carman says. He sees what he wants to.” David said and Alan smiled.

“That’s pretty wise talk for a 17 year old.” Alan said. David raised his eyebrows and turned around. He walked toward his house and stopped to look over at Alan as he reached the door. Alan smiled and waved. David waved back as Alan drove away.

It was 2 am when David stepped out of his house into the cool air. He took a deep breath and headed over to see Gabe as he had promised the day before. He quietly opened the door to the house. It was dark and quiet. He shut the door quietly and headed toward Gabe’s room. He steeped in and shut the door behind him. He took his jacket off and through it on the foot board of the bed. He quietly lay down on the bed facing Gabe. He could see Gabe in the moon light coming through the window and he could hear him breathing in his sleep. David stared at him for some time before gently moving a loose strand of hair from his face. Gabe's eyebrows twitched from the tickle it caused and David smiled. Gabe stretched in his sleep and his eyes opened into little slits.

"Hi." David said and smiled. Gabe smiled and closed his eyes.

"Hi." Gabe whispered and put his arm around David. David moved closer so Gabe could hold him. Gabe took a deep breath of David's hair and sighed. "Did you come to cuddle or fuck?" Gabe whispered in a sleepy drawl. David giggled and rested his forehead against Gabe's.

"Well, originally I came to fuck. But I would love to sleep." David said and closed his eyes. Gabe giggled and nodded.

"I know the feeling." David smiled and rolled over on to his back. He freed himself from his jeans and Gabe moved the blankets so David could join him. David lay on his back and Gabe put his head on David's chest. He also put his hand on David's lower abdomen. David sighed and shut his eyes. "Can I tell you something?" Gabe asked in a sleepy whisper.

"Of course." David answered. He could smell Gabe's hair and cologne. He smelled great.

"I never slept with a guy. I mean really actually slept." Gabe said and rubbed David's muscular stomach with his thumb.

"If you keep that up, this night won't be all sleeping either." David said referring to the rubbing and how much he liked it. Gabe giggled and kissed David's chest. He did, however, quit the rubbing.

"I would love to sleep with you." Gabe said and put his arm across David's body to hold him. David kissed the top of Gabe's head and closed his eyes. "I am kind of jealous of Alan." Gabe confessed and David giggled.

"Why?" He asked putting his left hand on the arm that held him. Gabe sighed and shook his head.

"Would you be here today if you didn't feel the way you do about him?"

"I don't know," David said and gently rubbed Gabe's arm. "Probably." He added. Gabe giggled and shook his head again.

"I doubt I would have grabbed your attention like he did."

"I wouldn't say that Gabe." David said and smiled. "I still would have thought the same thing when you answered the door that day."

"What did you think?" Gabe asked in a sleepy voice. David smiled and kissed Gabe's hair.

"I thought, wow, Gabe, what happened to you?" David said in a seductive voice and Gabe giggled.

"Nice."

"Besides, what there to be jealous of? Do you think Alan and I do what we do?" David asked.

"That's not it David." Gabe said in a serious voice. He lifted his head and looked at David. "You've got a thing for him I could only wish some dude would have for me." Gabe said and put his head back down on David's chest. David sighed and hugged Gabe.

"You would return the favor though Gabe, he doesn't"

"He doesn't know how you feel though." Gabe said and David sighed. He held Gabe and listened to him breath. He closed his eyes and thought.

What would he say if I out and told him, Hey Alan, I want you. I need you. I would do almost anything just too touch your hair or kiss your mouth. David sighed and shook his head.

"What are you thinking about?" Gabe asked half asleep.

"Nothing." David said and kissed the top of Gabe's head again. Gabe hugged David and sighed.

"You're gonna hate me." Gabe said. David giggled.

"Why?" David asked. Gabe propped himself up and kissed David. David closed his eyes and accepted Gabe's kiss. Gabe lay on top of David and kissed more deeply. David held Gabe as they kissed and could feel his excitement grow with Gabe's hungry movements. David moaned as Gabe pushed his growing erection against him. Gabe stopped kissing and looked down at David. David opened his eyes and looked into Gabe's. Gabe smiled and rolled off of David. David groaned as Gabe got back into his former cuddling position. Gabe giggled. "Your right, I do hate you." David said and Gabe giggled again.

"I thought you would say that." Gabe said and tightened his hold on David. David sighed and shook his head. He could feel the hard throb of an erection. He groaned again and Gabe laughed.

"And you say I'm a tease." David said and shut his eyes. Gabe sighed and shook his head.

"You are."

"Is this revenge or what?" David asked in a seductive whisper. Gabe shivered and David smiled.

"No." Gabe answered quietly. "That was just in case."

"Just in case what?" David asked. Gabe took a deep breath and then cleared his throat.

"In case you run." Gabe said in a nervous voice. David frowned and shifted his body.

"Why would I run?" David asked feeling suddenly very confused.

"I love you, David." Gabe said and held his breath. David smiled and then giggled. "What?" Gabe asked and David new he must have felt awkward for saying it.

"What a tangled web." David whispered and kissed Gabe's head. Gabe was silent. David held Gabe tightly for a few minutes and then said. "You know, Amanda said the same thing to me." Gabe sighed and nodded.

"I know." Gabe said and David could feel Gabe was uncomfortable with his situation. David smiled and rubbed Gabe's arm.

"It sounds better coming from you." David whispered. Gabe lay still for a moment then propped himself up to look at David.

"It does?" He asked. David smiled and ran his hand through Gabe's hair. It slid through his hand like warm, black silk. Gabe shut his eyes to savor the feeling. He stared at Gabe's pale features in the moon light. He was so beautiful at that moment, so David pulled him in for a kiss. Gabe kissed him with a passion he thought only existed in the movies. Gabe moaned as David pushed him onto his back and continued the epic kiss. "Don't fuck me, David," Gabe said as they kissed. "Just kiss me like this all night." He added. David smiled and kept kissing. David could feel Gabe's hands on his hips. He moaned as Gabe pulled David on top of him and raked his back with his finger nails. David pushed his hips against Gabe as they kissed. Gabe pushed back and David moaned again.

"Really? *Just* kissing?" David asked in an almost pained voice. Gabe giggled and stared into his eyes. This time Gabe ran his hand through David's hair. David closed his eyes and pushed himself against Gabe again. David opened his eyes to see Gabe had shut his.

"Just kissing." Gabe whispered and smiled. David groaned again and kissed the beautiful man that lay beneath him. They kissed for over an hour before it had calmed into a light make out session. David was now lying on his side facing Gabe. Gabe ended the kiss and sighed. "I like kissing you David. I like how it makes me feel." Gabe whispered. David looked down at both their erections.

"Yea, I like how it makes you feel too." David whispered. Gabe giggled and shook his head.

"Don't you like to be horny?"

"Lately, I'm horny all the time." David whispered and gently kissed Gabe again.

"Me too thanks to you." David giggled at Gabe's statement and then yawned. "Tired?" Gabe asked and David smiled.

"Aren't you?" David asked. Gabe nodded and kissed David again. David ran his hand down Gabe's side to his hip. "You wanna sleep?" David asked pulling Gabe's hips against his. Gabe smiled and nodded. David groaned again and Gabe laughed.

"You would fuck all night and day wouldn't you?" Gabe asked. David laughed and nodded. They kissed again and Gabe pushed David over on to his back. He lay his head on David's chest and his arm across his waist. David smiled and rested his hand on the arm Gabe held him with.

"Say it again." David whispered and Gabe hugged him.

"I love you." Gabe whispered. David sighed and closed his eyes. They were soon both fast asleep.

David awoke the next morning with Gabe still asleep on his chest. He smiled and rubbed the arm he still held him with. Gabe stirred and rolled over. David pulled himself up behind Gabe and Gabe giggled.

"I hate morning sex." Gabe said in a sleepy voice. David giggled and hugged Gabe. Gabe stretched and rolled over on to his back. David moved so he could stretch again. "Morning head, on the other hand." Gabe said and David laughed.

"You can live with your hard on sweet heart, I had to." David said and Gabe laughed.

"Touché." Gabe said and reached over for his cigarettes. He lit one for himself and one for David. They both lay in bed smoking. "So, how did your project thing go Friday night?" Gabe asked.

"Well, I got drunk and sang." David said thinking about the gaze Alan had held with him.

"You *sang?* Like in front of people?"

"Yea, I know." David said and ran his hand through his hair. Gabe raised his eyebrows and took a drag from his cigarette.

"Wow, that's weird."

"Alan asked me to." David said and then thought of Gabe's confession the night before. He felt like an idiot for saying it.

"See, that's the *thing* I was talking about."

"Come with me." David said and sat up. Gabe sat up too and they both through the clothes on they were wearing the night before. They walked quietly through the house and outside. Gabe followed David to his house and they went down to the music room. David sat Gabe down on the leather chair and pulled his stool up in front of him. He grabbed his guitar and sat down. He reached over and turned the amplifier on. Gabe smiled as David stared at him. He strummed the guitar and sang Think About You for Gabe. When he was finished Gabe smiled again and sighed.

"Wow." Gabe said and looked around the room.

"What are you looking for?" David asked leaning on his guitar.

"Something to say." Gabe said and stood up. He grabbed the old black guitar off the wall and plugged it into the amp. He sat back down on the leather chair and looked at David. "So, old stuff is all you like?" He asked. David smiled and shook his head.

"Play whatever you want." Gabe smiled and stared into David's eyes. He started to play Bed of Roses by Jon Bon Jovi. David smiled as Gabe played. When he finished David leaned over the two guitars and kissed him. Gabe giggled and sat back in the chair.

"I hate Bon Jovi." Gabe said. David laughed and started to play the Marilyn Manson version of Sweat Dreams. Gabe joined in and sang along with David. When they were done, Gabe giggled and shook his head. "I didn't know you were so good."

"I'm good at more than that." David said and Gabe laughed.

"Yes, yes you are." Gabe said and set the guitar aside. David did the same and they went upstairs. David made coffee and sat down at the table with a cup for Gabe and himself. "What do you think would happen if we told Amanda about us?" Gabe asked. David sighed and looked out the window.

"I don't know." David answered and looked out the window. It was a cloudy day and it looked like it might rain later.

"Think she would flip?"

"Probably."

"It would be easier than all this sneaking around." Gabe said and took a sip from his cup. David looked at him and then down at his coffee.

"Gabe, I don't want her to know." David said and looked back up at Gabe. Gabe stared into his eyes and raised an eyebrow.

"Why? Cause she's in love with you? So am I."

"I love her too, Gabe, but . . ." David stopped talking and sipped his coffee. Gabe leaned forward in his chair and looked at the hand David held his coffee cup with then at his eyes.

"But what?" Gabe asked. David looked into Gabe's eyes and sighed. He looked back down at his coffee but said nothing. "You're not *in love* with her, are you?" Gabe asked. David sighed and shook his head.

"How can I be? I mean, there's you and Alan in the mix, I can't love her like she wants but I don't want to hurt her either." David said and Gabe sat back in his chair.

"Maybe it's time you decide who you want and stick with *that person.*" David sighed and looked back out the window.

"I want to but it's not as easy as that." David said not looking away from the window. Gabe sighed and lit a cigarette.

"Well, it might not be easy, David. But, now you have two people in love with you and one that doesn't even know how you feel. You have to do *something.*"

"Ok, what did you have in mind?" David asked in an irritated voice. Gabe raised his eyebrows and took a drag from his cigarette.

"If I were you, I would figure that out before I jumped into bed with anyone else."

"Do you think I asked for this? Do you think I wanted you *and* Amanda to fall in love with me? Fuck Gabe! *No* one should love anybody as fucked up as me!" David yelled and stood up from the table. He walked to the counter and set both hands down on the cool top. He looked down at his hands and shook his head. Gabe got up and went to stand in front of David. David looked up at him with tears in his eyes. Gabe smiled at him and in a soft voice said,

"I'm fucking the guy my *sister* is in love with. There is nothing more fucked up than that." David sighed and looked back down at the counter. Gabe ran his hand across David's. "You can't decide who loves you David. And I know you didn't ask for this. But please think about what *you* want. That's all you can do." Gabe added and sighed. David looked into his eyes.

"Gabe, I want Alan." David said and a tear ran down his face. Gabe wiped it away and smiled.

"I know." He said and sat back down at the table. David sat down with him and they both lit a cigarette. David waited to see what Gabe would say. They sat in silence for a while before Gabe looked at David and smiled. "How can I help you?" David sat stunned at Gabe's question.

"Help me? Make Alan feel something for me, that would be a start." David said and Gabe laughed.

"You can do that. Trust me. I meant with Amanda." David laughed and shook his head.

"I don't think you can help there either."

"Well, what would you like from me then?" Gabe asked and David sighed.

"Just be Gabe."

Chapter 21

David awoke Wednesday, October 31 with Amanda sleeping next to him. Steve and Sandra had shown up the night before to get some things from the house, and Gabe thought it was best that Amanda and Little Mike stayed at David's house. Little Mike had slept in Nancy's room with her and Amanda stayed with David. David thought about the night before and the epic length of their love making. He sighed and grabbed his cigarettes. He lit one and lay on his back with the ash tray on his stomach. Amanda rolled over to face him and slowly opened her eyes.

"Good morning." She whispered and closed her eyes again. David smiled at her.

"Good morning." David answered and took another drag from his cigarette.

"It's nice to wake up next to you."

"Is it? I would figure for a non-smoker, it would suck waking up to the smell of a cigarette." David said rolling the cigarette on the edge of the tray.

"I don't mind. I think you make smoking look sexy." Amanda said and sighed. David laughed and shook his head. She lay next to him watching him smoke. When he finished his cigarette they both got up and Amanda went to the bathroom. David could hear Nancy and Amanda giggling in the hall way. He smiled and shook his head.

Fuck, my mom is cool. There is no way any other mom would be ok with their son having sex in their house. David thought. He could hear the shower come on and he went over to his desk. He put his homework in his bag from the day before and then collected his clothes for the day. He sat on the bed and waited for Amanda to be finished. When she came in she giggled.

"I thought you would join me." She said and lightly kissed his lips. David kissed back and smiled.

"I thought about it but I thought you would like to shower alone."

"Well, think differently next time." She said and sat down at David's desk to brush her hair. David laughed and headed to the bathroom. He took a pee and then had a quick shower. He got out and brushed his hair and teeth. He applied his cologne and deodorant and then went back to his room. Amanda had already headed downstairs and David could hear her and Nancy talking and Little Mike playing with something on the kitchen floor. He pulled on his jacket, grabbed his book bag and cigarettes and went down to join them. Nancy had a cup of coffee at his spot for him already.

"Good morning." Nancy said as he sat down.

"Yes it is." David said sending Amanda a lust look and Amanda blushed. Nancy giggled and passed Little Mike another Cheerio.

"So, the Fair starts tonight. Are you excited?" Nancy asked David as he sipped his coffee and smiled at Little Mike. Little Mike clapped and giggled.

"Well, it's gonna be cool." David answered and handed Little Mike a Cheerio.

"I heard about the sword play and stuff. I didn't think you would remember all that stuff." Amanda said and sipped her coffee. David looked at her and raised his eyebrow.

"Like riding a bike." David said and Amanda smiled. Nancy took a sip of her coffee and checked the time. It was 8 am.

"Well, it's been nice guys but I have to go now." Nancy said and took her cup to the sink. "I'll see you tonight at the fair." She added as she headed out of the kitchen toward the door. Amanda and David said their good byes and she left. Amanda leaned down and handed Little Mike another Cheerio.

"Do you know when Gabe is coming to get him?" She asked.

"I don't know. He said around eight." David answered recalling the talk they had a couple of days before. Gabe had remained himself like David asked and still flirted with him like the talk had never happened.

"Maybe we should call." Amanda said. David reached over to the phone and took it from the receiver. He dialed the number and waited.

"*Hello.*" It was Gabe.

"Hi." David answered and Gabe sighed.

"*Is it ok to tell you that your voice makes me hard?*" David giggled and nodded.

"I thought that only happened to me." He said. Amanda looked at him funny then went back to playing with Little Mike. Gabe giggled.

"*Well, it doesn't. I'll be there in a few minutes to get Mike. How was your night?*"

"Long." David said and winked at Amanda. She blushed and looked away.

"*I can believe that.*" Gabe said and cleared his throat. "*I'll see you in a minute ok.*" He added.

"Ok." David said and hung up the phone. "He's on his way." He said to Amanda and got up to get more coffee and a coffee for Gabe. "Want one?" David asked walking by and giving her a kiss as he passed.

"No, I still have lots." She said with her eyes closed. She loved it when he kissed her. David poured the coffee and looked out the window to see Gabe coming. He took the cups to the table and sat down. Gabe came in and walked into the kitchen.

"Good morning." He said and sat down between Amanda and David where his coffee was sitting.

"Hi Gabe. Look Mikey, It's Gabe." Amanda said and Little Mike reached up to him. He picked up Mike and sat him on his lap.

"So, fair day, David. Stoked or what?" Gabe asked raising his eyebrows up and down. Amanda giggled.

"Yea, I am actually." David answered.

"I can't wait to watch you do all that stuff I've been hearing about." Amanda said and sipped her coffee. David smiled and shrugged.

"Look at the modesty." Gabe said to Little Mike and Mike giggled. Amanda and David laughed. "The Iron Maiden thing he does is the coolest." Gabe said to Amanda.

"What do you do?" Amanda asked David and David smiled at Gabe.

"He gets in it." Gabe said and Amanda shot a look at David.

"You get *in* it?"

"Yea." David said in a quiet seductive voice. Amanda shivered and Gabe giggled. They chatted about the fair as they finished their coffee. Gabe left with Little Mike and Amanda and David left for school.

"Are they staying?" David asked looking over at Amanda's parents SUV. She sighed and shrugged.

"I have no idea." She said and grabbed his hand. They headed toward the school in silence. David thought about the knockout punch that Steve had given Gabe and felt instantly angry.

"Why can't they just go and stay gone?" David asked through clenched teeth.

"They won't stay long." Amanda said and squeezed David's hand. He squeezed back and opened the big glass door of the school for her. She walked in and led the way to their lockers. They collected what they needed and went to home room. They sat through attendance and went their separate ways. David's thoughts were consumed with Gabe and what his day must be like with Steve and Sandra there. At noon, David met up with Amanda at their lockers.

"You thought about it all day, didn't you?" Amanda asked seeing the anger in David's eyes.

"That obvious?" David asked as they headed out to the table.

"Yea, it is." She said and sat close to him on the table.

"It must be nice to just drop everything and fuck off." David said through clenched teeth. Amanda rubbed David's arm and sighed.

"It's better for Little Mike if they aren't around." They talked about the situation at Amanda's house for the rest of their lunch hour. David had finally calmed down when Amanda explained that she and Gabe were happier with things this way. When the bell rang, they headed into the school and collected what they needed for the afternoon. "Don't think about it so much. Gabe has everything under control. If it got too stupid, he would get us all out of there." Amanda said as they finished getting ready for the afternoon.

"I know." David said and kissed Amanda's forehead. She blushed and headed away to the library for her spare. David headed toward room 19 and Mr. Alan Black. He walked into the room and felt a warn sensation come over his body when he saw him. He was wearing his teacher's pants and a dress shirt again. David smiled and sat down at his desk.

"Big big night tonight, David." Alan said and handed David a worksheet. David looked it over and laughed.

"Thomas Edison?" He said. Alan rolled his eyes and nodded.

"I know." Alan said with a crinkled up nose. David laughed again and set the paper on his desk. Alan put a work sheet on every desk and walked up to the front of the class. "Thomas Edison . . ." Alan started the class with a little speech and some notes. Again he did three pages of notes like he always did to start a new section. At the end of class he stood at the front of the class, "I hope to see you all at the fair tonight. It's gonna be awesome. With that in mind . . ." He paused and smiled. "No homework, toss the work sheet in the trash on your way out." He said. The bell rang and everyone did as Mr. Black instructed. David stood up and stretched. "Ready for tonight?" Alan asked walking over to stand with David.

"I think so." David said and picked up his books. Alan smiled and nodded.

"You'll do great." Alan said and led David to the door with a hand on the back of his shoulder. David smirked.

"When we going over there?" David asked when they got to the door.

"Well, I'll pick you up at five so we can get Your Lady moved. Carman will be there with his truck."

"Sounds good." David said and left the room.

Alan rolled up at five like he said. David got in the car with him and they headed to the library.

"So, the guillotine is already there so it's just Your Lady that has to get there." Alan said as he drove.

"Carman is a god send hey?" David asked. He was both excited and nervous for the show. Alan smiled and nodded.

"He sure is." He said as he turned the corner. They could see Carman's truck parked in the front. They pulled up and got out.

"Did you find a ramp?" Alan asked Carman as he got out of the car.

"Yup, and I found your winch too." Carman said and smiled at David. They went into the library and collected the Iron Maiden. They walked it outside on the lift and set it just outside. Carman set up the ramp and Alan set up the winch. David took the hook from Alan and fastened it to the lifting apparatus the Iron Maiden was strapped to. Alan worked the winch while Carman and David slowly walked beside the iron coffin. When it made it to the back of the truck, Carman strapped it down. David and Alan road together in Alan's car and Carman followed.

"Thank you for doing this." Alan said as they drove.

"What? Again with the gratitude? Give me a break Alan." David said and giggled. Alan laughed and shook his head.

"You really are something, David."

"I know." David said. They could see the renaissance fair grounds up ahead. There were two large tents for the various shows that would be performed throughout the rest of the week. There was a smaller tent for the beer gardens and then behind that were the fair rides and carnival games. Alan pulled his car up beside one of the large tents.

David could see the guillotine set up and the various daggers, throwing stars and the long sword on a table. They got out of the car and Alan guided Carman back to the tent. Alan jumped up into the truck and Carman and David lined up the ramp. They unloaded the Iron Maiden the same way they had loaded it at the library. Alan walked it to where it would stand for the rest of the week. Alan got it off the apparatus and David looked it over for damages.

"Boy am I glad it's you I borrowed her to." Carman said to David as he watched him go over the Iron Maiden. David giggled and looked at him.

"Why?"

"She seems to be in good hands." Carman answered and Alan smiled. David shook his head and finished his inspection. When he was satisfied, they all decided to go down to the diner for supper. Carman took his truck and Alan and David rode together in Alan's car again. They got to the diner and picked a seat by a window.

"I'm Buying." David said shooting a look at Alan. Alan laughed and shook his head.

"The idea is to take off with the check before he gets his hands on it." Carman said and Alan laughed again. They looked over their menus and picked what they wanted. They gave the waitress their orders.

"So, when do we start?" David asked grabbing Alan's arm and looking at his watch. Alan smiled and looked at Carman. Carman laughed and shook his head.

"7:30." Alan answered and took his arm back. He looked at his watch as well. It was almost 6:00. "We have an hour to change our minds." Alan said and David and Carman laughed. They talked about the order of the presentations as they ate their meal. When the check came, Carman grabbed it right out of the waitresses hand and went up to the till. Alan laughed and shook his head.

"Man, he's quick." David said and finished the last sip of his pop. Alan giggled and they both stood up. They went out to their vehicles and all lit a cigarette.

"Well, wanna change your mind?" Carman asked David as they stood smoking.

"Nope." David said and Alan smiled. They finished their cigarettes and got into their cars.

"Nervous?" Alan asked as they drove to the fair grounds. David sighed.

"A little." He said and giggled.

"It will be fine. The first show will be the hardest. After that, it will get easier."

"There are two show's tonight and then one every night till Saturday, right?" David asked as they neared the grounds.

"Yep. Saturday is the last night." Alan answered. David took a deep breath as Alan parked the car. Carman parked beside them. They got out of the car and David looked around. There were already quite a few cars parked in the parking lot. Along with a big, black Hearse. David smiled and could feel his stomach flip. "Looks like Gabe is here." Alan said as they made their way to the tent. David nodded and looked away from the car. Carman helped Ron and Samantha get their podiums set up and Alan and David went over the order again. A tall man dressed in a knight costume came to the large opening in the tent.

"Five minutes to show time guys, you ready?" The man asked. Alan nodded and looked at David. David raised his eyebrows and took a deep breath.

"Don't be nervous, you'll kill somebody." Carman joked and David laughed. People started to fill the chairs that sat in front of the tent. Amanda, Little Mike and Gabe sat up front. David smiled at them as they took their seats.

"Are you sure you wanna sit up front?" David asked quietly and Amanda laughed. Gabe had Little Mike on his lap.

"We like to be right in the action." Gabe said and Little Mike giggled. David kissed Little Mike on the top of the head and squeezed Amanda's hand. Amanda smiled and David went up to the table. The sword was first. Ron talked about the history of the long sword while David did his closed eyed dance. When he finished the crowed stood and applauded. David bowed and Gabe whistled. Amanda laughed and Little Mike squealed. David demonstrated the daggers next as Samantha read from her notes. Again there was a standing ovation. Next, the throwing stars. Little Mike seemed to like those the best because he squeaked with each toss. The guillotine was after that and Amanda closed her eyes every time David let the release handle go to chop the melon. The melon had been Carman's idea. It was a hit. The crowed fell silent when David walked toward the Iron Maiden and slowly opened the door. Alan took the podium and referred to the Iron Maiden as David's Lady. The crowd didn't seem to get it but Gabe giggled. David stepped inside the coffin and placed his feet and hands in the appropriate places and stared at Alan. Gabe smiled and shivered. Little Mike yelled,

"Cowfull Davin!" The crowd laughed and David smiled. He closed his eyes and tilted his head back. Ron stepped beside the Iron Maiden and pointed out the spikes inside for the crowd as Alan spoke. David slowly stepped out and they replaced him with a large potato bag filled with red maple syrup. David closed the door and the syrup oozed out of the bag. The crowd said 'ewe' and giggled. They all stood and clapped again when Alan finished speaking. The four of them grabbed hands and bowed together. The crowd cheered and slowly dispersed. Gabe and Amanda walked up to David.

"That was awesome." Gabe said and winked at David. David smiled and thanked him. Amanda hugged him.

"That was kind of scary actually." She whispered as she held him. David laughed and shook his head. She let him go and David looked at Little Mike.

"Did you like it?" He asked. Little Mike giggled and clapped.

"Davin is my best!" Little Mike said and giggled again. David smiled at him and ruffled his hair.

"So now what?" Gabe asked.

"Well, I gotta get the maple syrup out of that thing for the 9:30 show."

"Ok, Little Mike wants a pony ride and Amanda wants to play the games. Catch you later?" Gabe asked with a hint of seduction in his voice. David smiled and nodded. Amanda led Gabe through the crowd and off to the games.

"Great job, David." Alan said and patted his back. David turned and looked at him.

"It was easier than I thought actually." David answered and took the cleaning supplies out from under the table for the Iron Maiden.

"I told you. You're a natural." Alan said as they cleaned. Ron and Samantha got the table set up again and Carman left to find pop.

"Alan, was the guys in the back from the fair committee?" David asked remembering seeing two men in suits standing behind the small crowd.

"You saw them did you?" Alan asked wiping the syrup out of the back of the Iron Maiden while David worked on the spikes.

"Yea I did. They seemed to be pretty impressed." David said with a cheeky voice and Alan laughed.

"Let's hope so." Alan said and sighed.

"You'll get your funding Alan. I would bet my life on it." David said as he seen the two men approach with smiles on their faces. Alan looked behind him and dried his hands. He walked up to the men and shook their hands. David continued cleaning.

"Very well done Mr. Black." The taller man said.

"Well, it was the kids. They did the work." Alan said and smiled. The shorter man looked around Alan at David then back at Alan again.

"You have your funding, Alan. The credits also and full college scholarships for all three students." The short man said. David dropped his wash cloth and Alan stood wide eyed at the two men.

"*What?*" Alan choked out.

"We've been waiting for a show like this from a school. We are tired of the essays and projections. You deserve it." The short man said and they walked away. David stood up and went to Alan who was still standing with a shocked look on his face.

"Did he say, *Full Scholarships?*" David asked. Alan blinked and looked at him. Ron and Samantha joined them now and they all stared at Alan.

"Yea, that's what I thought I heard too." Alan said. Samantha squealed and hugged Ron. Ron laughed and twirled her around.

"Like, pay for whatever we want in collage?" David asked still stunned.

"Yea, that's what that means." Alan said. David giggled and looked around. Alan laughed and sat down on the table. They all talked excitedly until Carman got back with pop.

"What did I miss?" Carman asked as he handed out the pop. Alan explained the whole thing and Carman was as shocked as everyone else. "That's awesome, Alan!." He finally said and hugged his friend. Alan laughed and hugged back. "Did you expect this?" Carman asked when they let go.

"No." Alan said. They talked a little longer while David finished cleaning the Iron Maiden. When he was finished, they all hit the fair grounds and played some of the games. Alan won the first one and his prize was a giant stuffed dragon. He gave it to Carman and they both laughed. When it neared 9:30, they headed back to their tent. Ron and Samantha got their papers in order and David stretched his shoulders. The crowd filled in and David saw his mother sit upfront with Gabe and Amanda.

"Hi mom." David said and she waved. They did the show the same as before and the reactions were the same. Nancy hugged David when it was over and told him how proud she was. He pulled her aside and told her about the scholarship. She practically jumped up and down. When she calmed down, she thanked Alan for taking such good care of David and thanked him for offering him such an opportunity. They decided it was time to go by the beer gardens. David told them he would catch up after he finished cleaning the Iron Maiden. Carman stayed to clean with him and David forced Alan to go.

"So, Alan sure got more out of those blow hards than he expected, huh?" Carman asked as they finished cleaning the Iron Maiden and putting the steel able things away.

"No kidding. He seemed pretty shocked." David said. Carman laughed and nodded.

"You know, he was worried they would come up with some excuse why they wouldn't give out the credits or the funding."

"Really? Than this should have been a surprise."

"You're not kidding." Carman said. They chained the Iron Maiden and the guillotine to large hooks in the ground. They decided it was time to meet everyone else at the beer gardens. They walked past Alan who was talking to some students David recognized from his class. Alan smiled at them as they walked by. David smiled back and Carman waved. They walked passed Amanda and Little Mike. He was going for his last pony ride before it was time to go home. Amanda waved and David and Carman waved back. They got to the beer Gardens and sat down at the table where Gabe and a few other people were.

"Some show, kid." One of the guys said. David smiled and nodded. He looked around the room while the others at the table chatted. He saw a few women dressed a little slutty that he didn't recognize. He watched a ridiculous arm wrestle between a really huge guy and some kid who looked less than half his opponent's size. He looked back toward the entrance and seen a man arguing with a woman. She wanted to leave but he wouldn't let her. She said something that made the guy shake his head and David could see his side profile. It was his Uncle Carl. David got up and Carman watched him as he walked over to the arguing couple.

"Hey, get out of here." David said to the woman and she nodded and left.

"Well, if it isn't Mikes little girl." Carl slurred. David rolled his eyes but held his ground.

"What the fuck are you doing here?" David asked. Carl stumbled and laughed.

"Looking for your mommy." He answered and grabbed his crotch. David shook his head.

"Why don't you get the fuck out of here before I throw you out."

"Yea right little girl, you wouldn't dare." Carl slurred and pushed David back ward. David jumped forward and pushed Carl down to the ground. A couple young girls screamed and jumped out of the way. Carl got to his feet and smiled at David. "Looks like somebody needs a lickin'" Carl said and swung at David. David dodged the swing and hit Carl in the stomach. Carl coughed and punched David in the jaw. David stepped back and could taste blood. Carl swung and hit David again and David went down. Carl jumped on top of him and hit him in the ribs. David was winded and couldn't move. Gabe came out of nowhere and hauled Carl off of David. David heaved a breath and tried to get up. Gabe grabbed Carl by the shoulders and kneed him in the gut. Carl bent over and David could see him pull a long knife out of his pocket.

"Gabe!" David yelled but it was too late. Carl sunk the blade deep into Gabe's stomach. Gabe fell to the ground and Carl took off running. A few of the men that were watching chased after him. David crawled to Gabe and put his hand on the wound. Gabe coughed and blood splashed his lips. "Gabe, Gabe don't move." David said and looked around. Alan came running up behind them.

"David! What happened?" Alan yelled as he approached. He fell on his knees next to David and looked down at Gabe. Carman was on the phone with 911 almost instantly.

"Gabe! Gabe!" David yelled and Gabe's eyelids fluttered.

"I . . . I can't feel . . . feel my legs . . . I can't . . ." Gabe tried to say but the sound stopped coming.

"Gabe, the ambulance is coming; You need to just stay calm." Carman said. Gabe started to shake under David's hand.

"Gabe its ok. Are you ok?" David asked. Tears ran down his face. Gabe looked at him with glassy eyes.

"David," He whispered and coughed up more blood. David sniffed and winced.

“Gabe, don’t talk. Its ok.” David said and looked around. “Where the fuck is that ambulance?” David yelled. He could feel Alan’s hand on his shoulder. Just then, David could hear Amanda scream.

“Is that Gabe?! Gabe! Oh my God!” She screamed and Carman grabbed her. She hid her head in his chest and cried.

“David?” Gabe whispered. David looked down at him and noticed the shaking had stopped.

“Gabe! Gabe!” David yelled and shook the man on the ground. Gabe’s eye lids fluttered again.

“Hang on Gabe.” Alan said and squeezed David’s shoulder. Nancy knelt down beside David.

“You need to keep pressure on that wound David.” She said and felt Gabe’s forehead. “He’s getting cold. Someone get a blanket or something!” She yelled and then checked Gabe’s pulse. She looked at Alan and whispered. “His pulse is weak.”

“Weak? What does that mean?” David yelled.

“Just keep pressure on that wound.” Nancy said and kept counting Gabe’s heart beet through the pulse in his wrist.

“David.” Gabe whispered again. David looked down at him. His eyes seemed dark and looked as though they had clouds in them. “David.” He whispered again.

“Oh god Gabe. Don’t die.” David whispered and moved the hair out of his eye’s with his free hand.

“David.” Gabe whispered again and his eyes closed. David could hear the siren of the ambulance approaching.

“Gabe, the ambulance is here.” David said but Gabe didn’t move. “Gabe! Gabe!” David yelled and Nancy looked up at him.

“David,” Nancy said but David shot her a look that could kill.

“Gabe!” David yelled through his tears. The paramedics rushed in and knelt on the side of Gabe that Nancy was on.

"I've lost vitals." Nancy said and David looked at her again.

"What?!" David screamed and looked at the paramedics.

"Sir, you need to move your hand on three ok?" One of the paramedics said. David nodded and the paramedic counted to three. David quickly moved his hand and the paramedic replaced it with white cloth. David watched as they tried to administer C.P.R. They seemed to work on Gabe on the ground for what felt like hours. Then they stopped and shook their heads.

"No! No you can't stop!" David yelled and shook Gabe. "Gabe! Gabe wake up!" He screamed. Amanda wailed and Nancy had tears falling down her cheeks. "Gabe!" David screamed again and let his head fall on Gabe's chest. "Don't do this." David begged and cried. He could feel Alan touch his back.

"David, we have to let the paramedics take him." Alan said quietly. David stayed where he was and cried. "David." Alan said again and pulled him up by the shoulders.

"Don't Alan! Please don't let them take him." David begged. Alan turned David around and held him. One paramedic got up and went to the ambulance. He brought out a gurney and the two of them loaded Gabe's limp body onto it. They covered his body and face with a white blanket and loaded him into the ambulance. They drove away without their lights on. David stayed in Alan's arms and cried.

"I need to call his parents." Nancy said.

"Go, I have him." Alan said and held David tighter. David could hear Amanda crying and Little Mike asking,

"Gabe? Gabe go bye-bye?" David cried and held Alan. Alan took him to his car and Carman followed with Amanda and Little Mike.

"We gotta take them to Gabe." Alan said and Carman nodded. Carman loaded Little Mike into the back seat of his truck and sat Amanda in the front. Alan still held David as they walked to the car.

"We need to go, David." Alan said and opened the car door. David nodded and got in. Alan ran to the driver's side door and got in. He started the engine and squealed his tires as they pulled away. Carman followed. "I'm gonna call your mom and let her know what we're doing, ok?" Alan asked and David nodded. Alan dialed the number and David listened to Alan's side of the conversation. "Hi, we're going to the hospital with the kids . . . . What? No answer . . . . Ok, ... We will be there . . . . He seems like he just watched his friend die . . . . I will . . . . Ok see you there later than . . . . Bye." Alan hung up the phone and put it back on his belt. "She will be there after she gets a hold of Gabe's parents." Alan said and David nodded. They pulled out onto the high way and Alan caught up with the ambulance. He stayed behind it and Carman stayed behind them. "What happened? Who was that guy?" Alan asked. David blinked and swallowed hard.

"My Uncle." David answered and started to cry again. Alan reached over and put his hand on David's leg. David looked down at it and sighed.

"Why were you fighting with him?" Alan asked. David stared at Alan's hand.

"He killed Gabe." David said and hit the dash. Alan squeezed David's leg and David started to breath like he was panicking.

"David. David you need to calm down."

"He *killed* Gabe!" David said and started to hyper ventilate. Alan slowed the car and pulled over. Carman did the same behind him. Alan jumped out of the car and went to the passenger side. He opened the door and got David out. He held David and tried to calm his breathing. Carman ran over to them.

"What's happening?" Carman asked.

"He's panicking. Do you have a paper bag?" Alan asked. Carman ran back to the truck and grabbed a bag that had been from a fast food drive through and dumped its contents out onto the road. He brought the bag to Alan. Alan squeezed the top and handed it to David. "Breath into this, it will help." Alan said and David took the bag. He could see Gabe's blood on his hand and pulled the bag away. He threw up and Alan swore.

"I have some paper towel in my truck." Carman said and headed back.

"And some water!" Alan called back. Carman returned with a roll of paper towel and a bottle of water. Alan unscrewed the top and poured it on David's hands.

"Alan, Alan its Gabe's blood." David said through panicked breath.

"I know, come on, wash it off." Alan said quietly. David rung his hands under the water. When the bottle was empty, Carman ripped off a piece of paper towel and dried David's hands.

"David?" Amanda said quietly as she walked up to them. David looked at her and then looked away. She came up to him and put her hand on his shoulder. "David, are you ok?" She asked. Her voice was shaky as she spoke through her tears. David looked at her and sobbed.

"Amanda, I'm sorry." David said and looked away again. Amanda grabbed him and hugged him.

"You didn't do this, baby. Its ok, I love you." Amanda whispered. David held her tight and Alan and Carman got rid of the bloody paper towel. "I love you." Amanda whispered again and David cried.

"It was Carl." David whispered and Amanda nodded.

"I know. We need to get to him, ok?" Amanda said and David looked at her. Her eyes were puffy and she was shivering.

"Ok." David said and Alan nodded.

"Let's go." Carman said to Amanda and they went back to his truck.

"Are you ready?" Alan asked and David nodded.

Chapter 22

Gabe's funeral was planned by Nancy, David, Amanda and Alan. No one was ever able to reach his parents. Amanda had left messages with all the family she could think of regarding Gabe's death and the funeral plans. The fair committee had spoken with Alan and told him that the offer still stood and there would be no need for further shows. David and Amanda went over the music list to use while Alan and Nancy went over Gabe's life insurance.

"He's left you forty thousand, Amanda." Alan said as he leafed through the papers. Amanda nodded and kept flipping through Gabe's plethora of C.D.'s.

"And the car." Nancy said and Amanda nodded again.

"Does that stuff need to be done now?" David asked turning to face Alan and his mother from his spot on the floor next to Amanda.

"I'm afraid so, David. It's hard but the sooner the better." Alan answered and Amanda began to cry. David put his arm around her and sighed.

"Can't you deal with it?" David asked. Alan sighed and shook his head. Nancy started to cry too and David sighed.

"We can do most of it but Amanda will have to file the claim for the insurance." Nancy said and wiped the tears from her cheeks. Alan passed her a tissue and she smiled. "Thank you." She said and Alan nodded.

"I can't. He isn't even in the ground yet." Amanda said and got up. She went up to the bathroom and locked herself in. David got up and Nancy stopped him.

"You stay with Alan, dear. I'll go talk to her." Nancy said and walked up the stairs.

"Manda sad." Little Mike said from his play pen. David smiled at him and sat at the table with Alan.

"Thank god he isn't old enough to understand." David said and ran a hand through his hair. Alan nodded and cleared his throat.

"Are you ok?" Alan asked looking across the table at David. David sighed and shook his head.

"Not even close." He said at fought back tears. Alan sighed and shook his head.

"Well, it may not be any consolation, but he seemed to have everything in order from what I can see."

"Your right, it isn't" David said and rested his head on his hand. Alan bit his top lip.

"Got some songs picked out?" Alan asked. David raised his eyebrows and nodded.

"I think so." David answered and went to go get the C.D's he and Amanda had gone through. He handed them to Alan and listed off the songs from each disk they wanted to use.

"This should be lots David." Alan said and set the C.D's aside. "There was one thing I found in these papers I wanted to talk to you about." Alan said and pulled out a yellow piece of paper from the pile. "This is a piece of his Will." Alan said and handed it to David. David read it over and sighed.

"Is this a joke?" David asked and Alan shook his head.

"It was signed and dated with a lawyer about two months ago." Alan said and David shook his head.

"He wants me to drive his coffin in *his* Hearse?" David asked. Alan sighed and nodded.

"You don't have to David." Alan said. "It's a special request page. You don't need to do it." Alan added. David stared at the page and sighed.

"If that's what he wanted, that's what he gets." David said and put the paper down. Alan sighed and nodded.

"Ok then. We need to let the funeral home know then." He said and went into the other room to use the phone.

"Gabe see the angels?" Mike asked and David turned to look at him. He smiled at Little Mike and ruffled his hair.

"Yea, Gabe see the angels." David answered. Little Mike giggled and clapped. David smiled and turned to face forward in his seat again. He could hear Alan on the phone with the funeral home and Amanda and Nancy talking upstairs. He put his hand in his pocket and dug out the pick Gabe had given him. He twirled it in his fingers for a while. Alan came back into the room and sat down at the table.

"Well, they are aware of the situation. They said these kinds of things happen often." Alan said and lit a cigarette. David nodded and looked down at the paper work on the table.

"Any news on finding Carl?" David asked and clenched his teeth.

"Nothing yet." Alan said and took a drag from his cigarette. They sat in silence until Nancy and Amanda returned.

"What do I have to do?" Amanda asked in the bravest voice she could muster up. Alan helped her make the right phone calls and get the ball rolling on the insurance. Nancy and David put all the paper work that wasn't insurance or Will Kit stuff into shoe boxes and piled them on the table.

"Funny how your whole life can be filed away." Nancy said and rested her hand on the boxes.

"That's not Gabe, mom." David said and lit a cigarette for both her and himself.

"I know it isn't. But it's a part of him." She said as she took a long drag from her cigarette. Alan and Nancy took the boxes over to Amanda's house and David sat at the table with Amanda.

"How can this be?" Amanda asked. David sighed and shook his head.

"I don't know. I can't believe it either."

"What will we do?" Amanda asked looking at Little Mike.

"Well, you can stay here." David said and Amanda nodded.

"That's what your mom said too."

"Well, that's what you do for now. Tomorrow we burry Gabe, and then we just take one day at a time. Ok?" David said leaning across the table to offer Amanda his hand. She smiled and took it into hers.

"Ok." She said and squeezed his hand. David sighed and tried to smile at her. She did the same. They sat like that until Nancy and Alan returned with two Guitars, some music books and the keys to Gabe's car.

"Where?" Nancy asked. She was holding the guitars. David got up and took them from her. He carried them downstairs and went into the music room. He set the guitars against the wall and looked around the room. He looked at the black guitar Gabe had found for him. He touched the neck with his finger tips and sighed. He walked past the stools and a piece of paper floated to the floor. He bent over to pick it up. It was the score Gabe had given him. On the bottom was a note.

You play like a god . . . And god, I love you. David stared at the note and wondered when he had a chance to write it. He read it over and over until tears stung his eyes.

"God damn you Carl!" He yelled and crumpled the piece of paper. He grabbed the black Stratocaster guitar by the neck and swung it like a baseball bat. He collided with the drum kit and pieces of guitar and drums exploded around the room. He swung again and connected with the book stand of music books his father had collected throughout the years. The neck of the guitar snapped and books fell to the floor. David could feel Alan's arms around him. He struggled to get free but Alan held on. Soon he succumbed to the weeping and pain in his chest and collapsed. Alan went down with him still holding him. They knelt like that on the floor while David cried.

"Is he ok?" Nancy whispered from the door. David could feel Alan shake his head. "David, do you need anything?" Nancy asked from the door.

"Carl and a shot gun." David said through clenched teeth. Alan held him tighter and looked over at Nancy.

"This may be a bad idea, but get rum." Alan said.

"Scotch." David said and Nancy stayed at the door. Alan sighed and nodded and Nancy left. Alan held David and never let go.

"Are you ok?" Alan asked. David nodded his head and Alan slowly let him go. They stayed on the floor staring at each other.

"I wanna kill him, Alan." David said through his tears.

"I know you do." Alan said and got up. He went over and shut the door. David looked around the room and his shoulders slumped.

"What did I do?" David asked and Alan sat back down next to him.

"What anyone else would have done." Alan answered. David stood up and picked up the neck of his guitar. He stared at it and shook his head. Alan got up and stood beside him. David looked at him and sighed.

"Look at this thing." David said and looked around the room again. Alan put his hand on David's back.

"I think it adds character." Alan said and David laughed. They picked up the little pieces of guitar and drums. Alan piled the books and David put his now two piece guitar next to Gabe's beautiful untouched guitars. There was a knock at the door. Alan opened it and took two glasses and a bottle of scotch from Nancy. He thanked her and shut the door. He poured a shot into each glass and handed one to David.

"To Gabe." David said and they both took their shot. Alan and David both sat down and Alan poured another shot. They held their drinks and David looked around the room.

"It's not as bad as it looks." Alan said. David looked at him and shook his head.

"Your right, it's worse." David said and drank his shot. Alan poured him another one and sat back in the leather chair.

"You can't keep doing this to yourself." Alan said. David took his shot and handed his cup to Alan. Alan sighed and poured him another. "David, you need to talk more than you need to drink." Alan said watching David stare into the glass.

"Do I?" David asked and slammed the liquid back into his throat. Alan set the bottle down on the floor and leaned forward on the chair.

"Talk to me, David." Alan said. David shook his head and looked down to the floor. "You talk, I pour." Alan offered and David sighed.

"He was saving me . . . again." David said. Alan grabbed the bottle and poured David another shot. He handed the glass to David and he slammed it back again.

"This isn't your fault." Alan said. David handed the cup to Alan.

"Isn't it? Tell that to the little boy upstairs who is going to grow up without his big brother." David said. Alan poured another drink but kept the cup.

"Do you really think he blames you?" Alan asked.

"He's going to." David answered. Alan sighed and shook his head. He handed the glass to David but David didn't drink it this time. He held it in his hand and stared down into it. Alan sat quietly waiting for David to speak. "He just died, Alan. No fight, no gurgling in his throat, no jerking or screaming. He just died." David said. Tears filled his eyes again and he took his drink in one swallow again.

"Carl stabbed him in such a way, David, that those things would have never happened." Alan said quietly and drank his own shot. He poured two more and David sighed.

"His last word was David." David said and swallowed his shot in one tilt of his hand.

"I know, David. He was trying to talk. Your name was what came to him." Alan said and David nodded. They sat in silence for quite some time. David handed the cup to Alan after a while.

"I don't want anymore." David said and Alan smiled.

"Good for you." Alan answered and set the glasses down with the bottle. He stood up and walked over to David.

"Promise me you'll only come down here and drink this when I'm down here with you." Alan said. David looked up at him and sighed.

"Ok, Alan." He said and Alan held out his hand. David took it and Alan helped him up.

"You need to sleep. You'll need your rest for tomorrow." Alan said. David nodded and they headed upstairs. Nancy was sitting at the table reading her book.

"Where is Amanda?" David asked.

"She's sleeping in your bed. Little Mike is my room." Nancy added and smiled as they sat down with her.

"Sorry about the music room, mom." David said. Nancy's face fell.

"Oh, David. Don't apologize. There's nothing in that room that means anything to me anymore. I just want to know you're ok." Nancy said with tears in her eyes.

"I will be." David said. Alan smiled and looked up at the clock.

"I think I'm gonna head home. Will you guys be alright?" Alan asked. Nancy and David nodded. Alan stood up and headed for the door. David followed him.

"Thanks for everything, Alan." David said as Alan put his boots on.

"You're more than welcome." He said and stood up. David hugged him and smelled his cologne. He smelled even more amazing to him than he ever had before. "Please call if you need anything tonight, ok?" Alan said when David let him go. David nodded and Alan left. He sighed and went back into the kitchen.

"Mom, are you going to bed?" David asked. Nancy nodded and looked up at him.

"Yes, right now actually." She said and stood up. They walked up the stairs together and stopped at David's door. Nancy hugged David before letting him go into his room.

"Good night, mom." David said as he opened the door.

"Good night." Nancy said and stepped into her room. David stepped into his room and seen that Amanda had left the lamp on for him. He got undressed down to his boxers and climbed in next to her. He shut off the lamp and lay his arm over her.

"I wish this was all a bad dream." Amanda whispered. David sighed an nodded.

"Me too." David whispered and pulled Amanda closer to him.

"Have they found him yet?"

"No, no one has heard anything." David answered and hugged Amanda. She sighed and seemed to fall back to sleep. David lay staring at Amanda's hair in the moon light.

Damn it Gabe. I am so sorry. That blade was for me. God I'm sorry. Tears filled David's eyes and he closed them. He tried to fight the agonizing pain in his chest. It was to strong and he cried till he fell asleep.

David slowly dressed into his black suit. He stared at himself in the mirror as he got ready. Amanda was in the shower and Nancy was getting herself and Little Mike ready. He sprayed on his cologne and fixed his tie. He hair was slicked straight back and his teeth were brushed. When he finished he stared in the mirror at the well dressed man he saw.

"Why do people dress like this to burry someone?" He asked himself and sighed. He shook his head and headed downstairs. He went straight to the coffee pot and poured a cup for himself. He looked out the window to the Hearse waiting for him out front. Alan had washed it inside and out the night before and parked it there while he slept. He took a deep breath and sat down at the table.

"Hi Davin." Little Mike said as Nancy entered the room with him on her hip.

"Hi Mikey. You look handsome." David said and smiled at him. Little Mike giggled and clapped his hands. Nancy set him in his high chair and got him a bowel of dry Cheerio's and then got herself a coffee. She came and sat down with her son. "Mom, this is crazy." David said and pulled at his tie.

"I know dear. It all seems like it's something out of a movie or something, doesn't it?"

"Yea. Like a night mare." David said and sipped his coffee. Nancy tried to smile but it was a fail. Tears ran down her face and she left the room. David sighed and looked at Little Mike. "I wish I was you." David said and sipped his coffee.

"Davin pretty." Little Mike said and David smiled. Amanda came into the room and kissed David on the cheek. "Me to, me to." Little Mike said and David laughed. Amanda kissed Little Mike and got a cup of coffee.

"How was your sleep?" David asked as she sat down.

"Red." Amanda answered and David sighed.

"Red?" He asked and Amanda nodded.

"I just kept seeing all that blood. But it was worse in my dream."

"God Amanda. Are you ok?" David asked and leaned across the table to hold her hand. She nodded and took his hand and squeezed.

"Yea. I'm ok." She said and smiled. "Let's just get today done ok." Amanda added and looked out the window at Gabe's Hearse. She shivered and sipped her coffee. "Why would I want that thing after today?" Amanda asked. David sighed and nodded.

"I know Amanda, it's gonna be hard." David said. He felt lost and confused. Nancy came back into the room with the phone. She handed it to David.

"Hello?" David said.

"*Hi, how are you this morning?*" It was Alan.

"Well, not good."

"*Ok, I'm on my way to pick up Nancy, Amanda and Little Mike. Do you remember where to park the car?*"

"Yea, I remember." David said and sipped his coffee again.

"*Ok, when we get there, I'll wait at the doors for you.*" Alan said.

“Thanks Alan.” David said.

“*Of course. See you soon.*”

“Ok, bye.” David said and hung up the phone. “Alan’s on his way.” David said and Amanda took a few big gulps of her coffee. Nancy took their cups to the sink and took Little Mike out of his high chair. She looked at David and smiled.

“Are you ok with this?” Nancy asked. David sighed and looked outside at the car.

“Yea, I can do this for Gabe.” David said. Amanda hugged him and whispered in his ear.

“I know he would have been so proud to have you take him to his grave, David.” David hugged her tight and smelled her hair. He could feel his body shake and she hugged him tighter. She pulled away and went up to the bath room. Nancy took Little Mike to the stairs to get his shoes on. David stared out at the Hearse parked outside. He closed his eyes and took a deep breath.

God Gabe, I am so sorry. He thought and opened his eyes. The Hearse was still there and he was still dressed in his black suit. He sighed and shook his head. Amanda came downstairs and David went up. He looked at himself in the mirror and could see tears forming in his eyes.

“Keep it together David.” He said to himself and splashed cold water on his face. He could hear Alan’s voice downstairs. He came down to see Alan hugging Amanda. He was dressed in a priest collar suit that, under different circumstances, would have been instant erotica for David. He got to the bottom of the stairs and Alan hugged him.

“Are you ready for this?” Alan whispered in his ear.

“No.” David whispered back and pulled away. Alan sighed and escorted the other three out to his car. David closed and locked the door and walked slowly out to the Gabe's Hearse. He took the keys out of his pocket and unlocked the door. He felt Alan's hand on his shoulder.

"I will wait at the doors for you, ok?" He said. David nodded and got in the car. He looked around. There were still the pictures of Marilyn Manson hanging from the rear view mirror. David sighed and put the key into the ignition. He started the car and the roar scared him.

"God Gabe. This thing is a beast." He said and put the car in drive. Alan led the way to the funeral home. David followed listening to the Apocalyptica C.D. Gabe had in the stereo. He let the tears run down his face as he drove. Alan pulled up in front of the building and David pulled around to the back. He backed the car up to the doors and shut the car off. He held on to the steering wheel and took a few deep breaths. "Ok, Gabe. Almost there." He said and got out of the car. He slowly walked around the building and seen Alan standing by the doors. Alan walked over to him.

"Wanna stand out here for a second?" Alan asked. David nodded and Alan lit them both a cigarette. David could see Carman's truck pull up. He got out of the truck and came over to David and Alan.

"Hanging in there?" He asked David and David nodded. They stood smoking for a few minutes. David watched as people he didn't recognize walked into the building.

"Are the other Paul Barriers here yet?" David asked remembering the long conversations he had on the phone with Gabe's friends.

"Yes, I saw them inside." Alan said. David nodded and finished his cigarette. Alan and Carman put theirs out too and they went inside.

The funeral seemed long and David was happy to carry Gabe's casket out to the car. They loaded him in and David closed the door.

"We're right behind you." Nancy said and David nodded. Amanda kissed David and followed Nancy to the limo waiting on the street.

"Alan," David said as Nancy and Amanda walked away.

"Yes?" Alan asked.

"Ride with me." David said. Alan nodded and Carman hugged David.

"It's 10 blocks. And then it's over." Carman said and David nodded. Carman shook Alan's hand and headed to his truck. David closed his eyes for a moment then looked at Alan.

"Ready?" Alan asked. David sighed and raised his eyebrows.

"As ready as I'm gonna be." David answered. They got into the car and David looked behind him at the casket. He remembered the last time he had seen Gabe in the back of that car and tears filled his eyes again. He looked out the windshield and started the car. David closed his eyes and listened to the monster engine.

"David, let's get him there, ok?" Alan said and David opened his eyes. He put the car in drive and pulled out onto the street. The limo pulled in behind him as he headed for the grave yard. "Take all the time in the world, David. He's in no hurry." Alan said and David sighed. The lump in his throat was agonizing and he couldn't fight the tears from falling. Alan put his hand on David's leg and he shivered.

"I wish I wasn't doing this." David whispered and Alan squeezed his leg.

"I know." Alan said and they both stared out the windshield. They passed an old man on his porch that stood up and took his hat off. David looked away and cleared his throat. He counted the blocks as they passed them. "You should talk to him." Alan said and took his hand from David's leg. David looked up into the rear view mirror at the reflection of Gabe's coffin. His heart pounded in his chest as he stared at the red, oak box.

“What do I say?” David asked. Alan shook his head.

“That’s up to you.” Alan said then added. “It’s kind of your chance to say something without anyone around to hear.”

“You’re here.” David said looking at Alan. Alan smiled and shook his head.

“I’m not listening.” Alan said and looked out the passenger side window. David looked up into the mirror and out on to the road. He stopped at the stop sign before the grave yard and looked back up at the reflection.

“I know you’re gone, and it’s too late for this but . . .” David paused and looked at Alan. He still stared out the window. David cleared his throat and looked back up in the mirror. “Gabe, I was too proud. Too stupid. I’m sorry I never told you that . . .” David paused again and Alan shifted in his seat but never looked away from the window. “I think I felt the same.” He said and pulled ahead to cross the road. Alan smiled and looked at David.

“You know, that was probably perfect.” Alan said. David nodded and pulled into the grave yard to the freshly dug whole in the black earth.

The long weeks after Gabe’s funeral were frustrating. Little Mike asked for Gabe every day, Amanda had her ‘red’ dream almost every night. Nancy would tear up every time she would walk passed Gabe’s car that David had parked next to his dad’s old garage. And David hardly spoke, especially about Gabe. School days were long and the nights sleeping next to Amanda seemed even longer. Her nightmares would wake David every time she had them. He would sit up in bed and have a cigarette which would break up his sleep. His only rest seemed to be his Sunday afternoons with Alan. David couldn’t bring himself to play his guitar so they would talk about the living situation and how David felt about it. They would do David's homework or go for a drive. They learned every back road and old highway in the county. David talked to Carman every Friday night. They found they had something in common with Alan and would talk about him a lot.

Christmas was soon closing in and the excitement seemed to still Little Mike's questions. Nancy kept herself busy by planning a trip out to see her sister Nora. Amanda's nightmares slowly dissipated to once or twice a week and David even noticed her laughing a little more. David was still consumed with grief and guilt. The police still had not located Carl but the search continued. He found himself feeling more and more angry over the whole ordeal. Alan was a good help. He tried to talk to David about it but when David would get upset, he would quickly change the subject. At the last day of school before Christmas holidays, Alan stopped David in the hall way as he left.

"So, you heading out to your Aunt's tonight or tomorrow?" Alan asked. David looked him up and down and smiled. David had found himself just as sexually frustrated, as he was frustrated with the search for Carl.

"Um, tomorrow afternoon some time. Mom has to work tomorrow morning." David answered.

"Come shopping with me then." Alan said and David laughed.

"When? Now?"

"Well, no. I have a class in two minutes. But after that." Alan said looking down the hall way to the student's going into his class room.

"Yea, I gotta find something for Little Mike anyway." David said and smiled. Alan smiled back and winked. David rolled his eyes and shut his locker door.

"Great. I will pick you up at around 3:30 then." Alan said and walked away. David shook his head and smiled. He left the school and headed home. He stopped at the sitters and picked up Little Mike on his way.

"Hi Davin." Little Mike said and David smiled.

"Thanks Rita." David said and waved.

"My pleasure David. Say hi to Amanda for me." Rita said. Rita had been Amanda's sitter when she was younger so using her seemed to be a no-brainer. David took Little Mike home and put him in front of his favorite show. He went to the kitchen and got himself a pop and filled Mike's sippy cup. He took it out to him and sat down on the couch. He felt his eyes grow heavy as he watched Little Mike's show. He had just drifted off when there was a knock at the door. He looked at the clock. It was 3:00. He got up and answered the door. A young looking male cop stood at the door.

"Uh, Mr. David Smith?" The young cop asked. David nodded.

"Yes, can I help you?" David asked.

"Yes sir. I am Constable Chad Phillips. I have news for you. May I come in?"

"Yea, yea of course." David said and stepped aside to let Constable Phillips come in. David led him into the kitchen and offered him a chair. He sat down and took out a pad of paper from his shirt pocket.

"Mr. Smith, I was sent here to inform you that a Mr. Carl Smith is now in our custody." David blinked and leaned back in his chair.

"I'm sorry, what?" David asked in disbelief.

"We have a Mr. Carl Smith in our custody." Constable Phillips said again and David laughed. It was a strange reaction but he couldn't help it.

"Are you *shittin* me?" David asked through his laughter.

"No sir." The officer said. David shook his head and sighed.

"I don't believe it."

"Well, it's true, sir."

"So, you guys *actually* found *him?"* David asked again as if the officer's answer would change.

"Yes we did sir."

"Can you quit calling me sir, you're my new best friend. You can call me David." David said and slapped the table. The officer smiled and nodded.

"Well, David. We have him. And he isn't going anywhere." The Constable said and stood up.

"What? That's it?" David asked getting up with the officer.

"That's it David, we will let you know when trial has been set. He hasn't pleaded yet, but if he pleads not guilty we will need you and your party to testify."

"Of course. I'm sure I speak for everyone that was there." David said. The officer smiled and headed for the door.

"That is great news David."

"What happens if he pleads guilty?" David asked as the officer waved at Little Mike and opened the door.

"Then you guys can enjoy your New Years without setting foot in a court house." Constable Phillips said. David smiled and shook the officer's hand.

"Thank you, so much." David said.

"It's our pleasure, David." The officer said and walked back out to his squad car. David closed the door and ran to the phone. His hand shook as he dialed the number to the school.

"*Hello, North Hill High School, Judy speaking.*"

"Judy. This is David Smith."

"*Oh, hello David. How can I help you?*"

"Could you pull Amanda Moore out of class and get her on the phone please?"

"*Uh, that's not really allowed, David.*"

"Judy! It's an emergency." David said trying not to yell at the school receptionist.

"*Ok, just hold.*" She said and the line went silent. David stood tapping his fingers on the arm of the couch and Little Mike giggled. David smiled at him and he clapped.

"Davin so silly." Little Mike said and David giggled.

"*David? David what's wrong?*" It was Amanda's shaky frantic voice.

"Amanda! They got him!" David said and Amanda was silent for a moment.

"*Got him?*" She asked.

"Got Carl! Amanda they have Carl!"

"*What!?*" Amanda said and he could hear her starting to cry on the phone.

"They have Carl." David said again and she screamed. It was both happiness and sounded as though she was crying as well. "Baby, we got him." David whispered. Amanda sobbed on the other end. "I'm coming to get you." David said and hung up the phone. He picked up Little Mike and rushed out the door. He went to the back and looked at Gabe's car. "Let's go for a ride." David said to both the car and Little Mike.

"Wheee!" Little Mike squealed and David unlocked the passenger side door. He set Little Mike on the seat and did up the seat belt. Mike was such a good passenger that no one ever worried about a car seat for him, except Nancy. He shut the door and went to the driver's side. He got in the car and started it up. "Boom Boom!" Mike said and David laughed.

"Yea, boom boom." David said and pulled the long, black Hearse out from beside the garage and onto the road. He got to the school and got Mike out of the car. They ran in and met Amanda at the office.

"David!" She yelled and jumped into his arms. He held her tight and Little Mike giggled.

"Amanda, we don't have to wait anymore." David whispered into her ear. She hugged tighter and cried.

"Is everything ok?" The receptionist asked.

"Car is in sustady." Little Mike said and David laughed. Amanda picked him up and hugged him. David explained the news to the ladies in the office and they all clapped or cheered.

"We gotta tell Alan!" David said. Amanda nodded and they headed toward room 19. They could hear Alan addressing his grade twelve History class. Amanda and Little Mike waited outside and David busted in the door. Everyone fell silent.

"David? What are you doing?" Alan asked. David was breathless and Alan excused himself from the class and stepped out of the room. He saw Amanda and Mike in the hall way. "Ok, what's going on?" Alan asked. He noticed Amanda had tears running from her eyes. "David?" Alan said his name like a question and David smiled.

"They found Carl." David said and Alan blinked a shocked look.

"And?" Alan asked as if there was more to the story.

"They have him in custody waiting for a plea." David said. Alan shook his head and grabbed David and pulled him in. They hugged and David took in the smell of Alan's hair and cologne.

"That's incredible." Alan said and David nodded. They let go of each other and Alan hugged Amanda. David smiled at Little Mike who looked as though he was feeling left out. Alan looked down at the little boy and laughed. He picked him up and hugged him.

"Alan is stwong." Little Mike said and everyone laughed.

"This is great news." Alan said and David smiled.

"It made my day, I'll tell you that." David said and Amanda cried. David laughed and took her into a tight hug.

"I can't believe it." Amanda said and David nodded.

"I know." David said and Alan shook his head.

"When did you find out?"

"The cops showed up at my house like 20 minutes ago." David said letting go of Amanda and holding her hand.

"Wow, did you tell your mom?"

"Not yet."

"Oh, let me tell her." Amanda begged and David laughed.

"Of course." David said and squeezed her hand. They talked out in the hall about their new good news until the bell rang.

"Shit." Alan said under his breath and went into the room. He said Merry Christmas to everyone and sent them on their way. "Ok, shopping. Still wanna go?" Alan asked.

"Yes, go. I will wait for Nancy and tell her all about Carl. We have some shopping of our own to do." Amanda said and took Little Mike from Alan.

"Ok, sounds like a date." Alan said and Amanda giggled at David's slight blush.

"Want me to take you home?" David asked. Amanda looked at him.

"Did you bring his car?"

"I thought it was fitting considering our news." David said and looked back and forth between Alan and Amanda. Amanda sighed and then smiled.

"Your right, David. I can drive it home. You go with Alan." She said and Alan smiled.

"Ok, you two be good." David said and kissed both Amanda and Little Mike on the forehead. They both giggled and left for Gabe's car.

"Let's get out of here." Alan whispered and David laughed. They headed out to Alan's car and took off toward the high way. "So, what a Christmas present." Alan said as he turned onto the highway toward the city.

"No shit." David said. He felt like his insides were shaking loose.

"How do you feel?" Alan asked and David looked at him.

"I was asked that once, my answer was horny." Alan laughed at David answer and lit a cigarette. David did the same.

"Ok, I was looking for happy, maybe a sense of closure. But horny works." Alan said and David laughed. They sat in silence still trying to grasp the situation. Alan flicked his cigarette out the window and looked at David. He could see that David was deep in thought and smiled. "What are you thinking about?" Alan asked. David flicked his own cigarette out the window and then looked at Alan.

"Do they have the death sentence in Nevada?" David asked. Alan laughed and shook his head.

"I don't know. We will have to look it up." Alan said and David smiled.

"I hope we do." David said. Alan shook his head again and looked between David and the road.

"It's good to see you happy again."

"It's good to be happy, Alan." David said and smiled at him. Alan laughed and they drove into the city. As they pulled up to the mall, Alan's cell phone rang.

"Hello . . . . Yes I know, Nancy . . . . Yes I have him with me. We are shopping . . . . Ok, and? . . . . He did what? . . . . You're kidding . . . . Yea, I'll tell him . . . . ok . . . . You too, bye-bye." Alan hung up his phone and put it into the holder on his hip.

"Tell him what?" David asked knowing Alan had something to tell him. Alan looked at him and smiled.

"He plead guilty." Alan said. David's eyes grew wide and he could feel his body shake. "Are you ok?" Alan said with a giggle. David sat shaking in silence. "David?"

"Holy shit Alan!" David said and Alan laughed. They got out of the car and met at the front with a hug. Alan could feel David shaking in his arms.

"Will you be ok?" Alan asked as he held the teenage boy. David nodded and smelled Alan's hair. "Are you sure?" Alan asked and giggled still feeling David shake.

"Alan, I can't believe this day." David said and Alan squeezed harder. David took a deep breath and tried as hard as he could to keep his body from reacting to Alan's touch. When he figured he would lose the battle he let go. Alan smiled at David and they went inside. They weren't in long before they both found the gifts they wanted. They took them out to the car and got back in.

"So your mom wants to meet for supper at that new Italian restaurant." Alan said as they pulled away from the mall.

"Ok, when?" David asked. Alan looked at his watch and answered,

"Now." They both laughed and headed for the restaurant. They could see Nancy's car parked outside and they parked next to it. They got out of the car and went inside. They found Amanda, Nancy and Little Mike and sat down with them. They talked the evening away about Carl and his plea. Every once in a while David would steel a glance at Alan. Only Amanda noticed. She would giggle and go back to her meal. David would notice her reaction and giggle himself. When their meal was done and Little Mike started to get cranky, they all decided to leave. David decided to ride with Alan again and they went to their separate vehicles.

"What a night huh?" David asked as both he and Alan lit a cigarette.

"Yea, no kidding. What did you find for Mike?" Alan asked as David took a drag from his cigarette.

"Um, a puppy puzzle for toddlers and a whole season of his favorite show on DVD." David answered.

"Good picks. I got him a photo album that your mom is going to fill with pictures of Gabe." Alan said. David raised his eyebrows and smiled.

"Wow, Alan. That's a pretty awesome gift."

"Well, I didn't know what to do. I got Amanda a locket for the same thing."

"That's really cool." David said and smiled.

"It's not too much?" Alan asked.

"What? No. I don't think so."

"Ok, what did you get Amanda?" Alan asked and David smiled.

"I bought her a plane ticket to go see her cousin in Texas."

"Holy shit, David." Alan said and they both laughed. Amanda had been going on for so long about how much she missed her cousin Alison. They were always close until Alison's family had to move for Amanda's uncle's job. "What about Mike?" Alan asked.

"There is a ticket in there for him too." David said and giggled.

"Ok, mine isn't as big as I thought." Alan said. David smiled and shook his head.

"Your gifts to them two are amazing, Alan." Alan smiled and nodded.

"What did you get your mom?"

"Well, I was a little nicer to her." David said and giggled. He took out a statement from his pocket and handed it to Alan. Alan read it as he drove.

"How did you do this? I mean, you paid off the mortgage?" Alan asked and David laughed.

"It's actually from both Amanda and me. There was twenty two thousand left on it and Amanda came up with the idea to pay if off with the mortgage."

"So, it's really, Amanda's gift then." Alan said and David laughed.

"Yes well, dad left the house to me. When we paid it off, I signed the deed over to her." David said and Alan laughed.

"Wow. That's amazing." They laughed and talked about their gifts all the way home. When they arrived, David and Alan said their good byes and Alan drove away. David went into the house to find Amanda and his mom decorating a tree.

"Nice guys." David said and they both giggled. Little Mike was helping by handing Amanda ornaments. David joined them and soon they had the tree decorated and the living room looking as Christmassy as they could. They all went to bed at the same time. Amanda changed in the bathroom while David got undressed and climbed into bed. Amanda came in the room wearing a cute pair of little shorts and a night shirt. She climbed into bed and snuggled into David. David shut off the lamp and held her.

"I saw you checking out Alan at dinner." Amanda said and David giggled.

"You did?" David asked and Amanda nodded. "So?" David asked and Amanda giggled.

"I think it's sexy, David." Amanda said and David laughed.

"Why?"

"I don't know." Amanda said and propped herself up on his chest with her chin. "I just do." She added and David sighed.

"Your weird." David said and Amanda laughed.

"I wish we could have sex." Amanda said and David raised his eyebrows.

"Why can't we?" He asked and she looked at him like he was stupid or something.

"When can't we have sex, David?"

"Oh, that thing." David said thinking of Amanda's period.

"Yea, that thing."

"Well, thanks for bringing it up." David said and Amanda laughed.

"Sorry." She said and David giggled. David held her as she slept on him like Gabe had their last night together. He rubbed her back until she fell asleep. He thought about Gabe and the latest news.

He's going away forever, Gabe. I wish you could enjoy it with us. David thought. He sighed and closed his eyes. It wasn't long before he fell asleep.

Chapter 23

Aunt Nora reminded David of a hippy, but without the pot and the boogie van. She looked a lot like Nancy but had darker hair. She was older than Nancy by four years but looked younger. Nancy had gone to lay down with a migraine, so David and Nora sat in the living room talking and drinking eggnog with rum.

"So, where's Amanda this Christmas?" Nora asked.

"Well, she took Little Mike to her grandmothers. She has been ill and Amanda thought it was a good time to take Little Mike to see her before she dies or something." David answered. Nara laughed and shook her head.

"You have always been so good with the words and them coming out of your mouth thing." Nora and David laughed and sipped at their drinks. "Terrible thing with Carl." She said and David nodded.

"Well, he's in jail now and we don't have to worry about him anymore."

"Tell me about, Gabe." Nora said and leaned on her arm on the back of the couch.

"What would you like to know?" David asked. He and his Aunt had a truth or bust deal. They could both unload on each other and the other one had to take it to their grave. He was the only one who had known about the affair she was having with a man from work. When her husband found out, it had been going on for over two years. They never talked on the phone because it was too impersonal so they always tried to find time to talk when they were together.

"Just tell me about him and I'll ask questions as they come up." Nora said and David nodded.

"Ok," he said and set his cup down on the glass coffee table. "He was Amanda's big brother. He was about ten years older than us. He was a music major . . ." Nora cut him off with a question.

"What did he play?"

"He played piano and electric guitar. He was awesome." David said and bit his bottom lip. He recalled the time they had sat in the music room at David's house and played to each other. Nora noticed the bit lip and the distant thought.

"That awesome, huh?" She asked and smiled at him. David sighed and nodded.

"Anyway, he had long black hair and drove a long, black Hearse." David said and grabbed his drink to take a sip.

"Ah, yes. The car. Your mother told me about it." Nora said and David nodded. "That was a very brave thing you did, David. I couldn't have driven my friend in his own car to his grave." She added. David cleared his throat and looked down at his cup. He could feel a lump grow in his throat. Nora noticed his inner pain. "Was he more than a friend, David? Maybe your best friend?" David shook his head.

"Amanda is my best friend. Gabe was . . . Different." David said and finished his drink. He stared down into the empty cup. The thick nog slowly sank to the bottom of the cup.

"Different how, David?" Nora asked softly grabbing his cup and getting a new drink. She noticed Nancy's door was open and she reached over and quietly shut it. She finished pouring their drinks and came back to the couch. David thanked her for his and she stared into his eyes trying to figure him out. "How was Gabe so different?" She asked. David took a sip of his drink and set it aside.

"This is the biggest news you will ever hear from me." David said and Nora nodded. She got herself ready for impact and looked him in the eyes.

"Ok, David. I'm ready." She said. David looked in to her eyes.

"I slept with Gabe." David said. He felt a weight lift from him and he sighed. Nora stared at him for a second then said.

"Like in the same bed?" David laughed and shook his head.

"Auntie Nora, I fucked him." David said giggling. Nora raised her eyebrows and her eyes grew wide.

"Oh, David that's . . ." Nora stopped and David itched the back of his neck. "That's . . ." She stopped again and sipped her drink. David raised an eyebrow and said,

"Weird?" Nora frowned at him and shook her head.

"No, David. Not weird." Nora said and stared at him.

"Then what?" David asked. Nora bit the inside of her cheek as she thought.

"Its, unexpected." Nora said and David laughed.

"You're telling me."

"So? What was it like?" Nora was always so understanding no matter what the talk they had was.

"Amazing." David said quietly and looked down at his drink. Nora tilted her head and smiled at him.

"Does your mother know about this?" David laughed and looked at her as if she hit her head or something.

"No one but Amanda knows about me and guys. She doesn't know about Gabe, but . . ." David stopped and smiled. He shook his head and sipped his drink.

"This wasn't a one night thing? There are other men?" Nora asked.

"Well, yea, Auntie. I mean, there was Gabe because of someone else."

"Who?" Nora asked tucking her foot under herself and settling down for some long epic story she thought was coming.

"Well, it all started on the first day of school . . ." He told her the whole story about first seeing Alan and the bad date with Todd. He told her about how Gabe had saved him and confessed his sexuality to him. He explained the affair with Gabe and Amanda falling love with him. He told her about meeting Carman and the story about him and Alan's teacher Charlie. He told her about the weekend with Alan and the night in the hotel room when he took off his cloths and David could see almost everything. He told her about the night of the project group party and the staring match he had with Alan and the talk with Carman afterwards. He even mentioned the first time he had masturbated thinking of Alan. It had of course happened more than once but the first time was the most amazing. When he finished his story, Nora sat back and exhaled a big breath.

"Well, that is certainly the most erotic thing you ever told me." She said and took her first sip of her drink since his story started. David blushed and looked down at his drink. "David, do you think you're gay or bi-sexual?" Nora asked.

"Well, I like to sleep with Amanda still and the only dude I've ever been with was Gabe so, I guess bi-sexual so far."

"So far? What would change it?"

"Alan." David said. Nora nodded and smiled.

"I thought you might say Alan. He sounds like a babe." Nora said and David nodded.

"Auntie, you have no idea." They talked about Alan until his mother woke up. Nora cleverly switched their conversation to school when she saw the door open and Nancy emerge. The rest of the visit was a lot of Christmas stuff and their little family gift exchange. David gave his Aunt the season she was missing of her favorite show and gave his mother a new pair of scrubs and a gift certificate to the spa in the city. Nancy gave David two tickets to the upcoming Gun's and Roses concert and a bottle of his favorite Scotch. Nora gave him a new journal with leather binding and a card with two hundred dollars in it. When Boxing Day came along and it was time for David and Nancy to leave, Nora took David aside while Nancy loaded some things into her car.

"I know you said you gave up writing in your journal. But I thought in the one a gave you, you could write to Gabe." She said. David smiled and nodded.

"Not yet, but I will keep it for when I'm ready." He said and hugged his aunt. His mother said her good byes to her sister and they left.

They reached home at four pm and saw that Amanda was already back. She had parked the Hearse in the front and David smiled. They went inside and Amanda and Little Mike both yelled 'Merry Christmas!' Nancy smiled and picked up Mike and gave him a big hug. David kissed Amanda and whispered 'Merry Christmas' in her ear. She blushed and David giggled. He went to Little Mike and kissed him on the forehead. He giggled and clapped his hands. Just then, Alan came in and said,

"Merry Christmas." Everyone took their turns hugging Alan and saying their own Merry Christmases. When it was Little Mike's turn he said,

"Do Santa now?" Everyone laughed and took their seats around the tree. Nancy sat closest so she could hand out gifts. The first one was to Amanda from David. She smiled and opened it. When she saw the tickets for her and Mike, she screamed and kissed and hugged David.

"When can I use these?" She asked staring at them with wide eyes.

"They are dated for spring break." David said and she hugged him again.

"Oh thank you David." The next gift was For Little Mike from Alan. Amanda helped him open it. She gasped when she saw the picture of Gabe's car on the cover.

"See! See!" Mike said and opened the book. "Gabe!" He yelled. Amanda teared up and Alan smiled. Mike looked at every page and clapped.

"That's from Alan." Amanda said and Mike looked at him.

"You give me Gabe?" Mike asked. Alan giggled and nodded. Little Mike squealed and clapped. "Alan is my best!" He said. Everyone laughed and Nancy grabbed the next gift. It was for her from Alan. She raised her eyebrows and Alan giggled. She opened the wrapping and saw it was the collective works of her favorite writer.

"Oh my, Alan, thank you, this is wonderful." Nancy said and ran her fingers over the binding. David raised his eyebrows.

"I would have never thought of that." He whispered to Alan and Alan laughed.

"That's why I'm the master." Alan whispered back and got up to hug Nancy. Nancy sat back down and dug under the tree. The next gift was a huge box for David from Alan. David raised his eyebrows and laughed.

"You just stuck something small into a big box right?" David asked.

"Just open it you shit." Alan said and David laughed. He opened it to find a guitar case. He looked at Alan and Alan smiled. He set the bow down and opened it.

"Holy Shit!" David said and picked up the jet black Stratocaster guitar with a single dark red rose on it. Nancy and Amanda gasped and David looked at Alan. Alan smiled.

"Merry Christmas." Alan said and David swallowed hard. It was the most beautiful guitar he had ever seen.

"Alan, thank you." David said with a slight stutter.

"There's more." Alan said and David looked in the box. Inside was ten rock and roll music books.

"Wow." David breathed and Alan smiled. David leaned over and hugged the Man sitting beside him. "You rock Alan." He said and Alan laughed.

"No, now you rock." He said and Nancy and Amanda laughed. David set the books and guitar back in the box while Nancy took the next gift out from the tree. It was addressed to Amanda from Alan. David took a deep breath and waited as Amanda opened the little box.

"Oh my god." Amanda said as she carefully removed the locket.

"Open it." Alan said. She did and inside was a picture of her, Gabe and Little Mike. She held it to her heart and jumped up.

"Oh, Alan. I love it." She said and hugged him. The next gift was the gift to Nancy from David and Amanda. It was wrapped in a manila envelope and she giggled. David and Amanda both looked at each other and took deep breaths. She pulled the paper work out and read it carefully. He face turned white and then two shades of red.

"What? . . . ." Nancy said and looked at them both.

"Merry Christmas." Amanda said and giggled. Nancy looked back down at the paper work and started to cry. David got up and walked over to her.

"It's all your mom. No more mortgage. And see?" He said pulling out the deed. "It's *really* all yours." He said. Nancy looked from him to the paper.

"You kids . . ." She said and cried again. David and Amanda hugged her and she cried for quite some time. When she finally composed herself and David and Amanda were able to return to their seats. Alan cleared his throat and said.

"Nancy, I say sell and move to Florida." Everyone laughed. Nancy set the paper work on the mantel and dug under the tree for a gift for Little Mike. It was the gift from David. He was so excited; they had to put the first DVD in right away. When they got Mike settled with his show. Nancy handed Alan a gift from David. David smiled and leaned back in his seat. "This better be good." Alan said and David laughed.

"Just open it." David said and Alan laughed. He opened the wrap and looked at the box.

"Jakes Imports?" He asked and David giggled. The rest of the box was blank. Alan opened the box and looked inside. "You little . . . I could just kiss you." Alan said and pulled the starter for his Lotus Elise out of the box. He looked it over and shook his head. "I can't believe you." Alan said.

"There's more." David said and Alan looked in the box. He pulled out a coupon for Jakes Imports for 50% off any Lotus Elise body kit. Alan was stunned. David laughed and Amanda and Nancy looked at each other with confused gazes.

"Wow, David." Alan breathed. David closed his eyes and savored the moment and the sound of Alan's voice. "This is awesome." Alan said and hugged David.

"Merry Christmas." David whispered and Alan hugged tighter.

"This is too much, David." Alan whispered into David's ear and David giggled.

"Shut up and love it." David said and Alan laughed. He pulled away and stared at the coupon.

"I do, thank you."

"Anyone want to explain this gift?" Amanda asked and David and Alan laughed. Alan explained what the starter was and what a Lotus Elise was while David took a gift to Mike from Nancy. He opened it and squealed. It was a toy airplane with opening doors and landing gear and it came with a pilot. Nancy hugged the little boy and giggled when his first order of business was to crash the plane. Nancy dug under the tree again and brought out a gift for David from Amanda. Amanda giggled and sat at the edge of her seat. David laughed and opened the gift. He took one look at the box and then back at her.

"Shoes?" He asked. She laughed and shook her head.

"Open it." She said with a giggle in her voice. He opened the box and looked inside. He sat back in his seat and stared. Alan looked at him with raised eyebrows.

"What is it?" He asked. David reached a hand in to the box and pulled out a picture of Gabe lying next to his guitar in his trench coat with a lock of his hair tied to the frame with a ribbon. He stared at the picture and Alan put his hand on David's back.

"Keep looking." Amanda said. David looked up at her and back down into the box. He pulled out a small box that had a little red ribbon on it. He slowly opened it and inside was Gabe's ring. David choked and tears ran down his face. "One more." Amanda said and

Nancy sat down next to him. There was an envelope left in the box and David took it out. Tears burned his eyes as he opened the long white envelope. He pulled out a folded piece of paper. Amanda took a deep breath and Nancy smiled at her. David opened the paper and read. His heart sank as he looked over the paper. He closed his eyes.

"Oh my God, Amanda." David said. Amanda smiled and came over to kiss his forehead. She hugged him and whispered 'I love you' in his ear. She went back to her seat and Alan and Nancy shot each other confused looks.

"What is it dear?" Nancy asked and he handed her the paper. She read it over and looked at Amanda. "Oh, Amanda." Nancy said and handed the paper to Alan. He moved closer to David and read the paper. It was a bill of sale in David's name to Gabe's Hearse.

"Wow, Amanda." Alan said and handed the paper back to David.

"Why?" David asked knowing the car had been left to her. Amanda sighed and tears filled her eyes.

"The day I drove that car back here, I knew I couldn't keep it. But I wanted it to go to someone who would love it as much as he did. So I gave it to you." Amanda said. David closed his eyes again and shook his head. "Look in the box." She added and David did. In the bottom where the keys. David smiled and looked at Amanda.

"Thank you." David said and she giggled.

"The look on your face was thanks enough." She said. Alan looked at David.

"Can you guys excuse us for a second?" Alan asked. The two women nodded and Alan took David outside. David's breathing had picked up as he held the ring in one hand and the keys in the other. "David, get it out. Do it now." Alan said and David shook. "You don't want to do it in there." Alan said and David looked into his eyes.

"Alan." David whispered and the tears fell.

"It's Ok, just, do what you gotta do." Alan said and David stared at him. The tears stopped suddenly and he just stared at Alan. It seemed to David that Alan wasn't expecting this silence. David just stared at him. Alan ran his hand through his hair and stepped closer to David. "Are you gonna have a panic attack or something?" Alan asked quietly. David blinked and frowned at him.

"What? No." David said. Alan stood still in the cold air and David still shook.

"Are you cold?" Alan asked. David shook his head but said nothing. "Are you going to do anything?" Alan asked. David sighed and stepped forward. He stopped about a foot away from Alan and then looked down at his feet. "David?" Alan said still standing very still. David shook his head and stepped back.

"I wish we had that talk." David said and walked over to his new car. Alan stood stunned for a second then walked over to him.

"You mean the one that lays everything out on the table?" Alan asked. David nodded and put his hands on the hood of the car. Alan stood next to him.

"Why? Should I know something?" Alan asked. David stared at his hands for a few minutes than looked at Alan. Alan looked into his eyes and David felt like he might melt. He looked back down at his hands on the hood of the car so he wouldn't just lean over and kiss Alan.

"No, Alan. You don't need to know." David said and walked away from the car. Alan shook his head and caught up with David. He turned David around and held him looking straight into his eyes. David stared into his eyes in shock.

"Look, I wish I knew what to say to you or what to do for you. I know I'm missing something and it kills me to think I have to guess. David, . . ." Alan stopped and let David go. David stood where Alan had stopped him with wide eyes. "David, I need to know what's going on with you. Please tell me." Alan said and David blinked. He looked down at the ground then back at Alan. He could feel his heart pound in his chest. Then suddenly he blurted,

"I cheated on Amanda." He said and Alan blinked.

"Oh." Alan said and stood staring at David. "With who?" Alan asked. David rolled his eyes and shook his head.

"It doesn't matter. I just did." David said and stared at Alan. Alan sighed and raised his eyebrows.

"Are you still cheating on her?" Alan asked and David looked from Alan to the car parked on the road then down to the ground.

"No. Not really." David said and Alan nodded.

"What's not really?" Alan asked and David shook his head with an irritated sigh.

"I can't explain it right now, ok?" David asked. Alan stepped closer to David and smiled at him.

"Ok, David. But I would like you to try to explain it to me someday." Alan said. David nodded. "I won't say anything. Bro's before Hoe's or whatever." Alan said and David laughed. Alan put his arm around his waist and led him to the door.

"What would Carman say if you held him like this?" David asked. Alan giggled and looked at David.

"Well, he would probably say something like, 'Fuck Alan, I hope you plan on going all the way' or something like that." Alan said and David laughed.

"Come on! He would be way more clever than that." David said and Alan laughed.

"Ok, what do you think then?" Alan asked still holding David low on his waist. David turned to face him and Alan raised his eyebrows but he held his ground and left his hand where it rested on David's hip. David looked deep into his eyes and said in a seductive voice,

"Fuck Alan, if I knew you had this in mind, I would have brought my lube." Alan smiled and shook his head.

"Yep." He said in a shaky voice. "That's exactly what he would have said." He finished and David laughed. Alan laughed then too and they went inside. They walked into the living room to see Nancy and Amanda playing with Little Mike and the rest of the toys he had gotten for Christmas.

"Sorry guys, we didn't think he should have to wait." Nancy said. Alan and David agreed and sat down on the couch. Amanda smiled and handed Alan his gift from her. Alan raised his eyebrows and looked at the beautiful wrap job.

"I would hate to rip the paper." Alan said and Amanda giggled. Alan tore open the paper and pulled the box out from the wrapping. It was a little white box with nothing on the outside. David put Gabe's ring on as he watched Alan open the box. Inside was a box of new guitar strings for both of Alan's guitars and a year membership to the most prestigious, men only, gym in the city. "Wow, that's great Amanda." Alan said and hugged her.

"That membership is made to take a guest with you." Amanda said and winked at David. Alan laughed and sat back down next to David.

"You're coming with me right?" Alan asked. David giggled and looked at Amanda. She mouthed 'you're welcome' and David laughed.

"Yea, I'll go." David said. Alan laughed and looked at the strings.

"These are really good strings." Alan said.

"David helped." Amanda confessed and Alan smiled. Nancy handed a gift to Amanda that was from her. Amanda giggled and opened the gift. It was a certificate to the spa and a pair of earrings. Amanda giggled and hugged Nancy.

"How much you wanna bet it's to the same spa you got Nancy's from?" Alan whispered in David's ear. David laughed and nodded.

"My mom's friend works there and she probably told her I was in." David whispered back. Nancy shot them an evil look.

"Did you think I would want to go alone?" She asked and Amanda giggled. David and Alan laughed quietly to themselves. There was two gifts left under the tree and they were both for Alan. Nancy had him open the one from her first. He opened it and laughed when the paper was only half way off. David looked at him funny and he showed David what he could see. David laughed when he saw the box for an antique radio. He remembered when Alan had seen one and said how he would give his left nut to have one just like it. He opened it the rest of the way and stared at the box.

"This is excellent, Nancy." Alan said and hugged her. She laughed as he whispered something in her ear. He sat back down and Nancy handed the last one to him. It was from all of them. "What's this?" Alan asked. David laughed and shook his head.

"It's just a little something to show you how thankful we are to have you a part of this family." Amanda said and Alan smiled. He opened the red box and was silent when he looked inside.

"David picked it out." Nancy said and smiled at her son.

"Merry Christmas." David said and Alan shook his head. Inside the box was a gold pocket watch with *Alan* engraved on the front.

"This is excellent." Alan said and Amanda clapped, Nancy smiled and David just stared at him. Alan looked at David and sighed. "You picked this out?" Alan asked. David smiled and nodded. Alan shook his head and hugged him. "Thank you." Alan whispered and David closed his eyes. He smelled Alan's hair again as they hugged.

"You're welcome." David whispered and Alan pulled away. He hugged the two ladies and Amanda helped him fasten the golden clasp on to his belt loop. He put it into his pocket and hugged Amanda again.

After the gift opening was finished, Amanda and Nancy picked up the wrapping paper while David and Alan made drinks for everyone. Amanda carried Little Mike up to bed and then joined Alan, David and Nancy at the table. They talked and laughed over drinks until Alan was yawning.

"You're getting old." David said to Alan as he helped him carry his gifts out to his car.

"No, I had a long couple days with my sister and her husband. It was sort of one big party and I haven't really haven't had any sleep." Alan said as they stood outside having a cigarette.

"I was gonna ask you before." David said and Alan raised his eyebrows. "I got two tickets to Gun's and Rose's. Wanna go?" David asked and Alan laughed.

"Fuck yea I wanna go!" Alan said and David laughed.

"Ok then."

"Wow, you sure you don't want to take Amanda?" Alan asked. David smiled and shook his head.

"Trust me, she would be pissed if I didn't take you." David said.

"Alright then. That's really cool." Alan said and David giggled. Alan yawned as he put out his cigarette.

"You better go." David said and Alan nodded.

"Good idea." Alan said and hugged David one last time. "Merry Christmas." Alan said in a quiet seductive sounding voice and David sighed. Alan frowned and looked at him. "Why did you sigh?" He asked. David laughed and shook his head.

"Carman would kill me right now for this but," David said and stared at Alan. He stood his ground for a second then laughed and looked away.

"What?" Alan asked laughing.

“Forget it. I would be the new master and I would hate to steel your title at Christmas time.” Alan rolled his eyes and laughed.

“You wish.” Alan said and David laughed.

“Another time.” David said and smiled at Alan. Alan nodded and got into his car. David waved as he drove away and went back into the house. He went into the living room and sat down on the couch. He picked up his new guitar and held it on his lap. Amanda came in and sat beside him. David smiled at her and kissed her.

“What was that for?” Amanda asked in a sleepy voice. David took the keys out of his pocket and held them in the hand he wore Gabe’s ring on.

“This was the best Christmas I have ever had.” David said. Amanda smiled and he kissed her again.

“I know you will love that car David. The ring was cause it’s a man’s ring and Little Mike will get his graduation one. The picture was because; I wanted to see you look at him again. I know something happened with you two. I understand why you never told me.” Amanda said and held David’s hand. David looked down at his guitar and then back at Amanda.

“I should have told you.” David said and Amanda shook her head.

“No you shouldn’t have. I wasn’t ready to hear it David. I’m ready now.” Amanda said and Nancy walked in.

“When we go to bed.” David whispered and Amanda nodded.

“Well kids. I think its bed time.” Nancy said and David nodded. He and Amanda got up and hugged his mother before heading upstairs. They got ready for bed and climbed in together.

“Ok, tell me.” Amanda said as she lay on his chest again. He smiled and kissed the top of his head.

"Well, he used to lay on me just like you are." David said. Amanda hugged David tighter. David sighed and shook his head. "Are you sure you want to hear this?" David asked.

"David," Amanda sighed and looked up at him. "The first few weeks after Gabe's death, I thought he died sad, and alone. But when I thought about the way you trashed that music room. It came to me, it wasn't an act of anger or aggression. It was an act of passion. I've been trying to get up the nerve to talk to you about it for the last couple weeks. If he was happy before he died, because he was with you, then I'm happy." Amanda said. David sighed and hugged her.

Amanda looked up at him and they kissed. She moaned as he ran his hands down her back to her ass. David pulled her on top of him and she kissed more deeply. She pulled off her underwear and then pulled off his. She got a condom from the drawer and put it on him. She sat down on top of him and guided him in. He moaned and tossed his head back. She rocked her hips back and forth until they both climaxed. She lay down on top of him sweating and panting.

"Wow, Amanda." David said and kissed her hair. She giggled and kissed him again on the lips. David rolled her onto her back and slowly pulled out as they kissed. She smiled when he finished the kiss and looked down at her. He tossed the condom away and she giggled.

"I wish we could have sex all night." She said and David giggled.

"If you weren't so good, it may have lasted longer." David said and Amanda grinned. He kissed her again and lay down beside her. He thought about his confession to Alan and Amanda's feelings about him and Gabe. He held her until they both fell asleep.

Chapter 24

David and Amanda had been back to school for a month. David drove her to Gabe's favorite spot by the river every morning before school. He would wait in the car while she talked to the tree he had Little Mike's birthday carved into. She would run her fingers over the letters and read them every day.

Little Mike Moore
With us today
May 17. 2002
A ray of sunshine on
This very dark day.
We Love you Big Mike.

She would get into the car and tell him she was ready for the day. David remembered the day Gabe wrote the message on the tree. Steve had called Nancy that Sandra was in labor just as David had found his father dead on the bathroom floor. He had come to Gabe's Tree quite often in those days. He used to do the same as Amanda had done but, talked to his dad when he had visited. When he had finally written it in his journal, he quit coming. Amanda was now visiting Gabe's tree like he did. She was always so happy when they left. She stopped bringing up Gabe and him since Christmas even though she rode in his car every day and David never took off his ring. David played his guitar every day after school for Little Mike when no one else was home. He would clap and ask for Gabe's song. David wished he knew what this song was, but didn't want to ask anyone else and Little Mike didn't know what it was called. Alan and David spent their Sundays working on the Lotus Elise after their afternoon workout at the gym. Alan had picked up the kit on January second when Jakes Imports had their new year's sale. With his 50% discount, he paid almost nothing for his kit. They talked about Amanda and David's building relationship. David would never answer him when Alan asked if he loved her. Alan knew he had feelings for someone else, but couldn't get that information from David either. Carman still called on Friday's to talk to David after school. He slowed it to every second Friday after the middle of January when his father died. David and Carman switched their discussions from Alan to their fathers. David loved hearing the stories of how Carman's dad used to make up excuses for Carman to keep his sexuality from his mother until Carman moved his ex, Jan in. Apparently, she figured it out for herself. Nancy worked a lot of long hours at the hospital after Christmas. She was still dating some guy she never told David about. He had told her he didn't want to hear about it and to hold off until him and Amanda moved out before she moved him in or something. She would just smile and shake her head.

On the first of February, Preparations for David's birthday started. He wasn't supposed to know, but Nancy and Amanda were way too obvious.

"You know, you guys should really try to be a little more sneaky." David said to Amanda as they got they dressed after their morning shower.

"I don't know what you're talking about." She said and giggled. David rolled his eyes and pulled his shirt on.

"I think Christmas cost you enough money."

"Don't tell me what to spend that money on, David. What was I supposed to do? Keep it in the bank? I have ten thousand put away for a rainy day so don't worry, ok." Amanda said as she brushed her hair. David shook his head and finished getting ready for his day. He left the bathroom before Amanda and went into his room. He Ran his finger down the binding of the journal his aunt had given him then got his things ready for school. Amanda came in and did the same. They did their homework every night in his room at his desk before bed. David pulled on his jacket and walked past the closet where he could see Gabe's trench coat hanging. They had gotten it from the hospital in a clear plastic bag after he was killed. They put it on a hanger as is and hung it in the closet. Amanda wanted to get it cleaned but David wouldn't let her. He smiled at the jacket and went downstairs to the kitchen. Amanda followed behind him.

"Good morning mom." David said as he entered the room. She smiled at him and got them both a coffee. David kissed Little Mike on the forehead and he giggled.

"Remember Rita has that birthday party at her house today so you won't be picking up Mike until after five." She said as she handed David his coffee.

"Yea, I remember mom. Don't worry." David said and Amanda laughed.

"You know Nancy," Amanda said and Nancy looked at her, "David has a calendar in our room that is called 'Little Mike's schedule.'" Amanda said and David smiled and shook his head.

"Really?" Nancy asked and sipped her coffee.

"Yea well, I can't be expected to remember everything." David joked in Mike's direction and Mike giggled.

"Davin love Lill' Mike." Mike said and everyone laughed. Nancy looked up at the clock and then back at Amanda.

"If you're going to talk to Gabe today, you better go." She said. It was 8:00. David took two big sips from his coffee and got up. Amanda closed her eyes and shook her head.

"Sit down David. We aren't going today." She said. David raised his eyebrows but sat back down.

"Are you sure?" David asked and he and his mother shared a puzzled gaze. Amanda giggled and nodded.

"I've said what I have to." She said quietly and looked at David. He peered into her eyes wondering why she looked at him like she did. He never listened to what she said to him outside by the tree.

"Well, good for you Amanda." Nancy said and smiled. Amanda smiled at her and sipped her coffee. They talked about Valentine's day, which was also David's 18th birthday. David shook his head when the girls talked and thought they were being sly. She got up and took Little Mike to the stairs to get his shoes on.

"Davin wemember Gabe's song?" Mike asked as David tied his little shoes. He smiled at the boy and ruffled his hair.

"I don't think I ever knew it, buddy." He said and put Mike's jacket on him.

"You know, Davin. You do." Mike said nodding with doe like eyes. David giggled at him and picked him up.

"I do?" He asked and the little boy hugged him.

"Davin knows." Little Mike said and hugged David neck. He rubbed the boys back and took him back into the kitchen. Nancy and Amanda stopped talking when they came it.

"Smooth guys." David said as he put Little Mike down on the floor. The girls giggled but said nothing. Mike went straight to the fridge and pointed at the Gun's and Rose's tickets dated for August 19. 2005. David looked at him and smiled. "If he was older, I would have taken him." David said and Amanda laughed.

"He just started this David. Those tickets have been there since you got back from your aunts at Christmas time, but he started doing this about two weeks ago." Amanda said and Nancy nodded.

"He just keeps saying, 'Gabe's song' over and over." His mother said and David went to kneel next to the little boy.

"What is it, Mike?" He whispered and Little Mike hugged him.

"Gabe song. Gabe song." He said in David's ear. David held him staring at the tickets. Just then Amanda touched his shoulder.

"We have to go." Amanda said and David looked up at the time. It was 8:25. David got up and went to the table to grab his bag.

"I have Mike today. I don't have to leave until 9:00 this morning so you guys go ahead." Nancy said. They said their good byes to Mike and Nancy and went out to the long black Hearse parked outside. They got in and David started the car. He thought about Little Mike's chant of 'Gabe song, Gabe song' as he drove. They got to the school and David parked the car. They went inside and got to their lockers.

"So you wanna tell me what the plan is for Valentine's Day?" David asked as they worked at their lockers. Amanda laughed and shook her head.

"Isn't that supposed to be *your* job to plan?" David giggled and shook his head. They walked to home room and waited through attendance. When they left the room to go their separate ways, David grabbed Amanda and kissed her. "David!" She scolded through her smile. David laughed and went to his morning classes. At lunch time they sat in the Hearse because it was raining. David lit a cigarette and left his door wide open to let the smoke out.

"I really wish you and mom would lay off the birthday thing." David said and Amanda laughed.

"What makes you think we have anything planned for that? Besides, that's the day you become two years older than me for like five months."

"So?" David asked giggling.

"Well, you'll be 18 and I'll still be 16 until July. It's weird." Amanda said and David laughed.

"You don't want people to know you're with an older dude or what?"

"People already know I'm with you, David. There are even girls that are jealous." She said in a flirting voice. David giggled and raised an eyebrow.

"Really? Which ones?" He asked and she playfully hit him in the shoulder. He laughed and shook his head. "Seriously Amanda, I would be happy just to have a couple drinks with you and mom and maybe Alan."

"*Maybe* Alan?" She asked and David smiled. He thought it was so funny that Amanda still had such an interest in what he thought of Alan even though, they had been having sex quite regularly and sleeping together every night since her parents left.

"Well, of course Alan." David confessed and Amanda giggled.

"Your so cute, David." She said and held his hand, "How *are* things going with you two anyway? Anything physical?" She added the question with raised eyebrows. David laughed and shook his head.

"Don't you think I would have told you if *that* happened?"

"Who knows? Maybe it's a deep, deep secret." She said and giggled. David rolled his eyes.

"I would tell you." He said and squeezed her hand remembering how he had kept Gabe from her.

"Well, have you told him yet?" Amanda asked. David remembered back to the night that he and Amanda had talked about how much David hated keeping something from Alan. David and Alan seemed to talk about everything else except David's *real* sexuality. There had been times that he was going to say something to Alan, but never did. Amanda thought their little staring matches were sexy and if she were David, she would jump Alan when that happened. David thought back to Christmas time and he and Alan's talk outside and how he was going to kiss him by his car just before he left. Amanda thought he should have and got it over with. David just rolled his eyes.

"No, he doesn't know." David answered and Amanda sighed.

"How long did it take you to tell Gabe you liked him?" Amanda asked. David was so shocked that she asked. It had been so long since she had questions about him and Gabe.

"I didn't tell him, I just kissed him." David said remembering the night of Todd's attack and the kiss he laid on Gabe in his bed. Amanda raised her eyebrows and giggled.

"So, what's the difference with Alan then?"

"I knew Gabe was gay. I don't know *what* the story is on Alan."

"Well, you should find out." Amanda said and David laughed.

"What do you think I've been doing since September?" Amanda giggled and nodded.

"I know, David. I'm just talking." Amanda said. They spent the rest of the lunch hour talking about Nancy and Amanda's coming trip to the spa on the weekend. David tried to talk her into a Brazilian wax but Amanda wasn't going for it. When they went back inside, Amanda stopped David and kissed him in front of their lockers.

"Wow, that was very public of you." David said and Amanda giggled. They went their separate ways to their classes. David walked into his history class and smiled. Alan was wearing tight blue jeans and a button up shirt.

"Hi there." David said in a far more seductive voice than he meant. Alan laughed and shook his head.

"Are you *sure* you and Carman aren't related?" Alan asked and David laughed.

"God, let's hope not." David said as he took his seat. Alan giggled and started with his notes on the board. He had stepped away from regular studies to do a small section on Saint Valentine. David thought the whole idea of the holiday of love having such a dark history was hilarious. Alan felt the same way. At the end of class David collected his books and yawned.

"Tired today?" Alan asked and David nodded.

"Yea, Amanda doesn't let me sleep much lately." David said and they both laughed.

"Are things good with you guys?" Alan asked.

"Yea, I think so."

"Ok, that's good. You still thinking about this other person?"

"Every day." David said and left the room. He walked to his locker and got his homework packed into his bag. He got into his car and headed out to Gabe's tree. He got out and sat down leaning his back against it. "I wish you were here. I need your advice on Alan. I don't know what to do about him. He seems to be interested one minute then he's my teacher or friend or whatever the next. I just wish I had the balls to tell him or kiss him or something." David said and tilted his head back against the tree. He looked up into the branches and saw something around the large branch above his head. He got to his feet and jumped up to reach the branch. He was too short so he pulled the car up to the tree and climbed on top of it. He reached up and pulled the hangman's noose down from the branch. "What the fuck is this Gabe?" He asked quietly. He stared at the rope and rolled it in his hands. "God Gabe, What was so bad that you even thought about this?" He said and tucked the rope back up on the branch. He climbed down off the car and got in. He stared at the tree and shook his head. "Thank god you didn't do it." He said and started the car. He drove home and took his things inside. He got a pop from the fridge and closed the door. He stood there staring at the tickets. He remembered Little Mikes chant and then thought of Gabe's C.D. collection. He ran downstairs to the music room and looked through the shoe boxes that held his disks. He looked through them until he heard Amanda come in.

"David?" She called from upstairs.

"Shit." He breathed realizing he had lost track of time. "Down here!" He called and he could hear Amanda stepping down the stairs.

"Hey, you didn't come get me." She said as she came in the room and seen the stacks of C.D.'s David had been going through. "What are you doing?" She asked sitting next to him and tucking some loose hair behind her ear. David looked at her and sighed.

"Trying to find Gabe Song." David answered repeating Little Mike's words. Amanda smiled and shook her head. She reached into the yellow shoe box and dug out a Gun's and Rose's C.D. She handed it to David and he frowned. "I didn't think he listened to this stuff. Look at the rest of this music?" He said and read the back of the C.D.

There was a song circled on the back but he couldn't make it out. He opened the C.d. case and took the back cover out. He could see the song name better now. It was Sweet Child of Mine. David laughed and Amanda smiled.

"He used to play it on his guitar all the time for Little Mike when it was alive. Why didn't you just ask?" Amanda asked and rubbed David's arm.

"I wasn't sure how to ask." David said and Amanda smiled. They went back upstairs and Amanda started dinner. David went out to his car and played Gabe's song. He smiled as he listened to it over and over. Amanda came outside after a while and waved at him. He turned the stereo down and wheeled down the window.

"It's 5:00. Can you go get Mike?" She called from the door. David nodded and started the car. He cranked the stereo and drove to Rita's house. He stopped the disk at Gabe's song and paused it. He ran in to get Little Mike.

"Hey Bud. I have a surprise for you." David said as Little Mike jumped into his arms. David thanked Rita and took Mike out to the car. He started the car and turned on the stereo. Little Mike clapped and yelled,

"Gabe Song! Davin found it!" David laughed and drove slow enough for Mike to hear the whole song.

That night, David went up to his room early and sat down at his desk. He stared at the leather journal he got from his aunt. He grabbed a pen and opened the book.

Dear Gabe,

God how I miss you. I found your rope at that tree today. I can't believe

I never noticed it before. How long has it been there? Why would you tie it there? I wish you were here to tell me. Little Mike taught me something about you I never knew today. He calls it Gabe Song. Sweet Child of Mine? I would have never guessed you listened to G & R. I guess I'll have to play it on guitar for Little Mike like you used to. He sure misses you.

Amanda gave me the car and your ring. I never take it off. I don't know why but, it seems to help. Anytime I miss you I look at it. That seems to be a lot. I miss kissing you. I want you to hold me again. It sounds corny even to me but, I don't know how else to write it.

Alan is still sexy and seems untouchable. I can't get passed this fear of rejection or something I have. We go to the gym together now and let me tell you, Gabe, watching him work out is torture. Thank god Amanda has been so horny lately or I would die of severe blood loss. She wants to know if I loved you I think. I never know what to say when I feel like she's asking. I know I felt strongly for you and I liked it a lot when you said it.

She talked to your tree every day since you died. She just stopped today. She said she had told you everything she needed to. I hope she did.

I miss you. David.

David looked over his letter and smiled he closed the book and got into bed. He left the light on for Amanda. He lay on his side with his back to the door. He stared at the picture of Gabe Amanda had given him for Christmas. He ran his thumb over the hair on the frame. He smiled and closed his eyes. He was almost asleep when Amanda came in.

"Are you awake?" She whispered as she climbed in behind him.

"No." David whispered back and Amanda giggled. She put her arm around him and hugged him. He pressed his back against her and sighed. "How was the rest of your movie?" David asked still whispering.

"Sad, the girl died at the end." She said and cuddled in close to him. David rubbed her arm and reached over to shut off the lamp. "I love you, David." She said and hugged him again.

"I know." David said and yawned. Amanda giggled and closed her eyes. She fell asleep before David did. He lay staring out into the dark room.

I wish it was Alan lying behind me, holding me like this. It would feel so good to be touched by him. He looks like he would be such a good kisser. God, to kiss that man. David thought and felt a tug in his groin. He smiled and shut his eyes. He was happy that Alan could still make him hard with just a passing thought. He shifted to get more comfortable and Amanda rolled over. He sighed and tried to sleep.

God, I could fuck you right now Alan. He thought and sighed. He rolled over and closed his eyes again. He was soon asleep.

Chapter 25

David woke up the next morning with Amanda already in the shower. He sat up and lit a cigarette. It was the day before his birthday,. February 13. He rolled his eyes knowing that Amanda and Nancy must have planned something. He got up and went to the bathroom. Amanda laughed when David peaked in the shower.

"David! Privacy. Ever heard of it?" She asked and David laughed. He peed and got ready to get into the shower. Amanda got out as he got in.

"What? You don't want to shower with me?" David asked as slapped her butt as she walked by.

"That time of the month my friend." She said and giggled.

"Didn't you just do that?" David asked as he washed his hair. Amanda giggled and shook her head.

"Yes David, a month ago."

"Seems like the months go fast when you have a period to fight against." David said under his breath. Amanda heard it and laughed.

"Nice David." She said and left the room. He finished his shower and brushed his hair and teeth. He put on his cologne and deodorant and left the room. He walked into his bedroom and got his books together. He put on his coat and headed downstairs. Amanda and his mom where at the table giggling.

"Good morning." David said and kissed little Mike's forehead. Mike giggled and David went to get his coffee.

"So, tomorrow is Valentine's Day. You guys have any plans?" Nancy asked. David rolled his eyes and shook his head. He thought for a second while he came to the table. Then a smile crossed his face and he looked across the table at Amanda.

"Yes actually. I made reservations at Antonio's for Amanda and I." He lied. Amanda and Nancy's faces went white.

"Oh, David. Um, I planned a quiet night with Little Mike and us." Amanda said.

"Well, we could go out for dinner first couldn't we?" He asked. Amanda squirmed in her seat and looked at Nancy. Nancy looked at her and then at David.

"Who would watch Little Mike when you go? I have plans." Nancy tried and David smiled.

"I thought he would come." David said and looked at Amanda. Amanda smiled and rolled her eyes.

"Ok, David. Sounds excellent." Amanda said and got up to get Mike some more dry cereal.

"Well, of course it does. It's Antonio's." David said and giggled. Nancy smiled at him then shot Amanda a look. They didn't say anything else about it. Amanda and David dropped off Little Mike at Rita's place on their way to school and went the rest of the way in silence. When they got to the school, David got out of the car and Amanda followed.

"You don't have reservations, do you?" Amanda asked as they got to their lockers.

"You and Mom are planning a party, aren't you?" He answered her question with a question of his own. Amanda sighed and shook her head.

"If you aren't talking, neither am I." She said and headed to homeroom. David laughed and followed her in. They sat through attendance and headed to their morning classes. David was relieved to have a quick morning. It had seemed like a long time since the morning had gone by so fast. He met Amanda at their locker and they headed to the smokers table. David stared out at the black Hearse in the parking lot. Amanda ate a granola bar as David smoked.

"Why are you trying to hide this from me? I have never celebrated Valentine's Day because it's my birthday. Did you think that I would be dumb enough to except the crap stories you and my mom give me?" David asked with a hint of a giggle in his voice. Amanda sighed and shook her head.

"Can't you just wait and see?" Amanda said and looked down at her feet. David smiled and rubbed her back.

"Sorry, I will wait and see. I have no reservations." He confessed with a whisper in her ear. She giggled and kissed his cheek.

"Does this period thing mean I won't be getting laid on my birthday?" David teased and Amanda laughed.

"I lied about that." She said and David rolled his eyes.

"I thought it was too soon. Why are you saying no?" David asked smelling her hair and looking at her with a seductive glare. Amanda blushed and giggled.

"I thought if you had to wait a couple days, you would like it more."

"I always like it." David said and kissed her mouth. Amanda sighed under his kiss and ran her hand through his hair. David ended the kiss and looked into her eyes. "You are so cute." David said and kissed the end of her nose. Amanda laughed. They talked about the 'not coming' party and David had a rough idea that it was going to be pretty big. It was going to be out at Alan's place and there was supposed to be a D.J. and everything. By the time they got inside, Amanda had begged David about a hundred times not to tell anyone she told him. He promised before they went to their afternoon classes. David walked into his history class and went to his desk.

"Hi there." Alan said in a seductive voice. David laughed and shook his head.

"Carman would be proud." David said and Alan laughed.

"Got plan's for tomorrow?"

"Nope. Amanda said she wanted to have a quiet night in tomorrow." David said and laughed. Alan saw right through it and shook his head.

"She told you, didn't she?" Alan asked as the room filled with students. David smiled and shrugged. Alan laughed and shook his head. He went to the front of the class and announced the test for the day on the history of Saint Valentine. He handed out the test papers and the class got to work. David looked up at Alan once in a while. He was reading another novel. He was leaning back on his chair with his feet crossed at the top corner of the desk. He had his fist held in front of his face like he did at Carman's bar. He was rubbing his bottom lip with his thumb as he read. David stared at him and could feel his body reacting. He looked back down at his test and took a deep breath. He noticed Alan look up from his book and look at him. He looked at Alan. They stared at each other. Alan never moved his hand from under his chin as they held their gaze. David shivered and looked down. He closed his eyes for a second and then looked back up at Alan. He had gone back to his book. David took another deep breath to try to calm his body. He finished his test and sat back in his chair. Alan looked up and smiled at him. He got up and walked over to David's desk. "All done?" Alan asked and David nodded.

"It was easy." David whispered and Alan smiled.

"I better come up with a good midterm exam for you." Alan said and winked. The midterm exams where starting next week. David wasn't looking forward to spending the rest of the year with no classes with Alan.

"Why are the midterms so late this year?" David asked thinking they should have written them at Christmas time.

"The curriculum changed and we decided to run the first semester for two months longer." Alan whispered and squatted down next to David.

"So what about next semester then?" David asked.

"That's what changed. They took out half of the next semester's curriculum." David raised his eyebrows and Alan smiled.

"Don't you like spending 80 minutes a day with me?" Alan asked and David giggled. Alan got up and went back to his desk. David watched him look over his work and smile when he graded it. David knew he would get full marks. When the bell rang, David had English class and then went home. He picked up Little Mike on the way. He sat Mike down on his little chair and played Gabe's song for him. He yawned when David was done and David laid him down on the couch for a nap. He turned on the T.V. for him and put a blanket over him. He went into the kitchen and got a pop. He sat down at the kitchen table and thought about Alan.

I would like to know why he looks at me like that. Is he just as interested as I am? Why doesn't he say anything? Probably for the same reason I don't. I wish I had the balls to say something. Amanda thinks I should just kiss him and get it over with. I wonder what he would do. I wish he would give me some kind of sign or something. Is the long stares and our new flirting game during class his way of telling me? If I have to wonder than it must not be. Oh, well. Someday he'll crack, or I will. David thought and smiled. He looked out the window and stared at Gabe's car. He sighed and shook his head. Just then the phone rang.

"Hello?"

"*Are you picking me up today?*" It was Amanda.

"Mike is sleeping actually. Want me to wake him up?" David asked.

"*No, no. I'll walk. How was your afternoon?*"

"Good. Alan was . . ."

"*Alan is always hot, David. Did you find out about the no change in semesters?*"

"Yea, I'll tell you all about it when you get home." David said. They said their good byes and David hung up the phone. He went into the living room to shut off the T.V. Little Mike was fast asleep on the couch. David brushed the hair out of his face and left the room. He went outside and waited for Amanda. He sat on the step and stared at his car. The black paint reflected the light like black water. David smiled at the memory of being with Gabe in the back. He ran his hand through his hair and lit a cigarette. He looked down the street and watched for Amanda. It was still chilly but the sun was shining. He remembered Amanda telling him about snow at Christmas. He had only ever seen it on T.V. She was so happy to see the snow when she went to Montana to see her Grandmother. David could see her turn the corner. She was walking and kicking a rock as she walked. He stood up and she noticed him. She waved and he waved back. She got to him and they kissed.

"So, Mike is sleeping if you wanted to go upstairs." David said and Amanda giggled.

"My plan was to wait till tomorrow you know."

"I know, but I won't tell." David said and pulled her hips against his. Amanda giggled and kissed him again. Just then Alan pulled up. Amanda backed away from David and he laughed.

"Hi guys." Alan said as he came up to the house.

"Hi Alan." David said and Amanda smiled. David looked at Amanda and then back at Alan. "What brings you here?" David asked and Alan smiled.

"I came to get you." Alan said and winked at Amanda. Amanda giggled and David raised his eyebrows.

"Ok." David said and looked at Amanda.

"I have Mike. Go have fun. I'll see you later." She said and quickly kissed him on the cheek. She went into the house and Alan smiled at David.

"Ready to go?" Alan asked. David checked his pockets for cigarettes and his wallet. He had both so he said yes and they got into Alan's car.

"What's this about?" David asked as Alan drove.

"Can't I just spend some time with you?" Alan asked. David shook his head and stared at Alan.

"We spend time together on Sunday." David said and Alan smiled.

"Well, what's wrong with more?"

"Nothing." David said and looked out the windshield. Alan turned toward the city on the highway. "Where are we going?"

"I thought we would go into town and have coffee." Alan said. David raised his eyebrows.

"We never do coffee." David said and Alan giggled.

"Well, then. It's a good thing I thought of it, huh?" David shook his head and sighed.

"There is party stuff going on at home, isn't there?" David asked. Alan tried to look shocked but it was no use. David could see threw it. "Not you too." David said and Alan laughed.

"Sorry. I guess they have some baking or something to do. They don't want you there when they do it." Alan confessed and David laughed.

"Nice, Alan." David said and Alan laughed.

"I wanted to talk to you about spring break anyway." Alan said and David looked at him.

"What about it?"

"Well, Amanda and Little Mike are going to Texas, your mom has that convention in New York. I thought you might wanna go see Carman with me." Alan said. David smiled. He hadn't seen Carman since the funeral.

"Yea, that would be awesome." David said and Alan smiled.

"I thought you would want to. You guys still talk every second Friday?"

"Yea, it's his turn to call tomorrow actually."

"Well, it's a good thing he knows to call my place huh?" Alan said and smiled. David laughed and shook his head.

"You guys don't have to do all this you know."

"We know that. We want to David." Alan said and smiled. David shook his head and looked out the window as they entered the city. Alan pulled up to the little Russian coffee shop on Main Street and they went in. They sat down at a little table by the window and ordered their coffees.

"So, Carman isn't coming then?" David asked as he sipped his coffee.

"No, he wanted to but work is keeping him away. It was his idea that we go out for spring break." Alan said and sipped his own coffee.

"That's too bad. What does he do anyway?"

"He didn't tell you?"

"It never came up."

"What do you guys find to talk about then? All he does is work." Alan asked and David smiled.

"That is classified. If I told you, I'd have to kill you."

"Really? That good huh?" Alan asked and David smiled.

"Wouldn't you like to know." David retorted. Alan laughed and shook his head. "What *does* he do?" David asked.

"Well, he works with computers. He builds them and fixes them. He does a bit of programming too I think."

"Really? I would have thought he was in the porn industry or something." David said. Alan laughed and choked on his coffee. David laughed and apologized.

"I'll have to tell him you said that." Allan added and David laughed again.

"Did he go to school for that?"

"No, actually. He wanted to be a lawyer." Alan said. David raised his eyebrows.

"What happened?"

"Well, he failed the bar exam and never went back to write it again."

"So he *is* a lawyer, just isn't licensed."

"Pretty much." Alan said. David shook his head in disbelief. Alan smiled and kicked David under the table. David looked up at him. "Let him tell you about it ok? I have probably said enough."

"Yea, of course. What happens in the coffee shop stays in the coffee shop. Don't you know the rules?" David asked. Alan laughed and shook his head.

"No wonder you and Carman get along so well."

"Why?" David asked. Alan smiled and looked down at his coffee.

"You guys are a lot alike. Your personalities are almost the same. You can have a serious discussion a lot better than Carman can, but otherwise, you're a carbon copy."

"Well, not a *total* carbon copy." David said. He had decided after talking to his Aunt that he was bi-sexual. Carman was gay.

"Why do you say that?" Alan asked.

"Well, Carman is gay." David said with a crooked eyebrow. Alan nodded and smiled.

"I guess that is a difference, huh?" Alan asked. David smiled and shook his head.

"I think he's Carman *because* he's gay. He would just be some pervert dude if he wasn't" David said. Alan laughed and looked into David's eyes. They held the gaze for a while until David looked down to save himself the embarrassment of a public erection. "Why does that happen?" David asked and Alan blinked. David's stomach flipped waiting for Alan's answer.

"I don't know." Alan said. David looked back up at Alan's face. Alan smiled and cleared his throat. "I don't know why that happens David." Alan said and left the table. David watched him walk to the bathroom. David took a deep breath and told the waitress to refill the cups for when they got back. He walked into the bathroom and seen Alan standing at the mirror.

"Are you ok?" David asked. Alan turned around to face him.

"Yea, I just needed a minute. Sorry about that." Alan said and turned around to wash his hands.

"I just wanted to know why those stares happen. If you don't have an answer, you have nothing to apologize for, right?" David said. Alan looked at the reflection of David in the mirror.

"No, I guess I don't" Alan said and dried his hands. They went back to the table and sat back down. They both put their own cream and sugar in. Alan was stirring his coffee when he looked up at David and said, "It used to happen with Carman too." he looked back down at his cup. He set the spoon aside and sipped the hot liquid. David looked at him and cleared his throat.

"So, you have an eye fetish or something?" David asked. Alan looked up at him and smiled.

"I don't know. Just blue ones I guess." Alan said. He seemed so uncomfortable with the conversation. David felt sorry for him. He knew what saying something you didn't want to felt like. He sighed and kicked Alan under the table. Alan looked up at him and David caught his gaze. They sat like that for a few seconds before Alan looked back down.

"Don't look down." David said. His hands were sweating and his heart pounded in his chest. Alan looked at David with a puzzled gaze but found himself lost in David's eyes again. David smiled. "See, it's cool, ok?" David said. Alan smiled and nodded.

"You are far to wise for your age." Alan said. David laughed and sipped his coffee.

"Not wise. Wise is for old guys. I like to think I'm clever." David said. Alan laughed and shook his head. "Speaking of old, I hear your birthday is during spring break." David added.

"Any planning and you die." Alan said. David laughed and raised his eyebrows.

"Revenge is sweet."

"Really, I hate my birthday. No party." Alan said. David smiled and looked around.

"It will cost you." David said and Alan laughed.

"How much?" Alan said and David looked deep into his eyes.

“I’ll think about it.” David said and looked away. Alan sighed and sipped his coffee. They talked about the trip to Carmans until Alan’s cell phone rang and he was told it was safe to come home. David paid for the coffee and they went out to the car. Alan drove out to the highway in silence.

“Why are you so quiet all of a sudden?” David asked. Alan looked at him and smiled.

“Am I?” he asked. David giggled and shook his head.

“Yes you are.”

“Sorry, just thinking.” Alan said.

“Wanna share?”

“Well, I was thinking about Carman.”

“Oh, what about Carman?” David asked and Alan smiled.

“I am just curious to what he says about me. He’s been a little weird with me on the phone.”

“Ok, so you want me to find out why?” David asked. Alan looked at him and nodded.

“Would you? He’s always told me everything. I think I may have said or done something to hurt him. Something he doesn’t want to tell me.”

“No problem.” David said. They talked about all the things that could be bothering Carman the rest of the way home. When David got home, Amanda and Nancy where sitting at the table.

“Hi guys.” David said.

“Hi David.” They said in unison and then laughed.

“Wow, it’s like you guys practiced that.” David said. Amanda and Nancy laughed again. David sat down with them and smelled the air. “Smells like cake in here.” David said. Amanda got up and went to the counter. She brought back a cup cake and put it in front of him.

“That’s what you smell.” She said and Nancy giggled.

"Wow, hours of solitude and you guys make *one* cup cake." David said and Nancy shook her head.

"Be grateful you got it." She said and David and Amanda laughed. He ate his cupcake while Amanda and Nancy told him about the weird police activity that was going on in town. They weren't sure what was going on but they seemed to be looking for someone. When they were finished the casserole Amanda had made, they retired to the living room. Little Mike had fallen asleep on the reclining chair. David took him up to Nancy's bed and laid him down.

"I love Davin." Mike said as David covered him up. David smiled and shook his head.

"Look at that, three for three." David said and kissed the little boys forehead. He went back downstairs to join Amanda and Nancy. He sat down on the couch next to Amanda.

"Did he stay sleeping?" Amanda asked.

"Oh, yea. He only woke up long enough to tell me how wonderful I am." David said. Nancy and Amanda laughed. "But, I'm going to bed, ok." David said. Amanda kissed him and he said good night to his mom and headed up to his room. He went straight to his desk and opened his journal.

Dear Gabe,

Today was awesome. Alan and I went for coffee and had a funny little discussion about the way we look at each other. He was all wierded out that I asked but I told him it was cool. I told him I thought it was an eye fetish or something. He said just for blue ones. Can you believe that? It was sexy anyway. One of those, 'you had to be there things'. He wants me to have a talk with Carman. Apparently he's acting weird and Alan wants to know why.

Amanda and mom baked a cake for my birthday tomorrow. I wish you were here for that. I can only think of one thing I want and it's something I would like unwrap with my teeth. Anyway, you know what I mean. I wish Alan would let me unwrap him with my teeth. God! That would be so hot. He is certainly one guy I couldn't have a night of just kissing with. I barely made through it with you.

I miss you
David.

Chapter 26

David's morning was unusually usual. He was expecting a crap load of 'Happy Birthdays' and that sort of thing, but everyone in the house seemed to have forgotten. He ignored it and went about his day as he normally did. Amanda got Little Mike ready to go while David got their books ready for the day. Nancy left for work early. When David and Amanda were ready to go, they loaded Little Mike into the big black Hearse and headed off to Rita's.

"Study for the math test?" Amanda asked. David shook his head.

"You know I did. We studied together. What's going on with everybody today?" Amanda shrugged and looked out the window. David giggled and parked the car in his usual spot at the school. They went in and got their things together at their lockers. David stopped Amanda before they went into their home room.

"What is it?" Amanda said. David smiled at her and handed her a little navy blue box. Amanda's eyes were wide as she took the box.

"Happy Valentine's Day." David said. Amanda slowly opened the box and looked inside. She gasped when she saw the little gold bracelet inside.

"Oh David." Amanda said and David smiled. He took the bracelet out of the box and put it on Amanda's wrist.

"Look at that, it fits." David said quietly and kissed her. Amanda giggled and looked at the new jewelry.

"You didn't have to do this. You're the one that is supposed to get presents today." She said and David laughed.

"Its Valentine's Day Amanda. Did you really think I would forget to get you something?" Amanda giggled and they went into the home room class. They sat through attendance and went on with their morning. David's math test was just as hard as he thought it would be. When he was finished, he felt satisfied with his work. The rest of the morning was long and boring. He felt like he might fall asleep by the time the lunch break bell rang. He met Amanda at their lockers and headed out for lunch.

"Here." Amanda said and handed David a card.

"What's this?" David asked reading the front. It said Happy Valentine's Day on the front.

"Open it." Amanda said in an excited voice. David smiled and opened the envelope. He pulled out the card and read the front.

For the one I love.

David smiled at Amanda and opened the card.

If there were words to describe the way I feel,
They could only be spoken by angels.

My heart cannot hold all the love I feel,
Only god can know what I mean.
Please know that I love you more than all in the world.
And I will until it ends.

David raised his eyebrows and closed the card. Amanda sat looking at him. She seemed to be waiting for him to say something.

"That's beautiful." David said and Amanda smiled.

"So you like it?" Amanda asked. David kissed her and she hugged him as he did it.

"Of course I do." David said when the kiss ended. Amanda giggled and looked away. They talked about the math test and they both decided they probably passed. Amanda was worried about a few questions she had memorized to ask David. When she explained them, David said he answered them the same way. At the end of their lunch break, they went in and headed to their afternoon classes. David went into room 19 and sat at his desk.

"Happy Valentine's Day." Alan said and David laughed.

"Yea, you too." David answered and Alan laughed.

"I hope you didn't get me anything."

"Like wise." David said and Alan laughed. He went to the front of the room and told the class it would be an easy day due to the holiday. He told everyone they could study for their midterm exams for the class. The students took out their books and got to studying. David did the same.

"Hey, I'm picking you up at your place after school." Alan whispered to David. David looked up at him and smiled.

"I don't know how Amanda would feel if I had a date with someone else on Valentine's Day." David whispered back. Alan laughed and shook his head.

"She likes me, it should be ok." Alan and David both laughed and David went back to his studying. Alan went over some papers on his desk. David looked up at him after going over his history notes for a second time. He seemed to be grading something but he looked at David too. David smiled and Alan shook his head. 'Are you done studying?' Alan mouthed. David giggled and shrugged. 'I'm bored.' David mouthed back and Alan smiled. 'Me too.' Alan mouthed and David laughed. Some students looked up and Alan laughed. David looked down at his binder and giggled. He went over some notes from science class until the bell rang. Alan came to his desk and smiled at him.

"Go shower and get pretty, you're in for quite a treat tonight." Alan said and David smiled.

"Are you hitting on me?" David asked. Alan laughed and shook his head. He patted David's shoulder and leaned in close to his ear.

"You would like that, wouldn't you?" Alan whispered in his seductive drawl. David smiled but didn't answer. He left the room and headed for English class. It was another study period. David was so tiered of studying; he thought he would fall asleep going through his English notes. He thought about Alan's question and smiled.

I would like that, Alan. More than you think. Hit on me PLEASE! God I would love to reciprocate if it wasn't just a game to you. Why can't I just tell you? You wouldn't hate me, would you? God I have to stop thinking like this. I can't tell him yet. It's not the right time. There will be a moment when the time will be right. David sighed at the thought and went back to his studying. He forced himself to pay attention to what he was doing until the bell rang. He collected his things and headed to his locker. He put on his jacket, put all his books in his bag, and left. He got home and headed up to the bathroom. He quickly showered and went to his room to get dressed. He dressed in a pair of light colored blue jeans and a tight black t-shirt. He brushed his hair and put on his deodorant and cologne. He went down stairs and out to his car. He drove to Rita's to pick up Little Mike. Rita met him at the door.

"Oh, David hi." She said.

"Mike ready?" David asked. Rita leaned against the door jam and smiled.

"You can't have him." Rita said and David laughed.

"You're in on this 'not birthday party' thing too?"

"Afraid so my dear. I am under strict orders to keep this boy until Nancy picks him up tomorrow." Rita said. David sighed and shook his head.

"Ok, see you Monday." David said. Rita waved as he got into his car and left. He pulled up to the house and seen Alan's car parked outside. He smiled and parked the long car. He got out and walked over to Alan's car. He got into the car and looked at him. "You know, I'm not good at acting surprised." David said. Alan laughed and pulled away.

"You won't have to act." Alan said. David shook his head and sighed. "Besides, your 18. What else is there to be excited about? You're legal." Alan added. David rolled his eyes.

"21 is legal Alan." David said and Alan laughed.

"Maybe, but 18 means you're an adult. You can get away with a lot more now." David laughed and shook his head. "Happy Birthday, by the way."

"You're the first one to say that." David said.

"I know, The rules were not to say it until we got to my place."

"So, you broke the rules."

"Rules were made to be broken." Alan replied and David laughed.

"Nice." David said. Alan smiled and turned onto the highway. "Wanna tell me what to expect?"

"And ruin the surprise? No way." Alan said. David sighed and shook his head. Alan giggled and slowed the car. "You can expect a surprise." Alan said and David smiled.

"Ok, some heads up, Alan."

"What's a surprise party, without the surprise?"

"A party." David answered and Alan smiled. They drove in silence to Alan's turn off. Alan turned onto the gravel road and reached behind David's seat. He pulled out a green box and handed it to David. "What's this?" David asked. Alan smiled and slowed the car to a crawl.

"Open it." Alan said and David did. Inside were six music books inside.

"Oh, cool." David said as he leafed through them.

"Happy birthday." Alan said and pulled into his drive way.

"Thanks." David said and looked over the books. All six of them were old rock books. He smiled at Alan and Alan smiled back. They parked in front of Alan's house and Alan stopped the car. "Are they gonna jump out or something?" David asked as they got out of the car. Alan laughed and shook his head.

"No, but that's all I'm saying." Alan said and led David to the big shop. David saw all the cars parked outside with car covers on them. He looked at Alan and raised his eyebrows. Alan giggled and opened the man door. David stepped in.

"HAPPY BIRTHDAY!" Everyone yelled and David laughed. Everyone was dressed in blue jeans and leather jackets. There was a D.J. set up at the far end of the shop that started to play Its Your Birthday by The Beatles. David walked over to the crowd of people and thanked them. The young men who were Gabe's Paul Barriers were there along with Nancy and Amanda. Amanda's cousin Lexy, who David got along with pretty well during the summer holidays, was there. Then someone caught David's eye. It was Carman.

"Holy shit! Hi." David said and Carman laughed. He came over and hugged David. "I thought you weren't coming." David said as Carman hugged him.

"And miss this? Not in this life time." Carman said and let David go. Ron and Samantha came over to him next.

"Happy Birthday." They said and David thanked them.

"This is really nice, thank you." David said to his mom. Nancy smiled and hugged her son.

"Of course." She said and handed him a card. David opened it to find a hundred dollar bill inside.

"Mom, what is this?"

"I didn't know what to get you. I thought you could just get something for yourself." Nancy said. David laughed and thanked her. He went over to the table that was set up off to the side of the makeshift dance floor.

"We invited some other people, is that ok?" Hank, one of the Paul Barriers, asked.

"Of course. The more the merrier." David said and Amanda nodded. David sat down and Carman brought him a drink.

"Wow, thanks." David said and Carman sat down with him.

"So, what do you think?" Carman asked. David smiled and nodded.

"This is pretty cool. What's with the leather jackets?"

"Ah, that was Amanda's idea. She thought it should be 'David Themed' or whatever." Carman said. David laughed and looked over at Amanda. She was visiting with Samantha.

"Well, it's pretty cool." David said. Carman laughed and shook his head.

"You know something? Alan told me if I didn't come, he would never speak to me again."

"What? He did?" David asked and took a sip of his drink.

"Yea, you're pretty important to him, you know." Carman said and smiled. David rolled his eyes. "I'm serious." Carman stated and David looked down at his drink.

"I know Carman." He said and Carman smiled.

"Trust me, David. I know exactly what you're feeling right now."

"I know that, too." David said and smiled. Carman put his hand on David's lower back.

"Don't let it hurt you, David. Alan is a really smart and understanding guy."

"I know, you told me all this on the phone."

"I think you should tell him. He'll understand." Carman said and took his hand away from David's back.

"I can't." David whispered and Carman smiled. Alan came over to them then.

"Well, are you impressed?" Alan asked David and David smiled at him.

"Yea, actually. Good job." David said. Alan smiled at Carman. Carman got up.

"I'm gonna go get another drink." He said and left the table. Alan sat down next to David and leaned close to him.

"Your gonna have to do better than that." Alan whispered and David smiled.

"This is great, Alan. It really is."

"Ok, that's better." Alan said and winked at David. David smiled and shook his head. They watched people dance and visit. Hanks friends started to come in. They came over to David one by one and introduced themselves. David said his hello's and Carman took them to the table where the booze was kept.

"I guess these are Gabe's friends." David said. Alan smiled and looked at him.

"When they said they had people to bring, I told them they had to ask you first." Alan said and David smiled.

"No, it's cool. They should fill your dance floor." David said and giggled. Alan rolled his eyes and laughed.

"That was Amanda's idea. She thought just sitting around would bore you."

"Why? I don't dance." David said and Alan laughed.

"She is a woman, David. You will learn to just do as you're told."

"Yea, I'm learning that." David said and they both laughed. More people joined the table and the conversation turned to cars. They visited and people danced. David watched Amanda dance with Carman and laughed. Alan followed his gaze to where he was looking. Alan smiled and shook his head. They looked so funny together. Carman was so much taller than her that it looked like a child was dancing with him. They seemed to be talking about something but David couldn't make it out. Amanda seemed to be having such a good time.

"How is it that you sing the way you do but, you don't dance?" Alan asked. The floor had filled with more dancers. It was a slow Bon Jovi song.

"I don't know." David answered. Alan smiled at him and shook his head. Carman was dancing with Nancy now and Amanda was dancing with Gabe's friend Hank.

"You should dance with her." Alan whispered. David smiled and shook his head.

"If you dance, I'll dance." David said. Alan laughed and sat back in his chair.

"Well, I guess you won't be dancing then." Alan said and David laughed.

"How is it, that you can sing like you do, but you don't dance?" David asked sitting back in his own chair. Alan laughed and shook his head.

"Because, I hate dancing. It's like foreplay." Alan said as David took a sip of his drink. David laughed and Alan smiled.

"Wow, that doesn't sound so bad."

"It does when you can't control it." Alan said. David looked at him and shook his head.

"What?"

"I can't explain it. I just get so into it and then next thing you know . . ." Alan stopped talking and David laughed.

"Yea, I get that." David said and looked back at Amanda. Hank was talking to her and she was laughing. The night went on like that until midnight. There had been a few speeches and the D.J. tried everything to get David up on the dance floor, but nothing worked. People started saying there good byes and leaving with their designated drivers. Nancy was one of those drivers and was taking a load of people to the city. Amanda left to take Ron and Samantha home. By 1:00, the only people left were David, Alan, Carman and the D.J. He was packing up his equipment and Alan was helping him. Carman sat down at the table with David.

"So, have a good time?" He asked and David smiled.

"Yea, it was good." David said. Carman smiled and whispered in David's ear,

"If you could have one thing for your birthday, what would it be?" Carman asked. David stared at Alan and then leaned over to Carman.

"One kiss." David said. Carman giggled and looked at David.

"Can I do it?" Carman asked. David laughed and shook his head.

"One kiss from him." David said quietly and Carman laughed.

"I know. I was being funny. Well, trying to be."

"I know. But yea, that's what I would ask for." David said. Carman smiled at him and looked at Alan.

"Want me to go ask for you?" Carman asked. David shot a look of death at Carman. Carman laughed.

"Don't you dare." David said.

"I was kidding." Carman said and David laughed. Alan and the D.J. were finished and the D.J. started loading his equipment into his van. Carman went to help and Alan came over to David.

"So, have a good time?"

"Why is everyone asking me that? It was great, Alan." David said and Alan smiled.

"Good. Got any birthday wishes?" Alan asked. Carman heard the question and laughed. Alan looked at him funny and then looked back at David.

"Uh, well. I think I'm good." David said stuttering. Carman laughed again and went out with a speaker.

"What's his problem?" Alan asked and David laughed.

"It's Carman. I'm sure there's lots wrong with him." David answered and Alan sighed.

"I'm glad you had a good time." Alan said and hugged David. David closed his eyes and smelled Alan. He smelled so good to him. He held Alan for a minute and then let go. "Happy Birthday." Alan said.

"Not anymore. Look at your watch." David said. Alan pulled out the gold pocket watch and looked at the time.

"I see. Oh well, Happy Birthday anyway." Alan said and put the watch back into his pocket. David smiled and shook his head.

"Thanks." He said and Alan smiled.

"I hear Amanda has something planned for you."

"What? There's more?" David asked. Alan laughed at his sarcasm.

"I think you'll like it." Alan said and went over to help move the last of the equipment. When the D.J. was paid and gone. Carman and Alan joined David at the table.

"So, have we practiced?" Carman asked as he sat down. Alan laughed and shook his head.

"Practiced what?" David asked. Alan and Carman both looked at him as if he lost his mind. He thought of the game they played and giggled. "Oh, that." David said and Carman laughed.

"Yea, that."

"I can imagine that David would rather just drink." Alan said and David laughed.

"Are you kidding? I live for this." David said in a seductive voice. Carman laughed and Alan looked at him.

"Oh, really?" Alan asked and leaned close to David. "How much have you practiced?" He asked in his own seductive drawl. David could feel his heart pound. Carman smiled and watched them stare at each other. David sighed and leaned closer. Carman giggled.

"Every night." David whispered. Alan swallowed hard and bit his bottom lip. Carman giggled again.

"So have I." Alan whispered. Carman looked at David and waited for his response. David squinted his eyes but held his gaze.

"And what have you learned?" David asked in his seductive whisper. Alan leaned a little closer and David could feel his hands sweat. Alan looked deep into his eyes and parted his lips. David's breathing picked up and Carman sat forward in his chair.

"I find that, leaning close to you, makes you nervous and ups my chances of winning our little game." Alan whispered. David leaned close enough to kiss Alan and Alan's eyes went wide.

"And I have found that, leaning closer does the same to you." David breathed. Alan cleared his throat and shifted in his chair but didn't pull away. Carman sat still and quiet. David held his ground as well and waited for Alan's rebuttal. They stared at each other not even blinking. Alan swallowed and then sighed. Carman giggled and Alan pulled away. David threw his hands up in the air and Carman laughed.

"I win." David said. Alan laughed and shook his head.

"Very good David. You should get a medal or something." Alan said and David laughed.

"That was awesome." Carman said and winked at David.

"See, play chicken." David said to Alan referring to the conversation they had on their drive home from Carman's house a few months ago.

"Yea, I guess I'll have to do better than that, huh?" Alan asked. David laughed and Carman shook his head.

"You guys are amazing. I thought Alan would never meet his match."

"Neither did I." Alan said and laughed. David looked at Allan and smiled. Carman stood up and went to the booze table.

"What was your next move?" David asked in a whisper. Alan looked at him and smiled.

"I'm not sure I had one." Alan answered. Carman poured three drinks at the booze table.

"Not *sure?*" David asked and giggled. Alan smiled and shook his head. Carman came back to the table with the drinks. He passed them out and sat down.

"Wanna know what I would have done?" Carman asked and Alan laughed.

"You would have cracked long before I did." Alan said. David giggled and looked at Carman.

"What would you have done?" David asked. Carman smiled.

"I would have said, 'kiss me.'" Carman answered. Alan laughed and David shook his head.

"Nice." David said and took a sip of his drink. Alan looked at David and giggled.

"What would you have done if I said that?" Alan asked. David looked at Carman and then back at Alan.

"I would have . . . broke." David said and looked down. Carman smiled and shook his head.

"Well, I'll have to remember that then." Alan said. Just then, Amanda came in.

"Ready to go?" She asked. David looked up at her and smiled. She was wearing a long black trench coat that was tied tight at her waist.

"You better go." Alan said and David giggled.

"Have fun." Carman said and David smiled at him. David got up and followed Amanda out to the big black Hearse parked outside. They got in and Amanda drove out of the drive way.

"Where are we going?" David asked. Amanda smiled but didn't answer. David stared at her as they drove. She had make up on which was strange for her. David thought she looked gorgeous. Amanda looked over at him and giggled.

"You're staring at me." She said. David smiled and nodded.

"You look amazing." David whispered. Amanda smiled and pulled the car over. David looked around. They were parked next to a farmer's field. David looked at her and laughed. "What are we doing here?"

"I thought you would like to get your birthday present now." Amanda said and undid the trench coat. She was completely naked underneath of it. David raised his eyebrows and smiled.

"It isn't even wrapped." David said and Amanda blushed.

"Well, you wanna play with your new toy or what?" Amanda asked. David giggled and pulled Amanda on top of him. She kissed him deeply and moaned as he touched her. She pulled his hair and moved her hips in a grinding motion. David shook and kissed her neck. Amanda reached her hands down between them and fumbled with David's pants button. David lifted his hips and undid his pants. He pushed them down his legs and his full erection was freed. Amanda smiled and guided him in. David moaned.

"I'm not wearing a . . ." David tried to say but Amanda kissed him.

"So, you pull out." Amanda whispered. David moved his hips and Amanda moaned. He put a hand on each of her butt cheeks and lifted her up and down. She moaned louder as her ecstasy built. David moaned as she pulled his hair with her climax. She leaned her head down and kissed him. David's body began to stiffen and shake. Amanda rocked her hips faster and David closed his eyes. She moaned louder and louder as she climaxed again. David's eyes shot open and he gripped Amanda's hips. He moaned and Amanda moaned with him. He lifted Amanda off of him and ejaculated between their sweating bodies. Amanda buried her face in his shoulder and panted. David hugged her and kissed her neck. "Happy Birthday." Amanda breathed and David giggled.

"Yes it is." David said and Amanda kissed him gently on the lips. She lay herself against his chest and sighed.

"I love you, David." She whispered. David rubbed her back and sighed. She looked up at him and smiled. "I don't say it looking for an answer. I say it cause I feel it." She said and smiled.

"I know, Amanda. I just feel bad not saying it back." David said and looked down at Amanda's sweaty chest. He ran his finger between her breasts and she smiled.

"I would rather you felt it before you said it." Amanda said and grabbed his hand. She pulled it up to her mouth and kissed it.

"I do feel it, I just don't think it's fair to say it." David said. Amanda smiled and climbed back into the driver's seat.

"Why?" She asked and smiled at him. David shook his head and pulled his pants up. "Because of Gabe? He's dead, David." David looked at her and frowned.

"What? No, not because of Gabe."

"Then what, David?" Amanda asked. Her tone was short and upset. David sighed and shook his head.

"You're gonna be mad at me because I'm not ready to just give my heart up to you?" David asked. He tried to keep his voice even but he heard the anger in it as well as Amanda did.

"No, I am mad because I am in competition with my dead brother!" Amanda yelled. She started to cry.

"Is that what you think? I felt for Gabe but not the way I feel for you, Amanda." David said. She looked at him and blinked.

"Then why won't you just love me, David?" She asked. David sighed and shook his head.

"You deserve to be loved by someone who doesn't feel the way I do about someone else. Ok." David said and looked away. Amanda held her breath for a second and then gasped.

"Are you in love with Alan?" She asked. David looked at her and frowned. "Oh my god, David. You are aren't you?" She said. David sighed and looked away. He dug in his pocket and took out his cigarettes. He lit one and wheeled down the passenger side window. "Why won't you answer me? It's a simple question. Are you in love with Alan or not?" Amanda said. Her voice was harsh and there were tears in her eyes. David looked at her and shook his head.

"I don't know how I feel, ok! I can't answer your questions! This whole thing is so fucked up. I wish I could love you like you want me to, but I can't." David said. Tears filled his eyes and he got out of the car. He walked down the road and sat down on the shoulder. Amanda got out of the car and walked over to him. She sat down next to him and sighed.

"David, I'm sorry. I just wish I understood were you were at with all this. I mean, you don't even talk to me about it hardly any more." David sighed and looked at her.

"I know, I'm sorry. I laid it all on Gabe because you said you loved me. I thought it wasn't fair to talk about it with you anymore."

"Are you kidding? I want to be the one who hears it all. Just like always, David." Amanda said. She leaned against him and sighed. "Tell me everything." She said.

"Well, Alan and I play this game . . ." He explained where he was at from what he felt she missed. When he was finished talking Amanda smiled and looked into his eyes.

"I think you *are* falling love with him David. That's what it sounds like to me anyway."

"How do you feel about that?" David asked quietly looking down at the ground.

"It doesn't change how I feel about you. I think it's important for you to figure it out though." Amanda said. She shivered and David smiled.

“Let’s go home.” He said. Amanda nodded and they got back into the car. Amanda drove them home. Nancy was already in bed when they got home. They went up to their room and Amanda dropped the coat down on the floor. David giggled and sat down at his desk.

“It’s nice to see you writing again.” Amanda said as she crawled into bed.

“You’re not reading it, are you?” David asked. Amanda giggled and shook her head.

“I wouldn’t without asking first.” Amanda said and closed her eyes. David smiled at her and turned back toward his journal.

Dear Gabe,

My birthday was awesome. Everybody dressed up in leather jackets and they played all my favorite bands all night. They got a D.J. to come in and do it. It was pretty sweet.

Remember our ‘fucked up’ conversation. I just crossed over. I had sex with Amanda in your car. I win in the fucked up department I guess.

Carman asked me what I wanted for my birthday. I said a kiss from Alan. I just about got it too. It was so weird. We were plating our little game and we were close enough all I would have had to do was lean a little farther over. I just don’t got the balls for it. Kissing you the first time was way easier.

Amanda thinks I'm falling in love with Alan. I think she's right. I just hope I'm not ruining a good thing with her by not figuring this shit out.

I miss you,

David.

Chapter 27

With the exams over and the second half of the school year finally underway, David found himself looking forward to his Sundays with Alan more and more. The count down for spring break was underway as well. After the year everyone had, they were looking forward to the break. Even Nancy was looking forward to her trip to New York. Even though it was business oriented, she was becoming more excited about getting away. With only a week left to wait, everyone was buzzing.

"Why don't we take my car?" David asked Alan as they drove back to David's house Sunday afternoon. They had been talking about their upcoming trip to go see Carman.

"We could. Are you sure you want to?" Alan asked.

"Yea, it would be nice to take her out for a nice long drive." David said and smiled. Alan laughed and shook his head.

"Ok then."

"You don't want to ride in that car, do you?" David asked. Alan smiled and shook his head.

“I just haven’t been in it since . . .” Alan fell quiet and stared out the windshield at the high way.

“I know. It’s different now though. I’ve got my own personal touch in there.” David said. Alan laughed and shook his head.

“Ok, we’ll take your car.” Alan said. David smiled and looked out the windshield too. Alan pulled up to David’s house and sighed. “Will you bring your guitar with you?” Alan asked. David looked down at his feet. He hadn’t played for anyone but Little Mike since Gabe had died.

“If you want me to.” David said quietly. Alan smiled and nodded.

“I would really like to hear you play it.” Alan said. David smiled and got out of the car. He understood Alan’s feelings considering the guitar did come from him. David waved at Alan as he drove away. David went into the house and found Nancy and Amanda at the kitchen table.

“Hey, how was your day?” Nancy asked as he entered the room. David sat down and raised his eyebrows.

“Well, Alan out bench pressed me again but I can still out run him on the cardio machine.”

“How did working out together become a cock battle?” Amanda asked. Nancy giggled.

“Oh, I don’t know. Cause we’re guys I guess.” David said and laughed. Amanda shook her head and went upstairs. “Is she ok?” David asked as Amanda ran to the bathroom.

“I think she’s getting the flu.” Nancy said. David raised an eyebrow.

“We’ll all be sick by spring break then.” David said. Nancy shook her head.

“Poor thing. It seems pretty violent too.” David got up and went to the fridge. He took out a pop and got his mom an iced tea.

"Should we take her to the doctor?" David asked as he returned to the table.

"She has an appointment booked with her cousin's doctor in Texas." Nancy answered and opened her drink.

"Why doesn't she see a doctor here?"

"She wouldn't say." David sighed and got up. "Were are you going?" Nancy asked.

"I'm gonna go see if she's ok." David answered and headed upstairs. He walked to the bathroom door and he could hear Amanda crying. "Are you ok?" He asked from behind the door.

"Yea, it's just the flu. I'll be fine." Amanda answered through the door.

"Can I get you anything?"

"No, I'll be down in a minute." Amanda answered. David sighed and went back downstairs. Nancy was still at the table.

"How is she?" Nancy asked.

"Sick, I guess." David said and sat down. "When did this start?"

"Well, she said it started yesterday. But after she gets sick, she says she seems to feel better."

"Yea, that sounds like the flu to me. Maybe she should stay home this week." David said sipping at his pop.

"That's probably a good idea. I'll go up and talk to her about it." Nancy said and headed upstairs. David sighed and went into the living room where Little Mike was playing with his air plane.

"Hi Davin. Manda has yucky." Mike said. David smiled and sat down next to him.

"Yes she does little buddy." David said and picked up a toy.

For the next week, Amanda staid home and fought a flu that never seemed to get any worse than occasionally throwing up. David brought her some school work every day and helped her with it. He found it funny that they had a few classes together for the last half of the year and she was missing it. He still took Little Mike to Rita's every day so Amanda could rest. She said she slept for most of the day and that seemed to help with the pain in her stomach. Nancy kept a good supply of Rolaids and other kinds of stomach medication on hand for her. When Friday came along, David was worried that Amanda wasn't well enough to fly.

"Are you sure you should go?" David asked her as she packed. Amanda rolled her eyes and looked at him.

"David, I will see a doctor when I'm there. Besides, Mike is so excited to ride on the airplane. I'm fine, it's only a two hour flight."

"I know but . . ." David tried to argue but she stopped him.

"David, I appreciate your concern, I really do. I want to go." Amanda said and closed the suit case. David did it up for her and she smiled. "You'll hardly miss me while I'm gone anyway. You get to spend a bunch of time with your two favorite guys."

"I would stay home if you wanted me to."

"Yea right. I wouldn't do that. You're chomping at the bit by Wednesday to spend time with Alan on Sunday. Now you get to spend a whole week with him. I wouldn't make you stay home. I wouldn't even ask." Amanda said and put her coat on.

"Can I at least ask that you call me when you hear from the doctor?" David said.

"Of course I will David." Amanda said. There was a knock at the door.

"Are you ready to go, Amanda?" It was Nancy. It just so happened that their planes left within hours of each other.

"Yea, I'll be right down." Amanda said to the closed door. "I'll miss you baby." She said and kissed David. David smiled and opened the door for her. He carried the suit case downstairs and out to his mother's car.

"When will Alan be here?" Nancy asked as she put Little Mike in the car seat.

"Actually, we're taking my car so I'm going to go pick him up after you guys go." David said as he put Amanda's suit case in the trunk.

"The Hearse? Wow." Amanda said. David rolled his eyes and closed the trunk.

"It's just a car." David said. The words tasted like poison.

"Well, I'm sure you guys will have fun." Nancy said and hugged her son.

"Good luck at your thing." David said as they hugged. Nancy giggled and got into the car.

"I love you." Amanda said as she hugged David.

"Please let me know what the doctor says, ok." David said as she pulled away.

"I will, David." Amanda said and got in the car. Nancy honked the horn as she drove away and David waved. He went into the house and dialed Alan's phone number.

"*Hello.*"

"Hello to you." David said in a seductive sounding voice. Alan laughed.

"*Are the ladies off to the airport?*"

"Yup, you ready to go?"

"*As ready as I'm gonna be.*" Alan said. David smiled.

"Ok, see you in ten minutes."

"*Ok.*" Alan said. David hung up the phone and grabbed his bag and his guitar. He took them outside and set them down. He took one last look inside the house for any lights on. When he was satisfied, he went out and locked the door. He took his bag and guitar case to the car and put them in the back. He got into the driver's side door of the car and drove to Alan's.

Alan was sitting outside smoking when he arrived. He had one suit case, his amplifier and one guitar case. David smiled as he got out of the car.

"Packing light?" David asked. Alan smiled and grabbed the guitar case and suit case.

"Shouldn't have to pack a guitar for you anymore, should I?" Alan asked as he walked up to the Hearse. David smiled and picked up the amp. He took it around to the back of the car and opened the wide back door for Alan. Alan saw the guitar case in the back and smiled. They loaded Alan's things and hit the road. Alan was surprised how different the inside of the car seemed. David had replaced the Manson pictures on the rear view mirror with black dice. There was a new five disk changer in the dash witch seemed to completely change the inside of the car. "It looks good, David." Alan said as he looked around. David smiled.

"I told you it was different. I couldn't leave it the same. I find it easier to drive it when it doesn't have Gabe written all over it." David said as he drove down the highway.

"Well, it's a nice car." Alan said. David smiled again and nodded.

"Yes it is."

"Did you talk to Carman like I asked?" Alan asked. David looked at him and giggled.

"That was random."

"I'm sorry, I just don't want things to be weird when we get there."

"Well, I did." David said and felt instantly on the spot. Carmans problem was Alan's innocent flirting. David had argued with him that Alan was only doing it because he thought it was safe to. Carman was feeling sorry for David. He didn't think it was fair that David would have to be left sexually frustrated every time Alan was done with him. David had laughed at him and told him he liked it, but Carman didn't think David should have to grow up with it like he did.

"What did he say?" Alan asked. David sighed and tried to think of something good.

"Well, it's complicated." David said trying to buy himself more time.

"It's a long drive." Alan said. David laughed and shook his head.

"It's not even a big deal. I think it's funny he didn't tell you himself."

"Well, you tell me then."

"I would, but I don't want to." David said. Alan laughed and playfully hit David in the shoulder. "Hey, don't bug the driver." David said still laughing.

"You guys are alike, you know that?" Alan asked and shook his head.

"Oh come on. Don't you like a little mystery in your life?"

"No, not when it comes to Carman." Alan said. It seemed like a pretty serious answer. David looked at Alan and sighed.

"He thinks our little game is a dangerous one." David said. His hands sweat on the steering wheel and his heart pounded in his chest.

"Why?" Alan asked with half a giggle in his voice. David sighed and turned the corner toward the Oregon border.

"He thinks I might get the wrong idea." David said and almost choked. He wanted a deer or something to jump out in front of the car but nothing happened. The highway was clear and the weather was beautiful. He stared out the wind shield and waited for Alan to say something. Alan seemed to stay quiet for a life time. David started to feel as though Alan would never speak again for the rest of the trip until Alan finally asked,

"Would that bother you?" David just about swerved off the road and Alan laughed.

"Would what bother me?" David asked with a shaky voice. Alan looked out the windshield then back at David.

"If I was like Carman," Alan said. David blinked and looked between Alan and the road.

"How do you mean, 'like Carman'?"

"Would it bother you if I was gay?" The question hit David like a kick to the groin. He wasn't sure how to answer.

"Are you?" David asked instead of answering it with 'are you kidding, thank god' and pulling over the car for an epic make out session.

"Just answer the question David. Would it bother you?" Alan said. David sighed and shook his head.

"No, no it would not." David said. He looked over at Alan. He was staring out the windshield. "Why do you ask?" David added the question without thinking.

"I just wondered if it would make things weird or not."

"So are you or aren't you?" David asked. Alan laughed and shook his head.

"Don't you think you would know if I was?" Alan asked. David raised his eyebrows and shook his head.

"Some people can hide it pretty good." David said smiling at his own mastery.

"You can usually tell, David." Alan said and lit a cigarette for both himself and David.

"Gabe hid it for almost 28 years." David said as he wheeled down his window and took the cigarette from Alan.

"Is that right? I saw it right away."

"That's because he thought you were hot." David said and Alan laughed.

"Really?" He sounded surprised. As if he had never heard of someone thinking he was attractive. David took a drag af his cigarette and giggled.

"Oh yea." David answered and Alan laughed.

"That's funny." Alan said. David laughed and shook his head.

"Why, you're a good looking dude." David said and felt his stomach flip from saying it. Alan smiled and shook his head.

"Well, thank you, David." He said. David sighed and stared out onto the long highway. Alan messed around with the stereo as they drove and finally figured out how it worked. David laughed at how proud he was of himself. He put on 5 of David and his favorite C.D.'s. Alan sang along with some of the songs as David drove. They reached Portland Oregon at 6:00 pm exactly.

"Told you." David said tapping the clock in the car with his finger. Alan shook his head. David had bet Alan the day before that they would get there by six. Alan thought it would be closer to seven.

"What were the terms again?" Alan asked as David giggled at himself.

"The terms were, that if I won, I got to do something for you for your birthday tomorrow." David said and smiled.

"Oh yes. Well, thank god you don't have a lot of time to plan anything." Alan said and giggled.

"Ahh, yee of little faith. I knew I would win. I've had Carman working on this all week." David said and Alan looked at him as though he just shot his best friend. David laughed and pulled onto the freeway that led the way to Carman's house.

"You didn't." Alan said. David looked at him and stuck out his bottom lip. Alan laughed and shook his head. "You ass holes." Alan said and David laughed again.

"You love it. Besides, how many times do you turn 40?"

"Only once, thank god." Alan said and looked out the window.

"Oh don't worry, Carman and I are a lot kinder than you and a couple of women." David said and Alan looked at him.

"Yea right."

"We are. Carman seems to know exactly what you want for your birthday, so that's what we're going to do."

"And what's that?" Alan asked. David smiled and shook his head.

"You'll have to wait and see."

"Come on, tell me." Alan said. David laughed and rolled his eyes.

"Oh like how you told me?" David asked. Alan bit the inside of his cheek.

"I had TWO WOMEN to answer to."

"I have CARMAN to answer to." David said and Alan laughed.

"Yea, ok." Alan said. They listened to the rest of the last C.D. as they drove. David turned off the freeway and they could see Carmans house.

"Holy shit, I'm excited." David said and Alan laughed.

"Me too actually." Alan said as David pulled the big car into the driveway. He parked next to the garage and they both got out of the car. They got their things from the back and set them down at the foot of the steps.

"DEAD MAN WALKEN!" They called in unison. The door flew open and there stood Carman. He laughed and came down the stairs with out stretched arms. Alan hugged him and he moved to David.

"It's good to see you." Carman whispered as they hugged.

"You too." David whispered back. They let go and Carman picked up the amplifier.

"Who needs a drink?" Carman asked as they went in. Alan laughed and David smiled. They went in and took the guitars and amp into the music room. David took his bag downstairs. He walked slowly through Carmans collection of death and smiled. He saw his Iron Maiden standing with her sisters. He set his bag in his room and came back out to see her. He opened the door and stepped inside. The cold iron smelled good to him and felt as though he had just come home from a trip that took way to long. Then Gabe flashed in his mind. He stepped out of the machine and closed the door.

"Not the same since Halloween, huh?" Alan said from behind him. David turned around and looked at him.

"No, it's not." David answered and latched the lock on the door of the big iron coffin.

"You know, you could stay upstairs with us." Alan said. David smiled and shook his head.

"No, it's ok. I like to be down here."

"Ok, are you alright?" Alan asked.

"Yea, of course."

"Well, I was supposed to come down here and tell you the bartender was in." Alan said with a smile. David laughed and they headed upstairs to the music room. Carman was standing behind the bar with a towel flung over his shoulder.

"Howdy boys, what are you havin'?" Alan and David took their seats and read the makeshift menu that Carman had just made. David laughed at the ridiculous names of the drinks. Alan scratched his head and looked at Carman.

"What's a, Big German Cock?" David laughed and looked at Carman. He surprisingly kept a straight face.

"A good start." Carman said. Alan laughed and looked at David.

"You want a 'Big German Cock?" Alan asked. David raised an eyebrow and looked at Carman. Carman winked and David giggled.

"That depends," David said and looked at Alan. "Are you German?" Alan's eyes grew wide and he shot a look at Carman. Carman burst out laughing and Alan giggled.

"Actually, I am." Alan said quietly. David kept his face as straight as he could.

"Bar tender, I think I'll have one of those." David said looking straight at Alan. Alan sighed and composed his face. Carman giggled and made his mystery drink. Alan looked over the menu and smiled.

"I will have, The Young Lover." Alan said. David fought the smile and Carman laughed. Carman mixed the drink and handed them across the bar. He sat down on the stool he had moved to the other side of the bar. He spun the menu around and looked it over. Alan giggled as he seemed to peruse the menu as if he had never seen it before,

"I will have, the One Who Walks Away." Carman said. David laughed and Alan smiled.

"That's not on the menu." Alan said.

"I know, but it sounded good coming after your guys' orders." Carman said. David laughed and Alan smiled.

"Yea, it was pretty good." Alan said. Carman mixed his drink and leaned on the bar. He stared at David and Alan laughed.

"Oh crap." David said and took a big sip of his drink. Alan giggled and watched David compose himself.

"You ever heard of a whispering orgasm?" Carman asked in a surprisingly sexy voice. Alan smiled and put his fist over his mouth. David stared into his eyes.

"No." David answered in a low voice.

"I hear, it is the most intense orgasm a guy can have." Carman whispered. David raised his eyebrow and stared at Carman.

"Is that so?" David asked. Carman leaned closer across the bar to David.

"I hear that once you have one, nothing else compares." Carman whispered. David leaned on the bar so they were almost nose to nose.

"And I suppose you can do this?" David asked. Carmans voice spread into a seductive grin.

"No, but I know who can." He whispered. Just then Alan leaned over and moaned quietly in David's ear. David held his breath and closed his eyes. Alan and Carman waited for his reaction. Finally after a few moments, David laughed and Carman cheered.

"Since when is tag teaming aloud?" David asked. Alan laughed and took a sip of his drink.

"Since you won last time and Alan wanted his title back." Carman said giggling. David looked at Alan.

"This was your idea?" David asked. Alan smiled and nodded. "Nice, very clever." David said and looked at Carman. Carman smiled with puppy dog eyes as if to say 'I'm sorry'. David shook his head and looked at Alan. "What's the most you've ever done to win?" Alan raised his eyebrows and shrugged.

"I don't know." Carman rolled his eyes and cleared his throat.

"He once ran his hand all the way up my leg till he almost touched my dick." David giggled.

"What happened?" David asked.

"He broke." Alan said and smiled.

"I thought it was no contact." David said taking a sip from his drink.

"It's no contact when we play with kids." Carman said as a dig to David.

"Well, lucky for you, I'm not a kid anymore." Alan laughed and shook his head.

"Oh, so you think you can play with the big boys?" Carman said. David took a sip of his drink and then looked at Alan.

"That depends."

"On what." Alan asked.

"The rules." David said. Carman came around the bar and sat on the bar stool behind Alan and David. They turned in their seats to face him.

"The rules are simple." Carman said and took a sip of his drink. "No outside interference, no reference to sex and, as always, he who breaks first loses." Carman listed the rules and David smiled.

"That's way easier than just talking."

"Don't get too excited, it's harder when you can't talk about sex." Alan said.

"I'm usually the one who wins at this game." Carman said. David looked at Alan and Alan nodded.

"Ok, show me." David said. Alan giggled and sipped his drink. Carman moved his stool close to Alan and Alan looked at him with wide eyes. David laughed.

"Me?" Alan asked. Carman nodded and Alan shook his head. "Ok, Carman. No wimping out." Alan said. He cracked his neck and stared at Carman. David giggled and watched Alan.

"I was thinking," Carman said and put his hand on Alan's thigh. Alan raised an eyebrow but never looked away. "You and I never really got to know each other the way I would have liked." Carman said and slid his hand up farther. David giggled and watched Alan. He held his straight face and looked into Carman's eyes.

"And what did you have in mind?" Alan asked and moved his face closer to Carman's. David sat staring at the incredible restraint Alan had from laughing. Carman looked at him and moved his face closer to Alan's. David giggled again and tried not to laugh.

"Well, I thought you might be interested in taking a tour of my bedroom." Carman said. Alan ran his hand up Carman's arm and David smiled. He could see Carman breaking. Carman took a shaky breath but didn't laugh. Alan bit his bottom lip and played with Carman's hair.

"When does the tour start?" Alan asked in the sexiest voice David ever heard. Carman sighed and then laughed. Alan laughed and David gave Carman a mock dirty look.

"You suck, Carman." David said and Alan laughed.

"Think you could do better?" Carman asked and sipped his drink. David sighed and turned Alan in his seat. Alan looked at him with wide eyes and composed his face. David leaned in close to Alan's ear and whispered.

"The tour of *my* room starts whenever you're ready and ends when you beg me to stop." David pulled away to see Alan's face. His eyes were still wide but he just stared at David. Carman put his hands over his mouth and held back his laugh. Alan fixed his eyes and leaned forward to David's ear.

"I would *never* beg you to stop." Alan whispered. Carman waited to see what David would say.

"Man I wish you guys would speak louder." Carman whispered. David looked at him and then back at Alan. Alan bit his lip and David swallowed hard. Soon they both started laughing.

"Damn it, Carman." Alan said and David laughed harder.

"Sorry, did I wreck it?" Carman asked. Alan shook his head and took a sip of his drink. "What did you say first David?" Carman asked.

"He said, the tour for his bed room started whenever I was ready and ended when I begged him to stop." Alan said. Carman giggled.

"That's stepping dangerously close to breaking the no sex talk rule." Carman said and David laughed. What did Alan say?" Carman asked David.

"He said he would *never* beg me to stop."

"Wow, you guys should just do it and get it over with." Carman said and laughed. Alan shook his head and got up off his stool. He went over to the guitars and took his out. David joined him and they played until Carman was tired and his throat was sore from singing. "Well, guys. I am bushed. See you tomorrow." Carman said and headed off to bed. Alan set his guitar aside and looked at David.

"Can I ask you something?" David looked up at him from his guitar.

"Sure." David said and put his guitar aside. Alan leaned against the bar and cleared his throat.

"Why do you think I always win with Carman?" David shrugged his shoulders and lit a cigarette.

"Cause he's no good at the game." David answered. Alan laughed and shook his head.

"He's good at that game. He is also scared to beat me." Alan said. David found and looked into Alan's eyes.

"Why?" David asked. Alan sighed and took David's cigarette. David giggled but let him have a drag. He handed it back and smiled.

"Cause we have a bet."

"What are the terms?" David asked suddenly very interested in the kind of bet that would force the loss of a game like the one they played.

"What do you mean?" David asked. He leaned over totally engrossed in Alan's explanation. Alan giggled and shook his head.

"It was a stupid bet, but he says it still stands."

"What does he get if he wins?"

"A night in bed with me." Alan said. David was shocked. He sat back in his seat and almost fell off. Alan giggled and then sighed. David composed himself and looked at Alan.

"Doesn't he want that?" David asked. Alan nodded. "Can he beat you?" David asked. Alan sighed and took the last sip from his drink.

"I think he can." Alan confessed. David looked at Alan in disbelief.

"If he wants you, why doesn't he beat you then?" Alan smiled and looked at David.

"I think he's afraid he'll ruin our friendship if I had to pay up." Alan answered. David blinked a few times and then cleared his throat.

"Would it?" David asked. The question felt like a murder confession but he thought it was the best way to get the information he needed from Alan.

"Well, it would certainly change it anyway." Alan said and stood up. "Look, it's a touchy subject with him. Keep it between us, ok?" He asked. David nodded and took the last big sip of his drink. Alan smiled and touched David's shoulder. "Don't stay up too late, huh?"

"No, I'm going to bed now." David said and stood up. "What did you say when Carman told you he was gay?" David asked as they left the room. Alan sighed and looked at David.

"I think I said, 'I know'." Alan said and smiled. David sighed and raised his eyebrows.

"Did you know?"

"I was pretty sure." Alan said. David nodded and walked toward the basement stairs. "David," Alan called quietly and David looked back.

“Yea.” He said. Alan sighed and walked up to him. He put his hands on David’s shoulders and looked him straight in the eyes. David swallowed hard but held his ground.

“I want you to know, that no matter what your secret is, it’s safe with me.” Alan said. David shifted where he stood and nodded. Alan let his shoulders go and sighed.

“It’s not a secret Alan. You just don’t know about it.” David said and went down the stairs. Alan didn’t follow and David was happy for that. He went into his room and slumped down on his bed. He lay there staring at the ceiling.

Why did I say that?! I’m such an idiot. He fucking knows and he wants to hear it from me! He got up and opened his bag. He searched through it and realized he had forgotten his journal at home.

“Shit.” He said out loud and lay back down on the bed.

I guess keeping a record of stupidity isn’t a good idea anyway. I can’t believe I forgot my fucking journal. I’m so stupid sometimes. What the hell was I thinking saying that to him? He’s going to ask about it. What am I gonna say? David racked his brain for an answer until sleep took him.

Chapter 28

David and Alan's visit was pretty full with Carman's plans. Alan's birthday was an amazing surprise for him. Carman had invited some old buddies of theirs and they played poker for the whole night. Alan won by default. The next few days were full with horseback riding, trips to the city for various things like going to the movies or going to town for coffee. On the Friday before they had to leave, Carman was called to work for a few hours. Alan and David decided to go for a walk around Carman's property.

"Well, Carman isn't talking. What's this not so big secret?" Alan asked as they crossed the make shift bridge Carman had built across the little creak on his property. David sighed and shook his head.

"It's nothing." David lied. Alan rolled his eyes and stopped at the end of the bridge. David had crossed first and was up ahead a bit. He stopped walking and faced Alan. He sighed and walked back to where Alan stood. "It's really nothing." David said. Alan lit a cigarette and looked at David with disbelieving eyes.

"You tell me everything else. What's so wrong with this?" Alan asked. David looked down at the ground and sighed.

"Why don't you guess?" David asked. Alan laughed and shook his head. They started walking again and Alan looked at David.

"Are you an axe murderer?" David laughed and shook his head.

"Be serious." David said. Alan giggled.

"I was."

"Well, no. I'm not an axe murderer." David said and giggled. They passed an old run down granary and Alan looked inside. David peaked in the little window with him.

"Are you secretly a woman?" David laughed and shook his head.

"I wish." David said and Alan laughed.

"Are you secretly a woman axe murderer?" David laughed again and stepped away from the window.

"Are these really your guesses?" David asked. Alan sighed and looked into David's eyes.

"No they aren't" He said and continued walking. David followed and he felt his heart speed up. He took a deep breath and tried to prepare himself for what was coming.

"Ok, ask for real then." David said and wished he hadn't. Alan stopped and turned to face him. He looked over to a log and went to sit on it. He patted the space next to him and David joined him. Alan sighed and looked out into the trees.

"I think you're toying with the idea of being with men and you're too scared to tell me because you think I would look down on you for it." Alan said. David looked down at the ground. There was a little bug crawling away from the log. He wished he was the bug. "Your silence suggests that I'm right." Alan said but never looked away from the trees. David sighed and looked at the trees Alan stared at. "Well, if I am right," Alan said and looked at David. David closed his eyes and waited. “Then you’re wrong. You could talk to me about this. I would *never* look down on you for that.” Alan said and looked back out into the trees. David reopened his eyes. He felt like his chest was split open for the world to see his bleeding heart. Alan sighed and looked back at David. “Please talk to me.” Alan said quietly. David looked at him and shook his head.

“I can’t, Alan. I can’t talk to you about it.” David whispered. Alan looked away and sighed.

“Why?” Alan asked. David stood up and walked over to the nearest tree. He put his arm around it and leaned his head against it. Alan stood up and walked over to him. “When you’re ready to talk, I am here for you.” Alan said. David looked at him and sighed.

“I wish I could Alan, I just can’t” David whispered. Alan smiled and rubbed his back.

“Now I get what Carman’s problem was.” Alan said. David giggled without meaning to.

“Don’t be different because of this, ok.” David said facing Alan with pleading eyes.

“Of course not. This makes the game way easier to win.” Alan joked and David laughed. They decided to head back to see if Carman was home. He wasn’t so they went into the music room and picked up their guitars. “Will you sing for me?” Alan asked in a sexy voice.

“You’re a dick.” David said and Alan laughed. “But, yes I will.” David said and played While my Guitar Gently Weeps. Alan smiled as David sang. When he was finished Alan sighed and shook his head.

“You a really good guitar player David.” Alan said. David smiled and looked away. “Don’t think about it, David. Just be you.” Alan said and strummed his guitar. They played together until they heard Carman yell,

“DEAD MAN WALKEN!”

"What do you say if you *are* getting laid?" David asked quickly and Alan laughed.

"IF YOU WALK IN, YOU *WILL* BE DEAD!" Alan yelled and David laughed.

"That's not really it, is it?" David asked. Alan laughed and shook his head.

"No, we never thought of anything." Alan answered. David laughed and Carman walked in.

"I thought you were pulling my chain." He said. Alan laughed and shook his head.

"It was David's idea." He said and David giggled.

"Rat." He said and Carman laughed.

"I have a surprise for your last night here." Carman said and took his bag behind the bar. Alan and David took their seats at the bar and watched Carman's back as he poured three drinks. He turned around and handed a glass to David. "Try it." Carman said and winked at Alan. Alan giggled and watched David take a sip.

"It's Scotch." David said and smiled.

"I thought you could use a man's drink after a week with us." Carman said. Alan laughed as Carman handed Alan his cup. Alan took a sip and looked at Carman.

"David thinks he can beat you with some new rules we made up." Alan said. David looked at him with a puzzled gaze and Alan winked at him.

"Oh really. Lets hear it." Carman said and sat down at his stool that was set for him beside Alan.

"Well, the rules are simple. No talking, no touching and as always, He who cracks first loses." Alan said.

"Out side interference?" Carman asked.

"Allowed." Alan said. David giggled and looked at Carman. Carman took a deep breath and locked eyes with David. Alan took a sip of his drink and leaned forward. He slowly ran his hand slowly up Carman's leg and stopped just short of the center seem in the groin. He squeeze Carman's thigh and Carman giggled. David laughed and Carman shot a dirty look at Alan.

"Outside interference sucks." Carman said and laughed. Alan smiled and took another sip of his drink.

"That's the rules." Alan said.

"Why didn't you do it to him?" Carman asked. David giggled and looked at Carman.

"Cause I wouldn't crack with something like that." David answered. Alan laughed and shook his head.

"My ass." Carman said. David giggled and shook his head.

"Lets see." Alan said and David's eyes shot over to his. Alan leaned forward and put both hands on David's thighs. He slowly moved them up and David stared at him without blinking.

"I think that's shock you see, Alan." Carman said and David laughed.

"Damn it, Carman!" Alan and David both said. Alan pulled his hands away and David took a deep breath. Alan noticed it and winced. After an hour of chit chat, Carman got up to go to the bathroom.

"I am so sorry." Alan whispered. David looked at him with confusion while he poured three more drinks.

"For what?" David asked as he came around the bar and handed Alan his last drink for the night. He set Carman's drink down on the bar and kept his in his hand.

"For that leg thing earlier. I saw the deep breath you took after. I'm sorry." David giggled and shook his head.

"You just keep thinking that." David said. Alan laughed and shook his head.

"Ok, so what was the sigh about then?" Alan asked. David looked at him and smiled.

"Alan, you are incredibly naive for a 40 year old man." Alan blinked and was about to say something but Carman walked in.

"What did I miss?" He asked as he grabbed his drink and sat down.

"We were discussing hand jobs." David said and Alan burst out laughing.

"Why do you guys always have the good talks when I leave the room?" Carman asked. David and Alan both laughed.

"Cause you interrupt with stupid questions." Alan said. Carman laughed and shook his head. David looked at Carman and Carman caught his gaze. Alan smiled and shook his head. He took the last sip from his cup and set it on the bar. David looked back at Alan and smiled. "Well, on that note, its time." Alan said. He got up and David downed the last of his drink.

"Me too." David said. Carman looked at his full shot and giggled. He tipped up the glass and downed the whole thing. He shivered as the hot liquid went down.

"Don't puke." Alan said and David laughed.

"You should try shooting a hit of Scotch like that." Carman said and held his breath for a second.

"I know someone who can drink it like water." Alan said and winked at David. David smiled and shook his head.

"Well, whoever that is has balls of steel." Carman said and they headed out of the room together.

"Good night, David." Alan said as they passed the hall way Alan's room was in.

"Good night." David said. Carman sat down at the table in the living room and blew a kiss at Alan.

"You wish." Alan said as he went in and shut the door. David turned and looked at Carman.

"Fuck Carman, he knows." David whispered and sat down at the table with him.

"Everything?" Carman asked in a whisper. David shook his head.

"He thinks I'm toying with the idea of being with a guy." David answered. Carman raised his eyebrows.

"Was that a guess or did you tell him that?"

"It was a guess." David answered. He ran his hand through his hair and Carman smiled.

"That's great!" Carman said. David looked at him puzzled.

"What? How?" David asked. Carman leaned closer to David and sighed.

"Cause now, you can talk about your 'curiosity' with him" Carman said making his fingers into quotations around curiosity.

"How is that a good thing?"

"I think he has always had a skeleton in his closet banging on the door. Maybe you can let it out."

"What?" David asked. Carman giggled and shook his head.

"Look how he plays that game. No perfectly straight dude is *that* comfortable with his sexuality." Carman said. David sighed and shook his head. Carman's logic did make sense but it made David nervous to think about it for some reason.

"Carman, I couldn't do that." David said and sighed.

"Why not?"

"Well, because of you, for one thing. And Alan is like a fantasy. A scary, untouchable fantasy." David said. Carman smiled.

"David, don't worry about me. I could never be with Alan. The size of his cock frightens me." Carman said and giggled. David raised his eyebrows and looked down the hall. Carman laughed and shook his head. "Fantasy's shouldn't be scary David." Carman added and David looked back at him.

"This one is." David said and leaned back in his chair.

"Why?"

"What if something *was* to happen and I choked?" David asked. Carman smiled and ran his hand through his hair.

"I doubt you would."

"You can't know for sure though." David said and sighed again. Carman smiled and leaned against the table.

"Come here." Carman whispered. David leaned close to Carman and Carman kissed him. David was so surprised he almost fell off his chair. Carman giggled and shook his head.

"Why did you do that?" David asked still stunned. Carman smiled.

"I wanted to see if you would choke under the element of surprise. Trust me, if Alan does anything, it will be his first move and you won't expect it." David sighed and swallowed hard.

"I see." David said. Carman giggled and looked into David's eyes.

"Plus, I've wanted to do that for a while." Carman confessed. David laughed and shook his head.

"Well, that sucked though." David said. Carman laughed and cracked his neck.

"Wanna do over?" Carman asked. David looked at him and giggled.

"Yea, I kinda do." David said. Carman leaned across the table again and this time, David kissed him. Carman closed his eyes and gently kissed David. David whimpered under Carman's kiss and Carman moaned. David pulled away and looked at him. Carman opened his eyes and looked into David's. "I better go to bed, Carman." David whispered and Carman giggled.

"I know." Carman said. David sighed and shook his head.

"That was way too good to keep going." David said and stood up. Carman stood up too and smiled.

"Your speed David. If a kiss is all you want. I can live with that." Carman said. David smiled and shook his head.

"It's not that, it's Charlie."

"Charlie?" Carman asked. David sighed and looked down. "Oh, he told you about that, huh?"

"Don't say anything to him." David said. Carman smiled and shook his head.

"There is *a lot* more to that story than you think." Carman said. David looked up at Carman. "Don't worry about it, David. Alan isn't as easy to aggravate as you would think."

"I'm not worried about aggravating him. I'm worried about pissing him off." David said. Carman laughed and walked down to Alan's room. David shook his head and watched what Carman would do.

"Hey Alan!" Carman called through the door.

"*What Carman?*" David heard Alan's tiered voice say.

"Would it piss you off if I kissed your puppy?" Carman asked. David rolled his eyes and gave Carman the finger. Carman giggled and waited for an answer.

"*Yes it would. He is MY puppy.*" Alan answered. Carman laughed. David smiled and shook his head.

"PLEASE!" Carman begged outside the door. David laughed and ran a hand through his hair.

"*If you touch him, I'll have to kill you.*" Alan's voice said behind the door.

"What if he kisses me?" Carman asked. David shook his head and Carman giggled.

"*He wouldn't, he thinks you're a dick.*" Alan said. Carman laughed and shook his head. Alan opened the door and looked at Carman. "Did he?" Alan asked. Carman giggled and shook his head.

"I surprised him with it and he whined about you." Carman said. David shifted where he stood. Alan looked over at David and smiled.

"You whined about me?" Alan asked as if he were touched by the hand of god. David sighed but said nothing. "See how well behaved he is." Alan said and closed the door. "*No more corrupting my puppy.*" Alan said from behind the door.

"Yes dear." Carman said and walked back over to David. "Guess you're off the hook." Carman said and David laughed.

"That was the stupidest thing I've ever seen." David said. Carman giggled and shook his head.

"He loves you, David. He only wants the best for you." Carman said and winked at him. David shook his head and Carman went to his room. David sighed and headed toward the basement stairs.

"David." Alan said from behind him. David winced and turned around. Alan was wearing a pair of blue jeans but no shirt. He looked amazing. "Fill your boots. You could learn a lot from him." Alan said and smiled. David walked over to him and shook his head.

"Are you kidding?" David said through clenched teeth. Alan raised his eyebrows and looked down the hall.

"Come on." He said and took David down the stairs to his room. He shut the door behind them and looked at David. "Are you ok?" Alan asked. David looked around the room and realized he was alone with Alan in a bedroom. His heart jumped into his throat and he felt faint. "David, are you ok?" Alan asked.

"Yea." David whispered and sat down on the bed. Alan sat next to him and David whimpered.

"You don't look ok." Alan said. David sighed and looked at him. "So you kissed a guy, that's ok." Alan said.

"Oh, Fuck Alan! It's not the first time." David said and got off the bed. Alan sighed and looked up at David.

"Then what's the matter with you?"

"It's Carman, Alan!" David yelled.

"Lower your voice. Calm down. I know who it is. What's the matter?" Alan said in a calm level voice.

"It was stupid. All that shit with Charlie you told me about. I feel like . . ." David stopped talking and laid his head against the wall.

"David, you are *nothing* like Charlie. Don't think that." Alan said and got up. He walked over to David and turned him around. He looked David in the eyes. "You are not Charlie. Carman is my best friend and I would never have walked away had it been anyone else. Charlie was a dick, ok?" David sighed and looked down. "You can't keep doing stuff like this to yourself." Alan said. David looked up at him and frownd.

"What do you mean?" David asked. He was fighting the urge to touch Alan's bare chest.

"You told me once you cheated on Amanda, remember that?" Alan asked. David cleared his throat and nodded. "Well, after our talk today, I got thinking. It was with Gabe wasn't it?" Alan asked. David sighed and nodded his head. "You were in the kind of pain that a partner feels when they lose their mate and you wouldn't talk about it. *Don't* do it to yourself again. Ok?" Alan said. David nodded again and Alan hugged him. David's eyes rolled back in his head as he felt Alan's naked torso touch him. David shook in Alan's arms. Alan pulled away and looked at him with a puzzled gaze. "Are you cold?" Alan asked.

"I'm tired." David said. Alan smiled and stepped out of David's way.

"We are leaving tomorrow so get a good sleep ok?" Alan said. David nodded and Alan opened the bedroom door.

"Alan." David said as he sat down on his bed.

"Yes, David." Alan asked.

"I miss history class." David said and Alan smiled.

"I miss having you in there." Alan said and left the room. David sighed and shook his head. He undressed down to his boxers and crawled under the blankets.

God save me. Alan knows and now Carman is kissing me unannounced. What the fuck is going on with me? How could I have forgotten my journal? I can't believe this is my life. Shake lose Alan's skeleton? What is he nuts? I am such an idiot. I can't wait to get home and have normal day. David thought to himself as he fell asleep.

The morning after was bizarrely normal. David woke to find Carman and Alan laughing over morning coffee. He showered and got his things ready to go. He came out to the kitchen to see Alan making him a coffee.

"Good morning." Carman said and winked ad David.

"Good morning." David said and went into the music room. Alan followed him in and handed him his coffee.

"It doesn't have to be weird David." Alan said as David loaded his guitar. "Apparently you're an awesome kisser." Alan said. David looked up at him from buckling his guitar case.

"You guys *talked* about it?" David asked. Alan smiled and nodded.

"He won't shut up about it actually."

"It was just a kiss." David said under his breath and Alan laughed. Alan set his coffee on the floor and packed up his own guitar.

"David, you don't need to freak out about this." Alan said quietly. David looked at him and shook his head.

"Look, the kiss was great, ok. *That's* what's weird about it." David said and picked up his guitar. Alan raised his eyebrows and picked his own up.

"How is a good kiss, weird?"

"Cause its *Carman."* David answered.

"Ahh, I see." Alan said and rolled his eyes. David laughed and picked up his coffee.

"You're a dick." David whispered. Alan giggled and nodded.

"I know I am."

"Don't forget your coffee." David said. Alan picked up his coffee and smiled.

"Don't leave here with out being normal, ok." Alan said.

"I am being normal." David said. Alan shook his head and stepped out of the room. David sighed and called Carman into the room. Carman came in but looked nervous. "Its weird cause your Carman." David said. Carman laughed and shook his head.

"That's funny cause I thought it was awesome because it was you." David sighed and shook his head.

"What?"

"David, I am going to be 40 in September. Kissing an 18 year old hotty was the highlight of my year." Carman said. David smiled and shook his head.

"Really?" David asked.

"Trust me, I wanna get out of here so I don't have to hear about it anymore." Alan said from the kitchen. David and Carman laughed.

"Not weird, ok." Carman said.

"Yea, ok." David said. Carman hugged him and David giggled when Carman grabbed his ass. "You're a dick too." David said. Carman laughed and walked David out of the room.

"He's all yours, boss." Carman said. Alan smiled.

"Good. I thought I wouldn't get him back." Alan said and David giggled. They loaded their bags and things with Carman's help and then said their good byes. Alan waved as they drove down the drive way. David sighed and looked out the window.

"Sad to go?" Alan asked.

"Nope, I need a normal day." David said and Alan laughed.

"Why do I get the idea that your normal and my normal are two different things?"

"Well, cause my normal is not talking to you about my interest in men. Your normal is wondering why." David answered. Alan smiled and ran his hand through his hair.

"Ok, then. Normal it is." Alan said. David looked at him and smiled.

"I don't have to talk about it?"

"Talk about what?" Alan asked and smiled. David laughed and turned the stereo on. They talked about their sucky new classes, cars, Amanda, Nancy and anything they could think of. Alan kept his promise and never brought up David's sexuality even once. When they got to Alan's, David helped him unload his things. They talked for a few minutes about Amanda again and David promised Alan he would call him with what the Doctor said. David drove home and unloaded his car. It was 4:30pm and he didn't expect Amanda and his mother until after midnight. He went up to his room and opened his journal.

Dear Gabe,

What a fucking week! Alan knows I'm into guys. He guessed it actually while we went for a walk around Carman's place. He guessed about you too. The guy can read me like a book. I don't know why I never seen it coming. He seems cool with it at least. He doesn't know how I feel about him though. Carman thinks I should give that some time. He said that if anything is gonna happen with me and Alan, it would have to be Alan's first move. That kind of reminds me of us. Remember that first kiss? Only this time, I get to wait for it.

Speaking of kissing. Carman kissed me. I didn't like how I reacted so he gave me a do over. Apparently I'm the high light of his year. It was a good kiss, don't get me wrong but, I didn't know I was that good. You never really told me. Anyway,

Amanda is sick and won't tell me what's wrong. I hope everything is ok. I won't know until she gets home.

God I miss you

David.

Chapter 29

David woke up early the next morning. He could feel Amanda cuddled up behind him. He rolled over and hugged her. She smiled in her sleep and kissed his chest.

"Hi baby." Amanda whispered. David smiled and kissed her forehead. "What time is it?" She asked. David leaned over Amanda and looked at the clock.

"5:30." David answered. Amanda groaned and rolled over. David giggled and rolled over to reach for his cigarettes on the side table. He opened them to find the pack empty. "Crap." David whispered to himself. He got up and got dressed. He quietly left the room and closed the door behind him. He went downstairs and put his shoes on. He stepped outside and quietly shut the door behind him. He took a deep breath of the cool, spring air. He walked down the side walk and headed toward the Little Indian's store. He knew he had at least a half hour before the store opened. As he walked, he thought about Alan.

I wonder if Carman was right. I wonder if he really would make the first move if I just got the idea in his head. I wonder what it would take. I wonder what he would like. He's probably into long make out sessions like Gabe was. I bet he would love to have his hair pulled. David smiled at the thought and turned the corner towards the store. He walked up the glass doors and tried them. They were still locked so he sat down on the bench outside. He looked around at the quiet morning and smiled.

"What a day." David said out loud. He looked toward the library and seen a lady jogging with her dog. He smiled at them. She seemed to notice and waved. He nodded at her and she kept running. Just then, the Little Indian pulled up in his funny little car.

"Good morning David." He said as he got out of his car.

"You need some new wheels, Indie." David joked.

"Oh, you are funny like daddy was." The Little Indian said and opened the door for David. David smiled and walked in. "Smoke?" The Little Indian asked.

"Yea, thanks." David said and waited as the man unlocked his cigarette cupboards and started up the till. He grabbed a pack of cigarettes for David and handed them to him. David handed him the money and smiled.

"Thank you." The Little Indian said. David smiled at him and left the store. He stepped outside and opened his new pack of cigarettes. He lit one and took a long drag. He started his walk home. He passed the lady that was jogging with her dog.

"Hey, aren't you Nancy Smith's son?" The lady asked. David raised his eyebrows and was surprised that his mom knew someone in town.

"Yea." David said and pet her dog. The lady smiled.

"Could you tell her that Kelly says hi?" The lady asked.

"Yea, sure." David said. The lady thanked him and continued her jog. David thought the lady was pretty good looking for one of his moms friends. He shook his head and continued on his walk. He passed by the library and stopped outside. He stared at the doors and remembered the last day he had walked in to the building. It had been Halloween. He sighed and shook his head. He walked past the old building and continued on his way home. He turned the corner and seen Alan's car parked outside his house. "Little early for a visit." David said to himself. He picked up the pace and walked up the side walk. He tossed his cigarette aside and walked in. He looked into the kitchen but didn't see anyone. He raised an eyebrow and heard something in the living room. He walked over to the living room doorway and stopped dead in his tracks. He stared into the living room at Alan and Nancy entwined in the kind of kiss you only seen in the movies. Nancy's hands played with Alan's wavy, sandy hair. Alan held Nancy low around the waist. David could see the side profile of both of them. They both had their eyes closed and looked like they were in love. David looked up the stairs to see Amanda standing on them.

"David." Amanda said. David looked back into the living room. Nancy and Alan were both staring at him. His heart pounded in his chest and his eyes burned with tears. Nancy and Alan just stood staring at him. David looked back at Amanda. "David." Amanda said.

"Did you know about this?" David asked. Amanda nodded and looked down. "You *never* told me." David's hands were sweating and he felt like the room was spinning. David looked at Alan. Alan tried to say something but David cut him off. "Don't Alan! You only pretended to care about me to get with my mom! I have spent the last seven months replacing my father and Gabe with YOU! I should have just waited for my mom to do that, huh?" David yelled and shook his head. Tears rolled down his face.

"David . . ." Alan tried to say but David looked at him and cut him off.

"Fuck you Alan!" David yelled and went out the door, slamming it behind him. Amanda sat down on the stairs with tears in her eyes. Alan opened the door and went out but David had already driven off in his car.

"Shit!" Alan said and came back into the house. Amanda was crying and rocking on the stair she sat on. "Damn it." Alan said and looked at Nancy. "We should have told him about us months ago."

"That wouldn't have made a difference." Amanda said through her sobs.

"What do you mean? I thought he would have been happy that Alan was with me. It's not like he's some strange guy that I just brought home someday." Nancy said. Amanda looked at both of them and shook her head.

"I cant believe you guys. You said you would tell him." Nancy sighed and shook her head.

"Amanda, David has always had a short fuse, just like his father. He will come around to the idea."

"I doubt it." Amanda said and shook her head.

"Amanda, why do you say that?" Alan asked. He kept looking out the window for David's car.

"Alan, he's in love with you." Amanda said and cried again.

"What?!" Nancy said. Alan closed his eyes and sighed.

"Where would he go, Amanda?" Alan asked. Amanda shook her head.

"I don't know."

"You need to think, where would he go?!" Alan yelled. Amanda shook under Alan's stern words.

"Alan, what is going on?" Nancy asked. Alan sighed and shook his head.

"David has been questioning his sexuality and . . ."

"Questioning?" Amanda said and coughed a laugh. "He was sleeping with Gabe. He has been in love with you for a long time. Questioning is an understatement."

"I didn't know any of this." Nancy said and sat next to Amanda.

"He is not going to take this well." Amanda said and cried again. She was holding her stomach and Nancy rubbed her back.

"We need to figure out where he would go. I need to talk to him." Alan said and looked out the window again. Amanda shook her head.

"I really don't know." Amanda said and rubbed her stomach.

"Oh god, Amanda, would David hurt himself?" Nancy asked. Amanda looked at her and shook her head.

"I don't know. I just know he really loved Alan and he doesn't love easy. Trust me." Alan paced back and forth and ran his hand through his hair. "Wait!" Amanda said and jumped up off her seat on the stair. She ran up to David's room and grabbed the Dear Gabe journal off the desk. She took it downstairs and handed it to Alan.

"What's this?" Alan asked and opened it. Nancy gasped and jumped up. She shut the book and held it to her chest.

"This is David's journal. We can't *read* this." Nancy said.

"If there is any place David would go, it will be in there. And, if he has any plans on hurting himself over something like this, it would be in there too." Amanda said and sat back down on the stair.

"I will read it and never repeat what I read. Ok Nancy?" Alan asked. Nancy nodded and slowly handed the journal over. Alan opened it and read. Amanda and Nancy watched him read. He swallowed hard and Amanda figured it must have been something about him. He read for a few minutes until he got to the page about Gabe's tree and what he found in it. His eyes filled up with tears and he shut the book. "Where is Gabe's tree Amanda?" Alan asked. Amanda swallowed and thought for a second. "Amanda!" Alan yelled. Amanda cowered and Alan sighed.

"Alan, please don't upset her." Nancy said. Alan looked at Nancy with a puzzled gaze. "She's pregnant." Nancy whispered. Alan squatted in front of Amanda.

"Is this true?" Alan asked quietly. Amanda nodded. Alan sighed and looked into her eyes. "Amanda, I read something in this book that scares the shit out of me. If you want that baby to have a daddy, I need to know where Gabe's tree is." Alan whispered. He closed his eyes and tears ran down his face.

"Its on Look Out Cliff." Amanda said. Alan smiled at her and looked at Nancy.

"That's where I will be." Alan said and left the house. He got into his car and drove off. He looked in his rear view mirror and saw Amanda and Nancy loading Little Mike into Nancy's car.

God please don't let David do something stupid. I love that kid. I can't stand that I've done this to him. God the stuff in that journal. And that's just since Halloween. How could I have been so blind? I spend the whole week spouting off shit about keeping secrets and 'David, you can tell me anything.'

"Fuck, I'm an idiot!" Alan yelled at himself as he turned the corner to Look Out Cliff. He nervously tapped the steering wheel as he drove. As he approached the cliff, he could see David standing on the back of the big black Hearse. "Shit!" Alan said and stepped harder on the gas. He stopped the car and got out. He ran to the car but David had already thrown himself from the car. "DAVID!" Alan screamed. He ran over to where David hung from Gabe's tree and grabbed his legs. He lifted him up and looked up at his face. David's eyelids twitched and his body jerked in Alan's arms. Alan held him up and watched Nancy come running over the hill.

"DAVID NO!" Nancy yelled and ran to where Alan stood holding her son up from a hanging death.

"Cut him down!" Alan yelled at her.

"How!" Nancy yelled back.

"In my car. In the back seat is a dagger." Alan said. He struggled to hold David's twitching body. Nancy dug through the car and found the dagger. She ran back over to the car and climbed on to the roof. Alan carefully moved David's body closer so she could reach the rope. She sawed through it and Alan caught David's falling body. Nancy jumped off the car. "Call 911. You'll have to go up to the road for service." Alan said. He handed her his phone and Nancy ran back up to the road.

"I . . . Hate . . ." David tried to say.

"God David! Hate me, love me I don't care but please live!" Alan cried and held David's vibrating body. David's eyelids fluttered. Alan stared at the life slipping away in his arms. "No David! Don't do this. I'm not worth this. Please live." Alan whispered in his ear. David breathed shallow and his body shook. Alan cried and rocked his body. "Please, Please don't die!" Alan yelled. David shivered and his breathing slowed again. Alan hugged him and cried in his hair. "David, I will never forgive myself if you die right now. I'm sorry I was so blind. Please fight." Alan begged. David coughed and wheezed. Alan looked at him. Blood had come up to his lips. "Oh God! David please. You have to live. You're a father!" Alan said. His tears burned his eyes as he stared at David. He looked up to Nancy. She was on the phone. He looked back at David. He could hear sirens coming down the high way. "Listen, Help is coming. Please hang on, David." Alan whispered in David's ear. David's breathing stuttered and Alan screamed, "GOD! DAVID NO!" Alan held David tight as his body fell limp . . .